Slave Camp
Nightclub

Happy reading!

David W. Goodwin

Slave Camp Nightclub

David W. Goodwin

Library of Congress Control Number:		2013902114
ISBN:	Hardcover	978-1-4797-9026-5
	Softcover	978-1-4797-9025-8
	Ebook	978-1-4797-9027-2

This book was printed in the United States of America.

To order additional copies of this book, contact:
Xlibris Corporation
1-888-795-4274
www.Xlibris.com
Orders@Xlibris.com
129349

DEDICATION

THIS STORY IS lovingly dedicated to all of my wonderful housemates at the Zoo during an amazing year and a half in the mid 1970's. Yes, these are all real people but their names have been changed, not so much to protect the innocent but to make a half-hearted attempt not to embarrass them and their children too much. You all conspired (unknowingly, I'm certain) to change my life and mostly for the better as a result of some of the almost unbelievable experiences we shared during that time long ago.

I owe a special debt to both Eric and Iggy for their friendship over the years and for being good sports about my using them as the two other main characters in this story. I hope you will forgive my indulgence and continue to be my friends after you read this. Remember, this is fiction but there was no real disguising of your wonderful and quirky personalities. If you think I got too many of the details wrong, I encourage you to write your own books and make me look like a moron (which would be fairly easy). Thanks from the bottom of my heart, guys!

ACKNOWLEDGEMENT

SLAVE CAMP NIGHTCLUB had been brewing inside me for a long time. The motivation to finally write it came after an illness forced me off my bike for a few months and I had to channel that energy into something constructive. I asked my partner/girlfriend/fiancée Suzanne Ryan to listen to each chapter as I wrote it and read it aloud to her. She was a wonderful sounding board. She laughed at parts that I too thought were funny but most importantly, told me honestly when something fell flat and needed a major revision or needed to be thrown onto the scrap heap altogether. To keep her interested in the story, I wrote her into it (and we're not talking about Jackie here). Otherwise, who wants to read a tale about your partner's old girlfriends, real or imagined?

Suzanne was a great editor, provided limitless encouragement and enthusiasm and really made me feel like this story showed perhaps a glimmer of promise. I might not have had the motivation to stick with it if you hadn't been there for me. I thank you, sweetie, from the entirety of my heart.

CHAPTER 1

"WHAT'S THE NAME of that guy that has to roll a boulder up a hill for the rest of his life?" I asked my housemate Kate the morning after I woke up from my crazy dream. As usual, she was only barely dressed on this beautiful warm and sunny day. We were sitting together at our beat up dining room table having breakfast. Kate was one of seven other housemates that I shared a vegetarian communal household with during the summer of 1976 in Boulder, Colorado. There were four men and four women who lived upstairs in the main part of the house, three male downstairs renters and a rotating cast of additional characters that came and went that summer. I was one of the four men and we were all college students. No one else was awake so we had the room to ourselves, which was a rather uncommon occurrence.

"You're thinking of Sisyphus and that's kind of a random question," Kate replied. As an English major, she obviously knew a lot more about Greek mythology than I did. Before I could respond, she added, "He was the King of Corinth and was being punished by Zeus for trying to outsmart the gods. Hades condemned him to spend an eternity rolling a massive boulder up a long hill. Why do you ask?"

"I just had this dream last night and it was pretty bizarre. I guess I asked the right person. Sounds like maybe you just read about him in one of your textbooks. What else can you tell me about this dude?"

"Every time he reached the top, his boulder would fall back down to the bottom so he would have to repeat this task over and over again, each time with the exact same result."

"Doesn't sound like he was too bright if he couldn't figure out how to position it properly at the top."

"Or mysterious forces were at work to conspire against him. That's kind of the way things go with mythology. There's not always a rational explanation for the ways of the gods. In the case of Sisyphus, he was being punished for his shady business practices."

I must have been subconsciously channeling Sisyphus in my dream. My friends Eric and Iggy were there with me and we had to take our boulders and roll them up a series of switchbacks. Unlike Sisyphus, however, our boulders stayed at the top. Unfortunately for us, there were a lot more boulders where these came from so we had to walk back down to get the next boulder to wrestle to the top.

We weren't being punished for anything in particular; we were simply slaves condemned to work at the quarry. Another apparent twist on this myth was that our reward was to spend each night in the quarry nightclub so we probably didn't mind the tough work as much as Sisyphus did since he didn't really have anything to look forward to. At the end of my first tough day, all of us slaves shuffled into the filthy and sparsely furnished nightclub. We were a sorry sight in our torn and dirty coveralls and hardhats, our dust covered faces streaked with sweat. When the door opened that evening, we dragged our sorry selves in to take our places around the crappy looking tables. We looked like bit characters that might have escaped from the set of *The Grapes of Wrath* and our group was sporting a seriously bad attitude.

Big ugly, smelly waiters came around and slammed dirty mugs filled with a questionable looking liquid on each table. We all looked around to see who would take the first taste. Being extremely thirsty from our grueling day working in the quarry, I gave my beverage a tentative sip and decided it was drinkable, not refreshing, but at least drinkable. My coworkers followed suit. At the moment when all of the drinks had been drained, a spotlight turned on and was trained on a far wall. In walked a guy with a massive old-fashioned microphone in his hand wearing the world's ugliest and most ill fitted tuxedo in the entire history of bad tuxedos.

"Welcome ladies and gentlemen to the Quarry Nightclub! I'm Knute Fisticuffs, your Master of Ceremonies and, man, are you in for a treat tonight! Not only do we have the finest drinks this side of the Mississippi but for your entertainment, you'll be treated to the fabulous song stylings of Mr. Vinny Bayonne!"

Apparently, Knute was expecting an appreciative audience but instead was greeted by dead silence. He put his hand over his brow to shield his eyes from the harsh glare of the spotlight and looked out at the assembled slaves. "I can tell we have a rough crowd here tonight. How do you like your special drinks?"

"They suck!" shouted a burly guy sitting at the next table.

"Sorry to hear that, sir. By the way, where are from?" Mr. Fisticuffs asked coming over to him, followed by the spotlight.

"Boulder," he responded when the microphone was thrust in his face.

"Ah, Boulder, city of sin, land of a thousand ex-virgins, the best place in a five hundred mile radius to get an industrial strength hickey, my favorite city that's named after a rock, yes indeed, you are one lucky man to call Boulder your home, just don't ever invite me over for dinner. It's a long story and involves a short lady, if you know what I mean. But seriously folks, I'd like to introduce you to a person who needs no introduction, in fact she doesn't even need a conclusion, bibliography or title page because she's all body. She's guaranteed to raise your red blood cell count higher than a pig in a china shop! You all know her by day as my lovely assistant but tonight, appearing on this very stage, ladles and germs, I give you the always vivacious Valerie, Queen of the Quarry!"

This got the audience to perk up their attention level a bit; from near brain dead to just a little shy of comatose. Vivacious Valerie came sashaying out to join Knute in the spotlight and was looking decidedly dowdy and frumpy. She was dressed in an evening gown that might have looked better on Totie Fields or Mama Cass. It was at least ten sizes too big, fit poorly in all the wrong places and was the nastiest shade of pink ever.

"Hello everyone, thank you Knute," Valerie said with a million dollar smile that was missing about $950,000 worth of teeth. Taking the microphone, she continued, "It's great to be with you all tonight here at the Quarry Nightclub. In addition to Mr. Vinny Bayonne, we've got another great treat because your Master of Ceremonies Mr. Knute Fisticuffs has agreed, after an overwhelming outpouring of requests, to do the Dance of the Seven Veils! That's got to be worth the price of admission right there. But before we launch into that, however, a little birdie tells me that today is someone's birthday." Valerie started walking around the tables like maybe she was thinking about playing "Duck Duck Goose". When she got to the table next to us, she stood behind one of my coworkers and started singing "Happy Birthday". I'm certain she hoped everyone would join in but when no one did she ended up toughing it out on her own, completely off key and with somewhat random timing. Thankfully, the song finally came to a screeching halt and Valerie put a gold plastic crown on the guy's head and walked back to the stage, followed by the spotlight.

Valerie and Knute were standing on their makeshift stage, looking like rejects from a parody of a grade school talent show while the audience had the enthusiasm one might experience at the funeral of a disliked relative. Just when the entire scene was spiraling down into the deepest recesses of embarrassment, Knute walked over to a massive Frankenstein switch on the wall. Using two hands and a significant amount of effort punctuated by a sizable grunt, he moved the switch handle from the side that said "OFF" in three inch high red letters to the "ON" side. There was a loud pssstttthhhhhzzzzttttt as the power surged through the circuit followed by a huge flash of lights all around the room. It took more than a few seconds for my eyes to adjust to the new brightness.

The first thing I noticed was that the space had been magically transformed from a dark, dingy and dank supply building to a glittering, shiny, totally upscale fancy nightclub with black pedestal tables set on stylish, curving stainless steel legs. Our chairs had somehow become beautiful matching tall stools with ergonomically designed backs and armrests. The makeshift stage had become a real stage with perimeter lighting, a gleaming black floor, a fancy backdrop and professional quality stage lights. Knute Fisticuffs had been transformed from country bumpkin to a Las Vegas-like emcee with a fitted and tasteful tuxedo. He had on stage makeup; a full head of coiffed hair; white, gleaming teeth and a nuclear tan. Valerie truly became vivacious and went from grungy to glamorous with a stylish hairdo, professional looking makeup and an evening gown to die for.

Our scummy glasses had been replaced by beautiful crystal with delicious-looking martinis and olives on a glass swizzle stick. Additionally, all of my fellow slaves' outfits were transformed as well to contemporary tailored suits for the guys and fancy dresses for the ladies. Everyone looked like they had fallen out of the pages of a fashion magazine. The rest of the room was fabulously appointed, with a beautiful sumptuous wood bar in the back of the room, lots of mirrors, intricately carved paneling, tasteful artwork and fresh cut flowers in tall vases all around the room.

There were two more things to note. First, our surly waiters had all become smiling, human sized mice, walking upright and wearing perfectly tailored rodent tuxedos. They were walking around the tables to make sure everyone was being properly served and attended to. Second, as I looked around the room, all of us had big long penis shaped dildoes for noses, sticking out horizontally. Each dildo had a clothespin clamped onto the end. As the entirety of this scene became apparent to all, riotous laughter and applause broke out.

I had this dream the night after my first day working at a rock quarry. Before I accidentally landed this job, I was killing time during the country's bicentennial summer between semesters. There were a lot of interesting distractions in my life and I was planning to look for a job more seriously soon. The one application I put in so far was for a lactation consultant I had seen in the newspaper but I hadn't yet been contacted to schedule an interview. In the meantime, most of my time was spent hanging around with various housemates and friends that showed up on a regular basis that summer. Our most popular activity was playing Frisbee out in the street in front of our house. This consumed a high percentage of my waking hours.

We lived up on the "Hill", the most quintessentially student infested neighborhood in Boulder. The area of mostly large older homes had been turned into small student apartments but also consisted of a few scattered fraternity and sorority mansions that were mostly well maintained and raised the aesthetic of the area considerably.

It was a typical sunny 85° Wednesday afternoon in Boulder. Iggy asked Eric and me if we wanted to go out and "wing the wham". You have to understand the lingo on this one—the Wham-O Company makes the Frisbee so, well, I guess the rest is rather obvious. The last thing I heard before I felt the Frisbee whack me on the side of the head was "Hey Beans, look out!" My attention had been drawn down the street towards a woman in a very skimpy pair of shorts and tight tank top getting out of a strange looking vehicle. She went over to talk to a bunch of fraternity boys tossing a football around in their front yard. After a brief discussion, they all started shaking their heads in unison, looking like they were all watching the same ping pong game between two Olympic caliber players. She then slowly shook her head, went back to her car and then drove down the one-way street towards where I was standing nursing a sore noggin with a Frisbee on the ground by my feet.

I usually recognized most of the cars driving down our quiet street but not this one. Its light blue paint job was weathered from the sun and it had strange, fake rocks set on the roof. As the car pulled closer, I could see that it said "SUGARLOAF QUARRY" on the side door in large block letters. However, what really grabbed my attention was the image underneath the letters. There was a smiling rodent cartoon character sitting at a table of a nightclub hoisting a martini glass. The rat was dressed in a tuxedo, had a lit cigar in his other hand and looked completely toasted.

The car slowed down as it approached and pulled up right next to where I was standing along the edge of the street, driving over my Frisbee. I probably had my mouth open as I stared at the car, trying to be as discreet as possible. "You looking to make a few bucks, college boy?" the woman asked me from behind large, mirrored sunglasses. I don't think that I had actually ever heard someone say those words before, at least not in real life.

"Ahhh, what do you have in mind?" I asked in my coolest voice, trying hard to make sure that it didn't crack and only barely succeeding.

Standing beside the rodent mobile gave me the opportunity to get a closer look at her. I had noticed her outfit from afar when she was talking to the frat boys but now that she was right there in front of me, I could see that her tank top had the same cartoon rat as was on the sides of her car. I could also take a closer look at the rodent, distorted as it was by the way it clung like a serpent around her very curvy body. He seemed to be waving his martini glass in the air and dancing in his bar stool as she moved around inside the car. This was especially pronounced when she wiggled a bit to grab some papers from the back and handed one of them to me. By this time, my friends had joined me next to the vehicle.

"Here, this describes our business. I've been going around town stapling them to telephone poles. Why don't you and your pals hop in my car and I'll take you up the canyon to our quarry? Once we're there, we can discuss the details of the job and you can decide if you want to work with me," she said somewhat provocatively. "If you don't want the job, I'll be happy to drive you back down here and you can get back to your game. I'm guessing you'll decide to stay." She got out of her car to put the rest of the papers in the trunk which gave all three of us the chance to stretch our primitive, college boy imaginations a bit.

"Sounds interesting," I said to her and passed the flyer to Iggy. "You guys want to go work at a quarry?"

"Sure, why not?" Iggy said, nodding to Eric who also thought it sounded reasonable. All of us were running pretty low on cash and there was still over two months of summer before the fall semester began. I think the woman's sex appeal and take charge attitude might have helped some too. "It says here they specialize in curbing, stone walls, gravel and decorative stonework. That's always been something that's appealed to me, especially if it involves a rat in a tuxedo!"

DAVID W. GOODWIN

"Hey, are you guys all somehow related?" the woman asked as she walked back to the driver's side of her car.

"No, fortunately," Iggy answered. "But it's surprising how often we're asked that."

Iggy was a local Colorado kid, having grown up in a nice part of Denver. He was the youngest of five children. His mom was a first generation French immigrant. Ignace, or Iggy as everyone called him, was a big guy, not fat, and had an imposing presence. I would guess that he was a few inches taller than six feet and probably weighed close to two hundred pounds. He had a big barrel chest, long, thin straight hair and usually had some sort of creative facial hair. Today he was sporting a well trimmed and manicured beard. Usually when I see this, I think that the person has too much time on their hands but this wasn't true in Iggy's case. He always had a lot of things going on. During the school year he had a part time job at a local restaurant as a cook and also did volunteer work in the judicial system rubbing elbows with some hardcore people. In contrast to his facial hair, the rest of his appearance was somewhat disheveled. I assumed this was because he really didn't care too much about what others thought of him.

The woman said we didn't have much time so we should grab whatever clothes we needed and get going. We disappeared inside to get some shoes and shirts and then piled into her car. I sat in the front after clearing away some old dusty tools and a couple of equally dusty looking six packs of beer. Eric and Iggy hopped in the back and the car accelerated quickly down our street. She was driving west out of town, towards Boulder Canyon, when she stopped at a hardware store. "Feel free to drink these beers if you'd like." We opened three cans and watched with rapt attention as she danced across the parking lot.

"She is one fine looking lady, wouldn't you agree, Beans?" Iggy observed. Even I was a little fuzzy on the evolution of this nickname he had given me but it must have had something to do with the occasional "burrito research" parties we had or the fact that it rhymed with my name.

"Down boy! I saw her first and besides, she's old enough to be your older sister," I said. "This whole situation seems a bit on the bizarre side."

"What seems bizarre—the rocks, the squirrel in a tuxedo, these evil looking chisels, or her non-existent pants?" Eric asked.

Eric, in contrast to Iggy, was pretty calculating with his time, appearance, and general approach to life. He grew up in a wealthy suburb of St. Louis with a younger sister and brother, a mom named Ann who I think might have been the inspiration for Beaver Cleaver's mom June and a father who was the president of a local bank. On my previous trips through St. Louis, his family welcomed me with open arms and made me feel like a member of their family—even when I showed up once unannounced at six in the morning on a weekday looking and probably smelling like hell when I embarked on a spur-of-the-moment hitchhiking trip last summer from Boulder to visit my sister in North Carolina. Eric's dad was one of the sweetest and unassuming fathers that I ever met, even though he drove a Mercedes Benz 450 SL convertible with a vanity plate that said "MAN". Okay, those two statements sound contradictory but it was an acronym for his bank and tied to an advertising campaign.

Eric and I first met when we were both freshman. I had applied to the University of Colorado at the last minute, literally a few days before my high school graduation, when I hadn't been accepted at the various East Coast colleges that I'd wanted to go to. When I showed up as a freshman in late August, there weren't any dorm rooms left so they put ten of us temporarily in a rundown five bedroom house on the edge of campus, with a promise to move us into dorms as spaces opened up. About a month into our first semester there were five of us left, each with our own bedroom. After some discussions with the housing administration staff, we convinced them to allow us to stay in the house for the entire school year. One of the stipulations was that we had to eat our meals at a nearby dorm. This happened to be where Eric lived.

I saw Eric on occasion during our freshman year but our paths never really crossed. However, I did admire him from afar; he had long blond hair, a sparse blond beard—typical Scandinavian looks. He was about Iggy's height but with a slighter build. Towards the end of the spring semester, after everyone in our house had a brush with the law, in spite of being on University probation for our transgressions, my housemates and I decided to host a party. Unlike any of our friends, we had an actual yard so we fashioned a cooking pit from cinder blocks and invited a swarm of friends down for a beer and barbeque fest. Even though he wasn't invited, Eric showed up with some other friends of mine, wearing a cool leather vest.

Back in the Sugarloaf Quarry car, we drank our car temperature beers and gave the woman our full attention as she came back across the parking lot. "Couldn't find what you were looking for?" I asked when she got back in empty handed.

DAVID W. GOODWIN

"Nah, I ordered some special items but they weren't in yet. By the way, my name's Rhonda. What are your names?" We told her and then Eric asked about the work we would be doing. "I was wondering when you were going to start asking me some questions. I work at the Sugarloaf Quarry but you probably figured that out already. We found ourselves a little shorthanded today and my boss, Big Larry, asked me to go into town to round up a few strong college boys to help us out. You guys lift weights or something to stay so buff?"

Now I knew something wasn't quite right. It wasn't as if Iggy, Eric and I were 98-pound weaklings but our idea of lifting weights was to pick up one of our friends and drag them kicking and screaming into the reservoir during a rowdy picnic. Since our neighborhood was littered with fraternity houses populated by guys that all looked like they spent more hours lifting weights than going to classes and studying combined, she could have easily found other guys that fit the description a lot better than us. I did, however, witness one group of buff boys that turned her down.

"That's right Rhonda. We're doing some serious training this summer hoping to qualify for the '80 Olympics in naked three-man luge. I think we have a pretty good shot. Trials are this fall up in Breckenridge," said Eric winking at me when I turned around to look at him in surprise.

Rhonda ignored Eric's joke and continued talking. "If Big Larry says it's alright, you guys can help us with our landscaping. We're trying to spruce the place up a bit for an inspection next month by the U. S. Fish and Wildlife Service. They're on our asses to make sure that we've complied with the federal migratory insect laws. You see, our quarry is on the flyway for the black rumped pygmy gnat and we've got to make sure they have adequate habitat on their long journey from Downer's Grove, Illinois to Waco, Texas. There's a certain type of rock outcrop they like for resting spots and as it turns out, our quarry is loaded with them."

"I've got lots of landscaping experience from last summer. I operated a hedge clipper before the crew chief decided that perhaps my talents were best utilized driving the other workers around to various job sites and getting coffee and donuts for them. I kind of thought the homeowner would have appreciated my creative hedge work but I guess not," I said.

"Yeah," said Iggy "and I worked for the Lazy Cow Restaurant last summer. One of my jobs during slow times was to water the gardens in front and pick the flowers for the vases."

Not to be outdone, Eric mentioned the time that he was allowed to mow the lawn at his parent's spacious suburban estate once when the lawn service's trailer broke loose from their pickup truck on the way to their house and crashed into a police car.

"Okay, I get the idea. It sounds like you're all pretty well qualified for the job. Do any of you have PhD's?"

Assuming this was a rhetorical question, we all decided to keep quiet. Rhonda was speeding up the canyon and narrowly missed a few hikers along the way. While chugging one of the warm beers with her right hand and steering with her left, she crossed the road lines as if she was entitled to both lanes, in spite of oncoming traffic. She told us that we would be taking the turnoff to Sugarloaf Mountain Road. One of our friends lived on Sugarloaf and we hung out there a lot so we knew the area pretty well. Rhonda continued her fast pace up the canyon and took a right. From the turnoff, it was another two miles before she hung a left at the quarry entrance.

"Is that arch new?" I asked. "I was just up here last week and I don't remember seeing it before."

"Big Larry decided it was time to make things look a bit more polished. He's gone a bit crazy—from this arch, to the new logo on everything, to the rocks on the car roof and of course the new uniforms that he makes us all wear."

"I hope we'll get some tank tops just like yours," Iggy commented.

She turned around to look at Iggy in the backseat and gave him a quick death stare. "You guys will get overalls and a tee shirt but if you were a gal, you'd get a tank top and shorts or jeans. I like wearing the tank top if it's hot out but since I find jeans too restricting, I prefer these shorts, with a little modification. Sometimes, though, even this outfit makes me too hot."

I'm sure all of us were thinking of the exact same thing but luckily, we kept it to ourselves. This behavior was unlike a recent experience where we were interviewing for a new housemate. Since our house maintained an even gender mix, when someone moved out we would replace them with a person of the same sex. Iggy was one of the three basement renters and was technically a guy but since everyone loved him, he was welcomed to join us for meals and shared all other responsibilities. In essence, there were five men and four women that formed the nucleus of our home. Most of us were still holding onto the late 60's/early 70's hippie look and lifestyle even though it was 1976. The contrast between the hippie wannabe's and the fraternity/sorority crowd in Boulder was pretty obvious. In this situation, a woman named Sandy was moving out so we were trying to find another woman to fill her spot.

Two women responded to our ad in the school newspaper. One would easily fit in philosophically and had the right look going. During her interview, Jackie gave all of the correct answers and we all agreed that she would be a good housemate. The other woman, Cyndi, was a drop dead gorgeous sorority girl who for some reason was interested in living in our house. During her interview, she had on more makeup than most of us had ever seen on a Boulder college woman and was dressed to the nines. After she left, the eight of us were discussing her strengths and weaknesses. Of course the three women agreed that Cyndi would be a terrible choice and us five guys were trying hard to keep the drool inside our mouths.

"She would absolutely not fit into the scene here," said Crystal.

"And did you see her clothes? She was actually wearing a bra!" said Hazel. She and Crystal were a lesbian couple and I think all of the guys in the house were kind of turned on by them.

"Yes, sadly, I did notice the bra but she is a Business major and has an internship at the *Daily Camera*. She could be a great asset to our household and you may recall that she said she knew someone whose sister was a vegetarian," I noted.

Wayne is the one that actually spoke the unspeakable. "I'm Wayne and I'm hot to trot! Let's choose Cyndi. I can't wait to get her in the sack!"

Needless to say, Sandy was not replaced by Cyndi and there was a general uneasiness in the house for a while after this. We of course went with Jackie and everything eventually got back to normal. Wayne, on the other hand, was the butt of a lot of our jokes and many times one of us would say "I'm Wayne and I'm hot to trot!" in any situation where it was only mildly appropriate but it would never fail to get a hearty laugh. The ironic part was that Wayne was the least successful trotter of all the guys in our house and our wide circle of friends, which made this even funnier, at least to us, but Wayne probably got tired of hearing it.

Back in the car, Iggy, Eric and I were enjoying our own private thoughts about how hot Rhonda was. The mood, however, was shattered when she jammed on the brakes and veered off to the side of the long driveway that wound its way back into the quarry. She came to a screeching halt just barely managing to keep all four tires on the road and was dangerously close to a steep drop off into a stream below.

"Damn, I forgot to get something in town. Big Larry's going to kill me! I've got to go back to Boulder immediately. Why don't you guys just walk the final stretch? When you get to the main building, just ask for Big Larry and tell him you're the guys Rhonda picked up to work on the landscaping crew. Tell him that I'll be back in about half an hour."

We started to extricate ourselves from the car and felt the effects from our Frisbee exertion, being out a good chunk of the day in the sunshine, chugging several warm beers and the crazy thoughts rumbling around inside our heads. Without Rhonda to introduce us to Big Larry, it seemed like the situation had somehow become just a bit sketchier. With some reluctance, we started walking towards our destiny, much like Dorothy and her three companions as they skipped through the snowy field of poppies and made their way to the Emerald City. Iggy started singing the lyrics in a high pitched voice and seemed to know all the words.

He was quite theatrical, having spent a lot of time in high school plays and musicals. He also played all sorts of stringed instruments and wasn't shy about singing in public or in front of us. I think he had even been in a production of the *Wizard of Oz* recently, maybe even translated into French. His mom taught French at a local college in Denver and Iggy was often recruited to play the male lead in plays when she couldn't find anyone else that spoke French and sang. Plus, he was also kind of a ham. Every once in a while, a bunch of us would pile into someone's car, bomb down to Denver, smoke some pot along the way and catch one of his plays. They were always very entertaining, made more so by our giggling the entire time and cheering wildly any time Iggy was on stage.

Eric and I started skipping up the road and tried to sing along with Iggy except we only knew a few of the lyrics. Eric, who was even more tone deaf than me, was singing the wrong tune entirely. My version wasn't a whole lot better. As we rounded the final bend and the quarry came into sight, we stopped dead in our tracks.

"I'm not sure this is the first impression we want to give Big Larry," Eric said.

"Umm, yeah, I think you're on to something there Mungo." I responded. There remains to this day some disagreement about the name Mungo. The three of us often went hiking or camping together and decided that instead of using our regular names, we should have names of mountain men, those tough guys from Colorado's earlier white guy history. Three names were decided on—Mungo, Jacque and Poindexter. Of course nobody wanted to be Poindexter, that name was thrown into the mix to describe the wussiest guy on each particular trip and changed depending upon the situation. If you were called Poindexter, you were being told that you had better toughen up a bit. Mungo and Jacque were used interchangeably. Over the last year, Eric just kind of grew into Mungo although he insists that it was more my name than his. So really, any of the three of us could be called Mungo or Jacque but hopefully not Poindexter.

Iggy was still into his little performance and sang it a few more times before he caught up to us. "Oh yeah, some buff college boys indeed, skipping along singing in girlie voices! I guess we should talk about this a bit before we get up to the quarry. I have a feeling that this isn't exactly what Big Larry is looking for in his new landscaping crew."

It was obvious which building was the office as it had a big "Sugarloaf Quarry" sign on the roof and an "Office Entrance" sign above the door in the middle. There were various buildings scattered around nearby. The quarry was visible over the rooftops and around the sides of the other buildings. We saw massive rock cliff terraces with lots of vertical drilling marks, some very steep roads that followed switchbacks from the bottom all the way to the top, piles of sorted rock and gravel scattered here and there and some very large slabs of rock stacked up by size. In the very center of the quarry was a large structure with lots of conveyor belts reaching into the middle from almost every conceivable angle, making the entire assembly look like a massive mechanical spider. In addition to all the noise we heard around us from the equipment and machinery, there was a lot of dust that was stirred up from all the activity. On the edges of the quarry were all sorts of vehicles, machines, and various old dusty parts that undoubtedly had some sort of function. The things I recognized were backhoes, front bucket loaders, forklifts, and steamrollers. Some of the other pieces of equipment looked like augers, large bins with some sort of screening and shaking device on top, crushers, tractor trailers and lots and lots of conveyor belts that seemed to be piled up at random locations.

"Alright boys, time to go meet Big Larry. Remember; try not to squeal if he puts you in a head lock. I think he's going to put us to a test right away to find out how macho we are," I advised.

"Quien es mas macho, Ricardo Montelban o Ignace Jambon?" Eric said in his best Mexican accent, imitating something we had seen recently on TV.

"Clearly it's Ricardo Montelban because it looks like Ignace just whizzed in his pantelones," I said.

As we were about to walk through the office door, a very small man came blasting out the other way yelling into a walkie-talkie. The four of us bumped into each other and bounced off backwards, taking a few stutter steps. Once everyone reestablished their personal space, Eric asked this guy if he knew where we might find Big Larry. There's a certain irony to some of the names of people you encounter out in the real world. There are the bald men called "Curly", the huge beasts with the name "Tiny", the slutty vixens named "Madonna". Well, Big Larry was in this category.

"You're lookin' at him. Who wants to know?" Big Larry's voice sounded like it belonged more to a medium sized gerbil than a grown man. It was high pitched and sounded like he wanted everyone to think that he was straight off a dude ranch, which might have been the case. I was trying real hard to stifle my laughter. Here was a guy who looked like he could have been a junior accountant at some backwater financial consulting office in Des Moines. Big Larry was about five feet tall, had slicked down black hair parted way too far on the side and clearly arranged in a way to cover a massive bald spot. He looked like he couldn't have weighed more than a hundred pounds, even after spending the morning at the All U Can Eat breakfast buffet at the Chow Down Rodeo Diner. He was dressed in baggy overalls and the Sugarloaf Quarry tee shirt that Rhonda had told us about.

Eric managed to explain our situation and Big Larry invited us inside. He motioned for us to have a seat around a big dirty wooden table. "Now, I hope that Rhonda explained everythin'. What we have here is a 'mergency sichyation. We've got about a month to clean this place up. Its hard work but you'll be well paid. If you agree to work here, I want a commitment of at least a month and if it turns out that any of you boys are worth your weight in horse manure, we might have enough work to last for the rest of the summer, that is, if you're innerested. Any questions?"

"Yeah, I've got a few questions. First, how much are you willing to pay us?" I asked.

"That depends on how much I think you're worth. Most of my employees get a buck over minimum wage to start. If I think you're any good, I'll bump that up to two. Minimum wage right now is $3.55 so I'll start you at $4.55 and if you play your cards right, you might be makin' triple fives in no time. However, I have to tell you up front that you should consider all the various perks of the job. I might not give you what sounds like a big hourly wage but its all part of a package deal," Big Larry stated.

"That sounds like pretty good pay. I was making $3.55 an hour cleaning dorm rooms and that job really sucked. What's included in the package?" Eric asked tentatively.

"Well, of course we'll supply you with work clothes, boots, gloves, hardhat, you know, the usual things you need to work in a quarry. In addition, we've got a bunkhouse where all of our workers park their carcasses at night during the week so you don't have to commute up here every day."

"We already have a place in town and have signed a lease for the next year so I'm not sure if that's a real plus for us," Eric explained.

"Wait, I wasn't done yet explainin' all of the perks so hold your horses before you go sayin' anythin' stupid. We also feed you all your meals while you're here—breakfast, lunch, and dinner as well as mornin' and afternoon snacks. But the biggest benefit of workin' at the Sugarloaf Quarry is our nightclub."

CHAPTER 2

"A NIGHTCLUB? UP here at the quarry? I've never heard anything about a mountain nightclub," I said.

"It's definitely not open to the public so you wouldn't know about it unless you worked here or someone squealed. Bottom line, this is a tough job and sometimes at the end of the day, you might be askin' yourself—why get up and do this job day in and day out? It was Rhonda who came up with the idea to convert the supply buildin' into a nightclub. At nine every evenin', we invite everyone to come to the nightclub for a few drinks and some entertainment, 'cept Friday, Saturday and Sunday. We try to unwind, let our hair down like you boys seem to have already done and just focus on havin' a good time. I guarantee that it will make the job worthwhile. You boys are all over twenty-one, right?"

"Oh yeah," we all answered quickly in unison. This wasn't technically true. Eric and Iggy had just turned twenty-one in the last few months while I had another two months to go but why quibble about details? I didn't want to miss out on any opportunities for free drinks. Colorado had a two step minimum drinking age. If you were eighteen to twenty, you could drink 3.2 beer, but when you are over twenty-one, you could drink normal beer and everything else. However, Colorado in 1976 was a pretty laid back place. Here I was, a twenty year old New Jersey kid who looked like I couldn't have been much older than seventeen. I usually couldn't get into a bar but could almost always buy alcohol at a liquor store.

One time, as a sophomore, I went into a liquor store with my slightly younger girlfriend to get a bottle of wine for a romantic evening together. Other than us, the place was empty. Lauren was really into plants and noticed a huge rubber tree that filled up almost the entire window of the liquor store. This window was enormous; the room had a cathedral ceiling so the tree had to be at least twenty feet high. Lauren asked the guy behind the counter how old it was.

"Somewhere around twenty years," he said.

"Wow, that's older than you, Dean!"

"Yeah, a few years ago, maybe," I skillfully responded, trying to save the moment from the humiliation of not being able to impress my girlfriend and hoping the cashier wasn't the sort of person that was good with numbers. Luckily for us, either he wasn't a math whiz or needed the business because he thanked us for the purchase and we left with our wine.

Big Larry's comment about the entertainment clearly had piqued Iggy's interest. "What sort of entertainment do you have?"

"Oh, sometimes we get a comedian, sometimes a band, sometimes dancers. It really depends on who's comin' through town and owes me a favor," Big Larry explained. "Then of course there's Rhonda. You can probably imagine how she might put a wrinkle in your shorts."

"How do you feel about bluegrass music?" Iggy asked. This wasn't the question I was going to ask.

"Sure, we've had a few bluegrass bands here. Last month we had Stubby Chester and the Flabby Hombres. Man, they were smokin'. I think everyone was on their feet dancin' except for ol' Stubby, of course. You ever hear of 'em?"

"Uh, no. Where are they from?"

"That I couldn't tell you for sure but my guess is that most of 'em are from Oklyhoma. If you've ever seen Stubby Chester, you'd never forget him. This guy lost all four of his limbs in a freak accident, somethin' to do with a go cart and flamin' marshmallows, I forget the details, but one of the Flabby Hombres wheels him on stage, he's got a microphone taped to his chest and this guy just sings his heart out. Unreal!"

"Hmm, sounds pretty interesting. So, Big Larry, tell us more about the job, what we'd be doing, what the work day is like, you know, stuff like this so we can make a decision about working here," I said.

"We start work each day at 7:30. You'll know that it's time to get your butts in here when you hear Sugarloaf Sam, our mascot—we play him over the loudspeakers. We expect you to be dressed and ready to work promptly. If you choose to stay here in the bunkhouse, you'll get a wake up call at 6:30, breakfast is served in the mess hall at 6:45 and then you report for duty at 7:30, like I already said. We all meet here in this room. I will assign each person to a work crew and then you'll work with that group of folks all day. Sometimes I switch crews around in order to make sure we get the proper group dynamics, if you know what I mean. However, some of the crews never change because we need experienced people for drivin', mechanical work and the technical quarry work. We have five crew chiefs and they're always in charge of their particular activity. I took a correspondence course a few years ago in Leadership and Group Psychology and I seem to have a talent for bein' able to read people pretty well. One crew might be out sortin' aggregate, one group might be doin' haulin' and deliveries, one group will be workin' in the quarry, one group on equipment maintenance but you boys will mostly be doin' landscapin'. Work ends every day at five; you'll hear Sugarloaf Sam which means that it's quittin' time. Any more questions, boys?"

"When do you want us to start?" Eric asked.

"You could start right now if you want. There's still a few hours left to the work day and we've got a lot to do. You can decide at five if you want to stay in the bunkhouse. Just remember, however, that if you choose not to stay here, you'll have to get yourselves back by 7:30 tomorrow mornin' and you'll miss out on the nightclub because this is only for folks who choose to stay here. I wouldn't want to be responsible for your hides if you tried to drive down out of the mountains after bein' here. And if you aren't back by 7:30, don't bother showin' up because you're fired, flat out, no excuses."

I looked at Iggy and Eric, trying to get a sense of what they were thinking. We all nodded to each other and I told Big Larry that we'd do it. He said he'd track down Alfonso and called him on the walkie-talkie that was strapped to his belt as we all went out into the parking lot. His voice suddenly transformed from cowboy to trucker.

"Biggie calling Scaper One, Biggie calling Scaper One, do you read me, over?"

"I read you Biggie. Do you need me on another 10-52, over?" a man's static filled voice responded.

"No good buddy, I've got this sichyation well under control. We've got three new perps here and I need to know your 10-7 so I can bring them up to you, over," Big Larry yelled into his receiver.

"I'm halfway up the Juiceway. We're moving some rocks out of the road and building a retaining wall at Switchback 3, over."

"Hold your position Scaper One. We'll be there in fifteen minutes, 10-4."

"We ain't goin' nowhere, Biggie, 10-4."

Biggie told us to come with him to get outfitted and we walked over to the largest building in the quarry complex. There was a little sign by the door saying "Supply Building" which was underneath a picture of Sugarloaf Sam in his bon vivant pose. The door had four different locks on it like something you might see in a New York City apartment. Big Larry had a massive key ring hanging from his belt loop that he unhooked and skillfully opened all four locks with four different keys. The building was windowless and pitch black inside. I could hear him feeling around the wall and he eventually found the light switch. The room was illuminated by a few dangerous looking dusty light bulbs hanging from wires suspended from the ceiling. As I looked around, I saw shelving units on three of the four walls. There were six really old and used-looking tables in the middle, each with four folding and partially painted metal chairs around them. The inside of the building looked a lot smaller than I expected it to look from the outside. Behind us, right near the door we had just come through, I saw another light switch next to a normal looking one. This was not an ordinary light switch—it was more like something you'd see in a horror movie—one of those massive, two sided metal things with a big handle in the middle and pivots on the side.

Big Larry noticed where I was looking and said, "Whatever you do, never, I repeat never, touch that switch." This caused Eric and Iggy to turn around and look where I was looking. "That's pure danger. You ever see in cartoons when someone gets electrocuted? Their body sticks straight out parallel to the ground, their hair sticks out and you can see their teeth and bones flashin' on and off? Well, if you touch that switch the wrong way that will happen to you except you'd probably die a painful death. Anyway, as you see over there, we've got all the clothin' and apparel that you'll need. Why don't you boys try some of this stuff on so we can get you up to Alfonso before the day starts lookin' like a flat tire?"

On the far wall, covering the entire space from floor to ceiling were three levels of metal shelves with neatly arranged piles of overalls, tee shirts, tank tops, hardhats, leather gloves, and work boots. Each pile was clearly marked for size, from XXS all the way up to XXXL. The boots were arranged like shoes at a bowling alley and each pair was marked with the size on the back, from 4 up to 14.

"Here, try some of this stuff on for size. Make sure it fits before we head out. Even though we supply these clothes, we expect you to return all of it when you leave. Understood?"

"Fair enough," Eric responded. "Where is a good place to change?"

Now, back in Boulder, Eric was always looking for opportunities to take pictures of his friends when they were naked or in some other sort of compromising situation. This never seemed to bother Iggy; Eric had a lot of pictures of him alone and some with various girlfriends over the past few years, pictures that could easily be used in the future for some sort of nefarious purpose like if he ever wanted to run for public office. I was the subject of some of Eric's photographs as well. I wasn't too upset by him doing this and tolerated it, thinking that he sometimes captured some pretty funny moments. However, if the tables were ever turned and it was me with the camera and Eric in some sort of embarrassing situation, he would have immediately tried to cover up or run away. He was a very modest person. I often accused him of showering with his underwear on. This probably explains why he was more comfortable being on the other side of the lens.

"Geez, don't be such a ninny! Right here is as good a place as any. Are you afraid that Rhonda might come in and see you in your skivvies? It's just us fellers and we all got the same plumbin' so get on with it!"

Not wanting to seem like ninnies, we striped off our shorts and tee shirts and pulled on some Sugarloaf Quarry clothes until we found the right sizes. Big Larry gave us each a pair of thick leather work gloves and a silver metal hardhat. We tried on work boots until we found a pair that fit and had the most life still left in them.

"The hardhats are adjustable so one size fits all unless of course you've got a gorilla head like Hector the Animal in which case nothin' fits. Okay, looks like we're ready to roll. Let's hop in the pickup truck and take you ladies up to meet Alfonso."

"Where can we leave our stuff?" I asked.

"Oh, just pile it over there next to the blenders," Big Larry said, motioning to one of the shelves that had a strange assortment of electric appliances and bartending supplies. We're not talking about a few random appliances; the middle shelf had four brand new blenders still in their boxes, a bunch of cutting boards, glass bowls, all sorts of glasses and stemware in various shapes and sizes, and shiny metal shakers and tumblers. The bottom shelf had a handful of toasters, electric knives and forks, two deli quality meat slicers and a couple of space heaters. The top shelf was filled with every conceivable and inconceivable sex toy. I had no idea what most of these things were used for although I could guess.

"Don't let you eyes bug out of your heads there boys," Big Larry said with a laugh when he noticed where we were looking. "Those are just some props. If you look over on that wall by the door, in addition to all the quarry tools, on the bottom shelf you'll see all sorts of costumes, hats, whips, you know, theatrical stuff. I don't have time to explain any of this now so don't go worryin' yourselves about any of it. Just so's you know, this is where we have our nightclub."

Big Larry started herding us towards the door and out to the pickup truck. As we came out into the bright Colorado sunshine, we saw Rhonda's car blasting up the driveway. Exhibiting a driving style that we were already quite familiar with, she braked hard, slid sideways a little and came to a stop about five feet from us. The cloud of dust enveloped us and I tried not to breathe until it had cleared out. Rhonda bolted out of the car, opened up the trunk and pulled out a large cardboard box festooned with white stickers with the words "CAUTION LIVE ANIMALS" in large red letters.

"Geez Rhonda, do ya think you could drive any faster?" Big Larry said in his little squeaky voice. "This car's gotta make it through at least another year before we'll be able to replace it."

"Calm down there, little man. These poor animals have been cooped up for way too long on their plane trip from Africa. Can't you hear them crying and squealing inside? I've got to get them out of this box and into their new quarters."

"I just ask that you try to take it a little easier there in the future, girl."

Rhonda stopped on her way into the office and took a long, exaggerated look at us. My guess was that she was impressed with our transformation from college boys to quarry men.

"Well, I'll be hog tied, slapped silly and folded like a pretzel. Look what we have here. Man, you guys look like you're ready for some real work! Not too shabby, eh Big Larry? These boys are just what you were looking for, wouldn't you say?" Rhonda asked with either pride in finding us and delivering us to Big Larry or was being blatantly sarcastic. I couldn't tell which and it made my scrotum tingle and not in a good way. I also had the sense that she was doing an imitation of Big Larry but I don't think he got it.

"We'll see about that. I was just about to run them up the Juiceway to Alfonso at Switchback 3. He could use some help up there since he's only got a skeleton crew today."

"Which skeletons did you assign to him this morning?" Rhonda asked.

"Um, let's see, I gave him Junior, Georgie and Joan," Big Larry said chuckling.

"That should be interesting. I'm gonna go spring these animals and get them settled in. I'll track you down on your walkie-talkie to see where you need me in a little while."

"Let's get this show on the road then boys. Hop in the back of the truck."

Dutifully, we all jumped into the truck, trying to find a comfortable spot to sit. The truck was filled with rakes, shovels, pick axes and sledgehammers so it was critical to find a good seat. Before we got too comfortable, Big Larry stomped on the accelerator. His driving style wasn't much different from Rhonda's so we had to hold on for dear life. After circling around behind the office building, he drove about a quarter of a mile down a dirt road to the edge of the quarry. He turned up another road that I assumed was the Juiceway. The road immediately became steep and all of us and the tools slid to the back of the truck. We got pig piled against the tailgate and it was a struggle to free ourselves of each other and the tools that had all become intertwined.

"Poindexter, get your nose out of my armpit!" Iggy yelled over the noise as he tried to push Eric off of him.

"No, I like it here. Especially since it smells like you haven't showered for several weeks. I can't get enough!" Eric responded.

Every time we would disentangle ourselves, Big Larry would hit another large bump that sent us all up into the air a foot or two only to land in another pile or he would skid around a switchback and we would all get thrown into one of the corners and have to reorganize ourselves all over again. After one of the switchbacks, Big Larry turned around to look at us through the back window and flashed us a maniacal toothy grin. He reminded me of a mini version of Jack Nicholson in *One Flew Over the Cuckoo's Nest*. We had all been to see it a few weeks ago at the Boulder Theatre during a Saturday matinee.

Unfortunately, before we went to the movie, one of our friends had us over for some treats that consisted of half a package of SureFine Fudge Brownie mix and about an ounce of some Colombian that for some reason he wanted to get rid of. The final product consisted of four brownies so jam packed with marijuana that they were green and you could barely even taste the brownie part of the mix. I was okay until right around the time that we purchased our tickets and found our seats in the theatre. The next two hours were just a blur of Jack Nicholson's crazed face, the line "if he's crazy, what does that make you?" rumbling around mercilessly inside my brain, and a thirst that was so strong that my tongue seemed to be glued to the roof of my mouth. Swallowing was a physical impossibility. Unfortunately, I was in such a stupor that I couldn't get out of my seat and sat there for what seemed like ten hours hoping the movie would end so I could get up and get something to drink after the lights came on. I knew I wouldn't be able to stumble out towards the back of the theatre, find the concession stand and speak to someone to tell them what I wanted since I wasn't able to form words. I was certain that on the way back I would get so lost trying to find my seat that I would accidentally end up sitting on someone's lap. When the movie finally did end and the lights came on, I managed to roll out of my seat and crawl around between the rows looking for drinks that people had left behind. I didn't really care too much what was left in the cups, as long as it was liquid. After three or four successes with cups filled with a small amount of something, I was finally able to get my tongue freed up which gave me the wherewithal to attempt standing up. Eric, Iggy and Steve apparently weren't in any better shape and I noticed the entire theatre was empty except for a few theatre staff making their rounds through the seats picking up trash that people had left behind. I searched around and eventually found my three friends as their heads would briefly bob above the height of the backs of the seats. They were all crawling around doing the same thing that I had done, trying to find the cups before the staff did. Eventually, we all had drunk enough to be able to walk out of the theatre without having the staff feel the need to call the police.

This was only the beginning of our challenges that evening. In our household, affectionately called "The Zoo", we had a rotating cooking schedule for dinner where everyone would team up with another person and was responsible for planning, cooking and cleaning up after one meal per week. There was a great expectation that, unless you knew beforehand that you wouldn't be able to make it to the meal, you be there and be there on time or suffer the collective wrath of the upset housemates. On this particular evening, we knew that Peter and Crystal were cooking and dinner was scheduled for six. Peter was a great cook, a committed vegetarian and the person responsible for all of us agreeing to have a vegetarian household in the first place. I don't think any of us were vegetarians before we moved in but agreed to follow these rules. It was a great education for me as I had very little awareness about my diet before moving in.

This evening, Peter and Crystal were cooking spanakopita. As anyone who has ever made this knows, it is very labor intensive. When Eric,

Steve, Iggy and I finally stumbled out of the theatre onto the streets of Boulder, the sun was still up so we knew that it wasn't really late. None of us had a watch, hell, nobody in Boulder in 1976 had a watch; it just wasn't cool. The obvious downside is that you never knew what time it was but since we prided ourselves on being tuned into the world around us, we felt we had a pretty good handle on the time based on the position of the sun and the length of the shadows. Clearly this wasn't going to help us much once the sun had set but we knew that it was close enough to six and that we needed to get back to the Zoo as quickly as possible.

I suppose it would be interesting if someone had mapped our route that night. Once we got out into the fresh air, our condition improved slightly, meaning, we were able to "walk" and marginally able to "talk". We knew this part of Boulder like the back of our hands and the walk from the theatre, while slightly circuitous, would normally have taken about ten minutes. After several conversations amongst ourselves about the best way to walk that any passing pedestrian might have thought was being conducted in a language that probably wasn't even invented yet, we went a way that to this day completely baffles me. I'm guessing that it took us anywhere from twenty minutes to two hours to get back to the Zoo but I don't think I could be any more specific than this. However, I do remember that it was dark by the time we arrived.

When we finally got to the Zoo, it was obvious that we were very late for dinner. We stumbled into the dining/living/music combination room and were "greeted" by our six other housemates and man, did they look pissed off, especially Peter.

Peter was a man of few words but he did his best to make sure each one carried a lot of weight. Just as we entered the room, he stood up, started clearing the table and said slowly, "I'm glad you guys finally made it to dinner."

Crystal, on the other hand, was Peter's polar opposite in the talking department. "You guys, you can't believe how much effort we put into this meal. Where have you been? We started over an hour ago. You guys knew we were making spanakopita tonight. At least you could have been here on time. You're lucky there's any food left because it came out so well. We set aside plates for you in the kitchen and we were about to go in and help ourselves to your portions. It might be a little cold but it's still awesome. So, where have you been? You all don't look so good."

The three of us looked at each other and got the uncontrollable giggles. Eric finally managed to say, "You wouldn't believe the afternoon we've been having."

Iggy added, "Yeah, hey thanks for saving us some food. I'm feeling mighty hungry so I think I'll go get my plate."

"I just need to get some water," I said. "Then I'll join you for dinner."

The original diners agreed to keep us company, even though they had already finished eating. When Eric, Iggy and I returned with our plates and drinks, three additional chairs were brought in and spaces made for us at the table.

"You guys look really stoned," Jackie observed, stating the obvious.

"We're beyond stoned," mumbled Eric. "We're hallucinating."

"Did you drop some acid?" asked hot to trot Wayne who suddenly perked up.

"No," I said in between gulps of water. I told them in clipped sentences what had happened with the brownies, our time at the movie, and our walk home.

"I can't believe you did that. Man, you guys are morons," Peter said. "By the way, how do you like the meal?"

Eric and Iggy were busy eating what must have been a fabulous meal and seemed to be thoroughly enjoying it. I, on the other hand, couldn't even begin to get my fork, food, mouth and brain to cooperate. The smell and sight of the food was giving me a visceral reaction that you might get if you were to sit down to a plate full of wiggling worms set attractively on a bed of dirt. I just couldn't do it.

"This is fabulous, I've just got to get your recipe," Iggy said with a rather effeminate lisp. Reverting back to his normal voice he said, "No, really, this is some good shit."

"Yeah, Peter, I agree with Iggy. How'd you and Crystal make it?" Eric was able to say between bites.

Peter's response was, "a little of this, a little of that."

"Peter, geez, that's all you can say? Okay, here's what we did . . ." Crystal went on to describe in detail the ingredients, including their time at the grocery store, the drive home, the unloading, and how each item was prepared, cooked and arranged for presentation at the dinner table. I was trying hard to keep my stomach under control.

When it became clear that I wasn't going to be able to try a bite, I told everyone that I needed to go lie down for a bit, apologized to Peter and

Crystal and said that if anyone wanted my portion, they were welcome to have it but if not, I would love to have some of it later.

This might explain why I had a sudden thirst when I saw Big Larry looking back at us doing his best Jack Nicholson imitation while driving up the road. We made it through two switchbacks without any of us falling out of the truck and by the time we were about to go screaming through the next one, he thankfully pulled off to the side and came to a halt. Me and my fellow passengers in the back felt like we had just been let out of a dryer. We tried to get out of the truck but our balance was completely off and we looked like we were a bunch of drunkards that were about to fail a field sobriety test. Luckily, after a short time standing next to the truck, our heads stopped spinning.

"You guys look like you've never driven on a mountain road before," Big Larry said.

"No, not true, we drive on mountain roads all the time, just not in the back of a pickup truck," Iggy said.

"With tools threatening to impale us," Eric added.

"Come on; let's go find Alfonso and his crew of skeletons. I tell ya, that Rhonda, she's a funny lady. They said they were at Switchback 3 but I don't see 'em here. Maybe they're workin' below the bank. I see their trucks so they can't be too far away."

Big Larry walked over to the steep drop off on the outside of the switchback and looked over the edge. He must have located them since I could see him talking and gesturing to someone. The three of us walked over and when I looked down the slope, I saw a bunch of people sitting on some rocks. Two of them were smoking cigarettes. Big Larry told them that break time was over and they should get their butts up here.

When all of the landscaping crew members were assembled, Big Larry introduced Alfonso, Junior, Georgie and Joan to us. He clearly didn't remember our names so instead he said, "Okay, Alfonso, here are your new workers; Mo, Larry and Curly. Why don't you all introduce yourselves?"

Alfonso was Hispanic, about forty years old, medium height and build and was wearing the Sugarloaf Quarry uniform. He had a few tattoos on his strong looking arms; a cigarette dangling from his lips and a neatly trimmed goatee. His hair was cut really short, almost military style, except for a long tail in the back. Junior was a Baby Huey clone, with a big round belly and I assume no diaper. He was really tall, probably weighed over three hundred pounds, had on the quarry outfit with one of the overall straps hanging off his shoulder. He had a brown afro and could have been anywhere from sixteen to thirty, it was hard to tell. Georgie was another story altogether. I'm not sure if he was a she or what. He/she was dressed in the overall and tee shirt combination so maybe that meant that he was a he. His/her height was around five and half feet tall, with shoulder length hair, no facial hair and slight curves that didn't sway my opinion either way. When we shook hands, it wasn't a firm manly shake nor was it a gentle womanly shake, very confusing. Finally, there was Joan. She was clearly a female with long almost white straight hair, tall, slender, tan and wearing the same tank top that we saw Rhonda in earlier but instead of shorts, she had on jeans. I found her very attractive.

Big Larry's walkie-talkie beeped so he went walking away out of earshot but we could hear his little voice yelling into his receiver. When it was apparent that he was going to be occupied with this for a while, Alfonso took control.

"I trust Big Larry explained the job to you guys," Alfonso said with a really cool sounding Mexican accent. "He told me that you'd probably be working with me most of the time. I'm a little worried about having college hippies working landscaping but let's see how things go. There's not much time left today but let me fill you in here. Last night, there was a little rockslide that covered part of the switchback. My crew and I have spent all day using this material to build a retaining wall over there and we're trying to complete the job by five so that we can get trucks up here early tomorrow morning. Junior here does a lot of the heavy work but we all help him out as much as possible. We've got lots of tools and this here Bobcat 763C Skid Steer Loader. This baby has a Kubota 46 horsepower diesel and 66" bucket. I'm the only one that's authorized to operate it but sometimes I let Junior or Joan do a few things. Joan's our *artiste;* she's especially good with things like rock wall building. She's got the eye, if you know what I mean. She's also our plant expert. Georgie is my all rounder, he will do just about anything you ask and never complain. A little funny in the cabeza though, right Georgie?" Alfonso said jokingly, giving Georgie a little push on the shoulder.

"So, how can we help out here, Alfonso?" Eric asked. "We're ready to get to work."

"Let's finish up building this wall. We've probably got a couple of tons of rock to move and stack. Now that we've got all this help, Georgie, why don't you take the truck without the trailer and do a complete drive through to see what condition all the roads are in. Biggie will want a full inventory at the meeting."

Big Larry started walking back towards us and yelled over to Alfonso that he needed to get back to the office. He turned his truck around and sped back down the hill.

"He's a character. Takes a little getting used to but I think you guys will find that he's a good boss. Just don't take him too seriously and be cautious 'cause he can turn on you if you get on his bad side. So, let's get back to the rocks. Joan, you do the stacking with the big guy, what's your name again?" Alfonso asked looking at Iggy.

"I'm Iggy and I'm hot to trot!" Iggy declared while Eric and I burst out laughing. Alfonso, Junior and Joan, on the other hand, just looked at us like someone had fouled the air.

"Inside joke," Eric said in our defense.

"Okay. Now you, Smith Brothers," Alfonso said pointing to Eric and me, "I want you to work with Junior to help load the rocks into the Bobcat. Use the crowbars to position the rocks so I can get the bucket under them and then when I'm moving them over to the wall, use the rakes and shovels to clear out the smaller rocks that we won't use in the wall and dump it over the side. Junior will show you what to do."

"You got it boss," I said, eager to appear like a model employee. "We're on it!"

Eric, Junior and I walked over to the rockslide while Iggy and Joan went about ten yards in the other direction to the mostly built retaining wall on the inside slope of the switchback. Alfonso climbed into the Bobcat and fired it up in a big cloud of diesel exhaust. The pile of rocks that was still in the road was about the size of a large car and a random assortment of shapes and sizes. I was a bit disappointed that Iggy was assigned to Joan duty and I was stuck with Baby Huey.

I had taken several geology courses during my first three years at CU and knew enough to appreciate the geological history of the region. We had taken several field trips up into the foothills and some of the nearby canyons. Anyone who has ever been to Boulder or seen pictures of it knows about the flatirons that form the western edge. These rocks are sedimentary sandstone but as you go further west, up into the mountains, the sedimentary rocks quickly transition to a mixture of harder igneous and metamorphic rocks. The rocks around the Sugarloaf area are mostly granite but are occasionally infused with silver, lead and gold veins. The discovery of gold caused a major prospecting frenzy in the 1860s and left its telltale mark on the landscape in the form of many old mines, tailings and old rusted metal equipment. One of my friends lived up Four Mile Canyon and her house was literally built on top of an abandoned gold mine from that era.

Iggy and Joan hit it off immediately. They had several dump loads of rocks to work with and a clear task. Iggy considered himself the consummate lady's man and thought he was as smooth as silk. In his mind, he knew how to talk to women and would absolutely turn on the charm from the very beginning. We could hear their interaction from the slide area. "So Joan, got a boyfriend?"

"Why would you ask that? I just assumed you're gay. Am I right?"

"Hell no! That's a good one. No, I'm definitely not gay but I have had a few special friendships, if you know what I mean." Eric and I looked at each other and started laughing again at Iggy's banter.

"How about we just concentrate on getting this wall finished. We can continue this conversation tonight at the nightclub if you want."

"The nightclub-man, I can't wait to check it out. However, I live down in Boulder with Eric, Dean and six other crazed lunatics. I wasn't really planning on staying here at night."

"That would be a bad decision," Joan said in a deadpan voice. "I don't care who or what you have waiting for you in town because if you decide not to stay the night, you would be making a real dumb mistake. But, enough of this chit-chat, I'll point to the rock that I want and you grab it and bring it to me. Do you think that you can handle that?"

Meanwhile, we were working hard to get the bucket of the Bobcat loaded with the best, flattest rocks, not an easy task when you're working with granite. Most of these rocks were blocks, uneven blocks at that, so they seemed like they would be hard to use in a rock wall. However, Junior seemed to have a plan and he made it clear to Eric and me which rocks we should load into the bucket. Most of them were light enough for one person to move, some required two people and a few required long crowbars to get into the bucket. Before long, we had cleared all the rocks out of the switchback and went over to help with the wall building. In about an hour, the wall was finished and our work was done. It looked good.

"Great job, guys," Alfonso said. "Perfect timing, too, 4:40. Let's head down to the office as soon as I load the Bobcat onto the trailer. We never leave any of our tools or equipment out on a job site."

We had some water from the big cooler that was sitting on the tailgate and then climbed in and drove downhill. Joan took the passenger seat while the four of us guys jumped in the back. Alfonso drove at a reasonable speed and got us down to the office without injury, even while pulling the Bobcat on a trailer behind the truck.

Down in the parking lot, everyone that we had already met was standing around by the office building. There were another ten or twelve other people congregating that we hadn't met yet. Big Larry was waiting by the front door, taking an inventory of his crew and when he saw that everyone was there, opened it and let us in.

Clearly, there were seats that everyone was used to sitting in around the big table in the center. Big Larry and Rhonda each took a seat at the two heads of the table and the five crew chiefs, I assumed, sat on one side while everyone else filled in the remaining seats. We waited until everyone grabbed a place and took the ones that were left over. Big Larry barked like a military man, "Okay, let's hear the crew reports. Quarry?"

"248 tons blasted, mostly granite, some ore," barked a big guy who looked like he might have played for the Broncos fifteen years ago.

"Good job, Sorting?"

The woman who gave the report was also a behemoth of a person. Her tank top clearly was being stretched to its limit. "11 yards of chips, 47 yards of gravel, 26 yards of stone, 19 small slabs and 6 large slabs."

"Excellent, Transport?" Larry said.

"Six deliveries, three residential, one commercial, one industrial and one to the County Highway Department," said a man who looked like he probably drove a truck from the time he was twelve.

"Fine work, Maintenance?"

"Changed the main seals on the dozer, hydraulics on the grader, new bearings on the crusher," reported a guy in greasy overalls who looked like maybe he was Big Larry's older, slightly larger brother.

"Good production, Landscaping?"

Alfonso said, "Cleared Switchback 3 from yesterday's rockslide, built retaining wall, all roads clear as of 16:45."

"Excellent. Now before I let you go, I want to introduce three new workers that will be here temporarily, Iggy, Eric and Dean. I'm not sure which one is which but I'll let you figure it out for yourselves. College boys all look the same to me. Have you rookies decided if you're staying here for the night yet?"

"Not tonight, we're expected for dinner and I've got other plans," Eric explained.

"And I didn't bring my toothbrush or jammies," I added.

"And it's my turn to cook," Iggy said.

The assembled group started making disapproving noises that included whistles and jeers just as Sugarloaf Sam's wild rodent screech blasted over the loudspeaker, signaling quitting time. With that, everyone started clearing out of the office.

Big Larry said in his loudest voice possible, "Anyone want to run these boys back into town? I'll pay ½ an hour of overtime." Turning to us, he whispered, "I hope for your sake that you come back to work bright and early tomorrow and will stay here tomorrow night."

CHAPTER 3

BIG LARRY AND Junior were having an animated discussion off to the side that I couldn't hear. Eventually, Junior was sent in our direction with an annoyed look on his face. Behind him, Big Larry yelled, "You needed to go into the big city sometime anyway, you told me so this mornin', right?"

"Yeah, I just wasn't really planning on doing it today." Looking at the three of us, he said, "Hop in the Sugarloaf Quarry car, I'll drive you home. Just give me a few minutes to get some stuff from the bunkhouse."

We got back into the car that just hours ago had brought us up here. Even though I had only worked a short time, I was feeling a bit tired from the effort so it felt really good to sit down.

"Maybe we should consider staying here tomorrow night. I'm not sure what this nightclub thing is all about but it sure seems like something that they all get pretty excited about," I said.

"For sure," Eric said, "but it has me kind of worried. You guys saw the supply building. It's a complete dump. How can you have a nightclub in a room that's so trashed and filled with shelves and a few crappy tables? And what's the deal with all the sex toys and blenders?"

"Good point Mungo but aren't you curious? You guys probably heard Joan say that we would be making a big mistake not to leave our lives in Boulder in order to stay up here. Weird," Iggy said while taking sips of water out of a bottle that he had brought with him from Alfonso's truck.

"Yeah and we also heard that she thought you were gay," Eric said.

We had a good laugh over this again until Junior came out and got into the driver's seat. The four of us drove down the driveway and onto Sugarloaf Mountain Road without saying a word. It wasn't until we hit Boulder Canyon that the silence was broken.

"Hey, man, thanks for taking us home," Eric said to Junior. "I take it you didn't really want to do this so we all appreciate it. It will be different from here on because we'll bring one of our cars up in the morning. Rhonda literally picked us up off the street this afternoon."

"Tonight's dance night and I had a few things to do before nine. I need to write a letter to my mommy and there's just not much time. Where do you live?"

"Up on the Hill," we all answered in unison and then starting laughing at how silly it came off, "on Pleasant Street between 10th and 11th," Eric added.

I was pleased to see that Junior was a safe driver like Alfonso. By the time we got into town, Junior took all the right shortcuts to get to our neighborhood so it was clear that he knew his way around pretty well.

"Are you from Boulder?" I asked.

"I grew up in Table Mesa and went to Boulder High. My mommy and daddy moved to Albuquerque a few months ago and I really miss them."

"What can you tell us about Alfonso?" Eric asked thankfully changing the subject.

"He's a great guy, a great boss, a really great person to work for," Junior said.

"Great," I responded.

"I've worked with all the crew bosses since I came to work at the quarry and I have to say that Alfonso is one of my top five favorites."

"But aren't there only five crew bosses total?" Eric ventured tentatively.

"Let me think about that some. Yeah, I guess you're right. He's definitely top five."

When we got to our neighborhood, Iggy told Junior which house was ours and he dropped us off at the curb. He barely came to a full stop and seemed quite anxious to be on his way.

"See you tomorrow," Iggy said as we got out of the car.

"Have fun at the nightclub," Eric called out. "Take it easy on the dance floor."

Kate, Crystal and Hazel were sitting on the front porch as we walked up to the house. They watched the car drive away and then focused on us quarry men with quizzical looks on their faces.

"What the hell was that?" Kate asked. "And where have you guys been all afternoon? Iggy, you and Jackie are supposed to be making dinner tonight. It's already 5:30. And why are you all dressed like identical Bozos?"

"It won't take long to throw dinner together. We're making Eggplant Surprise, your favorite Hazel. Is Jackie around?" Iggy asked. "We'll answer all of your other questions at dinner. You won't believe what Jacque, Mungo and I got ourselves into today!"

"I think she's already in the kitchen getting dinner going," Crystal said. "You might want to be careful what you say to her, she's not in a great mood."

Given our living situation and the typical hormonal surges of men and women of college age, it was inevitable that various relationships in the house would develop over time. The combinations of pairings were almost infinite, especially when you factored in friends of housemates, ex-housemates and potential housemates. In the current line up, Iggy had been in a casual relationship with Kate earlier in the year that was mostly one of convenience so it ended easily and, as far as I know, there were no hard feelings or jealously. The two of them had known each other since high school. Currently, he was having a rather stormy relationship with Jackie, one that either burned really hot or was painfully cold, for them and everyone else in the house. While Iggy's bedroom was in the basement, Jackie had gotten the best room upstairs. It was a two room suite with her bed and dresser in one room and her desk, a couch and lots of beautiful plants in the other. It was a corner room and both outside walls had huge windows that Jackie had turned it into a veritable greenhouse. When you entered her room, it was almost magical, very welcoming and visually appealing. She had a lot of interesting artwork and other wall hangings and a flair for interior design. Given the choice between sleeping in a dark, damp, cramped basement room or Jackie's room, I think Iggy might have been drawn to Jackie partly for this reason and was willing to overlook her moodiness.

When Iggy and I walked into the kitchen, he not only got the cold shoulder but also the cold back, front and entire lower body. Jackie's body language could have stopped a rhino in full charge. She was banging pots and pans around with wild abandon and had the dinner ingredients all laid out on the counter.

"Sorry I'm late, honey," Iggy said, tail between his legs as he bravely came up behind her and attempted to give her a hug. "Thanks for getting started on dinner. I've got a story to tell that you're going to find quite interesting."

"Get away from me. All I know is that we had a plan to start cooking at five and you didn't even bother to show up on time. You are one of the most inconsiderate and frustrating people that I've ever met. Have you been out playing with Dean and Eric again?"

"It will become clear when I tell you about my afternoon."

"It will, will it? And why are you and Dean wearing the same stupid costumes?"

"We all got jobs today."

With that news, Jackie's mood did a complete about-face and she snapped out of her funk. She threw the pan she had in her hand onto the counter, turned around and gave Iggy a big hug and kiss. "Oh baby, that's fantastic! What are you going to be doing?"

"Let's just get dinner started. We want to tell everyone the story while we're eating."

I abandoned this drama and tracked Eric down to see if he wanted to add his dirty clothes to mine to make up a full load of laundry. I went back into the kitchen where Iggy and Jackie were making up and made the same offer. Iggy stripped completely out of his quarry duds right there and handed them to me.

"Um, Iggy, why don't you quickly go shower and put some clean clothes on first. I'll start chopping the vegetables," Jackie offered.

After I was done showering and had put everything in the laundry, I grabbed a cold beer and went to the front porch to join my other housemates. They all knew that on a night that Iggy and Jackie cooked, the food was going to be really good. Crystal and Hazel were snuggled up together in one of the overstuffed and ratty chairs while Eric and Kate were looking a little cozy on the couch, Wayne and Peter each had their own chair and I grabbed the stump that was often used as a table. Say what you will about group living but for all its drawbacks there were some moments that were just perfect.

"So Beans, Eric here won't tell us anything about your new jobs," Wayne stated. "Why don't you at least give us a hint about what you're doing?" He had a summer job working at a pizza place, mostly doing food prep in the afternoon and deliveries during the evening. He timed his dinner break to be back at the Zoo in order to eat with us.

Before I could respond, Hazel said, "I'll bet you guys can't talk about it because either it's illegal or you're embarrassed, right? I mean, why would you want to go around wearing a tee shirt with a drunk mouse on it?"

"Yeah, this is a pretty cool shirt, for sure! We promised not to talk about it until we were at the dinner table," I said. "Besides, it's not really all that interesting, just a bit strange. By the way, Hazel, how are the music lessons going?"

"Okay, I guess. I've got a few clients that I'm seeing every week and once the public schools let out next week, I've got a few high school kids that will be starting up. I'm hoping it will be enough to live on this summer because I'm really grooving on having some free time. Plus, there's some overlap with the voice students that Crystal is tutoring."

"I've always wanted to learn to play the tuba," Kate interjected. "Maybe I could get my parents to spring for lessons. How much do you charge?"

"For you Kate, $12 per lesson and they run about forty five minutes. You've got to have big strong lungs and be able to blow hard though."

Iggy had just appeared at the front door and said, "She can, I'll attest to that. By the way, dinner's ready."

"Hey, shut up you creep," Kate said to Iggy giving him a friendly punch on the shoulder.

We followed Iggy back into the house and took our places around the table. Spread out before us were fresh flowers, a beautifully arranged salad in a large bowl with multiple dressing choices, several loaves of French bread and one of our perennial favorite meals, Eggplant Surprise. The surprise was the asparagus and goat cheese that was in the recipe. It was a spectacular dish and very pretty to look at.

"I'm salivating," said Peter, "I've been looking forward to this meal all day."

As the various bowls and baskets were passed around, Jackie said she was dying to hear about our new jobs. Her parents were quite wealthy and she never had to work during the summer if she didn't want to but somehow lived vicariously through those that did. It had been an issue between her and Iggy that he needed to get a job so they could do the kinds of things she liked to do without feeling obligated to cover his expenses.

"We were out winging the wham after lunch today," Iggy began, "when this crazy car pulled up to Beans. This dowdy woman gets out and starts talking to him so we went over to check it out. She ends up kidnapping us at knife point, takes us up to the Sugarloaf Quarry to meet this little midget who gave us special clothes to wear that most of you have already seen, promised to pay us $4.55 an hour and then he puts us to work moving rocks around. At five, the rat sang and they brought us back down here and told us to be there by 7:30 tomorrow morning if we wanted to work again."

"At knife point?" Jackie asked suspiciously.

"Dowdy woman?" Eric asked giving Iggy a fake doubtful look.

"Most of that is true except for the little midget part," I interjected. "I think he was actually a dwarf."

"You were actually kidnapped at knife point? Why didn't you just escape when you had a chance? And why would they kidnap you and then offer to pay you?" Jackie asked, exposing some of the obvious flaws in Iggy's version.

"Okay, we went there voluntarily," Iggy conceded. "But I'm sticking with the dowdy part."

"Oh yeah, Rhonda was dowdy all right and I'm Robert Redford!" Eric said knowing that he probably would never get mistaken for him even though the Sundance Kid had probably walked around our neighborhood regularly when he had been a member of the Kappa Sigma fraternity about ten years ago.

"Why would you lie about this woman, Ignace? She must have been quite a babe, right? What did she look like?" Jackie asked and since she called him Ignace, it was clear that her mood had reverted to the dark side.

"Well, let's just say that she wasn't a total dog," Iggy said digging himself in deeper. "I guess some guys might think she was attractive, like Beans, Wayne, Peter, or Mungo but I guess I didn't. My standards are a bit higher than that."

"I thought she was a babe," I offered, fanning the flames a little higher. "Iggy, I thought you got her phone number before we left."

"No, you must be mistaking her with Joan," Eric said.

"Who's Joan?" Jackie asked icily.

"We're getting off track here. Do you want to hear the rest of the story or not?"

Jackie sat there, legs pushed out far in front of her seat and her shoulders pushed way back. She resembled a plank of wood in the chair. Her arms were folded over her chest and she was making a pouty face to complete the look.

"Maybe Eric should tell you about the nightclub," Iggy suggested.

"Oh yeah, the nightclub," Eric began. "Well, apparently every night at nine they turn the supply shack into a nightclub. We saw this dive and I'm not quite sure what to make of it. They told us that the employees live at the quarry during the week, sleep in a bunkhouse and eat all their meals at a mess hall. It kind of sounds like summer camp to me. I know it sounds hokey but I swear everyone we met there today was so excited about the nightclub that they thought we were complete idiots for coming back to Boulder tonight. Big Larry, he's the dwarf or the midget or whatever, he's the boss and he told us that if we didn't stay at the quarry, we couldn't go to the nightclub."

"And we saw the supply building because Big Larry took us in there to get our clothes and equipment. The place looked almost as bad as Iggy's apartment. I can't imagine that it's more fun than being at the Zoo on any evening of the week," I said.

"But they have entertainment and free drinks!" Iggy added.

"Maybe you guys should check it out tomorrow night and see what you think. It sounds rather intriguing," Hazel said, giving Crystal a wink.

"I'm just annoyed that Iggy feels that he needs to lie to me about attractive women," Jackie said in a sulky voice. "I thought our relationship was stronger than that."

"I just didn't want to hurt your feelings or make you think that you had anything to worry about, honey," Iggy offered in his defense.

"Well, in the future, tell me the truth, okay?"

"For sure, man!" Iggy said, pretending to be a really stoned hippie.

Iggy wasn't the only one of us with challenging female relationships. Eric and I weren't exactly leading the bachelor life. He saw a few women on a semi-regular basis. One was a local woman named Tina who was a weaver. She lived in North Boulder in a beautiful house and a pretty good sized yard. We loved to be invited to hang out with Tina and her female housemates because they often sunbathed naked on their back deck and didn't really seem bothered enough by our presence to cover up. Since she mostly sold her artwork at craft fairs, she was away a lot of weekends so Eric didn't get to spend as much time with her as he wanted. His other love interest was a young woman that he knew back in Missouri who had just graduated from high school. Phoebe flew out to Boulder every so often to visit Eric so he needed to schedule his time pretty carefully since Tina and Phoebe didn't know about each other.

My love interests were a bit less complicated. For whatever reasons, I had shorter relationships, one at a time, which rarely overlapped. I was currently trying to foster a relationship with a next door neighbor named Lani who was from Hawaii. I think her real name was Noelani which she told me means "heavenly girl" but everyone just called her Lani. She was a few years older than me, having already graduated the previous year. Like Iggy, I had a very short fling a few months ago with my housemate Kate, before that with another housemate who moved out because she had about five other boyfriends and decided to sponge off one of them for a while. I think he also had a cool car, way cooler than my twelve year old Chrysler Newport.

More recently, I had been involved with a cowgirl from a small ranch town in Colorado whom I met in my "Human Sexuality" class. This was perhaps the most popular course on campus, not surprisingly. It was taught by a Sociology professor who was more like a standup comedian. His lectures were amazing and the class filled one of the largest auditoriums on campus. There was a lab for the course, each run by one of thirty or so teaching assistants who had previously taken the course. We were required to meet at the house of the TA one evening a week and were "encouraged" to supply enough alcohol to make sure that everyone was relaxed and lubricated enough to talk freely. Any subject was fair game. The women of the group ran full speed with the concept while most of us guys needed both the alcohol and constant prodding from the women to contribute much. The cowgirl and I started seeing each other outside of lab and began a small romance. Unfortunately, the end of the semester came and she went back home for the summer. I knew some things about her before we had our first date that really came in handy. These were the sorts of things that might have taken a complete lifetime to find out under normal circumstances and maybe even that wouldn't have been long enough. I knew how much she loved having the spaces between her toes probed with a tongue and I knew that making dog-growling noises at the right time could produce astonishing results.

Having grown up in the white, Republican New Jersey suburbs of New York City, I admit that I had lived a fairly sheltered life before coming to Colorado. Having never been away from home before and having never really met anyone that wasn't from the same socio-economic background as myself; my horizons had quickly expanded since I made my decision to go to college in Colorado. I was the only son of parents who grew up in the Midwest and moved to suburbia thinking it would be a good place to raise a family. I also had three sisters, one older and two younger.

Like Iggy and Eric, I, too, had long hair that was dark blond, a more-or-less full reddish brown beard that I was really happy to be able to grow considering that I was kind of a late bloomer. I was an inch under six feet and weighed about a hundred and forty pounds on a good day. Even though I was blessed with an unusual amount of energy during my waking hours, usually by the middle part of the evening when everyone else around me was just getting revved up, I was ready for sleep. When I was a kid and had sleepovers at a friend's house, I would often fall asleep on the couch way before their parents made us go to bed. Maybe this explains why I wasn't invited to a lot of these as a kid. One of my parent's favorite embarrassing stories concerned a particular New Year's Eve when I was probably around ten. From about 9:30 onward, I was struggling against seemingly impossible odds to stay awake until midnight. Apparently, I dozed off around 9:31 but managed to wake up with about ten seconds until midnight and shouted with great pride, "I made it!!" Years later, my sisters would tease me mercilessly telling me that I hadn't really made it but our parents had made them promise not to tell me the truth of my slumbers.

The Zoo dinner conversation went on to other topics and we confirmed that Hazel and I were cooking tomorrow night. After dinner, out on the front porch, we planned the night's activities while Iggy and Jackie cleaned up. Crystal and Hazel were going to a movie downtown. Kate and Eric were going for a walk around campus as Eric was meeting up with Tina and Kate was going to visit with her new boyfriend Elmo. Wayne had to go back to work and Peter and I were content to hang out and drink another beer. We assumed Iggy and Jackie would be busy for the rest of the evening processing their issues.

"Maybe we should head out to Tulagis," Peter suggested. "We could play some foosball. I think you have a score to settle from a few nights ago, remember?"

"How could I forget?" I said. Peter was so good at foosball that he was able to consistently beat me and whomever I recruited as my partner by himself. In fact, he was able to beat almost any other two people that he played single-handedly.

Tulagis was a bar on the Hill a few blocks from our house. They usually had pretty good musicians, even during the week, and it was a great place to have a few watered down beers, meet people and sometimes dance. Peter wasn't much into the dancing part, nor was I for that matter, but the other activities were more appealing. Knowing that I had to get up fairly early to head back to the quarry, I warned him that I might not stay very long.

The sun was just setting behind the Front Range and the sky became electric with spectacular colors. Everything came alive with the warmest red glow I had ever experienced and this happened almost every night. As we were enjoying this special time, one of our neighbors came walking by and joined us. Her name was Windy and if ever a name fit a person, it was Windy. She might have been born Gertrude, Eloise or Harriet but Windy was her true name.

"Hi guys, mind if I join you?" she asked in the sweetest wisp of a voice that sounded so adorable and vulnerable. She was clearly used to blowing in and out of situations and taking whatever she wanted before moving on. On many occasions, she would show up right at dinner time and of course we would invite her to join us. My theory was that she monitored the activities in our kitchen from her house as she had a direct line of sight and could time her visits perfectly.

"Of course not, Windy," Peter said, "would you like a cold one?"

"For sure, I can get one from the kitchen."

"You better let me get it. Iggy and Jackie are in there cleaning up from dinner and they're having a little argument. Would you prefer a bottle of the Arapahoe Amber or the Sunshine Porter?"

"Whatever you have the most of—I like them both."

After Peter left, I asked her what she had done today. I knew she didn't have a real job and earned most of her money as a street musician, either playing solo or sometimes with other musician friends of hers, always guys. I think she also relied on the kindness of her friends and acquaintances and we were almost always on her rounds through the neighborhood. When you looked like Windy, long wavy sun-streaked light brown hair, fabulous body with a good singing voice and a reasonably skilled guitar player, you could get by pretty easily.

"I had a really super day. I met my friends Joachim and Butch downtown around noon and we played for the lunchtime crowd. They're really good. We made about $25."

"Each or to split?"

"To split but we only played for an hour."

Peter came back with the beer and we enjoyed the last moments of the sunset. I mentioned my new job up at the quarry and asked if she knew about the nightclub.

"No, I've never heard anything about it. They have some sort of act every night?"

"Some of the nights, at least this is what Big Larry told us."

"Maybe I should go up and talk to this Big Larry guy. I could use a few more gigs and besides, I've got a whole new repertoire that I'm trying out. They're bawdy songs that I've written inspired by what I've learn about the old prospecting days. Maybe you'd like to hear one of them? I'll run home and get my guitar so don't go sneaking off."

After she floated off the porch, Peter said that we probably wouldn't see her again for a few days since she had a tendency to get easily distracted by something or someone and then forget what her original task was. To our surprise, she reappeared a few moments later.

"Just know this song is still a little rough, so be kind."

Windy spent a few minutes tuning her guitar and getting comfortable on one of the chairs. This alone had both Peter and me mesmerized. She was wearing a very loose, flowy sort of top that didn't hide much underneath, especially since the setting sun was behind her diagonally and we could easily see the outline of her breasts through the light fabric, even the deliciously faint outline of her areolas and nipples bobbing around inside looking like they were scouting out escape routes. Her short cut-off jeans, like Rhonda's, were probably illegal in some states. Before she started playing, she seemed totally incapable of actually producing anything musical but once she launched into a song, her persona underwent an amazing transformation. She frequently played for us so I figured there was a good chance we were in for a treat.

She played a bluesy sort of introduction and then launched into the song in a rough kind of voice.

> *Well I'm a Union Claim miner,*
> *I don't need no wife or gal,*
> *'Cause I've got ol' Sadie here,*
> *She's better than one of my pals.*
>
> *We huff and puff all day long,*
> *Workin' down in that ol' mine,*
> *Then we huff and puff all night long,*
> *Me and ol' Sadie and her warm vagine.*
>
> *Some might say it's wrong for a horse,*
> *To be givin' a man such a thrill,*
> *But when it comes to me and ol' Sadie,*
> *She always lets me give her a drill.*

"Here's the chorus." Windy quickly said.

So blow me away, blow me away,
And I'll work hard all day long,
Blow me away, blow me away,
'Cause I've got my Sadie and that can't be wrong.

"That's all I've got so far. What do you think?"

"I have to say, Windy, that song is pretty sick, funny but sick. You've built the entire song around a horse vagina. That takes some pretty serious cajones!" I said.

"But it's a great tune!" Peter said encouragingly. Windy was pretty fragile when it came to an honest critique so I should have taken Peter's tactic and found something positive to say.

"Thanks, Peter, do you like the chord progression?"

Peter played the guitar a bit so he could appreciate her musicianship. He said that he liked the way that it flowed and maybe the lyrics needed to be tightened up a bit but the framework was good and solid.

"Is this based on personal experience or did you write it about someone you know who was into bestiality and works as a miner or in a quarry?" I asked rather pointedly, half afraid of what her answer might be. "Luckily, I didn't see any horses up at the quarry this afternoon but I did meet some guys that could possibly be into this sort of thing."

"No," Windy said laughing. "It's based on a book that I read on the history of Colorado mining camps. It talks about how the men who worked there didn't have any girlfriends because the only women around were prostitutes and there just weren't enough of them to go around. The guys that were trying to save their money or were just plain repulsive for one reason or another had to get creative."

"Well, I think you're on to something. However, promise me that if you are ever asked to perform at the Sugarloaf Quarry, don't sing this one, okay?"

Windy sang a few more songs while we finished our beers. We invited her to go to Tulagis with us and surprisingly, she agreed. The night was cooling off quickly and the air was a perfect temperature. After Windy took her guitar home, she joined us for the walk down the street. The place was pretty quiet when we arrived but both of the foosball tables were busy so we played some pool instead. Before long, a band took the small stage. They started playing cover tunes from popular bands and sounded pretty good. Windy was starting to get a bit antsy and asked if either of us wanted to dance. Peter looked at me and it was clear that he was hoping that I would volunteer as nobody was out on the dance floor yet.

"I'd love to," I said with a little hesitancy.

I wasn't that comfortable enough yet in my own body to feel relaxed dancing but how many times would I get a chance to dance with Windy? I threw caution to the wind, so to speak, and headed out. The band was playing that super big hit and all round crowd pleaser *I Wanna Dance Wit' Choo (Part 1)* by Disco-Tex & the Sex-O-Lettes so I was able to fake it enough by flailing around more-or-less to the rhythm of the song. I was secretly hoping they'd play *I Wanna Dance Wit' Choo (Part 2)* because I was just getting warmed up. The next tune, however, was the slow song by the Eagles, *Best of My Love,* and I swallowed hard as I took Windy in my arms. Not surprisingly, she felt amazing as her body just flowed with the song and seemed to take me along for the ride. More surprisingly was how well we seemed to move together. She was making subtle movements that communicated to me how to lead her around the floor. This gave me a huge boost in confidence and I eventually relaxed into the moment. After another slow song, she leaned in and gave me a delicious little kiss. She said that she needed to leave but hoped that maybe we could pick up where we left off sometime soon.

Meanwhile, Peter found some of his friends from the Biology Department he was working with for the summer. After Windy left, I decided that I had better head home and get to bed early so that I would be well rested for work tomorrow. I said goodbye to Peter and walked home. My lips were all tingly and it felt like I had a mild fever.

As I was to discover the next day, all three of us quarrymen went to bed that night with smiles on our faces.

CHAPTER 4

THURSDAY MORNING ARRIVED way too quickly. I hadn't needed to set my alarm since the end of classes but I had to get up around six so it was an absolute necessity. I'm a morning person, luckily, since I'm not an evening person. Eric, on the other hand is definitely not a morning person. Iggy is both a morning person and usually an evening person, too. I have never figured out how he managed to get by on such little sleep. When I heard my radio click on, it was the beginning of the broadcast day at KUNK, the most alternative of alternative radio stations. One of our friends, John, had a girlfriend Effie who was one of the DJs there. One time, John and Effie went to the station after hours when the station wasn't licensed by the FCC to be on the air and decided to give the Boulder area a bonus broadcast. They just made scary Halloween sounds and giggled and, this part is contentious, maybe said some raunchy things. It seemed highly unlikely that anyone heard them because who's going to be listening three hours after they've signed off for the night unless you fell asleep with the station on? Apparently someone did; reported it to the station manager and Effie got fired.

KUNK always started their broadcast day with the same song. I only knew this because during the last two semesters, I had a work-study job on campus and needed to be there by seven on some days. When you're sound asleep, dreaming about your first kiss with Windy and everything is fuzzy and beautiful and you fly with her up into the clouds and then you kiss again and all of a sudden you hear the Steve Miller Band's guitar and drum introduction to *Keep on Rocking Me Baby*, you are awake and out of bed before Steve even starts singing.

My bizarre boulder-rolling dream was also fresh in my mind and I quickly reviewed the details, laughing out loud about some of the images that were clearly based on my quarry experiences yesterday. It took me a few moments to refocus on my morning tasks and went to see if Eric and Iggy were awake. Eric's door was closest and my knocking didn't get any response nor did a second louder knocking. Going in and physically rousing him from his slumbers seemed like a good idea. In his bed, I saw a familiar looking naked Tina sleeping on top of the sheet backward, feet on the pillows, and head hanging over the side with her panties over her head looking like a helmet as the leg holes were perfectly positioned over her ears. She didn't appear to be sunbathing this time. Eric, by contrast, had on his tee shirt, white briefs and socks and was on the floor next to the bed, curled up into the fetal position.

"Hey Poindexter, wake up! Time to get going to work."

"Hmmffffthththththth . . ." he said, followed by "gggllllgggg."

"This train is leaving at seven o'clock sharp. Better rise and shine if you want to catch a ride."

"Not going," he managed to say, "and get out of here."

"Alright man, your decision."

My next stop was Jackie's room. I listened at her door and heard voices so left without disturbing them. I went back downstairs, showered, dressed and made my breakfast. Kate was awake since she had a summer job to get to as well so we ate breakfast together. This was when she gave me the two-minute Sisyphus lecture that helped me to understand my dream a little better. As we were finishing up our meals, Iggy emerged, freshly showered and ready to face our first full day of our new summer jobs.

"Where's Mungo? Is he up yet?" Iggy asked.

"I tried to wake him without much success but he did manage to tell me that he wasn't going to work today. Let's just finish up here and head out. If he changes his mind and gets his ass in gear, we'll drive up together. We can take the Cruisemobile today unless you're planning on staying at the quarry tonight."

"No, I'm not. Jackie and I had a really nice night together. She read me some of her poetry and then we gave each other massages. Sorry for the tension last night but you know how she can be sometime. We have plans for tonight so if I stayed up there, I would be in some pretty deep shit with her again. Plus, I'm not sure if Gus has enough power to get up the canyon." Gus was Iggy's really old and feeble Volkswagen van.

Iggy and I said goodbye to Kate and headed out the door without any sign of Eric. We jumped into my car, I pulled the park lever up and was about to press the drive button—the Cruisemobile had a really funky push button transmission—when he appeared at the front door.

"Hey, assholes, wait for me!" he yelled so loudly that everyone on the block probably heard him. Eric clearly wasn't ready to go. He was still in his fashionable sleep wear and apparently had just gotten out of bed because his hair was still bedlike.

"You've got two minutes to get in this car because we can't be late. Remember what Biggie told us? 7:30 sharp or we're fired. Two minutes!" I reiterated through my window.

He ran back into the house and emerged shortly with his clothes, a glass of orange juice and an apple. Jumping into the back seat, he started getting changed as I drove away. We had just made the turn west onto Arapahoe when Iggy and I compared notes from our experiences last night.

"You're lying! Windy? I can't believe that she kissed you? You know any of us would give our left nut to make out with her? Man, you are one lucky guy!"

"Yeah, I'm pretty pleased about this turn of events but you know how she is. Remember that night a while ago when she was eating dinner with us and promised to come back later and play some songs?"

"And we didn't see her again for a week. Yeah, but she had some sort of explanation as I recall, something about a friend getting a last minute gig in Nederland and then it evolved into a four day tour through the mountain resort towns," Iggy remembered.

Eric was still struggling with his clothes and his juice. He managed to say that he and Tina had a great night together until I barged in and woke them both up.

"Would you have preferred that I left you alone? You'd be out of one of the best jobs of your life," I reminded him. "At least to this point."

"Yeah, you're right but at least you could have knocked."

"I did, twice. And by the way, Tina looks really sexy with her panties on her head. What the heck were you guys doing?"

"I don't remember but she's pretty embarrassed that you saw her like that."

"It's a memory I'll always cherish."

We continued up Boulder Canyon in silence, each one in our own private world of thought, except for Eric who kept nodding off only to be jarred back to consciousness every time I went around a turn. The reliable Cruisemobile clock said it was around 7:25 as I pulled into the quarry parking lot. Eric had woken up enough to put on his work boots as the car came to a stop.

We walked into the office building and saw a scene that we weren't expecting. Big Larry was there as were all of his crew chiefs, seated in the exact seats they were in yesterday. However, none of the other workers were around so it was unclear if we were supposed to be there.

"You guys wait outside until Sam croons his tune," Big Larry instructed, not unkindly. "This is our private time to go over the plans for the day but I'm glad to see that you boys got your carcasses here on time."

"Oops, sorry," Iggy said as we turned around and went back outside.

Within a few minutes, the rest of the crew came around the corner of the bunkhouse, just as the annoying screeching sound permeated the quiet, dustless, cool blue morning air of the quarry. Sam hit the final crescendo as everyone entered the building.

"Everyone, sit your kiesters down and get settled quickly. We've got another big day ahead of us with a lot of work to accomplish. You all did some fine work yesterday and some fine dancin' at the club," Big Larry added with a tittering little laugh. "How did you like that belly dancer? Me and Bernice the Flamboyant go way back to our high school days. She was in Denver attendin' a meetin' of the Flamin' Baton Twirlers Club of America and agreed to come up to give a little show. That's another hobby of hers in addition to twirlin'. I 'specially liked when she had Junior and Juan Antonio onstage and taught them some moves. So, before I discuss the day's assignments, any questions or things that need to be reported to the group?"

"Yeah, I can't find my shoes. I think I ended up with Junior's!" said a very small wiry guy who must have been the aforementioned Juan Antonio. "Two of me could fit into one of these."

"And I want mine back too. Yours are so small, my feet would feel like Polish sausages if I could even get them in!" said Junior.

"Why didn't you guys straighten this out last night after the nightclub?" Big Larry asked. Neither offered an explanation so Big Larry simply told them to switch shoes, calling them morons under his breath. "Here are today's assignments. Dickie, today your quarry crew will consist of Hector, Barbara and Buster. Zelda, you will have Georgie, Felix 1 and Yolanda on your sorting crew. Quesnal—well, you have your usual drivers, Frederick, JK and Laverne, and Harry you have your mechanics, Felix 2 and Juan Antonio. Alfonso, your landscapers are Junior, Joan and the Three Musketeers."

Iggy decided to speak up. "Excuse me, Big Larry; we've been called the Three Stooges, the Three Musketeers and the Smith Brothers. I don't

DAVID W. GOODWIN

really take any personal offense at this but it would be nice if you learned our names. I'm Iggy, this is Eric and that's Dean. I'll try to make it easier for you to remember us—when you see me, think of a ham because that's what my last name translates to from French and I'm kind of a ham so think Iggy the Ham. When you see Eric, think of Erik the Red's peace loving little brother Eric the White and when you see Dean, think of Obnoxious Dean because that was his nickname in high school and believe me, he can really be obnoxious. I don't expect that you'll remember this immediately but eventually you'll make the association—Iggy the Ham, Eric the White, and Obnoxious Dean. Make sense?"

"No promises," said Big Larry, "but I kinda like the Three Musketeers. Anyhoo, time to get movin' here. Each crew chief has their assignment and their crew so let's get to work. Your bag lunches and snacks are by the door; make sure to pick one up on the way out. Bunny assures me that you will love the vittles she prepared for you today."

We reassembled with the rest of our landscaping crew out by Alfonso's truck. Junior and Joan looked pretty tired but they were both drinking extremely large cups of coffee so I imagined the caffeine would jolt them awake soon. Alfonso came striding over after a brief conversation with Zelda. He yelled back to her good-naturedly as he approached us, "Well, that's your funeral, not mine, chiquita!" He told Joan to drive with me in the other pickup truck to the nursery and pick up a good variety of plants, some for wet sites but most for dry sites and get a nice height, color and texture mix because we were going to be working on the entrance today. He told the rest of the crew to come with him because they needed to get the tools from the supply building and gardening supplies from the composting area. "We'll meet at the entrance."

I was really pleased that I got this assignment today. I've always enjoyed plants and gardening and, based on the height that my marijuana plants got during my freshman year before I got arrested, they were my pride and joy. The other obvious benefit was getting a chance to work with Joan.

"This sounds like fun. What sort of plants will we have to choose from?" I asked.

"Well, Eric, you're in for a treat when you see what I've got growing over there," she said as we climbed into the truck.

"Remember, Obnoxious Dean and Eric the White? I'm not entirely pleased that Iggy decided to make that association but I'm Obnoxious Dean, not Eric the White."

"I know, I was just kidding. Eric looks a lot more like Whitey than you and I get the Iggy the Ham thing but I'm not sure about the obnoxious Dean part. I don't get an initial sense of that sort of energy from you but time will tell. Iggy took a bit of a risk laying out those nicknames. You never know how Big Larry's gonna react sometimes. Anyway, back to your question. I was hired here at the quarry right after I graduated from CU with a degree in botany. Big Larry gave me full control of the nursery; it was almost non-existent when I got here last year. He used to buy all of his plant supplies down in town so I convinced him to let me start propagating some of our own stock, telling him we'd save a huge amount of time and money. Plus, obviously, as a botanist, I love working with plants."

We were driving down the same road we were on yesterday on our way up the Juiceway but this time we took a sharp right turn past a stand of young ponderosa pine trees. Hidden behind the trees, I saw Joan's nursery. There were a few small greenhouses, a bunch of saplings and shrubs planted in neat rows and an area of all sizes, shapes and colors of grasses and small plants. On the far side were many rows of plants and flowers already in pots. Beyond the nursery were piles of sand, gravel and topsoil in addition to a few large granite block bins that held piles of compost in different stages of decomposition.

"I'm going to give you a little lesson today on landscape design," Joan began, sounding like a vocational high school teacher. "You heard Alfonso say that he wanted a mix of plant types, right?"

"Yes, I did. The area around the entrance arch looks like it's mostly a dry site but I did notice a little drainage swale that runs parallel to the road. I assume this area gets a little more moisture than the section further back."

"Hey, not too bad there OD!"

"OD?"

"Yeah, Obnoxious Dean. See, I remembered. You're right on with the site conditions. So tell me what types of plants you think might be appropriate there."

"Well, I'd start with some rhododendrons, mix in some pachysandra and myrtle, maybe a little mountain laurel for variety and then plant some arbor vitae in the back row."

"Geez, man, where the hell are you from, New Jersey?"

"As a matter of fact, yes I am. I was only kidding. I assume you want to go with native plants."

"You had me worried there for a second. Yes, not only do we use native plants but we also go for native landscaping so the final results look more natural and is easily supported by our climate. It works me into a lather when I see people bringing in vegetation that just doesn't belong here, then they have to spend all their time and energy watering and fertilizing just to maintain an artificial landscape. It's nasty looking too," Joan said while my mind was picturing what a full lather might look like on her naked, wet body.

"Sounds good to me," I managed to say. "What sorts of plants are you growing that we can choose from?"

She gave me a quick description of her inventory. I was instructed to go to the small storage shed, grab two shovels and meet her over by the saplings while she watered some plants in the greenhouses. Over beyond the nursery, I could see the other crew loading up shovelfuls of material into their pickup truck.

I waited by the saplings and watched as Joan walked back. Alfonso's truck pulled up next to her and they had a brief conversation. Joan looked into the back of the truck where Eric and Iggy were sitting, each on their own pile of something and I saw Joan nod approvingly and wave Alfonso on.

As she got close to me, she said, "Size and structure are important but we need to work with the natural contours of the land. You noticed the swale along the road but did you notice the little drainage ditch back beyond the front section?"

"No, I can't say that I did."

"Well that is a great opportunity for some wild plum bushes. They're almost like trees because they grow up to twelve feet tall and need a fairly moist location. Plus, the critters really love the fruit. We're going to dig up ten of them from over there," she said pointing to some plants a few rows over. "Now, along the road, in the swale, we'll plant some bluebunch wheatgrass because it likes to get its feet wet too. I've got some of that over in the pots. For the dry sites, we'll get a mix of prickly pear cactus, prairie coneflower, pussytoes, Whipple's penstemon and dwarf blue rabbitbush. That will be a nice mix of colors, heights and textures. You'll see."

We set off to dig up the plants and then wrapped their root balls in burlap before loading them into the truck. We then grabbed the rest of the plants that were in the pots and arranged them on a flat bed trailer. Within about thirty minutes, the truck was fully loaded with vegetation and we slowly made our way to the entrance.

"So, are you guys thinking about staying here tonight?" Joan asked.

"Well, none of us were planning on it. We've got pretty full lives in Boulder but tell me, do you stay up here all week at the bunkhouse with all these guys?"

"It's not quite like that. The bunkhouse is divided into two rooms, the guys have the big room and the women have the small room. It's only Rhonda, Bunny, Zelda, Barbara, Yolanda, Laverne and myself and Georgie sleeps in with the guys some of the time and with us other times. I'm not sure where she's more comfortable but nobody hassles her about it. I call her a her but I'm not quite certain, it's just easier that way. Nobody has seen her naked so we don't really know."

"Yeah, Alfonso called her a him and now you called him a her. Have you ever asked?"

"No, that would be rude. She does great work, is very quiet and we just let her go about her business in a way that seems to make her comfortable. I've kind of taken her under my wing; her protector you might say. Someone told me that she's worked here the longest of anyone, even Big Larry."

"I'm still kind of curious. We're also quite curious about the nightclub but aren't sure if it's worth giving up our personal lives for. Both Iggy and Eric have girlfriends."

"But that's what weekends are for. We all have homes and lives somewhere else but during the week, it's all quarry. You don't have a girlfriend waiting for you at home?"

"No, not at the moment. I was involved with someone during the semester but she's back in Montrose for the summer. There are a few women that I'd like to get know better but so far it just hasn't worked out. I guess you could say that I'm between relationships at the moment."

"Sometimes a little alone time can be a good thing. Anyway, I think it's important to be selective. You know, it's a bit of a sacrifice living here all week but if you just came to the nightclub once, you would definitely stay up here with us. I've got a few guys that I hang out with on weekends but I tell them up front that they just won't see me during the week. Either they accept it or they don't. If they don't, I just don't get involved with them."

I was dying to hear more about this subject but we were at the quarry entrance and parked right beside the other truck. Joan got out and went over to talk with Alfonso. "I've got a concept here so are you cool with me laying the plants out so we can see how well it comes together?"

DAVID W. GOODWIN

"Sí, claro," said Alfonso, "you know I always trust your judgment. Just tell me where you need the help and we'll get it done."

Just like the wall building yesterday, Joan and Alfonso took a position up high, this time by standing in the bed of the truck as Joan laid out her vision for the crew. Alfonso offered a few alterations and together they eventually agreed on a design. The upland site around the arch was currently just some sparse grasses, a few big chunks of granite, and some scrubby juniper bushes. The swale along the road had been scraped clean of vegetation, probably by repeated snowplowing in the winter but the little drainage in the back was thickly vegetated with some sort of plant that I'd never seen before. The morning was starting to warm up considerably and it was becoming a perfect temperature for work.

"Hey, Hambone, what the hell were you thinking in there?" I teased Iggy while walking over to where he was standing. "What's this Obnoxious Dean stuff?"

"I had to think of something quickly on the spur of the moment," Iggy said quietly to me. "I wanted to have them remember our names. I remember once you told me about your high school buddies calling you Obnoxious Dean. Sorry about that, it was completely spontaneous!"

"No problem, especially if it works, At least you didn't come up with Dean the Bean. I just wish you had thought of something else like Dean, King of the Universe."

"At least he didn't come up with Eric the White for you. I'd take Obnoxious Eric over Eric the White any day," Eric said joining our conversation.

"How about Obnoxious Eric the White?" I suggested.

Joan started directing the movement of plants to their initial location. We hauled the wild plums to the back along the low drainage ditch; the wheatgrass along the swale and then the rest of the plants were positioned on either side of the arch. When she approved of the placement, we were told to move over to the driveway so she could see how the plants looked in the context of the existing vegetation and rocks.

"Alfonso, I'd like you to think about what this area will look like in a year. It's tempting to overplant but then we'll spend all our time trimming things because we've planted too close. I'd rather have the plants fill out to their natural size without crowding other things out. Plus, our goal here is to make it look more natural without making it look like someone's suburban driveway entrance." My sense was that she was saying all of this for my benefit.

Alfonso walked down to Sugarloaf Mountain Road to get the view that visitors, workers and perhaps government employees would get as they approached the quarry in their vehicles. This, he explained, was the most important view.

"I think that will work really well and have a great impact without being at all gaudy," he stated. "Now comes the hard part."

Joan told us to go back to the plants and directed one person at a time to move one plant a bit in this direction and another plant in that direction until she felt that the arrangement was just right. She then instructed everyone to move each of the plants back about three feet from their current location and then start digging holes where the plants had been.

"Take a look at the root ball or the size of the pot of the plant you just moved and dig a hole that is about four times as wide and four times as deep," she said. This was a lot easier said than done and it took all six of us working for a few hours straight. In Colorado, you can't dig more than a few inches into the thin soil before you encounter rocks. Sometimes the rocks were too massive to dig out so there were a bunch of holes that needed to be relocated. This kept Joan busy because she constantly had to alter her design based on the unexpected geological reality. We were instructed to pile up the rocks removed from the holes near the end of the driveway because they were going to be used for another purpose. Once all of the holes were dug to her satisfaction, Alfonso told everyone to take a break.

There was a small stand of aspen trees about twenty five yards down the driveway that made a cool and comfortable place to drink some water and eat some of our snacks. I have to say, I was beginning to be impressed with the care that the Sugarloaf Quarry took of their employees. Junior carried over the big thermos jug of water and some cups for us. We all sat down and were snacking on some trail mix and apples while Junior handed out the water.

"Anyone care for a smoke?" Alfonso asked after he lit up. Junior took a cigarette from Alfonso's pack and accepted a light from our crew chief. "Thanks," he said very softly. The rest of us politely refused.

"So what can you tell us about last night at the nightclub?" Eric inquired. "Big Larry made it sound like it was quite a scene."

"I'm going to break this to you as gently as I can there Eric the White and I don't mean any disrespect seeing as you're a rookie," Alfonso began, "but we don't talk about what happens at the nightclub. I was a bit surprised that Big Larry said what he did at this morning's meeting, that's pretty unusual for him. You just have to experience it for yourselves and then it will all make sense."

We sat in silence for awhile, enjoying the rest, the shade, the food, the water and the beautiful view down from Sugarloaf Mountain across to the south side of Boulder Canyon; it was quite idyllic. A few magpies flew by and perched on the Sugarloaf Quarry arch. They are beautiful birds, one of my favorites, very colorful, quite large and have a very distinctive call that sounds like someone reeling in clothes on a clothesline that is connected to a rusty pulley. This was in stark contrast to the soothing sound of the wind as it whooshed through the upper branches of the ponderosa pines.

Alfonso told us that the next phase of the project was to mix up the topsoil, compost and sand in equal parts for the plants that liked a dry mix. The plants that liked a wetter soil would just get a topsoil and compost mixture. The gravel would be used to stabilize a few areas that had washed out. He told Eric, Iggy and me that once break was over, he wanted to give us a quick lesson in proper planting technique since this was a delicate process that needed to be done carefully. Right when he finished telling us this, his walkie-talkie beeped. "Scaper One here, over."

"Scaper One, this is Biggie. We've got a 10-52 at the office, come down here at once and bring Junior, over."

"I read you, Biggie, we'll be right down, over and out, 10-4."

"If you don't mind my asking," Iggy said, "what's a 10-52? I never learned my police talk."

"That means there's some sort of trouble and he needs help," Joan explained as Alfonso and Junior got up and started walking over to his truck. "Big Larry gets worked up a bit too easily if you ask me. Plus he likes to pretend that he's a tough guy cop, you ever hear about little man complex?"

"Oh yeah, I'm a psychology major. It's called a Napoleon Complex so I'm well acquainted with guys like Big Larry. That's one of the reasons why I challenged him this morning on his name calling. If you challenge someone early and don't let the pattern get established, they'll usually back down pretty easily. The hope is that they aren't offended by it but realize you're serious. You probably noticed that I tried to downplay it and make it sound like it wasn't a big deal."

"Yes, as a matter of fact, I did. I thought that you handled the situation very well."

"Thanks, I'm used to dealing with some fairly psychotic people from my past volunteer jobs and internships so it's not a big thing to deal with Big Larry. I actually find him rather amusing."

"What kind of trouble do you think is brewing up at the office?" Eric asked.

"Oh, it could be any number of things. Maybe Hector started running amok and threatened Big Larry with a shovel, maybe Juan Antonio got his hand stuck in one of the machines, that's happened before, maybe his baton twirling friend Bernice hasn't left the quarry yet and tried to show him a new move with a flaming baton that went haywire. I guess we'll find out when Alfonso and Junior get back. It's probably nothing too serious," Joan said. "So, why don't I give you guys a lesson in proper planting technique? I don't think that Alfonso would mind since I'm the one that taught him."

We followed Joan over to the planting area and she demonstrated on one of the prairie coneflowers. "You've got to be very gentle when you transplant so you don't shock the roots. Think of them as the plant's lungs, mouth and heart. They're very sensitive." She walked over to the truck and drew a pail of water from another jug labeled "Plant Water—Not for Drinking" and used a small container to carefully water the plant in its new home. "We'll have to water all of these transplants every day for a few weeks until they recover from the shock and get established."

"That seems pretty straightforward," Eric said. "Can I do the next one?"

"You all can do the next one—that's your new job. I'll go mix up a big pile of the soil mixture on the tarp and you can use these five gallon buckets to transport it over to the hole that you're working on. Oh, one thing I forgot to mention is that you should mix in some of the native dirt that you dug out originally. That will make a perfect mixture."

We all went about working on our new tasks. As my buddies and I would complete each new planting, Joan would come over and inspect it until she felt comfortable that we were doing an acceptable job. "You don't have to be that gentle, OD," she admonished me. "It's not made of glass. You show that cactus who's the boss!"

I took another cactus in my thickly gloved hands and pretended that it was a new recruit at boot camp. "You are nothing, your prickers aren't even sharp, you're mother doesn't even like you, I'm your new mommy, you will get in that hole and you will grow big and fast and I don't want to hear any complaining, do you hear me maggot?"

DAVID W. GOODWIN

"That wasn't exactly what I had in mind," Joan said, only vaguely amused. "Plants can sense negative energy but they don't understand sarcasm."

"How exactly do you know this?" I asked a little surprised.

"Oh, I just know. If you spend enough time around plants like I do, you can just sense these things. Each plant has its own personality. You'll understand what I mean if you just tune into them and pay close attention."

"Joan, come over here quick, this pussytoe just told me that she had a very unhappy childhood and really feels like she's a rabbitbush. She asked if I could help her get some therapy and maybe some experimental hybrid genetic material that would allow her to change species," Eric said with a comically sad look on his face. "I'm not sure what I should tell her."

"You should tell her to tell you to shut up and get back to work," Joan said laughing.

Joan was obviously used to dealing with wise ass guys like us. You could tell by the way she easily handled herself that she had honed her skills to a fine point. I'm sure working at the quarry was good practice for her. When you consider the other women that worked here, it was clear that she and Rhonda were probably the objects of most of the male attention and suggestive behavior. I was looking forward to getting to know them and understand their interpersonal dynamics.

The interpersonal dynamics between Eric, Iggy and me were another story. Here were three guys, the same age, the same political leanings, from similar backgrounds, all privileged white guys who had the good fortune to be going to a good college in a great place. However, in some ways, we were different as night and day.

On a late Saturday afternoon last week, we decided to hike up the Front Range from the south end of Boulder and spend the night in this cool rock formation we found on a previous hiking expedition. We called this place the "Bathtub" because it was a tub-like depression at the very top of one of the flatirons. This particular flatiron wasn't one of the more popular ones like the third flatiron with a big "CU" painted on it. Flatiron #3 was the one that almost any CU student who considered themselves an adventurous type had to climb—either with ropes and climbing gear if they were smart or as a free climb if they either were really good or had a death wish. I had climbed it with ropes and an experienced rock climbing friend within a few weeks of starting college as a freshman. Even under these circumstances it turned into one of the scariest experiences of my life. The climb took a lot longer than we anticipated and we didn't reach the top until well after dark. The repel off the backside at the top was about seventy-five feet of dangling in space before you eventually got down to a ledge. The second and third pitches were on rock so you were able to maintain contact with your feet almost the entire way. That first step into blackness as a complete novice after climbing for five hours was both terrifying beyond belief and one of the biggest rushes of my life.

The Bathtub was on the sixth or seventh flatiron, they become less distinct after a while and I'm not even sure they get numbered this far south. It wasn't a technical climb but involved a lot of scrambling up and over some pretty large slabs of sandstone. Plus, you had to know your way pretty well in order to find it. One other important detail was that you hoped when you finally made it up there no one else had the same idea because it literally was not much bigger than a large bathtub. If it was already occupied, you needed to either make friends with the other people immediately or head home because it was the only place where you could lie down for miles since it was flat and protected on all sides. It also had one of the greatest views of any place in Boulder as you could see the entire Boulder valley, south to Denver and east out to the horizon. It was a great place for three people to spend the night, even better for two, especially if it wasn't raining.

We made an impulsive decision to hike up to the Bathtub for the night as we didn't have any other big plans. It was about a two hour trip and we decided to travel really light to maximize the enjoyment. The skies were clear so we decided not to bring a tent even though we probably wouldn't be able to set it up if we had wanted to. Since each of us had a day pack rather than a full backpack, we only had enough room for a blanket instead of a sleeping bag. This still left some room for food, water and in Iggy's pack, a bottle of whiskey—all the essentials.

By the time we actually started hiking, the sun was just beginning to set. Eric and I started to get cold feet about the adventure while Iggy was all gung-ho. "Don't be such Poindexters," he said. "What's the worst thing that could happen?"

"We could die, get lost, or get lost and die," I answered.

"And since it will be dark by the time we get up to the Bathtub, if there are other people there, what do we do then?" Eric asked.

"Oh, yeah, good point there guys. Let's just get back in the car and go home. We don't want to have any fun now do we? We don't want to take a little gamble because there's a slight chance that we might have to be slightly inconvenienced," Iggy said with his voice increasing in volume. "This is the sort of thing I would expect from Jackie but not you guys. Here are my car keys, go home, I'll see you tomorrow and tell you about all the fun I had!"

"I guess it wouldn't be the worst thing in the world to hike up the last half in the dark. Arlo and I climbed up here a month ago. I'm pretty sure that I remember the way," I said.

"Well, okay, but let's all make sure that we stay together so nobody wanders off," Eric said referring to a time last year when the three of us and a bunch of other friends went camping at Rocky Mountain National Park in the winter. We lost Peter for the entire trip because we weren't diligent enough about keeping together on the first day. We had all eaten some psilocybin mushrooms and everyone became so preoccupied with the world around them that we lost track of each other soon after both trips started. We hiked higher and higher into the mountains and eventually found the perfect campsite. It wasn't until the next day we discovered Peter wasn't with us. On our long hike back the next day, we found him about two hundred yards from our car. He had hooked up with two women who apparently were out camping and 'shrooming as well. The three of them never left the meadow near the parking lot and were all in fine spirits when we came through and picked him back up.

"Hey, I think we can keep pretty close track of everyone on this trip," Iggy said as we began our journey to the Bathtub. "Just make sure that you can always hear or see each other."

We started hiking up towards the base of the flatirons. The trail was fairly well marked and worn so we were able to follow it quite easily. It wound its way through meadows and patches of forest, crossing little dry drainage channels and occasionally larger ones with a little water trickling through. We arrived at the base of the steep slope where the trail disappeared and the climbing went up sharply just as it was getting dark. The stars began to appear, the sound of the wind through the pines was hypnotizing and the rustle of leaves made by small animals and birds either settling in for the night or just waking up to begin their nightly activities kept the air full of interesting sounds. The smell of the night air quickly shifted from the hot and dry aroma of daytime and pine needles to the cool evening air with a hint of moisture that brought out the scent from the earth and vegetation.

"Beans, are you sure you're going the right way?" Eric asked after we had been hiking for about twenty minutes.

"I'm pretty sure. All we have to remember is to make sure to keep the flatiron on our right," I said. This was an easy thing to do since the edge of the flatiron rose sharply out from the hillside we were walking up and was almost as tall as some of the pine trees.

"Yeah but I seem to remember that at some point, we need to walk through a really tight slot canyon and cross over to the other side of the flatiron. Is that what you remember, Iggy?"

Iggy didn't answer so I stopped to see if he had fallen behind. Eric and I were standing still, the sky was full of stars at this point but the moon wasn't up yet so it was hard to see much beyond a radius of about fifteen feet.

"Hey Jacque!" Eric yelled out. "Are you coming?"

We didn't hear anything so he yelled out again.

"When was the last time that you saw him?" I asked.

"He was with us when we started hiking up the steep part because he ripped a really loud fart."

"No, that was me," I volunteered. "But maybe it was him too."

"Shit, do you think we should try to retrace our steps downhill and try to find him?"

We were startled by a laughing sound that seemed like it was coming from directly over our heads. Eric and I looked up and made out the figure of a person against the slightly lighter night sky standing up on the edge of the flatiron. We heard a familiar sound like the mating call of a wolf saying "Arrruuuuuu".

Eric and I both started laughing and said "arrruuuuu" back. This was the official greeting for all Zoo housemates when we saw each other away from home. The proper technique was to make a mini-megaphone with your hand, hold it up to your mouth to amplify the howl and strike a wolf pose, whatever that was but usually involved bending at the waist with head held high. It stemmed from a Valentine's Day greeting that I had placed in the *Daily Collegian* earlier in the year that said,

> *Roses are red*
> *Violets are blue*
> *Pleasant Street Zoo*
> *Says "Arrruuuu" to you.*

Somehow, Iggy must have slipped away from us when we weren't paying attention and climbed up the edge of the flatiron. I was worried that he might be in a bit over his head by climbing in the dark but this was a typical Iggy stunt.

"What the hell are you doing up there, man?" Eric yelled out.

"I think I found the spice route to India! Come up, I think we can get to the Bathtub this way!"

"Where did you find a way up?" I yelled.

"All you have to do is walk back down the hill about ten yards from where you are. There's a tree growing right next to the rock. Climb up there and about half way up, there's a crack with a ton of handholds. It's easy, I'll wait up here."

"Are you sure?" Eric asked.

"Absolutely. If you think it's too tough, I'll let you have my third of the whiskey," Iggy offered as encouragement.

Eric and I found the tree, shimmied up in the space between the trunk and the rock and were easily able to get up and over the first part of the rock ledge up to the crack. Iggy was right; it didn't require any extraordinary moves and was only about a 6.5 on the 10 point scale of stupidly dangerous risks to take. We got up to Iggy in a few short minutes. The slot continued up the middle of the flatiron as far as we could see into the night. It was a lot brighter on the rock face since it was above the tops of the trees and therefore not in night shadow plus the lights from Boulder were adding a little extra faint illumination.

"See what I mean?" Iggy asked. "Looks to me like we might have a clear shot at the Bathtub from here. Want to go for it?"

"I guess we could try. We can always retrace our steps back down if need be," Eric said.

We climbed up the crack for a couple of hundred yards, sometimes being able to walk upright, sometimes having to use our hands and feet to get around outcrops or places where the crack disappeared. Eventually, however, we got to a place where the flatiron had been split sideways and was separated from the upper half by a chasm that was about six or seven feet wide. This must be the top of the slot canyon that I had walked through previously.

"Beans, you should probably be the first one to jump across since you're the lightest and can probably jump the farthest," Eric reasoned. "Leave your pack with us and we'll throw it across once you're on the other side."

"I'm not too sure about this. In the light, I bet it isn't a big deal but I can barely see what's on the other side."

"I'll do it if you want," Iggy offered. "Here, take my pack and stand back."

"No, Mungo is right, I should probably be the first one. Let me make sure that I can get a bit of a running start. Heck, it's probably only a twenty five foot drop into the canyon. If I don't make it, there's a chance that I wouldn't die immediately, maybe twitch around for a few minutes first."

I surveyed the launch area and was silently trying to talk myself into this stupid maneuver. The flatiron wasn't really that steep here so I thought that I could get a good start. From what I could see on the other side, it looked fairly smooth but steeper and perhaps if I didn't make it cleanly across, I could at least hang on to the edge and pull myself up and over. After another thirty seconds of psyching myself up, I decided to do it. I was so pumped with adrenaline that I made it over the chasm with about two or three feet to spare and landed in a squatting position on the other side.

"Not too bad there, gentlemen," I said as they threw the three packs over to me. "Just make sure that your shoelaces are tied, that you have paid up your life insurance with me listed as your beneficiary and don't mind that there is a sheer fifty foot drop-off just ten yards up the flatiron."

"Is there really?" Eric asked with genuine fear in his voice.

"No, just kidding," I admitted. "But I wouldn't be too surprised."

Eric went next followed almost immediately by Iggy. Both of them also made it over easily. Iggy decided that we all needed a celebratory swig of whiskey and then another for good luck for the rest of the hike. I suggested that we needed one more to toast our friendship.

We continued hiking and climbing our way up the flatiron, making pretty good time. We could see the top off in the distance as the night got brighter but I knew from spending time previously at the Bathtub that the rock got way too steep to get to it from the front. At some point we would have to find a way off the face and get around to the back side. When we got to the steepest part and couldn't safely climb any further, we headed off to the side in search of a way down to the ground. After hitting a few dead ends, Eric found a route that showed some promise. There was a crack in the rock that went the direction we needed to go. If we faced towards the rock and used our toes to stay in the crack, we could use our arms and hands to maintain contact with the rock and inch along towards the inevitable drop-off, hoping that we would be able to get down easily. Iggy was in the lead and stopped when he got to the edge of the flatiron.

"This might work," he called out. "It looks like a ten or twelve foot drop-off though."

"What is your idea of a drop-off that wouldn't work, thirty feet?" Eric asked.

"Don't be such a wuss, man!" he said. "At least it's dark so you won't see how scary it is."

"I'm not going to jump off a twelve foot cliff, not knowing what's down there," Eric said, "unless you go first and then guide us to the best place to land."

"I'm not saying this is an ideal situation, I'm just saying that it might work, as you recall."

"Maybe we should just use this rope ladder?" I suggested nonchalantly having just found one attached to the rock with several metal pins. "I guess we're not the first humans to ever do this." I climbed down and we were at the bottom in no time.

Once on the ground, I knew the way to the Bathtub. All we had to do was climb around to the backside of the flatiron, scramble up to a narrow ledge, shimmy through another crack in the rock, friction climb over the top of a large boulder with a few strategic handholds, jump over another shallow chasm and then up one last easy pitch. I was the first one to the top and stood on the edge looking down six feet into the Bathtub. Fortunately, no one else was there so all of our efforts were rewarded.

"Now this is what I'm talking about!" Iggy yelled out into the vastness spread out before us.

"Unbelievable!" Eric exclaimed.

The view was spectacular. The stars were bright enough to cast faint shadows and just as we settled into the Bathtub, the moon rose on the horizon. There were several openings in the rock at eye level so that you could see out in various directions. It had the feel of a very well designed lookout spot where you could see enemy intruders coming from all angles. We unpacked our booty, got comfortable on the downslope edge so we could sit with our feet wedged into the rock for safety with the Bathtub behind us. Dinner was fabulous, as was the whiskey.

We spent a very enjoyable dry night. The sunrise woke us early and after a quick bite to eat, climbed back down and hiked back to the car the way that I had originally intended to come up. We were back at the Zoo before most of our housemates were even awake.

CHAPTER 5

OUR PLANTING PROCESS continued and Joan began to see that we were doing a good enough job so she could focus on her own plants. The quiet morning was interrupted by the sound of a car coming down the driveway as contrasted with the louder noise of the delivery trucks that went by periodically. As it got closer, we could see the Sugarloaf car with Alfonso at the wheel but there were two people in the car, one in front and one in the back. Junior followed behind them driving Alfonso's truck and they both parked their vehicles near us along the driveway. Junior got out and hopped into the backseat of the quarry car with the other passenger.

All of the windows in the car were rolled down and Alfonso called out to Joan. "You'll have to carry on without me and Junior for a while. I need to drive into town with these two." We could see Big Larry in the front passenger seat now and a woman in the back who didn't look familiar to us. "They got into a bit of a rumble this morning and I need to take them into town to get patched up a bit."

I looked into the car more closely and could see that Big Larry had a bloody towel wrapped around his head and the woman, sitting in the back with Junior, had her arm in a sling and a bag of ice on her shoulder.

"What happened?" Joan asked.

"Apparently, Big Larry told Bernice that he would send a check in the mail but she wanted cash. Things got a little out of control and she hit him on the head with one of her batons. Bernice slipped as she whacked him and might have broken her collarbone when she smacked herself on the side of the table as she was falling," Alfonso continued. "At least her baton wasn't flaming."

"Alfonso, spare the details and just get us down to the hospital," Big Larry squeaked, sounding both annoyed and impatient.

"And try not to hit any bumps if you can help it," Bernice said in a strained voice talking through clenched teeth. She clearly was in some degree of pain.

"It serves you right, you crazed bitch," Big Larry said, trying to turn around to face Bernice. He reached his arm around and tried to slap her but Junior caught his arm before any additional harm could be done.

"Oh yeah, you're a big tough guy, you little creep. I can't believe you were going to stiff me. Nothing changes, does it Lawrence? Just like in high school when you'd take me out for dinner and then pretend that you lost your wallet so I'd have to pay," Bernice yelled. She looked out the car window at the four of us watching this little drama and said, "I wouldn't work for such a cretin if I were you. This miserable excuse for a man can't even satisfy a woman, his name should be Microscopic Larry, if you know what I mean."

"Okay you two, that's enough," Alfonso interjected. Turning his attention to Joan, he said, "So, finish up with the plantings and if you finish that before we return, start on the wall like we discussed. We'll be back as soon as we can. I'm taking Junior with me because we need him to keep these two separated. I'm leaving you the truck so you can get more supplies."

Once they were gone, Joan started laughing. I could tell that she had been trying to suppress it. "Typical Big Larry behavior. That guy gets himself into more bad situations than anyone I've ever met. I'm sure he promised to pay Bernice a certain amount of money before she agreed to come up here and then tried to give her less this morning," Joan explained to us.

"Is this a common practice of his not to pay his workers?" Eric asked.

"Let's just say that he seems to have some money issues. He eventually pays up but not without a struggle. Anyway, let's see how many plants we can get in the ground before lunch."

We worked until noon and spent some time admiring the work we had done. Joan seemed pleased by her rookie college boy crew and suggested that we grab the lunch boxes from the truck. As we were sitting around by the aspen trees where we had taken our morning break, Eric started asking some more questions about the quarry.

"I understand that you would prefer not to talk about the nightclub for some reason and I'm cool with that. But can you talk about why Big Larry does this for the workers? Wouldn't it be easier for everyone if you all just commuted to work everyday like it was a normal job?"

"I suppose that's a fair question," Joan conceded. "Does this seem like a normal job? What did he tell you about the nightclub when he hired you?"

"Just that it was a way to give the workers a reward for putting in a hard day at the ol' quarry."

"That's right. What else can I say about it?"

"Where does he get the money to pay for the entertainment like Bernice the Flamboyant?" Iggy asked.

"That's not really any of my business. All I know is that I have a job, get paid at the end of every week, I'm given clothes, a place to sleep, good food and a fabulous nightclub to unwind at every night."

"I guess it's the fabulous nightclub part that I don't quite get. We've seen the supply building and it's far from fabulous. I have to say, it seems more like a dump," I said trying not to sound too critical.

"Since you're not willing to buy into the entire deal yet, I'll just say for now that you've just got to trust me, it is fabulous," Joan said with a kind smile on her face, the kind of smile that you might expect someone to use when they're talking to someone who isn't playing with a full deck.

"Alright, I guess we'll just have to experience it for ourselves. We'll stop asking questions now," Iggy said.

"Thank you."

We sat in silence, taking in the view, the sounds, and the smells. Joan said that she was going to take a little snooze and suggested we might want to do the same. I wasn't used to working all morning like this and was a bit sleepy. All of us dozed off for a while in the warm sunshine dappled with shadows from the aspen leaves. Our naps were interrupted by one of the dump trucks rumbling down the driveway heading out to deliver a load of rock somewhere. The driver saw us all taking our little naps and slowed down as they went by.

"Hey, `scapers! You going to sleep the whole afternoon just because the boss is away?" the woman yelled out her window at us.

"Yikes, what time is it Laverne?" Joan responded sounding a bit disoriented.

"1:15"

"Yeah, we laid down to take a brief nap after lunch but that was almost an hour ago. Thanks for the wake up call! Guys," she said to us, "let's get back to work."

Laverne threw the truck into first gear and started driving away. As she wound her big truck up, she yelled over, "Joan, when you see Big Larry again, tell him to give Bernice a kiss from me!"

Our afternoon was spent planting the remainder of the plants, thoroughly watering everything and cleaning the site up. We packed up the truck with the various tools and drove back to the office building. Big Larry, Alfonso and Junior were still nowhere to be seen. Rhonda, being second in command, took charge of the meeting. "I just got a call from Alfonso. He and Junior are still at the hospital with Big Larry and Bernice. He's got a head wound, nothing too serious, they gave him a few stitches. Bernice does have a broken collarbone. Apparently, they are still going at it and Bernice is threatening to press charges. So what else is new? Every time she comes up here, they fight like cats and dogs. You'd think he'd know better but I guess they like the making up part. But enough of that, let's get on with the reports."

After this was done, Rhonda said that she would see folks at the nightclub. Since it was Thursday, it was games night so she encouraged everyone to come with their thinking caps. She asked us college boys if we'd be putting in an appearance this evening.

"I've got some unfinished business in town this evening," I responded.

"Me too," said Iggy.

Yeah, me three," said Eric.

"Big mistake there college boys," Rhonda told us, echoing Joan's earlier assessment.

As we were getting into the Cruisemobile, Joan walked towards my car and complimented us on the work we had accomplished today. I drove away from the quarry, feeling tired, a little achy, but happy about the work that I was doing.

"She's pretty cool," Eric said. "Are you guys as attracted to her as I am?"

"Absolutely," Iggy answered. "Who wouldn't be?"

"I wonder if she's got a boyfriend," Eric asked.

"Don't you have enough to handle in your love life already?" I asked. "By the way, when's Phoebe's next visit?"

"Yeah, thanks for the reminder, Mungo. She's coming out to celebrate the Fourth of July. I'm not sure what I'm going to do about this. Tina's already talking about wanting to go on a camping trip since she isn't doing a craft fair."

"That's only a few weeks away. Plus don't forget about the Zoo party," I said.

As we reached the outskirts of Boulder, I pulled into the liquor store with the big rubber plant and each of us purchased a six pack of beer. Here we were, all dressed the same, covered in dust, dirt and dried sweat, each buying a six pack of beer. This image was not exactly what any of us saw as our future career path but was certainly our current reality.

"Yep, I'm goin' home to the missus to our new double wide at the trailer park. She just started her new job at the hair salon. Gonna cook me up some dogs on the Hibachi, drink this here beer and maybe watch *Let's Make a Deal* on the tube tonight. Yes sirree, I'm leadin' the good life," Iggy said in his hillbilly voice. "Maybe me and the little gal will have a romp in the hay tonight!"

The weather had gone from hot and sunny to cloudy and windy in the time since our stop at the store and arrival at the Zoo. There were often late afternoon thunderstorms in Boulder where the sky would go from blue to clouds to thunderstorm and back to blue in the matter of minutes. These little intense storms would whip over the Rockies without much warning but you knew it would be over almost as quickly as it started. Soon it was pouring outside and there was thunder and lightning all around, the perfect time to go sit on the front porch and watch the storm come and go.

"Another tough day in the ol' salt mine?" Kate asked.

"We had a great day, except when Bernice the Flamboyant opened up Big Larry's scalp with her flaming baton," Eric said.

"Seriously, did you guys have a good day? You look like you put in a hard one," Kate stated.

"Yes we did and I'm not lying to you about Bernice," Eric responded. "Both she and Big Larry ended up in the hospital. I think the highlight of the day, however, was when Joan let us fertilize her garden with our hoses. By the way, Kate, how was your time with Elmo last night?"

"Let's just say that my garden was well fertilized also."

"Excellent! By the way, Mungo, do you remember that Tina's coming over for dinner tonight?" Eric asked.

"I did." I responded thinking that I had better go track down my co-chef Hazel.

The storm appeared to be winding down and Hazel appeared at the front door. She looked a bit anxious and asked us if we thought it was safe to be on the porch during a thunderstorm. Before anyone could answer, a lightening bolt hit fairly close by and sent all of us running into the house.

"I guess the answer to your question is no!" I eventually said. "Give me some time to get cleaned up. Will you be ready to get started on dinner soon?"

DAVID W. GOODWIN

"Sure, but you should know that I have some ideas on a slight alteration to the menu." Leaning in close, she whispered, "I've got a little surprise in store. Crystal and I will meet you in the kitchen for a private consultation after you shower and get dressed."

Since we were planning on making the meal that I made almost every time it was my turn to cook, I'm sure that any variation would be welcomed. When I got back to the kitchen a little while later, Hazel and Crystal were in there having a little make out session in the corner.

"Dean, come join us," Crystal said, winking at me. "We need to discuss something."

Not sure what she had in mind, I went over and was brought into their intimate circle. Their strategy soon became apparent when they took turns whispering into my ears and started to explain the new dinner plan as I was sandwiched between them. Moments later, Jackie walked in on our little threesome.

"You guys, that is wrong on so many levels!" she reprimanded. "You can't be doing this here!"

"What we choose to do isn't really any of your business," Crystal responded angrily. "Besides, I don't know what you're thinking but we're just discussing tonight's dinner plan."

"The three of you are perverts!" With that, Jackie stormed out of the kitchen and went stomping out of the house. The three of us just looked at each other.

"Whoa, what the hell was that all about? Maybe she was jealous that she wasn't invited," Crystal said. "Let's pop into your bedroom and finish up this discussion in private."

We went into my room right off the kitchen and sat on the bed. Crystal and Hazel had put a fair amount of thought into the meal and filled me in on their ideas and the sequence of events. This meal was certainly going to be a change of pace from my usual broccoli, cheese and rice casserole.

"Remember when we were shopping for the ingredients and you said that you wanted to expand your culinary repertoire a bit?" Hazel started. "It got me thinking about a way to have a bit of fun with everyone. Here's what I want you to do—in a little while, go out and tell everyone that we're making the casserole but when we call them in to dinner, they have to be blindfolded. We will then lead each person to their place at the table. Tell them that we want to have a new type of dining adventure. In the meantime, Crystal should go out and socialize with everyone and pretend that everything is normal. I think most everyone has gone out to the porch since the sun is back out. After she's been there for a while, you go out and make the blindfold announcement, okay?"

"For sure," I said as we walked out of my bedroom. "Adios Crystal, see you in a bit.

"What just happened in here?" Iggy said as the four of us converged in the kitchen. "Jackie came down to my room and said that the three of you were having an orgy in the kitchen, a mighty fast one from the looks of things. What happened? Jackie is pretty upset."

"It hadn't quite reached the orgy stage yet but it was damn close!" I said. "A few more minutes and it would have gotten totally out of control. These ladies just attacked me when they saw me come into the kitchen in my shorts and NORML tee shirt. It usually has that effect on women—straight or gay. I just can't be responsible for the frenzy I cause!"

"Come on Iggy, look at him, could you resist?" Hazel asked.

"Hmm, somehow I'm managing. What really happened?"

"We were having a private meeting to discuss a change in the dinner plan. That's all, sorry, no orgy. Jackie totally overreacted and called us perverts because I think she thought the three of us were making out. That really wasn't cool. She owes us an apology."

"She can be like that. I just wanted to hear your side before I talked to her again. Sorry about that." With that, he disappeared and I heard him walk upstairs to Jackie's room.

Hazel and I began working on the meal. When everything was almost ready, I went out to the porch. Wayne had appeared for his dinner break, Tina had arrived and was hanging out on the couch with Eric but Iggy and Jackie were missing. I hoped to see Windy, especially after our time at Tulagis last night but she wasn't around either.

"I've got a special dinner announcement everyone. Tonight's menu will consist of your favorite broccoli casserole," I said pretending to be an English butler.

"Oh yummy," Peter said sarcastically. "Even though it is a great meal, Beans, one of these days you're going to have to learn to cook something else."

"You've got a point there Master Peter. Madam Hazel and I have special rules for tonight's meal. Please don't come into the kitchen or dining room until you are summoned. If you need anything from inside, Madam Crystal will be your waitress and is the only person authorized to be in the dining room until dinner is served. Also, when dinner is ready, you will be asked to don blindfolds and you will be individually escorted to your place at the table. Finally, the last rule we will insist upon is that you not speak unless spoken to. Do you all understand?"

"That's rather kinky," Kate said. "What's going on?"

"I can't say but Madam has created a bit of dinner theatre for your dining pleasure. Any further questions?"

"Yes," asked Tina, "do we have to wear the blindfolds while we're eating?"

"Yes, at least until you are instructed otherwise. Any further questions?"

"Will we barf?" Wayne asked.

"That depends upon you. My guess is no. If there are no further questions, I invite you to enjoy the evening and we will let you know when dinner will be served. One other thing, if you happen to see Master Ignace or Madam Jackie, please let them know they are requested to stay out of the dining room and kitchen for the time being. If you will excuse me now."

Back in the kitchen, Hazel was giddy with silliness. She was putting the finishing touches on the food and I could feel her excitement. She explained how she wanted the dining room set up, what sort of lighting, place settings and music. Crystal came in to get drinks for everyone and went back out carrying them all on a circular serving tray. Once Hazel was satisfied with the setup, we reviewed the order of the events and the role that each of us would play. Crystal came in and asked about Iggy and Jackie, wondering if they would be coming to the meal so I quickly ran upstairs and knocked on her door.

"Hey, are you guys going to be joining us for dinner?" I could hear them talking in her room but they didn't respond. I knocked again and said in a louder voice that we would be eating shortly if they wanted to join us.

"Why don't you go ahead without us," Iggy yelled from the deep recesses of Jackie's room.

"You're missing out on the meal of the century!"

The sun had almost set and the early evening twilight was upon us by the time I went out to the porch with a stack of silk scarves Hazel had given me. I announced that dinner was about to be served and that Crystal and I would lead them into the house in groups of two. Inside, I could hear the *Clockwork Orange* soundtrack come on over the stereo. Walter Carlos's haunting and somewhat disturbing synthesizer was a perfect accompaniment to the meal and atmosphere. I instructed everyone to put on a blindfold.

We first led Eric and Tina in, followed by Peter and Kate and then Wayne. Once everyone was settled into their seats, Hazel came into the room and motioned for me to turn the music down a little. The lights were off but there were a bunch of candles lit and placed strategically around the table and the room so we could see things well enough.

Hazel began to hum in a really low register. It wasn't a recognizable tune but I eventually realized it was the lower harmony to the song that was playing on the record. A few measures later, Crystal began humming the higher harmony. They must have practiced because it sounded fantastic. My role was to light some incense Crystal had given me earlier and walk around the table mumbling random Latin sounding phrases like I was a Catholic priest having a bad day. The overall effect was a bit freaky but pretty cool.

When the song ended, Hazel said in her deepest, evil sounding voice, "Welcome to the first annual Zoo sacrifice of our collective innocence. Tonight, you will be asked to join your hosts Crystal, Dean and me in the celebration of our bodies and souls. We will sample some foods, we will sample some potions and then we will sample each other. I guarantee you will leave satisfied."

The next song started and it was even darker and more foreboding. Hazel said that when we touched them on the shoulder from behind, they would be fed some food so they should open their mouths for a delightful treat. Surprisingly, everyone was being really obedient and didn't even make any stupid jokes.

Hazel announced that the first item to be served would be a fine Himalayan aphrodisiac made from the fruit of the tumtum tree. We circulated behind the five diners, touched them on the shoulders and placed a jumbo Kalamata olive on their tongues. Each person had a different reaction when they experienced the explosion of the distinctive olive flavor. Some gasped, some made yummy sounds and some laughed. Hazel then announced that the next course would be the potion of love and we went around with a carafe of champagne.

"Just today I was able to procure one of the finest delicacies this side of heaven. Ladies and gentlemen, for your pleasure tonight you will be sampling what many Persian scholars and clerics recommend eating every night before bed. These incredible morsels are guaranteed to make you men randy with desire, with the lasting power of a musk ox and the drive of a purebred stallion. For you ladies, you will become instantly aroused, reach previously unknown heights of passion and turn inside out with pleasure. Please prepare yourselves to receive the perfect mixture of the male and female essence, distilled into an elixir of sensuality."

Crystal and I took a plate of poached figs that were generously slathered with honey and fed one to each person. Sounds of delight were filling the room. Various other foods were introduced, separated by sips of the love potion, including avocado slices sprinkled with lime juice, asparagus with a generous amount of melted butter, grapes and then strawberries dipped in melted chocolate. It was clear that everyone was enjoying the taste sensations since the no talking rule was still being followed.

As Crystal changed the album to a sensuous jazz recording, Hazel said that the table would be cleared and everyone should keep their blindfolds on. We moved all of the candles to surrounding tables and shelves and laid down several thick blankets on the table. She then took all of her clothes off, unbeknownst to anyone but Crystal and me, and said that it was time to experience the beauty of the human body. Hazel was a solidly built woman, very athletic and strong. She played rugby.

"I have taken all of my clothes off," she said softly. "I am going to lie down on the table and when I say its okay, I want you to touch me, massage me, explore my body and experience me without the benefit of sight. However, you have to remain in your seat."

Crystal and I went back to the table as Hazel climbed on and lay down on her back. Once she was settled and comfortable, she said that people could now begin to touch her. Kate and Tina were the first ones to reach out and tentatively caress her while the guys were a lot more hesitant. I'm certain that Wayne and Peter were somewhat disappointed to be at her head and feet, respectively, but Eric and I were counting our lucky stars that we had seats across from each other in the middle.

"You don't have to be too gentle with me," Hazel whispered. "I'm pretty tough."

After a short while, everyone got more comfortable with the concept and Hazel began making little sounds of pleasure. I think it was safe to say that everyone else was enjoying her and themselves as well. She rolled over onto her front and the touching and massaging continued.

"I hate to be the only one to receive such pleasure," Hazel said. "Who wants to be next? I think it should be one of the guys."

It was a shame that Iggy wasn't here because there was no doubt in my mind that he would have been on the table in a heartbeat. I knew it wouldn't be Eric and it would take a lot of prodding to get Peter naked on the table. Wayne, on the other hand, might have volunteered eventually but I figured since I had a big role in this production, I had better step forward. "I'll be next," I said as I started to undress.

Hazel climbed off and took her seat. "After you get your turn on the table, you can take off your blindfold."

I had received a few amateur massages in my life, usually by girlfriends and some of them were pretty talented. However, having fourteen hands on me was a sensation unlike any I had ever experienced before. After I went, Crystal took a turn and eventually everyone became less inhibited. She was a fairly small woman and almost looked like a young boy as she had short black hair and a slender body. Hazel often called her "Peanut" so of course the rest of us called her that on occasion to be funny. I was quite turned on to see her naked. Peter was the next recipient, followed by Tina, Wayne and then Kate. When it was finally Eric's turn, all of us were sitting naked around the table without our blindfolds giving him a gentle massage by the warm glow of the candlelight.

Eric's moment of pleasure had just started when we heard footsteps coming down from upstairs. Iggy and Jackie came slowly into the dining room and undoubtedly saw something they weren't expecting. Now, it would be untrue to characterize the scene they walked in on as one of pure innocence. However, in our defense, it wasn't an orgy, just like the scene Jackie walked in on earlier in the kitchen wasn't an orgy. However, this scene was closer to an orgy than the previous non-orgy.

"Oh my god! What is going on here? Have you all completely flipped out?" she cried out as she turned on the harsh overhead light.

Poor Eric was left stranded on the table with his blindfold on, while the rest of the naked diners were trying to get our eyes to adjust to the bright light. Wayne stood up and walked past Jackie and turned the light off. When Jackie turned the light back on again, we heard someone open the front door and come into the house. We never locked our doors at the Zoo so people came in and out on a regular basis, even people that didn't live there. Standing behind Iggy and Jackie was Windy.

"Jackie, you were invited to this meal. Its fine that you chose not to participate but don't barge in here and ruin it for us," Hazel said. "I think everyone here is really enjoying themselves and if you weren't such an uptight bitch, you might enjoy it too."

With this declaration of war, all hell broke loose. Jackie charged at Hazel and started flailing away with her arms even before she made contact. Peter and Wayne caught her before she got too close.

"You get out of this house at once. I want you and Crystal to move out immediately!" she cried wrapped up in Peter and Wayne's arms.

By this time, Iggy came up behind her and took her off their hands. He tried to calm her down but everything he said just riled her up even more. "Let's leave them to their group massage session. You and I will go get some dinner somewhere else. We can discuss this some other time when everyone has their clothes on and is thinking more rationally."

"Get your hands off me. You are as sick as them. I don't know why I even spend time with you. I don't ever want to see you again!" she yelled in his face and bolted back upstairs.

"Hey, why is this my fault?" Iggy yelled after her.

So in one short moment, our first annual Zoo sacrifice of our collective innocence ended, and on a sour note, unfortunately. Everyone reluctantly put their clothes back on and Windy just stood there looking on in amazement.

"Hazel, I have to say, in spite of the way this ended, that was quite an amazing experience," Tina said. "I've never done anything quite like this before. What an incredible idea!"

"Too bad I didn't get the chance to fully experience it like everyone else," Eric said.

"Maybe some other time, Eric," Crystal said. "I think little Miss Crazy has some issues that she needs to work out and it's too bad that she reacts to things the way she does."

"The thing about Jackie is that she had a very conservative upbringing and some of the things that happen around here are pretty challenging to her," Iggy explained.

"I come from conservative parents too but you don't see me freaking out when I encounter something like this," I said. "I can understand some of where she's coming from but her behavior is completely over the top."

"I understand but it's a lot more complicated than that. To be honest, it's more than I can handle. I don't really need this kind of aggravation in my life. Maybe it's a good thing that this happened," Iggy responded. "I really would have liked to have been a part of this."

"What was going on here?" Windy asked in her sweet whisper of a voice.

"Its kind of a long story," I said. "We've got to clean up but I'm sure someone will fill you in."

Hazel and I started clearing the dishes and Crystal offered to help. Everyone else went out to the porch to talk about the evening's events and unwind a bit and Windy went with them.

"Thanks for all your help, Peanut. Until the part where Jackie showed up, that went really well. I think all three of us did a great job pulling this off," Hazel said.

"It was fun. It was especially interesting to see how each person reacted to the various foods and then the touching part," Crystal said.

The clean up went quickly and we went out to the porch to rejoin everyone where we got a nice round of applause. There was a lot of laughing and some good natured and embarrassed joking about the evening. Seeing that all the seats were taken, I went over to the steps and sat down with my back leaning against the railing. Windy was sitting on the arm of a chair with Peter and then came over to sit next to me.

"Wayne had to go back to work," Peter said, "but he asked me to tell you guys that this was the best meal ever served at the Zoo."

Windy put her arm around me and whispered into my ear, "I'm sorry I missed out on the fun."

"I'm sorry too."

"Maybe you'd like to come back to my house and we could have our own private massages."

"Well, to tell you the truth, I think that I'd rather go do an oil change on the Cruisemobile."

"Seriously?"

"No, not seriously. I can't think of anything nicer."

We got up and said goodbye to everyone. I reminded Eric that he needed to be ready to go to work by seven tomorrow and that I wasn't going to wake him up this time. He assured me he would be ready.

CHAPTER 6

TO GET TO Windy's house, all we had to do was walk through our back yard, into the alley and then across to her house. She held my hand as she led me there and I felt the excitement a child might feel when they were being taken to the circus. I was having a hard time believing that this evening was real. Windy's house was a funky little place that had originally been the garage of one of the bigger houses on Pleasant Street but at some point in the past was converted to a small one bedroom apartment. Given her financial situation, it was likely that someone else was paying the rent for her; an estranged husband, a current or former boyfriend, her parents, a trust fund, a sugar daddy, the mayor—anything was possible with Windy.

Walking in through the front door was like walking into a fancy home furnishings catalog. I had never been inside her house before so she gave me a quick tour. Her house consisted of a small living room, a tiny kitchen, her bedroom and a rather spacious bathroom with a big claw foot tub. She made the most out of every inch and clearly had put some time into the design and layout. Her possessions were about a hundred notches above the Salvation Army cast off furniture, cinder block and orange crate motif that most college students were used to. The living room had really nice furniture, a plush oriental rug, beautiful wood end tables, stained glass lamps, floor to ceiling bookshelves with leather bound books and framed artwork adorned the walls. The frames were almost as exquisite as the artwork they held. Her kitchen was immaculate with matching pots and pans, expensive looking glasses, and various sized plates and bowls that also matched and all arranged neatly on the shelves. The bathroom was spotless and the counter top had expensive looking lotions and various toiletries that looked like they were all purchased on the Rue Faubourg Saint-Honore. Beautiful house plants were everywhere that the space allowed. Finally, there was her bedroom. I can't tell you anything about it because the door was shut.

"Windy, your house is one of the coolest places I have ever been to."

"Thanks. I couldn't believe what I walked into this evening. Has that ever happened before?"

"Not even in my wildest dreams. Hazel and Crystal came up with the idea and they recruited me to help carry it out."

"Tell me about the people that you were massaging. Who was your favorite?"

"Well, it wasn't any of the guys, I can tell you that. I've never actually touched another man like that so it was a new experience for me, not altogether unpleasant but not as pleasurable as touching the women."

"Where were you sitting at the table?"

"Right in the middle. It was fun to massage Crystal and Tina but I have to say that I enjoyed Kate and Hazel even more. They're fleshier and I really like that."

Windy went into the kitchen and poured two glasses of red wine. She then directed us to her small couch and sat down very close to me. We toasted each other and then toasted group massages.

"Tell me what it was like to touch Kate—in detail," she half whispered. "I'll be honest, the thought of this is really turning me on. I really enjoyed dancing with you last night. I hope you didn't mind that I kissed you."

"Mind? No, in fact, I've been thinking about it all day. I'm really glad that you came over tonight."

"Back to Kate or Hazel, it doesn't really matter. Just tell me what it was like."

"So, I was right in the middle and was able to touch her pretty much anywhere from her knees up to her shoulders. I didn't want to focus too much on any one body part because I think we were trying our best to make this a non-sexual experience. However, when you're touching a voluptuous woman's tummy, hips, bottom, breasts and everything in between, I'm not sure that it could be a non-sexual experience."

"Were you getting aroused?"

"Are you kidding? I'm surprised that the guys didn't collectively raise the table when the women were having their turn. It was one of the sexiest experiences I've ever had!"

"What was it like to be the one on the table?"

"Unbelievable! Any worry or modesty that I might have started with quickly gave way to an overload of fantastic sensations. Having all those hands on me was amazing. Have you ever experienced anything like this?"

"Not exactly. Maybe we should go into my bedroom and give each other massages now. You just have to promise me that it won't be non-sexual."

"I think that's a promise I could keep."

She led me through the door and into her bedroom. The four poster bed looked like a family heirloom. The rugs were deep and rich and I felt like I was walking on clouds. Her night stand was neatly organized with several colorful ceramic containers with elaborate tops, a few books and another beautiful lamp. She kept her two guitars off in one of the corners on little metal stands near a tall wooden stool. She had an intricately carved chest of drawers that looked like it was made out of walnut and must have been worth thousands of dollars. In another corner was an overstuffed chair and matching ottoman. Her bed was covered with a handmade quilt that was gorgeous.

"Tell me about your bedspread. It's amazing!"

"That's probably my most prized possession. My grandmother made if for me a few years before she passed away. It's very special. I have a rule that you can't lie on top of it as it puts too much strain on the stitches."

"Yeah, I know. My mother makes quilts and has the same rule."

"Now, where were we? Oh right, you were telling me about touching Kate. How about we skip that part and you just start touching me?"

I went over and gave her a slow, gentle kiss. She responded in kind and after a short while, began taking my clothes off. I wanted to savor every moment of this experience so I wasn't in a big hurry to move it along any faster than necessary. I unfastened her hair tie so that her long wavy hair was free to cascade around her shoulders and her back. Slowly, I unbuttoned her shirt and slid if off down her arms, taking the time to carefully place it on a chair. She was wearing a very pretty bra with a few flowers embroidered on it. Windy was in the fleshy category, like Kate and Hazel. Her breasts were just the perfect size and bounced to their glorious fullness in the most delightful way when I unhooked her bra and let them loose. I made sure to give them the attention and respect they deserved with my hands, mouth and tongue. She seemed to be enjoying this almost as much as I was.

Somehow, Windy had managed to remove all of my clothes. I was standing there naked, at full attention, properly saluting the queen. Windy was topless and beautiful and I set about the delicious task of removing her jeans.

"Before you do that, Dean, I need to tell you something. I would love to make love with you tonight but you should know that one of my other friends is coming over later so you won't be able to spend the night with me. I just don't want you to have any hurt feelings."

I felt a slight stab of jealousy but had to ask myself what I had to be jealous about. I knew that Windy was a free spirit and to be given this gift of time with her was more than I had ever hoped for. Almost every guy and some gals I knew would have switched places with me in an instant, even under these conditions.

"I understand, let's just enjoy the time we have to the fullest," I responded as I unsnapped her jeans and unzipped them. As they slid to the floor, I gazed with utter delight at her very brief briefs, almost choking on my own breath and the wonderful aroma that immediately filled the air. As Windy's panties joined her jeans on the floor, it was obvious that this might be one of those experiences that I'd go to my grave with, smiling all the way.

"Let me prepare our bed," Windy said seductively. She pulled the quilt and top sheet back; it was almost like opening up an oyster, so pearly white and inviting. I watched her behind from behind and she was absolutely lovely in every way imaginable. We started hugging and kissing again while standing beside her bed and I thought that my legs might buckle beneath me.

"Would you allow me the honor of giving the first massage?" I asked.

"By all means. If you go over to my nightstand and look inside the bluish-green jar, there is vanilla massage lotion inside that I would like you to use. I hope you'll like it."

"Yum, that's one of my favorites scents."

Windy was lying on her stomach when I returned. I put some of the lotion on my hands and rubbed them together to warm it up before I touched her. I started at her feet and slowly worked my way up to her shoulders and neck. She wasn't at all shy and communicated with me freely what she liked and gave helpful suggestions when I was doing things that weren't exactly what she wanted. I could feel some tight spots in her back and shoulders so gave these areas some extra attention. Her skin was so soft and smooth and began to glow as I kneaded her muscles. I asked her to roll over so that I could give her front some attention. I almost couldn't even look at her body as she lay there for fear that I might get too excited and embarrass myself. Again, I worked my way up from her feet and eventually arrived at her face. The heat coming from between her legs was powerful and remarkable and seemed to produce a force field that my hands almost weren't able to penetrate. Her breasts moved around in a very sensuous way as I massaged first around them and then directly on them. Her nipples became pink nuggets of wonder when my fingers came into contact.

"Oh, that feels so good," Windy whispered. "You seemed to find all of my tight spots. Give me a minute here to get my head back on straight and then it will be your turn."

She slowly sat up in her bed and looked a little dazed. Once she had regained her balance, she slowly and sensuously moved her legs over the edge and stood up. Everything seemed to be happening in slow motion and I almost wanted time to stop completely. I then took her spot and was treated to a remarkable massage. She had very strong hands, probably from her years playing the guitar, and had a very good sense of just how much pressure to apply to various places on my body. After a fabulous massage, she lay down beside me and crossed one of her legs over mine.

"I hope you don't think it's too forward of me but I'd like to make love now," she said softly. Before that happened, however, there was a loud knock at the front door. I stopped doing what I was doing and Windy froze in place.

"Damn, if that's who I think it is, he's about an hour early. Who is it?" she yelled out.

"Hey, Windy, it's me, Wally."

"Wally, go away, you're too early, I'm busy."

Apparently Wally wasn't planning on going away. He continued to knock louder and harder and started yelling at Windy to let him in or he was going to kick the door in. Windy realized that he needed to be dealt with so she slipped out of bed and put on a silk bathrobe. I decided this would be a good time to get dressed as well.

"Stop being such a jerk," she said as she approached the door. "Calm down and I'll let you in."

Wally apparently calmed down enough from Windy's perspective so she opened the door. There he stood, about six and a half feet tall, dressed like a Hell's Angel and looking like he was under the influence of every drug you could find in Boulder.

"It's about time you opened the door," he bellowed as he barged in. Looking at me he said, "Hey, who's the pipsqueak?"

"That's my friend Dean. He and I were just getting comfortable when you appeared. What's going on?"

"Remember you invited me over tonight so that we could have a good fuck?"

"I doubt that I put it that way but there's been a change of plans and now I would like you to leave. You and I can get together some other time."

"The hell I'm going to leave. The pipsqueak is the one that's going to leave."

Now I was starting to get really uncomfortable. This guy was over a half a foot taller than me, outweighed me by at least a hundred and fifty pounds and was meaner and nastier looking than almost anyone I had ever met in my entire life. I wanted to leave but worried about what would happen to Windy.

"Listen pal," I said trying not to sound like a pipsqueak, "Windy has asked you to leave and I think that would be a good idea considering the circumstances. I was invited over to her house and I don't really appreciate the interruption."

"Well I was invited over too so unless you want to get pulverized, you should get the hell out of here now!"

"Windy, maybe we should call the police. I don't really want to get pulverized and you probably don't want Wally here even if I do leave in one piece."

"Wally is already in enough trouble with the law. If I call the police, he'll be carted off to jail since he already has a number of outstanding warrants. What's it going to be Wally?"

"I think I'd like to pulverize the pipsqueak and then do you," he said to Windy, taking full advantage of his limited vocabulary.

"That is absolutely not going to happen so I suggest you both leave," Windy said.

"I guess that's the deal. I'll leave if you agree to leave as well," I offered as a way to deal with the situation, thinking that once things settled down, maybe I would come back to Windy's house and pick up where we left off.

"Listen, Wally, your behavior here is really bad. I don't want to be with you tonight so I suggest you leave," Windy said.

With that, Wally turned around, slammed his fist on the wall, grabbed me by the arm and dragged me outside. When we were out of sight and earshot of Windy, he pushed me to the ground and kicked me in the side.

"That's a small price to pay for ruining my night with Windy, you little fucker."

"Hey, don't be such a bully or I'll hit you with my purse," I said trying to restore a few ounces of my dignity with some good old fashioned gay humor.

Wally went back through the alley, hopped on his hog and roared off into the night. I assessed the damage to my side and decided that nothing was broken. After considering my various options, I went back to Windy's house and knocked on her door.

"Who is it?"

"Dean"

She opened up the door and I could see that she had been crying.

"Are you alright?"

"Not really. You see, I used to be in love with Wally. He and I moved out to Boulder together from Ohio. He used to be a really nice guy. Unfortunately, he got mixed up with the wrong people and now I just don't want to be around him. I invited him over tonight because he told me that he was cleaning up his act but clearly that's not happening. I love being with you but things are just so confusing. I hope you aren't mad at me but I just need to be alone tonight to sort things out."

"Sure, Windy, I'm a bit disappointed, okay, very disappointed, but mostly I'm worried about you. What if he comes back?"

"Oh, he's not really as menacing as he tries to appear. If he does come back, I can handle him. Don't be worried. You go home and maybe we can get together tomorrow night. How does that sound?"

"It sounds like the last thing on my list of how I wanted this evening to end."

We said our goodbyes, exchanged a brief hug and kiss, and I walked back to the Zoo. Nobody was around when I got there so I went to my bedroom. On my desk was a note from Iggy. "Beans, I'm going away this weekend so I need to drive Gus to work tomorrow." I listened to some music for a while and eventually drifted off to sleep.

CHAPTER 7

FRIDAY MORNING WAS unusually cloudy and cool, rare in Boulder, especially in late June. After my morning shower, I had to put on my dirty Sugarloaf Quarry clothes since I had forgotten to do a load of laundry in the craziness of the previous evening. I put a sweatshirt on over my overalls, noticed that my side hurt like hell and went into the kitchen to scrounge some breakfast. There was other activity in the house and I was soon joined in the dining room by Iggy and Eric.

"Did you get my note?" Iggy asked me.

"Yes I did," I responded. "What's going on?"

"I've pretty much had it with Jackie. She's just too intense for me. I can't continue to make excuses for her behavior. I made some plans to go away for the weekend so I'll be leaving right from the quarry. Maybe by the time I get back on Sunday, when we've had some time to think things through a bit, she and I can discuss what happened yesterday a bit more rationally."

"What happened last night after your big blow out?" Eric asked, looking up with squinty eyes from his granola.

"I tried to talk to her about your group grope. By the way, that was totally cool and I'm pissed off that I missed it. Whose idea was that?" Iggy was talking in a near whisper since Jackie wasn't too far out of listening range.

"Crystal and Hazel's," I said. "Did you know about the blindfolded taste test that preceded it?"

"Yeah, Eric and Tina told me all about it after you left with Windy. By the way, I can't believe your good luck!" Iggy exclaimed.

"It was pretty amazing, although it didn't really have a happy ending. I'll tell you more about that later. First, I want to hear the rest of the Jackie story."

"Well, there's not a lot to tell, really. She wouldn't talk about it and said that she was tired of dealing with me and that we should go our separate ways."

"I'm sorry, man. I know how much you enjoy spending time with her when she's not a she-wolf but honestly, that's not very often," I said.

"Yeah but you know how I am with relationships. She is so far from the person that I first met that I can't believe she's still the same person."

"Maybe you'd like to get to know Joan or Rhonda a little better?" Eric asked.

"The thought has crossed my mind two or three hundred times," Iggy said, seeming more like his old self.

"Mine too!" Eric said.

Eric decided to drive up with Iggy so I drove the Cruisemobile alone. I arrived at the quarry entrance arch with time to spare so didn't feel like I had to hurry much. Iggy was behind me, actually, quite far behind me since he needed to be in second gear to get Gus up some of the steeper grades of both Boulder Canyon and Sugarloaf Mountain Road. I pulled off over to admire the plantings we had done the day before and to relieve myself by the trees. As I was walking back to the Cruisemobile, I saw Gus chugging up the road, even slower than I expected. I stood by the side of the road and waited for them to pull up even with me. Iggy and Eric were sitting in the front seats as expected but I noticed a large body that I eventually recognized as Junior in the back. Eric rolled down his window.

"Guess who we found along the road?" he asked.

"Hi Junior, what are you doing with these rookies?" I asked as I put my head through Eric's window.

"I'm not sure what happened. I woke up in a ditch down the road a ways," he said rather embarrassedly.

"Yeah, we were driving along when we saw Junior here climbing up an embankment to the side of the road so we stopped and picked him up," Eric explained.

Junior looked like he had rolled all the way down from the quarry, probably a distance of a mile or so. He was covered with dirt and debris and had various bits of vegetation stuck in his hair plus he didn't smell too good either.

"What happened at the nightclub last night, Junior?" I asked.

"I don't remember anything after the lights went dim," he responded.

"We've got to get to work, Beans. Let's talk later. See you up there," Iggy said as he accelerated away.

I jumped back into my car and pulled into the quarry parking lot right beside them. I could hear the muffled voices of the crew bosses inside the office so I took the time to make conversation with Junior, which was not an easy task.

"You really don't know how you got down the road, do you? Interesting. And what's this about the lights going out?"

"The lights go dim when it's time to, well, you know," Junior explained.

"No, I don't. That's why I'm asking. I've never been to the nightclub."

"Remember what Alfonso said. You aren't supposed to ask questions about it."

"Well, I wasn't really asking about the nightclub, I was asking about the lights. Is it usually dark at the nightclub?"

"That's a question about the nightclub."

"I suppose you're right. Sorry."

The rest of the quarry crew appeared from around the corner right on cue and marched into the office. Junior got a lot of slaps on the back and congratulations on his fabulous performance last night.

Whispering into my ear as we entered the building, he said, "I wonder what I did?"

Big Larry had a massive bandage wrapped around his head in such a way that both of his ears stuck out through the gauze, like Tina's panties, but were bent at an awkward angle. He looked like maybe he was planning on going out trick-or-treating later. My guess was that he might have added some extra bandages after the hospital staff got through with him to make things look worse than they actually were. His mood seemed particularly ornery and that was saying something. Everyone took their seats while Big Larry paced around in front of the table with an unusual amount of nervous energy. He kept looking towards the door as if maybe he was expecting Bernice the Flamboyant to barge in and whack him some more with her baton.

"Listen up people," he finally said, "we're going to keep the same assignments we had yesterday. Does everyone remember what they were?"

Most everyone nodded their heads or at least didn't volunteer that they didn't remember. Big Larry waited a few moments before continuing. "As most of you know, yesterday was a tough day for me. However, I think it might be safe to say that it was an even tougher night for Junior." Apparently, this was a big inside joke because the entire room, minus the four of us, started chuckling. Junior turned bright red while people again commended him for his antics. "Junior, if you ever want to hire yourself an agent, you should consider me. I know a lot of people in the business.

If this quarry thing doesn't work out for you, it's nice to know that a career in the entertainment industry might be an option."

"I hope someone eventually tells me what happened last night," Junior said rather sheepishly.

"Let's just say that you exceeded everyone's expectations!" Rhonda said to another round of laughter.

"Just keep in mind, everyone, today is Friday. You'll be getting your paychecks before you leave for the weekend," Big Larry said. "Okey dokey, now, on to the business of the day. We've got a lot of deliveries scheduled so I'd like the transportation crew to head out right after the announcements are done. Quesnal, keep things movin' so that you and your crew can finish up by five. If not, I'll pay overtime but I think you can fit it all in. Harry, the steam roller and the grader both need servicin' so you and your crew have a full day as well. Alfonso, the front entrance is lookin' downright bee-you-tee-full and I want to acknowledge the work that Joan and the boys did without help from you and Junior. Today you'll be buildin' the wall that we talked about. Rhonda, since I'm flyin' at half mast today, I want you to stick beside me as much as possible to help run this operation. Zelda and Dickie, I want you and your crew to stick around after the meetin' so we can review the priorities. If there are no other questions," Big Larry said without actually waiting for anyone to ask any questions, "this meeting is adjourned. See you all back here by five. Be sure to pick up Bunny's food bags on your way out."

Everyone seemed to be in high spirits and went outside to begin their work assignments, except for the folks on the quarry and sorting crews. The three of us college boys assembled by Alfonso with Junior and Joan in order to hear his briefing. Since we would need a lot of granite to build the wall out front, our first task was to load up several truck loads of prime rock from the sorting area on the other side of the quarry near the Fanny Packer Road. He instructed Eric and me to go with him in his truck and Junior and Iggy to go with Joan to get a large dump truck.

Since there was only room for two to sit comfortably inside the cab, I volunteered to sit outside in the truck bed. As we made our way over to the sorting area, I could see Alfonso and Eric were having an animated conversation inside the truck but I couldn't make out their words given all of the noise the truck made while bouncing over the rough road.

"So that's why I always make sure that my pants are on good and tight," Alfonso said, finishing up the tail end of the conversation as we all got out of the truck.

"Good idea," Eric responded looking at me with amusement as Joan, Junior and Iggy pulled up beside us.

"Let's start picking out the base rocks we need for the wall. Now, remember how the plants from yesterday are arranged. Think about where they are relative to the driveway and the arch and the topography of the area. From a design standpoint, give me your ideas about how we might want to build the stonewall," Alfonso asked, giving us a chance to weigh in on the matter.

"Well, if it were me, I'd build a wall right along the driveway to help define the entrance a bit more," I offered.

"That's a start," Alfonso said. "However, that might block out the lower growing plants we want our customers to see when they approach the driveway from the road. Any other ideas?"

"How about instead of a linear wall, we build a vertical wall, kind of like monuments, on either side of the archway to make the whole entranceway look grander and somewhat imposing?" Iggy suggested.

"Now you're getting creative. This is starting to evolve. Whitey, do you have an idea?"

"I was thinking kind of along the same lines as Hambone except I think we need to consider the intended purpose. Clearly, you are interested in aesthetics but you also want to showcase your primary product which is granite. I suggest that instead of a low wall along the driveway, we build a medium high wall behind the low growing plants using a variety of sizes and shapes of stone to truly show off the types, textures and colors of the rocks that you mine here. It should be high enough to rise above the plants in the dry section but low enough not to block out the wild plums lining the back edge. How does that sound?" Eric asked.

"¡Buena idea! That's close to the design Joan and I came up with last night. Maybe these college boys aren't such stoners after all," he said with a laugh. "Were you eavesdropping?"

"No, I was trying to have an orgy in Boulder but things didn't quite work out," Eric said.

"¡Qué lástima!" Alfonso said. "In order to build such a wall, we'll need a great variety of rocks. However, the most important ones are the base rocks. Since the wall will be about twenty feet long, our first few loads will be the base. Let's each take a load over and see where that leaves us. These rocks don't necessarily need to be super big, just fairly uniform in width. Since we will be setting this first course into the ground, we can adjust the size and shape of the hole. They just need to be flat on one side. Joan and I will pull the rocks out from this pile and the four of you will load them into the dump truck."

It was a sizable task to get the first load of the right rocks loaded into the truck. Joan and her crew headed off to the entrance when they had a full load while we went over to grab the tools needed for the day. By the time we had all reconvened at the entrance, a light rain had begun to fall and the temperature dropped about ten degrees. It wasn't cold out but certainly not warm enough to work in just tee shirts and overalls. Alfonso pulled out a bunch of yellow raincoats from behind his seat in the truck and handed them out to everyone. Joan had pulled the dump truck as close to the work site as possible.

"I know that it's not a lot of fun to work in the rain," Joan said, "but all the plants that we put in the ground yesterday will sure enjoy it. Alfonso, at least we've saved some time not having to water this morning."

"Es verdad," he said, "and since we'll get hot and sweaty from moving these rocks around all day, it might actually feel good."

I had taken Spanish in high school but really only remembered a few random phrases. Being around Alfonso, I was hopeful that I would be able to improve my language skills. It was helpful how he used a few Spanish phrases mixed into the context of English so I was able to understand a lot of what he was saying. In junior high school foreign language classes, the teaching method used was to memorize long dialogs with the hope that the students would eventually understand some of the patterns and be able to have very stilted conversations with each other. It was, however, hard to work the phrase "Meatballs, didn't I tell you?" into any normal conversation.

"Alfonso," I asked, "como se dice in Español, 'what is on the school lunch menu today?'"

"Why are you asking this, OD?"

"Because I want to be able to answer, 'Albondigas, no te dige?'"

At least Eric thought this was funny because apparently his school in Missouri used the same teaching method and dialogs. Before Alfonso had a chance to respond, Eric recited the entire dialog he was required to memorize probably four or five years ago.

"Not bad there Whitey!" I said, thoroughly impressed.

"Yeah, not too bad except your accent sounds like you're from somewhere north of Alaska. Okay, amigos, put on your raincoats and let's get to work here," Alfonso instructed. "Just be careful because the rocks will be a little slippery and the footing might not be so good either. Make sure that you have a good firm grip on each rock before you start moving it."

We transported the rocks from the trucks to the spot Joan was busy preparing for the wall. She told us to pile them on the slight upslope side of where the wall would go since it would be easier to work with the rocks if we had gravity on our side.

"Even though most of these rocks are fairly light, towards the end of the day after we've all lifted and moved hundreds of rocks, each one will feel like it weighs half a ton. The more we can do to help ourselves, the better," she explained.

Using a spade, Joan roughed out the twenty foot area where the wall would go. She consulted periodically with Alfonso to make sure that he agreed with her placement. The final layout was a bit undulating and seemed to follow their philosophy of landscaping. We got another load of rocks and unloaded them with the first batch. Eventually, Joan and Alfonso were satisfied they had the raw materials and right alignment and were ready to start building the base.

"Junior, I would like you to come with me to get the next load of stone. We'll probably be back with the next load before you need more rock," Alfonso said.

"Okay, Al," Junior said. Alfonso really didn't seem like an Al to me but didn't appear to mind. Maybe it was an inside joke.

The rain was coming down a little harder but it felt pretty good considering how hard we had been working to get the rocks moved over. With the combination of rain and sweat, I decided to pull my hair back in a pony tail to keep it out of my face. Eric and Iggy did the same, followed by Joan.

"Hey, we're all twins!" Iggy said. "Maybe we should start a band called Joan and the Ponytails!"

"I want to come up with a better stage name. Joan is kind of boring. How about Little Muffy and the Ponytails?" Joan suggested.

"How about Little Muffin and the Muffies?" I suggested.

"How about Big Muff and the Deep Sea Divers?" Eric said taking the joke in a different direction.

"How about Deep Muff and the Wet Guys?" Iggy offered.

"How about we forget the band concept all together and start digging in these rocks?" Joan said. "You guys already are the Wet Guys but I don't think I'd like to be Deep Muff."

We all seemed to be working together pretty well. By the time Alfonso and Junior returned, it was time for our morning break. The rain seemed like it was winding down so we took off our dirty raincoats and sat on the tailgates of the trucks to relax for a little while.

Junior and Alfonso smoked their customary cigarettes. Even though I was philosophically opposed to smoking, I had to admit that I kind of liked the smell of the burning tobacco. The combination of sweat, dirt, rain and cigarette smoke produced a strangely appealing combination of aromas. Alfonso pulled out a stack of metal camp mugs and a big thermos of hot tea that he shared with everyone. Each of us had a fruit pastry in the food bag that Bunny had prepared.

"Junior, I was wondering about something," Iggy began. "Since I'm planning to stay at the quarry on Monday and go to the nightclub, is there any advice you can give me? I have to admit, I'm feeling a little nervous about this whole thing."

Before Junior responded, Alfonso stepped in, "Hambone, it's really nothing to worry about. Just go with the flow, it will be fine, hombre."

"What was your first night like, Alfonso?" Iggy asked.

"Sorry, a rule's a rule. You'll just have to experience it yourself. My experience was different from what yours will be like, which will be different from Junior's and Joan's. It really depends upon the person and what goes on inside your head."

"If you don't mind my asking, what is it like for you living up here all week? Is it a difficult thing to do?" Eric asked getting us off of the forbidden topic.

"Yes, initially it was. I've got a young daughter from a previous marriage. She lives with her mom out in Longmont. I only get to see her on weekends anyway, that wouldn't be any different even if I had a job where I went home every night. So for me, it works out just fine. Being up here for the whole week is actually good for me, it keeps me out of trouble and when I'm home on the weekend, I spend almost all of my time with Maria."

"You guys should meet her sometime," Joan said. "She's an absolute angel. Such a darling."

"You see, I've made some bad decisions in my past but now I've got my life on the straight and narrow. Maria is a father's dream come true and I don't want to mess that up."

"I think I understand," Iggy said. "I've worked with a lot of men that don't have that kind of clarity."

"What about you Junior," Eric asked. "What's it like for you living up here during the week?"

"It's fine. I already told you that my mommy and daddy moved to New Mexico so I don't really have anyplace to go anyway."

"What do you do on weekends?" Eric asked.

"Sometimes I stay with my uncle and sometimes Big Larry let's me stay in the bunkhouse."

"All by yourself?" I asked.

"Sometimes. Sometimes other people stay here too."

"Really? I didn't know that," Joan said. "Who stays up here with you?"

"Once it was Georgie, once it was Felix 2. Georgie doesn't have a home of her own and usually stays with her brother. One time they got into a fight so Big Larry said that she could stay here."

Alfonso stood up and started to put things away. The rain had stopped completely and there were a few scattered patches of blue sky coming towards us from the west. Occasionally a delivery truck would rumble by and we could hear them coming from either direction. When things were relatively quiet, you could hear the quarry operation sounds all the way at the entrance where we were. After a short while, we were back working on the rock wall and heard a vehicle coming down the driveway from the quarry and saw the Sugarloaf Quarry car pull up. Rhonda got out and walked over to talk with Alfonso.

"Alfonso, I need to get your input on something," Rhonda began.

"Why didn't you just buzz me on the walkie-talkie?" Alfonso asked.

"Because I didn't want the whole danged quarry crew to be a part of our conversation. I don't mind if your crew hears since it will affect all of them but mostly I wanted to talk to you about something that Big Larry told me. It also involves Junior so I'd like him to be in on this as well."

"Sure, hey Junior," Alfonso yelled over, "would you come over here please?" Junior shuffled over, looking very guilty about something, or maybe this was just his general nature, it was hard to tell the difference. Looking at Rhonda, Alfonso said, "Que pasa?"

"Last night at the nightclub, there was a part of the evening where Junior went out on a little adventure with Laverne. Remember that?"

"Sure," said Alfonso. "That was really funny. They are two of the most unlikely people you would ever imagine together."

"Like I already said, I don't remember anything between the time when the lights went low and when I woke up in the ditch this morning."

"Understandable," said Rhonda, "but here's the problem. Apparently, Laverne insists on working with Junior now because she doesn't want to be away from him any longer than necessary. She told Big Larry that she's in love and can't concentrate on anything else. If she can't work with him, she's threatening to quit. She's one of our best drivers so we'd hate to lose her to a little puppy love. What do you make of all this Junior?"

"I've hardly ever even talked to her."

"Well that may be but here are the options—either Laverne could come work on the landscaping crew and one of you would work with one of the drivers. Another option would be for Junior to ride shotgun with Laverne because you don't have your commercial license, right Junior?"

"No, I mean yes. I mean no I don't have my license," he managed to say.

"Alfonso, if you give up Junior to the transportation crew, would you need someone in exchange for your landscaping crew?"

"Well, it's great to have Junior on our team. He really adds a lot of muscle. However, given the production that we are getting out of these guys, I think we could get by with just the five of us. That is if Junior doesn't mind," Alfonso responded.

"I like working with you guys but it doesn't sound like I have a choice," Junior said glumly.

"It really seems like the best option. It would be a shame to lose Laverne as a driver and I'm not sure if her talents are suited for landscaping. It also would be tough to lose Junior from landscaping but we could try it for a day or two and see how it works out. Maybe in the light of day, Laverne would have a change of heart, no offense Junior," Alfonso said.

"So everyone's cool with a temporary trial run? Junior, you just let me know if it creates an uncomfortable situation for you. You might actually like being Laverne's assistant. Its easier work than landscaping, all you have to do is help her with the loading, unloading, backing up, covering the load with the tarp, weighing in and out, delivering the customer the bill, you know, stuff like this," Rhonda said.

"Can't she do that on her own?" Junior asked.

"She can, most of the other drivers do but it's quite a bit more efficient and faster for there to be two people in each truck, the driver and the assistant. So, why don't you come with me and I'll drive you up to the quarry. I think Laverne's getting her next delivery loaded."

When they had driven away, Alfonso and Joan started laughing. It was certainly an interesting turn of events. Laverne was a middle age woman, very small with a big mouth. I was having a hard time picturing her and Junior together as a couple with their age, size and personality differences.

"Whoa, now that has to be one of the strangest pairings in the history of the Sugarloaf Quarry," Joan exclaimed.

"That's for sure," Alfonso agreed. "Love is a funny thing. Maybe with some time, Junior will feel the same way as Laverne. I've got to wonder what went on between the two of them last night. It must have been magical for Laverne. Did she wake up in the bunkhouse this morning?"

"Yes, just like always. But she was in a strangely happy mood so maybe all of this is starting to make some sense. She told me that she was ready to start living her life to the fullest again now that it's been a year since her husband died."

"Sounds like maybe she sowed some wild oats last night," Alfonso said. "But don't you think he would have remembered?"

"You know how things go at the nightclub, Alfonso," Joan reminded him.

"You mean that people get paired up and are sent off somewhere to have sex with each other?" Iggy asked. "I think I could get into this sort of thing!"

"Don't get your hopes up Hambone," Alfonso warned. "Strange things do happen. Alright, how about we all put our energies back into building this wall? Things are coming together nicely. Whitey, you and I are going to go up to the quarry and get another load of rocks. Joan, Hambone and OD should continue with the building process. Let's see if we can make some good progress by lunchtime. I'm not expecting we'll finish the wall today and I know it can't be rushed. This area is the first impression people will get when they enter the quarry so let's make it the best wall possible. I have no doubts that it will be muy fabuloso!"

After Eric and Alfonso drove off, Iggy, Joan and I got back to work fitting the various rocks into the wall. I could see that building a good wall took a lot of experience and patience. My initial inclination was to simply stack the flattest rocks on top of each other but Joan's approach

DAVID W. GOODWIN

was very different. It was like she had a vision that was totally invisible to me. Some of the rocks she wanted in the wall seemed totally wrong and out of place but as the new rocks were worked in, the wall began to transition to a thing of beauty. Instead of trying to force the rocks into a particular spot, it almost seemed like Joan let the rocks communicate with her where they should go, just like the plants. This wasn't exactly a straightforward process as sometimes she had us take some rocks out that just didn't quite fit. She was on her knees in front of the wall and would do the final adjusting. Occasionally she would stand up, walk around the wall to observe it from various angles and then make a few additional minor adjustments. I was finding it difficult to concentrate on my work when she started walking around, bending over to look at things carefully since it was so enjoyable to look at her. Iggy was having the same reaction because we both smiled broadly when our eyes met.

Alfonso and Eric eventually returned with the next load. "We saw Junior and Laverne up by the scale. They were sitting on the bench waiting for her new load to get weighed out before their delivery. She was giving him a back rub and the poor kid looked a bit confused," Alfonso said with a shake of his head and a little chuckle. "She sure seems to have been bitten by the love bug!"

"I'd love to know what he's going to write to his mommy and daddy in his letter home tonight. Do you think he lost his virginity?" Joan asked.

"Your guess is as good as mine but from the sounds of things, I would have to say that he did. I'm awfully curious, however, about why he ended up in the ditch," Alfonso said. "Given Laverne's experience, you couldn't find a better woman for your first time."

"Well, I'm not sure she would have been my first choice personally," Eric said, "but, I don't know her so maybe he's gotten really lucky. My dad tried once to fix me up with the wife of one of his friends when I was in high school. I think he thought I was a virgin too but that wasn't the case. She called me up when her husband was out of town and asked me to come over to help her with a little project. When I got there, she was wearing a see-through negligee and said that the project was to lose my virginity."

"What happened?" I asked.

"I told her that it was too late for that but I'd be happy to pretend that it wasn't."

"And you had sex with her?" Joan asked.

"At that point in my life, I would have had sex with almost anyone at any time."

"How is that different from now?" Iggy teased.

"Hey, at least now I restrict myself to women that aren't certifiably insane!" Eric countered.

"That's enough guys," Alfonso said. "Joan, start telling these hombres locos what to do."

We worked for a while until it was lunchtime, took our break and then worked the rest of the afternoon without any other further interruptions. The sun finally came out and the warmth felt good. It was hard work moving these rocks around and I was quite happy when it was finally time to call it quits. We loaded all the tools and miscellaneous stuff into the truck and drove back to the quarry. The wall was over half way done and was shaping up nicely.

Big Larry got all of the reports, including Quesnal's reference to the addition of Junior as Laverne's assistant. This got quite a few hoots from the quarry crew.

"This is none of your business. I don't want any of you to give me a hard time about this," Laverne yelled out with mock anger. "I just want everyone to know that Junior and I have made a special connection and would like some privacy to pursue our relationship. Please respect that and don't any of you dare make any jokes about this or I'll knock your blocks off. Junior's a grown man and even though there are a few years difference in us, it isn't a big deal. Right Junior?"

"Uhh, I guess so," Junior answered unconvincingly.

"So, one last thing," Big Larry said, wrapping the meeting up, "let's distribute your paychecks." One by one, he called out a name and Rhonda handed the person an envelope. The stack in her hand was gone before our names were called.

"What about us?" I asked.

"That's a good one there DO, or is it OD?" Big Larry cackled. "I've got some bad news for you buster. Payroll runs a week behind so you'll get paid next Friday for this week's work. Understand? Alright then, meeting adjourned. See you all on Monday. Try not to get into too much trouble this weekend."

We left the building and said goodbye to our landscaping crewmates. Eric and I chatted briefly with Iggy and said that we'd probably see him Sunday night when we'd all get back to Boulder. I told my friends that I was going away on a bike trip with my friend Rob and Eric said that he and Tina were heading up to a textile fair in Estes Park.

"Well I guess we'll all catch up later, then," Iggy said. "If you see Jackie when you get back to the Zoo, tell her that I was kidnapped by a roving band of Amazon babes or something."

CHAPTER 8

DURING THE SCHOOL year, I had a work-study job at a place called JILA on the University of Colorado campus. This was a high level government and University funded research organization that was involved in some top secret work that attracted some of the brightest and most eccentric scientists in the country and around the world. My guess was that a lot of the research was supported by the Defense Department. Most of the scientists were top shelf, internationally known and respected folks in the field of astrophysics. Their labs looked like they were designed for Hollywood movie sets. JILA stood for the Joint Institute for Laboratory Astrophysics, with an extra emphasis on "Joint". These folks were absolutely out there in space, metaphysically and astrophysically and fully exemplified the term 'mad scientists'.

My job was very high level. I had to pass an intense psychological profile screening, submit a character reference from at least one major elected official and eventually I took a loyalty oath and memorized the secret JILA tenets. Finally, I was inducted into the bosom of the JILA support staff and learned the secret handshake that was similar to the Phi Beta Kappa Honor Society handshake only instead of using the two finger wiggle on the other person's wrist, you used your middle finger and took turns inserting it into the other person's fist circle with an in and out motion.

My job was a never ending series of mindless yet completely cool tasks. First thing each morning at seven, I made a very large pot of turbo strength coffee. This was perhaps the most important task in the running of JILA, even more important than the research itself. There was a check list next to the coffee pot with each person's name and the five work days of the week in a matrix. For each cup of coffee consumed, the scientists would add one mark in the day's box. Most of the people consumed a few cups a day and their coffee bill would be around $3 per week. A few of the people consumed so much coffee that their bill would be around $10 per week or almost ten cups a day.

My next task was to go on the donut run. I would get the keys to the 1970 Dodge Monaco that looked like an unmarked police car and head over to Donut Heaven and pick up our daily standing order of four dozen donuts, assorted flavors, toppings and fillings. Before I returned to JILA, however, I had two more very important stops to make. The first was the National Bureau of Standards since they had a super computer that some of the scientists at JILA leased time on to run various simulation programs. I would drop off their stacks of keypunched cards containing all of their programs and pick up the 14" wide green and white striped print outs from their dot matrix printers and yesterday's keypunch cards from the big wire basket that said "JILA" on it. The next stop was my favorite. I had to drive up to the National Center for Atmospheric Research facility up in the foothills west of Boulder. This futuristic building, intended to bear a modern era resemblance to the Anasazi cliff dwellings of Mesa Verde, was designed in the 60's by the famous architect I. M. Pei and its claim to fame was that it was used in one of the scenes from the Woody Allen movie *Sleeper*. On most days, the sun would be rising up over the eastern plains of Colorado, illuminating the foothills with a beautiful pink glow as herds of mule deer grazed along the road. I did the same thing at NCAR as I did at NBS but the NCAR computer used a different programming language that most of the researchers preferred. I always felt like an important person when I showed my ID to be allowed into the facility.

I would rush back to JILA and deposit the donuts by the coffee machine. There was a second sheet next to the coffee sheet for donut consumption and this total would get added to the coffee total each week to complete their bill. I would then go around to each office to hand deliver their printouts and stacks of cards. These were extremely valuable items that you didn't want to leave just lying around in a mailbox or some other unsecured place. Even though I was 100% trustworthy, I'm not quite sure why I was trusted with such valuable things. I guess Brenda just knew intuitively that I was the best person for the job.

Brenda was my boss, office manager and a force to be reckoned with. She was probably in her mid thirties, marginally attractive, single, big and strong, dressed-for-success everyday with high heels, jewelry, stockings, dress, make up and perfume and ruled over every administrative aspect of JILA. If she liked you, you were set, if she didn't, your time at JILA was going to be very brief. The year I worked there, she had hired a stable of four work-study college boys. I'm not sure if she liked me but

I know that she loved one of my gopher colleagues, Kevin. To me, he was a nerdy, Bobby Goldsboro look alike with big glasses, a round goofy face, an annoying voice and mannerisms, a total suck up but he dressed really stylishly. In a word, he was a dork. In a few more words, he was a pre-disco era disco dork. Brenda had two female minions working for her full time and all three of them absolutely couldn't get enough of Kevin. He got all the really "good" jobs, I'm not even sure what they were but he was always hanging around in the office with Brenda and the gals. This guy could do no wrong even though I thought he was a total dirtbag ass kisser. The other two guys were Rob and Allen. Allen was a motorhead type of guy and spent most of his time working with the maintenance staff keeping the lab infrastructure and the three JILA vehicles serviced and running. I never really saw much of him. Rob and I pretty much had the same job and each worked half of the week with only a little bit of overlap when things got extra busy. Over the semester, we became good friends and started hanging out together a lot outside of work. He introduced me to the joys of riding a bicycle as an adult, similar to my friend Dean who was my biking buddy in my hometown in New Jersey when we first learned to ride tricycles together.

Dean and I were the same age and since we had the same first name and lived a few blocks from each other, we were inseparable from the time we were three. He had a long driveway that went right past their living room. I have vivid memories of riding our tricycles up and down that driveway for hours, from the street, past the house and to their garage. His mom had a rule that we had to stay in the driveway. One day, we were riding circles up and down the driveway and I noticed flames shooting out of their living room window. I remember asking Dean if he knew that his house was on fire. He casually responded that it was a new picture that his mom had purchased. I accepted this answer as legitimate even though I knew in my heart that it wasn't a picture. My fears were confirmed when a bunch of fire engines pulled up to his house.

Years later, in junior high school, Dean and I each got our own stingray bicycles. These were the bikes with a long banana seat and a sissy bar in the back so that you could lean against it when you were doing wheelies, big upward curling handle bars, and a slick tire in the back to maximize your skidding prowess. We would ride all around our town and beyond, sometimes to towns ten or fifteen miles away. In an absolute stroke of genius, he dubbed us the "Double Dean Wheelie Club" and said that our club motto was going to be "We pop wheelies and boners".

Rob loved to ride west out of Boulder for miles and miles up long, steep hills. Before I met him, I was physically active but I never really did anything that would be considered regular exercise. In college, my main activities were wham winging, hiking, camping or rock climbing. Rob had recently purchased a new ten speed bicycle and kept trying to get me to go riding with him. Not having a bike was certainly a limiting factor. However, one evening, he showed me a bike that a friend of his was looking to sell. We rode around his neighborhood briefly together and I was absolutely hooked from that first minute of riding. I bought the bike for $50 and it changed my life.

Rob became my personal trainer. We started riding together after work, first for thirty minutes, then forty five, then an hour, until my leg muscles slowly developed. He then set a goal of riding the ten miles from his house up to the top of NCAR. When I could do this without having to get off and rest, we would do this twice. The next goal was to ride the really steep hill from Boulder up to the top of Flagstaff Mountain, the small mountain just beyond the long gradual hill up to Chautauqua Park on the outskirts of Boulder. The road was a series of nine or ten tight switchbacks. We first rode until I could make it to the base, then part way up and then, after a handful of attempts, all the way without stopping. It was exhilarating and the descents were an unbelievable rush.

There's a little former mining town way up in the Rockies, right at the base of Guanella Pass, called Georgetown. Its elevation is around 8,600 feet above sea level. The town is super quaint, with lots of very well maintained and restored little Victorian houses, a few shops and a couple of bars. Rob had a couple of friends who lived there. This weekend, our plan was to ride our bikes from Boulder up to Georgetown on Saturday, spend the night, and then ride back to Boulder on Sunday. We had set this goal for ourselves when it was apparent to Rob that I was enjoying the challenge of riding. He had done it a time or two already so he knew what was involved and all the best, most scenic roads to take. The distance was around sixty five miles and the total elevation gain was around 3,200 feet from Boulder but probably a lot more due to the various undulations of all the roads.

With these weekend plans in mind, I knew that Friday night in Boulder should probably be a restful one. Eric and I were driving down from the quarry and were discussing our weekend plans and how good a few cold beers were going to taste after a long day of work.

"So, Mungo, this job at the quarry is turning out to be pretty cool, don't you think?" I asked.

"For sure, man. It sure beats cleaning dorm rooms like I did for a few weeks after the semester ended. However, that job did have a few perks."

"It did? Like what?"

"Well, for one thing, the stuff that was left behind. Even though most of it was trash, every so often we would find something good like a joint under someone's mattress or a bottle of wine or some dirty magazines. One of the best things I ever found was a ten dollar bill that someone had left behind stuffed into the cushions of a chair I was cleaning out."

"Cool! Hey, do you remember who's cooking tonight?"

"Nobody is, remember? Iggy's away of course, Jackie's probably locked in her room with a voodoo doll, Wayne is visiting his parents, Crystal and Hazel left this morning for a rugby tournament, Peter is working at the alumni geology weekend thing and so it looks like it might just be you and Kate. Maybe the two of you could get reacquainted?"

"I think I'd rather get reacquainted with Windy. The way things ended last night, I'd love to just pick up where we left off. She suggested that tonight was a possibility but you know her," I lamented.

"True, you never know. Remember the time when Peter talked her into going out to dinner with him. He got all spiffed up, made reservations and then she never showed up?"

"Yeah, that's kind of what I'm afraid of."

We stopped at our favorite liquor store and then drove the back streets to the Zoo. The place was unusually quiet. I assumed that everyone had already taken off for the weekend. Eric showered first, packed up some stuff for the weekend and then bolted for Tina's house, roaring away in his 1970 powder blue Pontiac Firebird. This car always surprised me. It seemed so out of character and I know that it embarrassed him a little but it had been a high school graduation gift from his parents.

After I showered and changed into some clean clothes, I went out to the porch to enjoy the solitude. I couldn't think of the last time that I had some time like this to myself. My mind began to think ahead to the possibilities of the evening with Windy, the bike trip, dinner, spending time with Rob, the upcoming Fourth of July festivities, the roving pack of dogs that just invaded the porch and began rough housing and knocking over chairs, tables, my beer and then me. "Hey, where the hell did these crazy mutts come from?" I must have said aloud.

"Hey Dean! Sorry! They aren't very well trained yet," said a voice coming from the driveway beside the house, recognizable as Windy even before I could see her. "My friend Fred asked me to look after his dogs this weekend and they aren't very disciplined."

"Yeah, I can see that! They just seemed to appear out of nowhere."

"I was just playing with them in the alley, trying to tire them out so that maybe you and I could go get some dinner together tonight. Are you interested?"

"Absolutely! I was hoping for that exact thing!"

These four dogs were a veritable canine tornado. They were so riled up that it was almost impossible to differentiate one from the other. They were running around, biting each other, knocking into everything, growling, jumping on top of each other—it was doggie mayhem.

"I'll try to get each of them on a leash and maybe then we can take them for a walk and hope that eventually they'll calm down," she said as she threw me two leashes while climbing the steps to the porch. "Try to grab one of these rascals and get a leash on him. The two light colored ones are Mandrake and Sunshine and the two darker ones are Max, he's the darkest one, and Yoffie, the girl dog."

"I'll see if I can get my hand in there without coming out with just a stump," I said somewhat tentatively.

When I tried to grab one of their collars, the entire herd turned on me and started biting my arms. It didn't seem like it was out of anger as they weren't biting hard enough to break my skin, more out of reflex and something new to gnaw on. Clearly this wasn't going to work so I let out with the loudest, highest pitched scream that I could manage. This got their attention immediately and they froze in place giving me the chance to attach two leashes while Windy nabbed the other two and snapped their leashes on.

"Good job there Beans!"

"Beans? You've never called me Beans before."

"Yeah, it seems weird. I hear other people call you that so I thought maybe that's what you liked to be called."

"Not really, it's just a dopey nickname that some of the guys at the Zoo call me. You can call me that if you want but I'd rather you call me Honey!" I said with what I hoped was enough humor that Windy would think it was funny.

"Hmm, that sounds delicious, Honey," Windy said in a sexy purring voice as she rubbed her body up against mine in a slinky, cat woman sort of way, or at least the closest approximation possible as we were holding onto two dogs each and were trying to control them now that they had recovered from their momentary stunning. "How about we go for a walk out in the cemetery? Maybe we can let them run themselves into oblivion and then we can snuggle ourselves into oblivion?"

"Sounds perfect! Would you like me to bring a few cold beers to drink once we're there?"

"Definitely!"

I handed her my dogs, went into the kitchen and threw a few beers into a backpack along with a blanket that I grabbed from my bedroom and then made a quick stop at the bathroom. It only took a few minutes but when I got back out to the porch, Windy was gone with the dogs. The only signs they had been there were several pieces of furniture that were still upside down and others that were out of position. I looked around the yard, I looked over towards Windy's house and I looked up and down the street but didn't see her. I walked over to her house, knocked on her door but there wasn't an answer.

I decided to start walking down the street towards the cemetery four or five blocks away, thinking maybe she decided to get a head start. Coming toward me was a middle aged couple and I asked them if they had seen a young woman walking four dogs. They said they hadn't so I assumed Windy hadn't gone this way even though it was the only logical way to walk to the cemetery from the Zoo. I knew that Windy wasn't always the most logical person to begin with so I continued walking until I got to the cemetery. I didn't see her or the dogs, gave up, kicked myself for getting so easily hooked by her charms and being willing to drop everything to spend time with her.

When I got back to the Zoo, feeling duped and dejected, I saw Kate sitting on the porch by herself. She had straightened all the furniture and restored order.

"Hi Kate, sorry about the mess. I was just coming back to clean things up."

"What happened here? The porch looked like there had been a fight. I was worried that maybe Iggy and Jackie had gotten into another argument."

I explained about the dogs, Windy, the cemetery and her confusing disappearance.

"Oh, that explains it. When I got home a few minutes ago, Windy was here and she asked if I had seen you."

"What did you tell her?" I asked full of renewed hope.

"Not much, I didn't know where you were. I thought maybe you were still at work but she told me that she had already seen you."

"Did she say where she was going?"

"Yes, she told me to tell you to meet her at the cemetery by the mausoleum in half an hour and she would explain everything. That was about five minutes ago."

"Crazy, that woman is certainly unpredictable. I was over her house last night, having a romantic evening when this Hells Angel biker dude barges in expecting to have sex with her and then she says that he and I both had to leave. It turns out he was a boyfriend of hers and they had moved out here from Ohio together."

"You want my advice, Dean? Avoid her like the plague. She's beautiful, sexy, a talented musician but she's trouble, do you know what I mean?"

"You're probably right but the pull is so strong. How can any guy resist that?"

"You'd be much better off staying here with me tonight. Remember that time last January when you and I were the first ones back from Christmas break and we spent the night together up in my bed and kept each other company? That was pretty nice, wasn't it?"

"Yes, it was," I admitted, remembering that evening. "But how would your boyfriend feel about that?"

"He'd probably get all bent out of shape," she admitted.

"I'm sure he would. You're a fantastic friend and I appreciate the offer but my heart just isn't into it the way it should be. I don't want to shortchange you. Say, would you like to drink a beer with me?"

"You're reading my mind."

I opened up my backpack and pulled out two beers and gave her one. We sat in silence for a while, watching our little corner of the universe go by. On Pleasant Street in late June when most of the students were gone, it wasn't exactly a beehive of activity.

"Have you seen Jackie today?" I asked.

"Yes, she was in a very grouchy mood. She was slamming things around in the kitchen and her bedroom but she wouldn't talk to me or anyone else for that matter. She just kept talking to herself muttering things like 'what a bunch of jerks' and 'if he ever tries to do that again' and a whole bunch of other things that I couldn't make out."

"I sort of feel sorry for her. There seems to be a lot of anger and sadness in her life, like maybe there was some critical piece of her childhood missing. Do you know much about her?"

"Not really, we've hung out together a few times since she moved in here but she never really talks much about herself. Mostly she's just critical of other people and likes to talk about their faults. Iggy probably knows her best at this point."

"And it seems like he's had enough of that relationship. Did you know that he decided to go away for the weekend?"

"Yeah, he's got some old high school friends that are getting together to play some music. I think one of them has a cabin up near Ouray."

"I guess I should probably go now to the cemetery and see if Windy actually shows up," I said after we finished drinking our beers.

I went into the kitchen to restock the beers in my backpack and came back out to the porch to say goodbye to Kate. Retracing my steps down to the cemetery, I saw Windy sitting near the mausoleum. I was actually quite surprised to see her there minus the dogs.

"Hi Dean," Windy said as she saw me approaching. "I hope that you're not angry that I left so unexpectedly."

"Not angry," I said taking the blanket out of my backpack and spreading it on the ground, "just a bit confused. I couldn't have been gone for more than five minutes and when I got back outside, you were nowhere to be seen. It was almost as if you vanished into thin air. I looked at your house; I walked down to the cemetery but couldn't find you. What happened?"

"Why don't you sit down here next to me?" Windy said as she positioned herself comfortably on the blanket. "Did you bring the beers?"

I reached into my pack and gave her one. We toasted each other and took a sip.

"Right after you went inside, my friend Tony drove by. He's one of Fred's best friends and asked if he could take the dogs with him until tomorrow. Knowing that you and I were hoping to spend some time together, I thought it would be a good idea to let him have them. He really loves Fred's dogs. Anyway, he asked if I would drive back to his house to help keep the dogs under control so it would be safe for him to drive. You saw how wild they can be. He lives near Pearl Street so we went down there, dropped the dogs off and then he brought me back home. I saw Kate but I didn't see you so I left her a message. Apparently, you got it."

"Yes, that explains it, although it would have been nice if you had let me know before you drove off. I'm glad that the dogs are gone, to be honest, so maybe we can go out for dinner together, my treat!"

"That would be cool!" Maybe we could go to the Hotel Boulderado, or is that a bit too pricey?"

"Well, I was thinking more along the lines of Señor Miguels. However, I promise that I'll take you to the Boulderado when I get my first paycheck. Big Larry didn't pay us today. Is that too disappointing?"

"No, not at all. I love Señor Miguels too," Windy said and it seemed genuine. The meals there were about a quarter of the price of the meals at the Hotel Boulderado. The Hotel was quite fancy while Miguels was low rent funky but with fantastic food.

Windy had taken a few sips of her beer and lay down with her body sort of wrapped around me from behind as I sat on the blanket. She asked about my day at the quarry and I told her about the wall we were building and the budding romance between Laverne and Junior.

"Oh, that is so sweet. I had a brief relationship last year with this really old guy, someone I met when I had a temp job cleaning houses to make a few extra bucks. He was so nice to me and ended up giving me a lot more money than he should have."

"Did you do more than just clean his house?"

"Well, yeah. He was kind of lonely, his wife was away a lot and he started making some crazy suggestions. I sort of felt sorry for him so I agreed to have sex with him a few times."

"Sounds a bit like prostitution."

"Not really," Windy said, "he wasn't really giving me money for sex. It was more like he was giving me money to spend time with him. He always seemed very appreciative."

"I can't blame him, a hot young babe like you and an old geezer who probably only gets to have sex with his wife a couple of times a month, if that. What a deal for him!"

"Anyway, it started getting pretty weird. He was really wealthy so he kept coming up with bigger piles of cash for me to do some kinky things. He didn't always want to have sex with me, sometimes he wanted to watch me do some things and sometimes he wanted me to watch him. It finally started creeping me out too much so I stopped going over. But, I have to say, the money was good!"

"Well, I don't think this is going to be the dynamic between Junior and Laverne," I said laughing, changing the subject as the thought of Windy having sex with an old guy for money wasn't working for me.

"Probably not but enough of this talk, when are you going to lay down here and start kissing me?" Windy asked. "I can only be patient so long!"

I immediately complied with her wishes and we eventually decided that it would be nice to go back to one of our houses and get comfortable in a more private place. We gathered up our belongings and slowly walked down our street hand in hand. I was feeling extremely happy to be spending time with Windy and I sensed that she felt the same way and it kind of surprised me. As we approached our block, we saw an ambulance and police car with their lights flashing. When we got closer, it was apparent they were parked in front of the Zoo. We saw a police officer going into my house. Only Kate and Jackie were home, as far as I knew.

"What do you think is happening?" Windy asked as we approached.

"Your guess is as good as mine. Let's check it out."

We entered the house and heard a lot of screaming coming from upstairs. The police woman we had seen previously entering the house stopped us in the hallway.

"Do either of you live here?" she asked.

"I do," I answered. "Can you tell me what's going on?"

"What is your name, sir?"

"Dean Morrison."

"What can you tell me about your housemate Jackie?"

"Well, it's kind of a long story but I know she's a bit on the psychotic side at the moment. She's very upset with all of us, especially her former boyfriend."

"What about?"

"Well, it would take a while to explain it all but let's just say that she disapproves of some of the things that go on around here."

"What sort of things?"

"Oh, recently she thought she walked in on someone making out with someone in the kitchen and another time it was someone getting a massage," I said.

"That doesn't sound too awful. Are you telling me the entire story?"

"Well, she thought the person was making out with two of his female housemates at the same time . . ."

"And?"

"And the person that was getting the massage was on the dining room table . . ."

"And?"

"And all of our other housemates were sitting at the table giving the massage . . ."

"And?"

"And they were all naked . . ."

"And?"

"Oh, and they were all blindfolded."

"And?"

"That's pretty much it."

"That could set someone off. Can you tell us where we might find her former boyfriend and give us a way to contact her family?"

"Her boyfriend's name is Ignace Jambon and he's on his was up to Ouray for the weekend. I could probably dig out some information on her parents. I'm in charge of dealing with the phone bill each month and I could look up the calls from past bills she made to them. They live in Greeley but they're currently doing missionary work in Africa." There was more screaming coming from upstairs and I heard Kate's voice try to calm her down some. I'm pretty sure I heard Jackie yell that she was the Queen of the Zoo and that she couldn't leave her throne without her court jesters. "Okay, that's weird. Can you tell me what's going on up there?"

"We got a call from your housemate Kate about fifteen minutes ago reporting that Jackie had become emotionally unstable. She requested assistance. By the way, my name is Officer Binswanger," she said pointing to her badge and nameplate.

"Thank you Occifier Banswinger," I said inadvertently as my tongue became a little tied with all of the excitement.

"That's Binswanger and its *Officer* Binswanger."

"My apologies, I wasn't trying to be disrespectful. You know how it is when you deliberately mess a word up for so long thinking that it's funny so when you actually have to use the correct word, you forget what it is? To this day, I forget which is the right word, genitinalia or genitalia."

"Can we get back to the situation at hand please, Mr. Morrison?"

"Certainly. By the way, this is my neighbor Windy," I said introducing Windy when I realized that she was just standing there without being a part of the conversation. I also realized that I didn't know her last name or if she even had one. "Windy, by the way, what's your last name?"

"Breeze," she answered.

"Hello Ms. Breeze. Mr. Morrison, how long have you known Ms . . ." Officer Binswanger said looking down at a notepad that she was holding in one hand and then at me, "Jackson?"

"Not a long time. She moved in at the beginning of the spring semester. She's the newest housemate and I have to say that she has seemed somewhat troubled off and on. She's very moody."

"Do you know if she is on any sort of medication?"

"That I couldn't tell you."

"Would you and Ms. Breeze wait down here? I would like to go upstairs and talk to Ms. Jackson and Ms . . . ah, let's see here, oh, . . . Ms. McDouglas. Please stick around Mr. Morrison as I'll need to talk to you in a little while. There's already an EMT up there."

Officer Binswanger began walking up the stairs so Windy and I went off to my room. My room was directly underneath Jackie's so it was a good place for privacy and a great place to hear a lot of what was going on upstairs. We heard Officer Binswanger's boot steps across the upstairs hallway and then knock on Jackie's bedroom door.

"Windy, this doesn't look too good for Jackie. If you don't want to hang around here, I'll understand. I'm not sure how long this little drama is going to last."

"Well, I was hoping to head downtown later tonight after dinner and play some music on the streets but we haven't even had a chance to eat yet. If you let me take your car, I could run out and get us some food."

"I'm not all that hungry at the moment, are you?"

"No, not really. Why don't we just hang out here for a while? If it drags on too long, I'll go get us some dinner. How does that sound?"

"That sounds good," I said feeling a bit relieved.

In the meantime, we lay down on my bed and tried to pick up where we left off in the cemetery. However, with the noise filtering down to us from upstairs and through the open windows, the mood was definitely not right for romance.

"Jackie, just sit down so the officer can talk to you," we heard Kate say calmly, like she was talking to a child.

"Tell her to bow down at my feet and kiss my ring before I will acknowledge her," Jackie said in a voice that was only barely recognizable.

"Ms. Jackson, I'd like to ask you a few questions," Officer Binswanger said.

"Not until you pay your respects to the Queen," Jackie yelled loudly.

"Ms. Jackson, can you tell me what you are the Queen of?"

DAVID W. GOODWIN

"Slave girl," she said "tell the intruder who I am."

"Officer Binswanger, Jackie thinks that she is the Queen of the Zoo. She believes we are all her subjects and that her job is to issue proclamations for all of us to follow," we heard Kate say.

"I don't *think* I'm the Queen, I *am* the Queen, slave girl. Go fetch me a cool drink at once."

"Ms. Jackson, can you tell me where you are?"

"I am on my throne inside my castle."

"And do you know who I am?"

"You are the intruder and I will have my guards remove you at once. Guards!" she cried out.

"I'm going to have the EMT take your vital signs so we can make an initial assessment of your status. Once we have this information, we will determine what the best course of action is for you this evening, Ms. Jackson," Officer Binswanger said.

"I will not permit such behavior," Jackie yelled. "Guards, remove them immediately!"

"Ms. Jackson, there are no guards, there are no slave girls, you are not a queen and I am not an intruder. I am Officer Binswanger from the Boulder Police Department, this is Kate McDouglas, your housemate and this is Dirk Feinbottom, an Emergency Medical Technician who is going to take your pulse, your temperature and check for a variety of other vital signs. If you choose not to cooperate, we will have to sedate you and take you to the hospital for observation. If you do cooperate, however, it will be a lot easier for all of us. Do you understand?"

"Off with their heads," Jackie screamed.

Apparently that was enough for Officer Binswanger because all we heard after this was a little scuffling, a few muffled grunts and then quiet. After a short while, we heard loud footsteps coming down the stairs. I went out into the hallway to investigate. There I saw Jackie strapped to a gurney as she was being wheeled out to the waiting ambulance by Dirk Feinbottom and Officer Binswanger. Kate walked down the stairs behind them.

"Kate, geez Louise," I said, "This is a huge bummer! I wonder if I should try to contact Iggy."

"I'm not sure that would accomplish anything. I would suggest that we just let this go for the evening," Kate suggested. "What do you think, Windy?"

"I think you're right. They must have sedated her to get her off her throne, right?" Windy asked.

"Yes," responded Officer Binswanger as they maneuvered the gurney down the front stairs. "Mr. Feinbottom administered 5 milligrams of haloperidol so she's gonna be out of it for a while. She's quite delusional and rather schizophrenic, in my unprofessional opinion. If you could try to contact any family members to let them know that she's at the Boulder General Hospital that would probably be best. Also, let this Ignace person know where she is because he'll probably want to check on her when he returns."

With that, Binswanger and Feinbottom took off with Jackie into the now dark Friday evening. Kate, Windy and I were left to sort things out for ourselves. I was feeling quite saddened by the way the evening had turned out, especially for Jackie but also a little for myself.

"Well, I can't say that I didn't see that one coming," Kate said. "She was like a time bomb waiting to explode."

"But on the other hand, maybe she truly is the Queen of the Zoo. Did she issue any proclamations?" I asked.

"Well, you and Windy weren't here for the start of it all. She came down to the porch right after you left and told me that from now on, there would be no nudity in the dining room. I told her that seemed a bit harsh. Then she told me that nobody could touch anyone else in the house. I asked if that applied to her and Iggy and she said yes, especially her and Iggy. Finally, she said that from now on, everyone was to address her as 'Queen Jackie, Ruler of the Kingdom of the Zoo'. I said that perhaps a better title would be 'Crazy Jackie, Biggest AHole in the Universe'. That pretty much sent her over the edge so I guess it's my fault."

"I don't think that's true, Kate. She was already over the edge in my opinion," I said.

"Maybe, but I wonder if there's anything we could have done differently."

"The bottom line is that nobody else was bothered by things around here."

"I think any normal person walking in on your naked group massage would have wanted to join in, not go nuts about it," Windy said.

"Regardless, it's way past time for dinner and I'm suddenly starving. Windy and I were about to head out to Señor Miguels for dinner before we walked in on this scene. If it's alright with Windy, would you care to join us Kate?"

"I don't want to intrude on your date," Kate said.

"No, it would be great if you came," Windy said. "I think we could all use a little down time and just relax for a while. Plus, Dean needs to get up pretty early tomorrow for his bike trip so we'll probably make it an early night."

"Great, let's go," I said.

We hopped into the Cruisemobile and drove over to Señor Miguels. Most of the usual Friday night crowd had already come and gone so the place was relatively quiet. They closed at ten so we were just barely able to get a table before it was too late. We had a great meal; a pitcher of margarita's and then made our way back to the empty Zoo.

"I think that I'll head over to Elmo's house again tonight. We have some catching up to do since I didn't see him yesterday. You two have a good evening. Dean, I'll see you when you get back from your trip. Bye Windy, thanks for letting me go out to dinner with you guys."

"Adios muchacha," I said.

Windy and I stumbled into my bedroom and I asked, "Are you still planning on going downtown to play music?"

"It's getting a bit too late for that and I'm a bit too full from dinner anyway. What I really want to do is just lie down on the bed with you and read for a little while until I digest my meal. Would it be alright if I spent the night?"

After a pause of approximately half a nanosecond, I said yes.

"Oh goodie! Let me go home and pick up a few things and then I'll be right back, I promise."

After Windy left, I used the time to prepare for my bike trip as best I could while daydreaming about the night ahead of me. My plan was to ride over to Rob's house so we could start our journey by nine, before the day got too warm and hopefully make it into the mountains by midday when the altitude difference would keep the temperatures at a more comfortable level. We needed to bring a change of clothes, some food, a few bike tools and spare inner tubes so I needed to get that stuff together. I also used the time to make sure that my bike was ready to go. Half an hour must have passed and I began to get a bit worried that Windy wasn't coming back. Just when I was about to go over to look for her, the phone rang.

"Hi Dean, you'll never guess who I found waiting for me at my house."

"Well, I hope that it's not your friend Wally. Is it?"

"No, fortunately, it's not Wally. It's my brother Turk! What a surprise, I haven't seen him for almost a year. He's just passing through town from Ohio for the night and is leaving for the west coast tomorrow. This is amazing! Would you like to come over to meet him and spend some time with us?"

"Thanks but it sounds like you two have a lot of catching up to do and I should get a good night's sleep."

"I'm sorry, honey. You sound a little disappointed. I'll make it up to you, I promise. It's just that I hardly ever get to see him."

"That's fine, I understand, really," I said, trying my best to sound like I understood, really, but knew that I must have sounded like I had just found out that my pet hamster was a serial killer.

"Hey, I really was looking forward to spending the night with you," Windy whispered into the phone. "Maybe I'll come over in the middle of the night after Turk goes to sleep. He drove straight through so he's pretty wasted. If I don't see you tonight, I'll see you when you get back, alright?"

"Sure, I'll be looking forward to it. Bye, Windy."

CHAPTER 9

S ATURDAY MORNING CAME and I woke up alone. Even though I was disappointed not to have Windy's company, it was a mix of excitement and fear that I felt about the bike trip that lay ahead of me. The morning was crystal clear, a bit breezy and a perfect sixty degrees when I got out of bed to get ready. The frustration that I experienced with Windy's untimely disappearances might serve me well in the huge task of riding my bike further and higher than I had ever done before. If I could channel that frustration into the bike, I could probably get up to Georgetown and back to Boulder before lunch.

Rob had advised me to make sure that I ate a really good breakfast. Even though I was a scrawny hundred and forty pounder, I could consume large quantities of food. Since I didn't need to get to Rob's house until nine, I had a good hour to tank up. I put some inspirational music on the stereo and was in the process of making a big bowl of oatmeal when Kate stumbled into the kitchen.

"Yikes," I exclaimed a bit startled since I thought I was the only person home, "sorry about the music. I just assumed that you were at Elmo's."

"Well, that was the plan but we had a little disagreement last night and I ended up coming home earlier than expected. Is Windy here?"

"No, her brother from Ohio came through town unexpectedly last night so I was abandoned."

Kate was a short woman with long perfectly straight red hair and satiny smooth skin. In addition, she was voluptuous, had beautiful, large blue eyes and also happened to be padding around the house in just her bra and panties.

"Good thing that Jackie isn't around to see you like this," I remarked, "because you're almost violating her first proclamation last night."

"Yeah and since she's not here, I can be as naked as I want in any room of the house. So take that Jackie!" Kate said as she whipped off her bra and threw it directly at my head. "And for that matter, take that too," she continued as she pulled off her panties and tried to fling them at my head, missing wildly and we both watched as they got stuck on a picture frame. "What do you think of that, Dean?"

"I say bravo, you sexy thing!"

"Come on, get naked with me! How often will we get the chance to run around the house, just the two of us without Jackie here?" Throwing caution to the wind and never one to pass up a reasonable dare, I stripped down as well.

"See if you can catch me, you scrawny love struck wimp!" Kate challenged as she took off through the house and bounced up the stairs to the second floor. She ran right into the bathroom which wasn't the room I was expecting her to head for. She turned on the water and we jumped into the tight shower stall together.

How was a guy not supposed to get ideas when there was a sexy, soft, soapy, slippery, squirming woman slithering all around him? We began to kiss and one thing led to another and then another and apparently we were both rather pent up from our respective evenings of disappointment. Pretty soon our kissing and fondling and groping got pretty serious and our sort-of-innocent shower quickly led to an impromptu stand up explosion of lusty passion that I dare say surprised both of us. Luckily there were several sturdy railings around the shower stall for us to steady ourselves on, in addition to each other. We held each other close for a long while afterwards while our breathing slowed down and the water gently rinsed off our suds and the heat our bodies were generating. We continued kissing for a while longer, looking into each other's eyes and then started laughing almost hysterically at what had just transpired. Eventually, we tumbled out of the shower stall and dried each other off.

"Wow, that was incredible Kate. I can't say that was even on my top ten fantasy sex list but it certainly should have been!"

"Yes, that was pretty amazing. What other things are on your list?"

"I'd have to give that some thought but right now my brain has been disengaged."

"Maybe when you get back you should tell me what they are and we can work on going through them together."

"Only if you tell me what's on your list too," I said.

"Deal! I keep a running top ten list in my head at all times."

"And have you crossed some of them off?"

"Absolutely! I have to keep revising it because once I've done it, I need a new one to take its place."

"That's awesome! You are one-of-a-kind Kate. I hate to shower and run but I really need to get going in order to be at Rob's house by nine."

"All right, Dean. I hope this was a proper sendoff!"

"The best, thanks Kate, I think that's just what I needed."

"Yeah, me too! Elmo was being a total jerk last night. When it was time to go to bed, he told me that he had work to do and that maybe we could see each other sometime next week."

Kate said goodbye and, I presume, went back to bed while I quickly tried to refocus on making my final trip preparations. After a hazy period of recovery and trying to remember what I needed for the trip, I rode over to Rob's house. He lived in one of the nicer neighborhoods in the older part of Boulder. There were lots of really attractive bungalow style houses made of brick with fabulous front porches. The streets were wide and lined with big old silver maple trees and inhabited mostly by University faculty types. Rob lived there with an older friend of his who had owned the house for a few years. When I pulled into his driveway, I saw Rob out by the garage doing some last minute maintenance on his bike. There was a small pile of rags, a bike pump, tools, and some small bottles containing various lubricants in a semi circle around his bike.

"Hey Dean, right on time. How are you feeling today?" Rob asked looking up as I rolled up to him on my bike.

"Excellent. I'm ready to begin our adventure!"

"Great, let's take a look at your bike before we leave so we can make sure everything is in good shape."

Since buying my bike, I had learned a lot about maintenance, even going so far as buying all the various tools that I needed to do a complete overhaul to give me the best ride possible. I may not have been the strongest rider in Boulder, but I might have had the cleanest and shiniest used bike.

"Looks good," Rob said giving it a quick going over. "You might want to put a little more air in your tires but not too much. Here, why don't you check the pressure with this gauge?"

I followed Rob's suggestion while he made a few final adjustments to his bike. "Do you need to use the bathroom before we head out or fill up your water bottles?"

"Good ideas, I completely forgot about the bottles. I had a rather crazy morning and I had the feeling that I was forgetting something," I said, heading into his house to tend to these details.

"Just be quiet because Zeke is still asleep," Rob said in a loud whisper.

Once we made our final preparations, we saddled up and made tracks out of Boulder by riding directly south towards the town of Golden. This is a route that skirts the Front Range and is a series of gentle and not so gentle rolling hills through rangeland with the high plains stretching out to the east and the mountains to the west. Twenty-two miles separates these towns and it was a nice way to start our long journey. The sun was to our left so the lighting was perfect. However, what wasn't perfect was the strong wind out of the southwest. Normally, this segment of the ride would take about an hour and a quarter but today it would take us a bit longer.

In Golden, we had a brief rest at one of the parks in town, drank some water and had a quick snack. Rob described the route from Golden to Idaho Springs and warned me that it was going to be rather hilly so we should ride at a comfortable pace. He also reminded me to make sure that I was in a low enough gear to spin my pedals at a fairly high cadence in order to try to keep my legs fresh and strong all day long.

"I've ridden that stretch from Boulder to Golden many times and it's almost always windy, although today the winds seemed like they were directly in our faces the entire way," Rob said. "That was a lot of work. I hope we have better luck when we get to Idaho Springs and start riding west."

The ride up to Idaho Springs followed Clear Creek and was a long uphill winding road that climbed through the small scenic canyon that the creek created over tens of thousands of years. The road was in great shape and didn't have a lot of traffic on it. Most drivers choose to stay on the bigger highways and interstates to make better time. By the time we arrived at Idaho Springs, it was around one in the afternoon and we rode for a while until we found a place to eat the lunches we had with us.

"This is pretty tough riding," I said as we settled into a grassy spot along the road beside a large stream. "The wind is really sapping my energy."

"You're doing a good job. I'm pretty tired too. The wind isn't usually this strong consistently. I think that as we get higher into the hills most of the stronger winds will be blocked by the mountains. Hey, I've been meaning to talk to you about something that recently happened at JILA. Do you mind talking about a work-related issue? I've got something that I want to ask you."

"No, not at all. What's up?"

"Well, I know that you were pretty upset when you weren't asked to continue working there this summer, right?"

"Well yeah, sure. I got along well with most everyone and I felt that I did a good job and had a good attitude. However, when Brenda told me she didn't want me to work there when the semester ended, I was really upset."

"Did she give you a reason?"

"Just that there were reduced demands on the staff during the summer so they could just employ you and the moron Kevin."

"Right, so I've been working there part time since May with Kevin, as you know. They told me some time ago that the reason they decided to get rid of you was because you were eating donuts and not paying for them. Is that true?"

"Not at all! I don't even like donuts. Why would they think that?" I asked.

"I think it was Kevin spreading rumors to increase his stature with the ladies there. He also had a thing for donuts and it probably embarrassed him to admit that he was eating four or five donuts a day so he would only mark down one or two. Almost every time I would see him, he had powdered sugar around his ugly mouth and stuck to his nasty beard."

"That's an interesting theory."

"Well, yesterday when I got to work, Brenda called me into her office and asked me if I was paying for all the donuts I was eating. I told her of course I was. She then said that there was a discrepancy of anywhere from ten to twenty donuts a week that weren't being paid for and that this couldn't continue. She said that I must have been lying."

"Did you tell her that it was probably Kevin that wasn't paying for the donuts?"

"Yes and she told me that it wasn't Kevin because he told her that it wasn't him. She believed his word over mine and she fired me!"

"What a couple of assholes! I think the two of them must have a little thing going on the side. I'm sorry to hear that you lost the job, Rob. I'll bet Mr. Dork is in trouble now without anyone to blame his donut habit on," I said feeling suddenly bitter about why I lost my job. "It's worked out pretty well for me though. Did I tell you that I got a new job this week?"

"No, doing what?"

"Working landscaping up at the Sugarloaf Quarry. Maybe you could get a job there too."

"Holy shit, you're working there?" That's the place run by this scrawny little guy with comb over hair and his foxy assistant, right?"

"Yeah, Big Larry and Rhonda. How do you know about them?"

"My housemate Zeke worked there a few summers ago. I would never see him during the week; he would just come home on weekends. It was kind of nice having the house to myself though. He left the job once the summer was over. He never talked about it much but there was something about that place that seemed really strange."

"Did he ever tell you why he stayed up at the quarry during the week? It's only about ten miles from your house," I asked.

"Yeah, I asked him that question a few times. It seemed kind of weird to me. While he was working there, he never really gave me much of an answer. He was always vague about it, once he said that it was just more convenient, another time he said that he liked the people there, once he said there were lots of perks like free food and a place to stay, you know, things that just didn't really add up in my mind. I mean, why wouldn't you want to come home every night, especially Zeke, because he has a really nice place? Are you living up there?"

"No, but I've only been working there since Wednesday. Everyone keeps trying to get me and my two housemates to stay over."

"Well, eventually, when Zeke left, it was like his old personality returned and he was willing to talk a bit more openly about his experience. He talked about some sort of nightclub the guy Big Larry and his sidekick ran. Do you know about that?"

"Absolutely, it seems like one of the main reasons people work there is just so they can spend a few hours at this dump of a supply building they call a nightclub. The whole thing is bizarre to me."

"Now that you mention it, after Zeke was back in school, he talked about this really swanky nightclub that was only open to employees. He told me that it was worth it to work there just to go to this nightclub."

"Swanky? Do you know why he left the job?"

"Donuts, I think," Rob said with a laugh. "No, seriously, it was just a summer job and he knew it was over at the end of August. One other thing that you should probably know about the place is that I don't think Zeke ever got paid all the money that he should have for working there. He said that Big Larry almost always shortchanged him."

"Yeah, I've heard a little about that sort of behavior already."

"The strange thing was that he never really seemed to care about it that much. He told me that it was such a blast to work there that it really didn't matter that much to him. I can't imagine that! Zeke is the sort of guy that watches every penny."

"Well, if you're interested, I could ask Big Larry if he needs any more help this summer."

"Thanks. I've got a few other possibilities for jobs to get me to the end of the summer. But if for some reason they don't work out, I may ask you to check into it for me," Rob said. "How do you feel about taking a little nap here? The last stretch up to Georgetown is the toughest. Even though it's only about fifteen miles from here on the interstate, the way we go makes it twenty. The last two miles are on the highway and even though it's illegal to ride there, I've never been stopped before but we need to ride as fast as we can and hope the cops don't give us a hard time. Two more hours of riding time if all goes well."

"A little snooze sounds like a good idea to me," I agreed.

We must have both fallen asleep because the lighting looked different when I woke up. Rob was sound asleep with his head on his backpack and his mouth wide open. My muscles felt a little tight from riding and the somewhat uncomfortable position that I must have slept in.

"Hey Rob," I said softly.

"What, where am I?" he said loudly, sitting up quickly, clearly not yet amongst the living.

"You're at JILA in a closet with Brenda and she wants you to smear her naked body with the cream from your donut."

"Right!" he said now fully awake. "Wow, how long were we asleep?"

"Good question."

"I told my friends to expect us late in the afternoon so we should probably get a move on."

We got up slowly and walked around a bit to loosen up before getting back on our bikes. I wasn't looking forward to more bike riding since my body was pretty sore, especially the part that touched the saddle, but once I started riding again things loosened up. The shoulder of this part of the road was wide so we were able to ride two abreast for a while and slowly get back into our rhythm. The highway paralleled the interstate at this point and then we turned onto the frontage road when the state highway and the interstate merged.

"In several miles, we're going to take a right turn and head away from the highway. It's a bit of a steep climb in the beginning but it gets us away from the noise and the sight of the highway. Besides, the frontage road comes to a dead end up there in a while. I found out the hard way the first time I did this ride and had to backtrack for about five miles to get back to the turnoff."

The wind was really blowing by now. Not only were we going up a hill but the wind was making it almost seem like we were climbing up Flagstaff Mountain. Pedaling was really hard and our progress had slowed considerably.

"Maybe it will be easier once we get away from the wind tunnel that the interstate creates," Rob said wishfully.

After what seemed like five miles of riding, we took the turn that Rob had mentioned. The next climb seemed more like a wall. I didn't have low enough gearing to ride up it while seated so I had to stand in order to slowly work my way up. When even this wasn't enough, I rode in large radius zigzags to reduce the steepness. Fortunately, there were hardly any cars that used this road so I was able to use both lanes to weave my way upward.

When the road finally became less steep, we could look out and see the interstate far below and the Continental Divide off to the west. It was a beautiful sight. I was exhausted by this effort and spun my pedals easily to catch my breath and recover a little. The road continued to climb for a while and then gradually flattened out. It was carved into the side of the mountain and continued to give us spectacular views along the way. Rob said that pretty soon the road would split—one direction went up over another pass while the other one went towards Georgetown. Most of the climbing was over and I was looking forward to some easy riding since I was near exhaustion.

We passed the turnoff point, stayed left and came around a blind corner to begin the last stretch of four or five miles before we met up with the interstate. As we rounded the bend, an even more intense blast of wind hit us squarely in our faces. I almost felt like it pushed us backwards. These weren't just gusts; these were sustained winds of thirty or forty miles per hour. Making headway against this almost felt like swimming against a riptide. Even though we got as low and aerodynamic on our bikes as possible, since we had backpacks on that stuck up into the air, we were not able to knife through the wind very well.

"Just think about the cold beer and the fabulous dinner that await us in Georgetown, Dean," Rob yelled above the roar of the wind.

"I'm trying but the wind keeps blowing the image out of my brain," I yelled back.

DAVID W. GOODWIN

With a huge amount of effort and cursing, we finally arrived at the junction with the interstate and were two miles from our destination. I wasn't sure I had enough energy left in my legs to make it.

"Hey Rob, does Georgetown have a taxi service?"

"You can make it. You've come this far. We'll be there in ten minutes!" Rob said encouraging me. "Just remember to ride fast!"

We rode up the on ramp to the highway and battled the fierce headwind and the crazy confusion of traffic whizzing past us at seventy miles per hour. Even though we kept as far to the right of the wide shoulder as possible, the speed and noise created by the passing cars and trucks was mind numbing. The green interstate sign said two miles to Georgetown, then a mile, then a half mile and then we rode the exit ramp into Georgetown; Elevation 8,489, Population 217. I was about as happy as if Windy's brother Turk hadn't showed up in Boulder last night.

The entire town was probably about eight blocks long and two or three blocks wide. I had seen it from the interstate before but never actually had been there. It was quaint beyond belief. Each house was perfect, like there was a townwide competition to see who could make their house look the most adorable. They were perfectly painted, each one had a beautifully manicured tiny front yard with a low white picket fence, flowers were everywhere, perfectly clean streets and sidewalks; the place was immaculate and I felt like I had accidentally stumbled into a fairytale. My body was screaming to get off my bike and go lie down somewhere and my brain felt like it had been caught in both the Mind Eraser and the Mind Scrambler.

"Wow, what an incredible place!" I exclaimed as I caught up to Rob who was waiting for me at the only intersection with a traffic light.

"Yeah, I love Georgetown. It's like Aspen might have been fifty years ago. I always feel like I've entered a doll house village or something."

"It is somewhat surreal. Where do your friends live?"

"Follow me, we're just about there."

We pulled up to one of the houses that must have been boycotting the cute house competition. It wasn't exactly a dive but it looked like a Boulder student rental that had been transposed to Georgetown. The house needed fresh paint, some of the windows were cracked, the front lawn was a patch of packed dirt and there were a few junky cars parked in the driveway.

Rob leaned his bike up against the porch railing so I did too. The front door was wide open and he went in yelling, "Hey Jimbo, Orville, its Rob. Anyone home?"

Music was coming from somewhere deep inside the house and Rob followed the sound. He continued to make our presence known by yelling out "hello" periodically. Since there still wasn't any response, he walked entirely through the house and out the back door. There we saw a group of four, two men and two women and they were sitting in lawn chairs drinking festive beverages out of tall glasses with a lot of colorful fruit slices.

"Hi everybody!" Rob said as the group turned to look at us.

"You guys finally made it. Welcome!" said a man who came over and gave Rob a big hug.

"Hi Jimbo, great to see you man!" Rob said. "This is my friend and new cycling partner Dean. That was one hell of a trip!"

"Come on over, have a seat, have some sangria and meet everyone. You guys must be wasted," Jimbo said.

The other guy, presumably Orville, brought two more chairs over and introductions were made. The women were introduced as Sarah and Candy. Candy poured us some sangria from a nearby table. "So, tell us about your trip," Sarah said as we took our seats in their circle.

"First, I should probably explain to Dean who you two ladies are. I wasn't sure if you'd be here or not so I only told him about knowing Jimbo and Orville in high school. Candy is the former Student Council president and hottest girl from Coolidge High School in Arvada. We all went to school together, except for Sarah, who is a friend of Candy's and now the rest of us. She's out from Yale this summer working as an intern at the Aspen Shakespeare Festival. Orville's been trying to get a date with her but she hasn't yet agreed to it. Have you finally caved in?" Rob asked as he looked directly at Sarah.

"Not yet, but if I drink many more glasses of this sangria, I just might let my defenses down," Sarah said with a wink.

"Let's have another one then!" Orville exclaimed.

"Sarah, I'm going to have to keep a pretty close eye on you tonight if you're thinking about finally giving in to Orville. The two of you together would be like oil and water or Janis Joplin singing with the Beatles, it just seems wrong," Candy said in kind of a mean way, I thought.

Candy was super cute and Sarah was drop dead gorgeous, very curvy with long straight light brown hair. She had flawless skin, high cheekbones and big beautiful eyes with a subtle touch of makeup. I rarely saw women like her in Boulder even among the sorority girls and Boulder had way more than its share of beautiful women. She was dressed in a very sexy short light summer dress that framed her legs perfectly. I was trying hard to take her in without all of my circuits overheating.

"This sangria is excellent," I said becoming vaguely aware that I was drinking way too quickly. The combination of thirst, fatigue, hunger and being in an unfamiliar social situation conspired to encourage me to drink without giving any serious thought to what I was actually drinking. "I have the feeling this is pretty potent stuff. What's in it?"

"Oh, the usual ingredients—wine, rum, citrus juice, fruit. This is a pretty tasty batch, I'll admit," Jimbo responded.

Rob told everyone about our trip and how the wind made it even more challenging. The conversation started moving away from me as the effects of the drink and our day were hitting me hard. My legs were starting to tighten up and I realized that I needed to get up and walk around a bit.

"I'm sorry to be antisocial but I really need to stretch my legs a bit as they're starting to feel like they're made out of wood," I said. "Maybe I'll take a quick stroll around town. Would that be cool with everyone?"

"Sure, just make sure that you come back soon as dinner will be ready in about half an hour," Orville said.

"Perfect, I'll be back before then."

I careened through the house using my hands for guidance because I felt very light headed and couldn't see very well in the relative darkness of the house. It was early evening, the wind had finally died down and the sun was already behind the mountains although the upper hills surrounding the town were fully illuminated. I stood in front trying to decide which direction I wanted to head when I heard a voice behind me.

"Do you mind if I walk with you? I need to go into town to pick up a few things."

I turned around and saw Sarah standing there. Given the events of the day, I felt like I was only partially present in the moment as my body and brain were feeling both buzzed and numb at the same time. Sarah's offer to walk into town with me put all of my corpuscles on high alert and a big goofy grin on my face.

"Sure, that would be great. Maybe you can show me around town. Do you know it pretty well?"

"You guys rode through it just a short while ago. That's about all there is to it. Georgetown is tiny; you could almost carry on a conversation with someone on the other side."

We walked down our street to the main road we had ridden in on. Sarah pointed out various town landmarks like the oldest house, the mayor's house, the town park with its feeble spitting fountain, the post office, the old saloon, all the highlights and all within a three block area. Sarah ducked into a little pharmacy saying that she'd just be a moment. I sat down on a bench and waited for her return thinking about what she might be buying inside. Tampons? Condoms? Mace? Make up? Pantyhose?

"I'm sorry that I'm probably not the best company at the moment," I said apologetically when she came out of the store.

"That's fine. I'll take that into account. I don't really know Jimbo, Orville and your friend Rob all that well. I've only hung out with them a time or two. It almost feels like I'm hanging out with friends in high school. I get the sense that Orville and Jimbo have never quite let go of that time. Rob seems like a really good person but I think he and Candy still have some unfinished business to attend to, if you know what I mean."

"I don't really know Rob all that well either. We worked together last year and we ride our bikes together a lot, but he doesn't really talk much about himself."

"Yeah, he seems like kind of a private person. I met Candy earlier in the summer when I first got out to Aspen. She was friends with someone from the cast and came out to one of our dress rehearsals. We all went out for dinner afterwards and she and I just hit it off. She's an intense person but really nice. I like her energy. Hey, perhaps we should head back to the house now. We don't want to miss dinner."

As we were rounding the corner to the street that Jimbo and Orville lived on, two people, a man and a woman, were walking towards us on the sidewalk. One of them looked very familiar to me. As they got closer, I recognized Joan from the Sugarloaf Quarry but I didn't recognize the man.

"Hey, it's OD!" Joan exclaimed giving me a friendly hug.

"Joan, what a surprise! What are you doing in Georgetown?"

"I should ask you the same thing," she replied.

I explained the bike trip and introduced Sarah. Joan introduced her friend Willie and explained that he lived in Georgetown and that she was visiting for the weekend. Since Sarah knew next to nothing about me, I gave her a brief synopsis of who Joan was and how I knew her.

"We really need to get back to dinner," I explained. "It was a great to run into you Joan. Nice to meet you Willie. I'll see you at work on Monday and maybe even at the nightclub next week."

As we shuffled back to the house, Sarah said that she was curious about the nightclub reference but I told her that it was kind of a long story and that I'd have to tell her about it later. "Just so you know, I haven't been to it yet. However, I'm curious to hear about your theatre job," I said as we walked through the front door of the house.

"I'll save that story for later as well," she replied.

The smell of dinner was so strong that it caused my hunger level to blast through the roof. We had eaten a fair amount of food along our journey but this was something altogether different. I followed Sarah into the dining room and saw what delicacies were waiting for us.

"You two are just in time," Jimbo said. "Please, have a seat. I hope you like chicken enchiladas!"

"This is their signature dish," Rob explained. "They definitely have perfected chicken enchiladas as you're about to find out."

We all sat down around the table and began serving ourselves. There were bowls filled with Spanish rice and salad, as well as smaller bowls with sour cream and plates with avocados and lime wedges. Another full pitcher of sangria was on the table. Dinner was outrageously fantastic, even after factoring in my deprived taste buds. I had to hold my appetite in check to avoid embarrassing myself by being a total glutton. By the end of the meal, I was starting to fade out so rapidly that I wasn't even sure that I was going to be able to hold my head up. Rob must have noticed because he pretended to be really tired too and inquired about the sleeping arrangements.

"Dean, you'll be sleeping on the couch on the back porch so feel free to head there anytime. I've put out a bunch of blankets that should be more than enough to keep you warm tonight."

"Thanks, I think everything finally caught up to me. I'd like to help with the dishes after this great meal before I pass out," I said.

"We'll do the dishes, don't worry about that. It looks like you wouldn't be able to stand in front of the sink long enough to clean more than a few spoons anyway," Candy said laughing.

"I think you might be right but I don't feel like I've been a very good guest."

"Well, we didn't ride our bikes all the way up here so you've got a special, one time pass," Sarah added. "Besides, when we come to visit, Jimbo and Orville cook and Candy and I clean up."

"Good night then everyone. Thanks for the great meal and company. You guys live in a really cool place. See you in the morning," I said getting up to go to bed. I probably was sound asleep on the couch within two minutes. My dreams started almost immediately and all of them involved pedaling. I must have ridden farther in my dreams that night than I did in real life.

CHAPTER 10

DAYLIGHT CAME QUICKLY and it seemed impossible to me that an entire night could have passed in such a short time span. When I got up to go to the bathroom, my muscles were barely functioning and my entire body ached. I felt like I was in a full body cast. Panic filled me when I remembered that I had to ride all the way back to Boulder today. At least it was mostly downhill.

I didn't hear the sounds of anyone else up yet and managed to drag myself into the kitchen to get a large glass of water without running into anyone. Gradually, on the way back to the porch, my body was starting to loosen up a bit and I could walk more like a scarecrow and less like a mummy. This was a bit more promising. Hopefully, by the time we were ready to ride back to Boulder, I would be able to bend my knees. My mouth was absolutely parched so I drank the glass of water before I even reached the porch so retraced my steps back to the kitchen for another one. Eventually I began feeling a bit more human as my cells starting absorbing the much needed liquid.

Returning to my couch on the porch, I was surprised to see Sarah sitting in the backyard reading the newspaper. I wasn't sure if I should go talk to her since I still wasn't moving very well and thought she would think that I was a total head case or a spaz or both. Against my better instincts, I walked slowly and awkwardly down the back stairs into the yard.

"Good morning. I thought I heard someone up," Sarah said as she motioned for me to sit down in the chair next to her. "I slept in the room right next to yours and I heard you talking in your sleep a lot during the night."

"Oh no, that's embarrassing," I said sitting down like I was a woman who was nine and a half months pregnant. "Could you hear what I was saying?"

"No, I don't think you were actually speaking in English. It sounded more like Russian." She then did some imitations that were so funny that we both started laughing really hard. That didn't feel too good since I ended up getting cramps in both sides, my neck, one calf and the little toe on my left foot.

"You're kidding, right? I really made those sounds?" I said when I was able to get my laughter under control and stretch out a few of the cramps. Sarah must have thought that I was stark raving mad. "Did you call the CIA?"

"I thought about it but I figured the chances of you being a Soviet spy were so slim that I was willing to take a risk. Besides, most spies can hold their liquor better than you do," Sarah said, thankfully choosing not to say anything about the weird positions I had to move my body into to stretch out the cramps.

"Have you known a lot of spies?" I managed to say.

"Only a few and they were kind of dopey. By the way, there was one word you said in the night that seemed different from the Russian mumbo jumbo."

"Uh oh, I almost hate to ask. What was it?"

"It sounded like Window or Wanda or something like that."

"Oh shit, was it Windy?"

"Yes, that's it! Was it because it was really windy on your ride yesterday?"

"Well, it was windy and I had bicycling dreams most of the night but I'll have to admit that I was probably talking about a woman that I know. Her name is Windy and she's a neighbor of mine in Boulder."

"Is that her real name and is she your girlfriend?"

"Those are both good questions. I'm not sure about either one. Why, did I say anything incriminating?" I asked worried about some of the things that I might have actually said.

"No, I was just curious. So, tell me how you're feeling today," Sarah asked, tactfully changing the subject.

"Pretty stiff. Every muscle in my body is sore. I'm not quite sure how Rob and I are going to ride back today. Well, let me rephrase that. I'm not sure how I'm going to ride back today. Rob probably isn't sore today. He's a much stronger rider than I am."

I tried unsuccessfully not to stare too obviously at the little tank top and boxers that she was wearing. The tank top was baby blue, it had dark blue satin ribbon around the scoop in the front with a little bow that was nestled perfectly between her breasts and since she wasn't wearing anything underneath, her nipples were protruding enough for me to see

DAVID W. GOODWIN

that she had delightful nipples that formed the apex of her two delicious fleshy mounds. The tank top ended way before her boxers began so that her tanned and fleshy tummy was exposed in the most appealing way. Her boxers were rolled down on the top a time or two that allowed her to wear them lower on her hips than a guy would. They were striped blue and white like a man's oxford shirt and the overall effect was stunning. I was completely captivated by her and would probably do anything she asked me to do at the moment, that is, if my achy body were capable of doing it.

I was sitting there lost in a fantasy about Sarah. I imagined that she would be strong and tender, soft and warm and if her mouth got close enough to me, I might even have the chance to breathe in some of her sweet smelling girl breath. Then, as our faces came close to one another . . .

"Hello, anyone home in there?" Sarah said loudly, I think for the second time as the first time didn't entirely register.

"I'm sorry, did you say something?" I responded, coming abruptly out of my lovely thoughts.

"Yes, I asked if you might want me to give you a little neck and shoulder massage since you seem to be pretty tight this morning."

"You're serious? You would do that for me? That would be awesome. You must have been reading my mind."

"I do have special talents, that's true, but I think the homeless person in the town park could have read your mind on this one."

Sarah walked over to my chair and stood behind me. She started touching me gently, giving me a very light massage through my tee shirt. I tried to attempt some humor and mumbled some imaginary Russian words but she ssssshed me and said to relax. When she was done, I told her how great that felt and asked if I could return the favor.

"Maybe some other time. Perhaps our paths will cross again and then I'll take you up on it. You clearly needed some attention more than me."

"I'll look forward to it. Hey, would you like to go get some breakfast? That is if there's a place in town."

"That's a great idea, now that you seem to be loosened up a bit. I was about to go take a shower and I assume you're going to take one this morning as well, right?"

"You're reading my mind again," I responded thinking that maybe I was going to have another experience like the one I had with Kate yesterday.

"Let me go first and then we'll go get something to eat when you're done."

I took the newspaper and went back to sit on the porch while Sarah showered. After a while, she walked by the door to the porch with a towel barely wrapped around her body and another one on her head. She told me that I could find a fresh towel in the hall closet. After I showered and dressed in the only outfit that I brought, I quietly walked through the house to track her down. I found Sarah in the kitchen, very nicely dressed in another stylish outfit, this time it was black and white silk blouse, open at the neck and a short black skirt that had a lot of movement to it. She was also wearing a pair of high heels, long sparkly earrings, a turquoise necklace and a lot of silver bracelets on one wrist. She looked very sophisticated and it made me a little nervous but I was impressed that she took the time to look good. Was it for me or was this just her general sort of look?

"I'm afraid this is the only outfit I was able to pack so you're going to have to be seen in town with me twice wearing the same duds," I lamented.

"Don't worry about it, you look fine. Let's go before anyone else wakes up and wants to join us."

We snuck out the front door and walked three or four blocks before we came to the Great Guanella Granery or, as I learned later, the Three G's. It was a funky little breakfast place run by a husband/wife or boyfriend/girlfriend team that was a non-stop comedy show. They kept up a banter that was better than the best sitcom you've ever seen. He was the cook and she was the waitress but the dynamic between them was that they would hurl innuendo-laden insults at each other and the clientele constantly from across the small restaurant so that everyone in the place was both their target and their audience. There was a cooking area off to one side, a small counter with four stools and maybe six tables. When Sarah and I arrived, there was an empty table off in one of the corners.

"Hey Sarah, great to see you," the man yelled out. "You're looking super hot! If Betty and your boyfriend don't mind, I'd like to take you out back and show you how we make our bacon."

"Watch it there Ricky," the woman who must be Betty yelled out from across the room, "I doubt Sarah wants anything to do with your bacon. I know I don't!"

"Hi guys," Sarah said, "Ricky, Betty's right. No bacon for me today but I wouldn't mind some sausage!" This set off a loud round of laughter from all the customers and it was clear to me that Sarah knew how to take care of herself. "This is my new friend, Dean, he and Rob rode their bikes up from Boulder yesterday. I'm hoping to convince them to stick around Georgetown today for a while before they head back down."

"Well, this is your lucky day, Dean. First, coming into my restaurant, second, having the good sense to become friends with Sarah, the second hottest woman in Georgetown and third, being our millionth customer of the morning. That means that coffee is on the house!" Ricky said with a lot of enthusiasm and fanfare.

"Excellent, can I have tea instead? Should I ask who the hottest woman in Georgetown is?" I asked knowing I could easily get myself into hot water with all of the women inside the restaurant if I were to throw out any suggestions. However, one look at Sarah and there wasn't any doubt in my mind that he was absolutely wrong.

"You're lookin' at her, sailor," Betty said as she sashayed over to me and pulled one of the straps from her waitress uniform down off her shoulder. She then sat on my lap and began to gyrate her hips all around. The combination of my body soreness, the embarrassment and the erotic nature of this performance left me feeling conflicted on almost every level imaginable.

"Hey, leave the poor guy alone," Ricky yelled out. "Can't you see that he's had a rough night? Can you imagine how a man must feel after spending the night with Sarah? I do and I'm extremely jealous!"

"Not so fast there, big guy!" Sarah protested. "You're making some pretty wild assumptions!"

"Just going on history," Ricky said laughing.

"He's making this stuff up," Sarah whispered to me.

Betty brought us over our beverages and the world's smallest menu. It had one omelette, one pancake, one French toast and one crepe special listed.

"Trust me, hon, anything you order here will be the best breakfast you've ever had. I guarantee it. If you aren't completely satisfied when you leave, I'll make sure that I satisfy you myself," she promised to the chuckles of the customers who probably weren't hearing this line for the first time.

"Sounds like a win-win situation," I responded.

"So what will it be?"

"I'd like the omelette special with rye toast, a side of sausage and home fries," Sarah said.

"Me too, exactly the same thing."

"Yeah, and I want what he's gettin'," Ricky chimed in.

"Dream on Ricky honey," Betty yelled.

"Is this scene too much for you? It looks like you're enjoying yourself," Sarah said.

"You're nice for asking. This is great entertainment," I replied.

"Wait until you try the food. It's really a treat. I hope you aren't offended by all the comments about you and me. This really is a small town and most everyone knows each other and their business."

"No, that's cool. I'm flattered that people might think that I'm your boyfriend."

"You're sweet! I really do hope that you'll hang out here for a while today. There's a really cool swimming hole and hot spring that I'd love to show you."

"I'll have to check in with Rob to find out how soon he wants to go. My only time constraint is that I have to be at work tomorrow morning by 7:30. How about you?"

"It's not too often that I get a weekend off from the theatre but we're between shows right now. I just need to be back there by tomorrow afternoon. That's why I'm hoping to make the most of today."

"That sounds excellent! However, I'm sort of at Rob's mercy."

"I understand. Let's just take the day as it presents itself and see what happens," Sarah said, leaning over to pick up her napkin that had fluttered off her lap when one of our fellow diners opened up the front door to leave. From Ricky's vantage point, it looked like something else was going on.

"Hey Romeo," Ricky yelled out. "Do you want your breakfast to go? Looks like you might have other things on your mind!"

"Wouldn't you if you were dining with the second most delicious woman in Georgetown?" I asked.

Sarah stood up and I thought for a minute that she was offended and was going to leave the restaurant. Instead, she made a big show of coming over to me and giving me a big wet kiss on the mouth and made sure that Ricky got a good view of her performance.

"Yum!" I said like a moron.

"Yum, indeed. See, we could have a lot of fun together today, don't you think?" Sarah asked.

"There's no doubt in my mind."

DAVID W. GOODWIN

Betty came by with our breakfast dishes. We attacked our twin meals with a passion that might have been slightly misplaced, at least on my end. The food was extremely tasty and I loved watching Sarah's delicate table manners. She was unlike any woman I had known growing up or since I had been a college student.

"Tell me a little about yourself, that is, if you're willing. I'd love to hear your story," I said.

"Are you sure? It's not all that interesting."

"I doubt that but do you mind if I try to guess first?"

"Not at all. I'd be curious to hear your version."

"There are a few things that are absolute certainties. First, you are from royalty and second, you are a very sensual person," I began.

"Right so far," Sarah said with a smile.

"Then here are the details. You were born to the Duke and Duchess of Luxembourg, the oldest child in a family with two younger brothers, Franc and Henri. Due to a freak weather event at the annual jousting tournament, you were separated from your family and kidnapped by gypsies who held you for ransom. You were able to escape and took refuge with a wealthy childless couple who moved to America and raised you. They were theatre buffs and since you displayed a natural talent for acting, they encouraged you to become active in the theatre. Eventually you became a famous actress which brings us right up to the present day. The only unknown part of the story is why you haven't gone back to Luxembourg."

"Because, sadly, all of my family was killed in the freak weather event when one of the jousting poles got swept up in a huge wind vortex and skewered them all like a giant shish-kabob."

"Gross!"

"You're close but here's the real story. I grew up in Minnesota, got active in theatre at a very young age, graduated from high school and went to Yale on a full scholarship. I just finished my sophomore year and got this great opportunity to spend the summer interning at the Aspen Shakespeare Festival and here I am."

"That's cool! What plays are you doing this summer?"

"We just finished performing *Twelfth Night* and start rehearsals for *The Tempest* tomorrow night. You should come to one of our performances. These are big budget, high quality productions. I could get tickets for you and Windy perhaps."

"Let me tell you about Windy before you get the wrong idea. She's got so many boyfriends that you almost have to schedule time with her a month in advance. Just when you think your time has finally come, she gets blown off course by something and you won't see her again for weeks. It's very frustrating. I've known her for about a year and we recently started spending some time together but I'm trying to be realistic about what kind of relationship I might expect."

"Sounds like you need a girlfriend that's a bit more predictable."

"Predictable sounds good. How about you? You must have a whole closet full of men."

"Interesting choice of words. Most of the men that I know are definitely not in the closet anymore. I'm almost always surrounded by theatre guys and most of them are gay so it's rather slim pickings for a healthy heterosexual like me. To be honest, I don't get a chance to meet men like you too often so it's refreshing."

"Thanks, that's a compliment, right?"

"Yes it is."

Betty dropped off the bill after asking us if we wanted anything else. Sarah grabbed it off the table before I had a chance to respond.

"It's my treat!"

"Alright but the next one is on me. I think by the time I leave here today, I'm going to owe you a lot of favors. I guess we'll have to see each other again."

"I would like that but there is one condition. You can't be wearing that same outfit!"

We said our goodbyes to Ricky and Betty after Sarah paid the bill. Betty asked me if the meal was satisfying enough or if she needed to spring into action.

"Not necessary but thanks for the offer, Betty."

We walked out into the bright morning sunshine and made our way back to the house. By the time we arrived, it was probably around ten and everyone else in the house was up and eating breakfast in the kitchen.

"Where have you two been?" Rob asked.

"We were both up early so we went over to the Three G's," Sarah said.

"That place is outrageous," I said.

"Yeah, it's almost worth the trip up here," Rob added.

"We thought we might see all of you over there," Sarah said.

"We thought about it but nobody really felt like getting dressed. Clearly, that thought didn't occur to you, Sarah," Candy said. "You're always willing to get dressed up. By the way, you're a knockout, as usual."

"Thanks Candy, and you're looking quite fetching in your nightie," she responded. "Rob, do you have an idea when you and Dean need to head back to Boulder?"

"My guess is that it will take us about five hours of riding so we should probably leave by noon. I'm in no great hurry to leave, how about you, Dean?" Rob asked.

"As long as we're back by dark, I'm fine."

"Well, let's plan for one and if we get going by two, that still leaves us enough time. How does that sound?"

"That's great. I'll try to get my body ready to go by then."

Sarah and I left the kitchen to give ourselves some time to digest our breakfast extravaganza. I also wanted to have some time alone with her to discuss the plans for the rest of the morning and followed her out to the porch. We went to sit down on the couch together and had an awkward moment trying to decide just exactly how close we should be.

"You realize that we don't have a lot of time together today and it's going to be difficult for us to get together much this summer. I get the feeling that we could have some fun hanging out but since you've already got a girlfriend, maybe this discussion isn't even necessary," Sarah said a bit matter-of-factly.

"What you say is all true and there's a chance that things could work out between me and Windy but it's highly unlikely. If there was a way for you and me to see each other and spend some time together, I would really like that. How long are you in Aspen for this summer?'

"Until mid August. We've got two more shows to do so I'll be around for about a month and a half. I then head back to spend a week with my family in Minnesota and then back to New Haven for the start of the fall semester."

"I would love to see you again. I know this is going to sound really crazy, but I have this feeling that there's something special between us."

"You're right, that's crazy talk. Why don't you shut up and kiss me?"

Not one to question a directive like that, we started kissing and it was like I had become supercharged with electrical pulses from the hair follicles on my head down to the cuticles on my toes and everywhere in between. I was having an out-of-body experience and was being transported to another dimension. Kissing Sarah was right up there with eating lobster.

"Maybe this would be a good time to head out to the swimming hole that you mentioned," I whispered. "I'm not sure if Jimbo and Orville would appreciate us doing this in their house. Sorry, it just seems a little anti-social."

"So if we were to leave, it would seem less anti-social?" Sarah teased.

"Good point but for some reason, I just started feeling uncomfortable even though that was one of the best kisses I've ever had in my life."

"You're right, that was a pretty nice kiss. Maybe we should make ourselves scarce. Let's go out for an adventure."

We walked through the house and saw that the kitchen was empty. As we passed through the front door, however, we saw Candy and the guys hanging out in the sunny front yard drinking coffee.

"Dean and I are thinking about going to the hot springs. Does anyone want to join us?" Sarah asked.

"That sounds like a great idea," Candy replied. "Let's all go!"

I was a bit disappointed but tried hard to keep a smile on my face. I realized that it was the right thing for Sarah to do, especially since we were guests here and they had been so generous. Orville jumped up out of his chair and said that he would go grab some towels.

"The place is swimsuit optional so we don't really need anything else," Jimbo said. "Besides, who's going to be there this early on a Sunday morning? I'll get some drinks to take with us."

The six of us jumped into Candy's truck. It was a big Chevy Blazer so we were able to squeeze inside. Rob told me that the swimming hole was only a ten minute drive up Guanella Pass Road and that there was a place on South Clear Creek where some hot springs drained into the main branch. It was a pretty popular spot with the locals because the water was icy cold in the creek since it was fed by glaciers and hot in the pools created from the springs. There were big flat rocks where the two met so it was an ideal spot for sunbathing, swimming and relaxing. There weren't any other cars at the parking lot when we arrived.

"This is great, we can stake a claim to the best rock!" Jimbo exclaimed as we got out of the truck and began walking up a pathway along the stream.

It was apparent which rock he was referring to since it was the biggest, the flattest and right at the confluence of the stream and the water from the hot springs runoff. The water in the stream was moving very fast around it but since there were lots of other rocks, it was easy to hop along out to the big one. Just upstream, there was a big deep pool about the size of someone's backyard above-the-ground pool. There were a series of steaming hot water pools off to the other side where the springs bubbled up from below the ground. The water was crystal clear and I could have never imagined that such a fantastic place existed as a kid growing up in New Jersey.

Jimbo gave everyone a towel and we unpacked and got comfortable. I've never been a prude but I certainly wasn't going to be the first one to get naked. Even though the sun had made its way over the edge of the surrounding mountains, the air temperature was still a bit on the cool side so it felt good to keep my clothes on.

"I'm going to check out the springs. Who wants to join me?" Orville said as he stripped down to his birthday suit.

"Give us a full report there Orville," Candy said. Turning to us as Orville jumped over the series of rocks to the hot springs she said, "It doesn't matter how many times I see someone naked, it still gives me a bit of a shock!"

"Yeah, well, especially Orville. He's so white! Doesn't he ever get outside?" Rob asked.

"He does, as you see, but he just never seems to tan," Jimbo said.

"That's got to be the whitest butt I've ever seen!" Rob said.

"Hey, it's a perfect temperature. Come on over," Orville yelled.

"Well, I guess we should join him," said Candy as she too stood up, took off her clothes and followed the route that Orville had just taken.

"And that's one of the sweetest butts I've ever seen," Rob said as Candy bounced away. "I'd better join them to make sure that Orville doesn't try any funny stuff!"

Jimbo was next which left Sarah and me together on the rocks.

"What do you say, want to join them?" I asked.

"I'm a little shy about these sorts of things. I've been naked on stage a time or two in my career but for some reason, getting naked in front of you seems like a big step. How do you feel about it?"

"You should definitely get naked," I said with mock seriousness.

"No, I meant how do you feel about getting naked in front of me?"

"In a heartbeat but there is something that I have to warn you about first."

"Do you have a microscopic penis?"

"Not at the moment."

"Is that what you want to warn me about?"

"Yes."

"Hmm, well I guess I should say that I'm flattered but are you sure that it's in my honor and not Candy's?"

"Hard to say exactly but if I were to come up with a guess, since I just saw Candy naked and she's not only very attractive but has a great body and I haven't yet seen you naked, I would put it at 20/80."

"Who's the 80?"

"You, so if you were to get naked, it, meaning the percent, would climb to 100 and it, meaning the other thing, would probably climb to 100 percent as well. It reminds me of a joke my friend Eric's mom told me once."

"Is it about Adam and Eve?"

"Yes, how'd you know? You've heard it apparently."

"Is the punch line, 'you'd better stand back, I don't know how big this thing is going to get'?"

"That's it! I'm just warning you."

"It must be hard to be a guy," Sarah said.

"You've got that right. Maybe I should go for a quick dip in the cold water."

Sarah stood up and whipped her clothes off. She stood in front of me in her full naked glory and looked even better than I had imagined. She had a dancer's body and clearly took good care of herself as every part was toned and well defined, especially her breasts. They actually defied any definition that I could have come up with except perfect.

"That's not going to help my dilemma at all! You're just tormenting me!"

"Hey, I can't help it. It would be anti-social of us not to get naked and join the others, don't you think?"

"Yeah except I've got to find a way to clear my mind. The more I try to think about something else, the harder it gets, so to speak."

"Come on, take off your clothes, you can immerse your vitals in the ice water. That will undoubtedly do the trick," Sarah said as she helped me to stand up. I realized there was no place to hide so just decided to deal with the embarrassment straight on. "Oh, I see what you mean! Good heavens!"

"Now you understand," I said with equal amounts of embarrassment and pride.

"Oh, poor boy, we should get you into the stream at once before you fall over on your face! However, if we were alone right now, I think that I could come up with a different solution."

"Stop, you're making it worse!"

"Or better."

I walked over to the edge of the swimming hole and climbed down into the cold water. I think that as my privates hit the water, I heard a sizzling sound and saw the release of steam. Sarah stood above me looking down from one of the rocks.

"That's a no-fail solution," I said as I emerged from the stream. "Quick, let's get over to the hot spring before he gets a change of heart. You'd better let me walk in front."

"Good idea. I like the view from back here anyway," Sarah said.

We arrived at the hot springs and got in with the rest of our new friends. The water felt great, especially on my achy muscles and I immediately felt relaxed.

"How does your body feel today?" Rob asked.

"Like I've been dragged along the train tracks for a few miles. How about you?"

"Only for a few hundred yards. My past experience is that once we start riding again in a little while, things will loosen up although sitting in these hot springs will help a lot too."

"You should have seen him earlier this morning. He was walking like he was a marionette," Sarah said.

"Good description, that's kind of how I felt," I said and then changed the subject asking Orville and Jimbo, "What do you guys do for work up here?"

"Mostly drive. I've got a job in Denver as a social worker so I spend a fair amount of time driving there and back each day," Jimbo said. "It's my first job since I graduated from Regis College a few months ago so I see it as a learning experience."

"And I work at Vail, just on the other side of the pass. We do a lot of trail maintenance and development in the summer and then I work driving a Snow Cat during the winter on the grooming crew," Orville explained. "I didn't go to college so I've been working there for a few years, working my way up the ladder. I can't see myself working there forever but for the time being, it's a good job."

The conversation continued until everyone felt the need to go cool off in the stream. There was some back and forth for a while, some sunbathing and then Rob announced that it was probably time for us to head back to the house and get on our bikes. This was the moment that I was dreading as hanging out on the rocks and the hot springs was perfect. We put our clothes back on and began walking downstream over the rocks and along the trail to the car. Sarah and I were bringing up the rear of the parade.

"I've really enjoyed meeting you Sarah," I began. "Maybe we could find a way to hang out some this summer. I think you're pretty cool."

"I would like that too. Why don't I give you a phone number where you can reach me when we get back to the house and we can see if there is any free time that might overlap. You've basically got weekends free and I have weekdays open with an occasional weekend so I'll warn you that it's not looking too good. We have matinees on Saturday and Sunday as well as performances on those nights and then at night during the week except for Monday and Tuesday. Like I told you earlier, we're on rehearsal schedule now and this will last for another week. We basically keep to a normal work schedule, Monday through Friday with next weekend off before we start back on the performance schedule."

"It sounds like you're quite busy! Do you have the Fourth of July off by any chance?"

"That's a week from today, right?"

"Yes, next Sunday. We're having a big party at my house in Boulder."

"Actually, I do. I would be free after rehearsals on Friday and then I don't need to be back until Tuesday because they're giving us the next Monday off."

"Maybe you could come down for the weekend. I'm not sure if I have to go to work on Monday or not but if you'd like, you could come down and stay for a little while. I know this is all a bit presumptuous but it would be a chance to spend some time together. I'd love for you to meet some of my friends and I know they'd like to meet you, especially my friends Eric and Iggy."

"Let me think about it and I'll give you a call. I've never been to Boulder before. Make sure that you give me your phone number too, okay?" Sarah instructed. "By the way, how does Windy fit into this whole plan?"

"That's a good question. I guess I'll have to figure that little detail out too. We can talk during the week to see if it can possibly work out. To tell you the truth, I don't think that it would really bother her at all if we went back to just being friends."

We arrived at the car and just as we were leaving, three cars filled with a large gaggle of rowdy high school boys pulled up. We had timed our visit perfectly. When we arrived at the house, Rob said that we should get our stuff together and get going. I pulled together the few items I had brought, filled my water bottles and put on the clothes that I had ridden up in. Sarah and I exchanged phone numbers, I thanked Jimbo and Orville for their hospitality, and said goodbye to them and Candy. I then gave Sarah a hug.

"It was great to meet you. I hope that I might see you next weekend," I said.

"That could be really great. Let's talk during the week."

Rob and I mounted our bicycles and began pedaling down the street to retrace the route that we had just ridden yesterday. Was that even possible? It seemed like it was days ago. The ride down the stretch of interstate went a lot quicker than going in the opposite direction. We managed to get to the off ramp in a matter of minutes even though we were again pedaling against a slight headwind but at least it was downhill. Rob was riding in the front and gave me hand signals to indicate which turns to take. I followed him but since the route was burned into my brain and legs from yesterday, I had a good sense of where we were going. My body was still pretty sore from the previous ride and my butt bones were very tender but my soul was soaring from spending time with Sarah so I wasn't feeling much pain.

We had been riding for about thirty minutes and were up at the point on the hillside road that had the fantastic view of the Continental Divide. Rob pulled over to take a whiz and take in the view. "Got to recycle some of this coffee. I must have had three or four cups this morning and it goes right through me," he said.

"I know exactly what you mean. I had a few cups of tea at the Three G's."

"I see that you and Sarah really seemed to hit it off. For some reason, I didn't think the two of you would have that much in common but apparently I was wrong."

"Yeah, it surprised me too but I think the fact that we are opposite genders helped some."

"You know what I mean. You're kind of a scruffy hippie college student and she's a sophisticated East Coast actress who wears make up and matching outfits. How many girlfriends have you had in the past that actually have nail polish on both their fingers and toes?"

"None. Speaking of toes, do you think that I stepped on any? Were Jimbo or Orville interested in her?"

"Of course! You knew about Orville and I think Jimbo might have had a few ideas as well."

"How about you?"

"I'm still trying to figure out things between Candy and myself but there's no denying that Sarah's a very attractive woman."

"So it probably wasn't cool that Sarah and I were spending time together. I didn't intend to upset our hosts. They're really great people and I'm very appreciative that they let us stay there and also to you for inviting me along. It's been an incredible adventure so far!"

"Well, I wouldn't worry about them too much. When something clicks between two people, it just can't be denied, I guess. Orville is used to it and Jimbo will get over it too," Rob said. "I hope for your sake that things work out. The summer is almost half over already and Sarah is only around until mid August, right?"

"Yep, that's what she told me."

"Let's get going, Dean," Rob said as he got back on his bike and started pedaling away.

The next stretch of road was one of the fastest descents imaginable. Luckily, there were hardly any cars on the road as we needed most of the lane to get through the curves at the speeds we were reaching. Around one of the blind bends, I was hugging the yellow line in the middle in case something was coming the other direction, as was Rob, and I saw him suddenly brake hard and veer across the road into the other lane. As I came up to the apex of the curve, I began braking as well since I assumed there must have been a good reason for his reaction. In the road ahead of us were two cars parked on the shoulder of our downhill lane and one of them was almost totally engulfed in flames. Rob and I had come to a complete stop by this time and leaned our bikes against the rocks on the other side of the road to figure out what was going on.

The non-flaming vehicle was a pickup truck and there were two men standing in the road near it. The flaming vehicle was teetering on the edge of the road and a steep drop off where there wasn't a guardrail. The flaming car looked like it was an abandoned vehicle. It only had three doors, one of its tires was missing from the wheel, it didn't have a windshield and it had weird symbols painted on the side. The guys motioned for us to stay away.

"You might just want to watch what happens here 'cause it's going to be really cool," one of the guys yelled at us, laughing like a maniac. He was dressed in greasy blue jeans and tee shirt that accentuated his bloodshot eyes and made him look like an escapee from an insane asylum.

"Yeah, we're about to push this car over the cliff and when it lands down below, it will probably explode!" the other guy yelled almost incoherently. He looked like the first one's twin only with a few more teeth. "Our friends are down on the frontage road and are watching so either help us push it over the cliff or get the fuck out of the way!"

These guys were so wasted that they could barely stand up. Even from a distance, they reeked of alcohol and gasoline. Both of them were smoking cigarettes. Everything made them laugh like lunatics. I couldn't figure out why they weren't engulfed in flames themselves.

Rob and I kept our distance and watched. By this time, the flames were everywhere and I was curious to see what these nut jobs had in mind to actually push the car over the cliff without severely burning themselves. One of them tried to get close enough to the car to push with his hands but eventually discovered that his hands were getting blistered from the heat. He started laughing hysterically at the fact that he had just scorched his hands as apparently the pain wasn't registering yet.

"Hey, assholes, come over here and help us push," the other one yelled at us.

"Yeah, or we'll blow your brains out," said the first one as he pulled a rifle out of the bed of the pickup truck. He accidentally fired the gun while trying to lift it out of the truck and the bullet ricocheted off the asphalt and nearly hit his buddy in the foot.

"You stupid jerk!" yelled the almost gun shot victim. "What the fuck did you do that for? You could have fuckin' killed me, you idiot!"

"Fuck, man, I'm sorry. I meant to shoot these idiots!"

These idiots were us and we wasted no time getting on our bikes and pedaling down the road as quickly as our trembling legs could take us. They were laughing loudly as we put some distance between us and then we heard the crack of gunfire, which made us duck low on our bikes and pedal even faster. After we had gone a few hundred yards, we heard a loud explosion. Both of us stopped and looked up the road to see that the Bobsy Twins got what they wanted, only without having to push the car over the cliff. Both cars were now in flames and the car that was destined for a flaming journey over the cliff was now upside down on the pavement with most of its various parts blown all over the roadway. I shuddered to think what happened to those crazies.

I heard the sound of sirens coming up the road towards us. Within thirty seconds, a police car came tearing up the road and we got as far over to the side as possible to let it pass. The car screeched to a halt beside us and the cop rolled down his window.

"Do you guys know anything about what just happened up here?" he barked.

"Yes," Rob answered.

"Good, don't go anywhere. I'll need to talk to you after I get up there to investigate."

With that, he patched out to get up to the burning vehicles, his siren wailing all the way. Coming up the road were a few more police cars, followed by an ambulance and two fire engines. Rob and I figured that we would slowly walk back up the road to make ourselves available for questioning. I was feeling a bit squeamish about what sort of grizzly scene we might find so I wasn't at all anxious to get there too quickly. Since we didn't want to get in the way of the emergency vehicles, we stayed on the other side of the road and kept our distance.

Up the road I could see all the emergency vehicles near the flaming and smoking mess. The police and EMTs got busy doing something while the firemen got their hoses out and began spraying the vehicles down. There were tall columns of thick black smoke emanating from both vehicles and now several white columns of steam from the water that was arcing in and intersecting from the fire engines that were parked on either side of the road.

"What do you think happened to our friends?" I asked Rob, worried what his answer might be.

"I think they're probably crispy critters by now."

"That's what I think. I can't imagine they could have survived that fireball."

We decided to park ourselves far enough away from the action so that we couldn't see the grim details of what was going on. We got comfortable along the side of the road and used the time to eat some of our food and drink some water. There was a lot of activity around the ambulances, a lot of opening and closing of doors but since they were parked mostly out of our sight, it was difficult to tell what was going on. After a few minutes, the EMTs jumped into their vehicles, turned on their flashing lights and sirens and came barreling past us.

"That doesn't look too good," I said.

"Crispy critters," Rob repeated.

The fires had been extinguished and a couple of flat bed trucks were called to the scene to take the wreckage away. At this point, the policeman who had instructed us to hang out got into his car and drove down to where we were and began the interview.

"Officer," Rob asked, "did those guys survive?"

"They're pretty badly burned. They're both still alive but just barely. Can you tell me what you witnessed?"

Rob described in detail what happened from his perspective and I added a few of my own observation.

"That information is very helpful," the officer said. "When we arrived on the scene, both of them were lying on the road and smoldering. It was difficult to ascertain what exactly had transpired."

"Not the brightest humans I've ever run across," Rob observed.

"No, I think that's a fair assessment. You boys can continue on your way in a moment but first I want to get your addresses and phone numbers in case we need to follow up with any questions. Could I see some form of identification?"

He wrote down the information and thanked us for our cooperation. We put our licenses away and continued with our ride back to Boulder. The rest of the trip was rather uneventful after this. The weather was good, warm and breezy but again, most of the time the wind was in our faces so it was another big effort to get home. After a few stops along the way for food and drinks and rest, we finally pulled into town as the sun was beginning to set. I arrived back at the Zoo just as the last of the daylight was disappearing.

Most of my housemates hadn't returned yet from their weekend activities, I wasn't sure where Jackie was and the only people I found any evidence of were Eric and Tina who were tucked away in his room. I went to my room to deal with my bike trip stuff and got ready to take a shower. On my bed was a note from Windy. It said, "Hi Dean, I decided to go with my brother to California for a few weeks. Very spur of the moment. Sorry!! I'll look forward to seeing you when I get back to Boulder. Windy". I was somewhat disappointed by this but considering that I just met the woman of my dreams, it simplified things considerably.

CHAPTER 11

MONDAY MORNING ARRIVED. It was late June. With about five minutes before my alarm was due to go off, I was awake and in a contemplative mood as I lay in bed thinking about my life and the various relationships that were developing. What if Windy decided that all of her other boyfriends were more appealing to her than me and that I was ninth on her top ten list or not even on her top ten list? What if Sarah was just looking for a little weekend fling or worse, a platonic weekend or even worse, not even looking for a weekend with me at all because she had a sudden moment of clarity and realized our relationship was nearly impossible? I barely knew her but I had the sense that a relationship with her could be delicious and satisfying but quite limited in terms of duration given her short stay in Colorado this summer. I must have slowly drifted back to sleep.

Out of bed, time to face the day and get ready to go to work at the quarry. Should I stay over and go to the nightclub? What was Eric going to do? Did I have any reason to want to come back to the Zoo tonight? Windy was gone for a few weeks and Sarah was back in Aspen for the week, so, hey, why not go to the nightclub? Time to track down Mungo and Jacque. Wait, that means that I'm Poindexter! Time to track down Mungo and Poindexter.

The house was quiet except for the noise that I was making inside my head. I went about my morning routine and heard the door to Eric's room open. "Hey Poindexter," I said, "You don't look too good. What happened?"

"I think its poison ivy. Tina and I were camping in this field near the craft show for two nights and I must have gotten exposed to something that has irritated the hell out of my neck, chest and back. Man, does it itch!"

"Did you put anything on it?"

"Yeah but now I need to shower and get her to put more stuff on me so that I can go to work today," Eric said unenthusiastically.

He shuffled off to the shower while I continued on with my breakfast. I heard footsteps and then saw Iggy entering the dining room. He didn't look all that good either. In fact, he looked like he was sleepwalking.

"Hey Poindexter," I said to the other Poindexter, "You going to work today?"

"Wouldn't miss it for the world!" Iggy said with some life in his voice and seeming to come out of the trance he was in. "Are you staying over tonight?"

"That's my plan," I said as I put my breakfast together. "You and Mungo should come too."

"That's my plan, too," he said as the phone rang. I wondered who would be calling the Zoo this early in the morning.

"Are you expecting any calls?" I asked Iggy.

"No, unless it's someone from Jackie's family to see if we can give them any more information about her status."

"Maybe you should answer it then. I don't know anything about her."

Iggy walked over and answered the phone. "It's for you, Beans."

I cleared my throat and had a brief moment of panic thinking about the potential bad news that might be on the other end of the phone. "Who is it?" I whispered to Iggy. "Does it sound like the cops?"

"I don't think so but she has an awfully sweet voice."

"Hello," I said tentatively.

"Hi Dean, its Sarah. How are you?"

"Hey, what a great surprise! I'm fine. What's up?"

"Two things. First, I just wanted to make sure that you got back home safely and it sounds like you did."

"Yes, it was a long day but we got home alright in spite of being shot at by two crazy drunk pyromaniacs who might actually be dead now."

"You're kidding, right?"

"Unfortunately, no. What's the second thing? I can't talk very long because I need to leave for work in a few minutes."

"That's why I'm calling you this early. I wanted to catch you before you left. I'll be quick. I wanted to tell you that a bunch of us from the cast are going to be in Denver today to do some radio promos for the play and thought we'd stick around and go to a cool bar where we hang out sometimes. I'm wondering if maybe you might want to meet me there?"

"That would be awesome! What time and where is the bar?"

"We'll probably be there around seven and the place is called the Oxford Hotel and it's on the corner of 17th and Wazee."

"Excellent! Hey, this is a great surprise. I'm so glad that you called. I've been thinking about you a lot since yesterday. I'll be there if at all possible and if I can find it on the map. But I have to warn you, I'm not old enough to get served so I might have to drink cokes."

"Me too but we've never had any problem at this place before and half of the cast is underage. I won't keep you any longer. I hope to see you there!"

"Bye and thanks for calling!" I said feeling happy as I wrote down the information.

"Who's Sarah?" Iggy asked while he was chewing on some toast.

"A budding Shakespearian actress from Yale that I met this weekend."

"It doesn't sound like you'll be staying at the quarry tonight. What's Windy going to think about all this?"

"She blew out to California on Saturday for a few weeks. She left me a note."

"Pretty good timing, I'd say."

Eric emerged from the bathroom with a towel wrapped tightly around his lower body. His rash looked pretty bad, especially since he had just gotten out of a hot shower and it looked more inflamed than it probably was under normal circumstances.

"You've got to hurry, Eric, we've got to leave in about fifteen minutes. Iggy is going to stay at the quarry tonight but I'm not. How about you?"

"No, Tina and I have dinner plans," he responded. "Maybe on Tuesday. Iggy, can I drive up with you and get a ride back down later with you Beans?"

"For sure, man," we answered in unison.

We all got ready to go, that is, everyone but Eric. I walked out to my car right around seven while Iggy was sitting semi-patiently in Gus waiting for Eric to come out of the house.

"See you up there, Iggy. I hope you guys aren't late," I yelled at Iggy from across the street.

"I'm leaving in a minute, with or without him," Iggy said. "I'm definitely not going to be late and get fired because of him."

My thoughts focused on the day ahead as I drove towards the canyon. I was really looking forward to seeing some of my coworkers. Most of them were very likeable people; a few were at the other end of that spectrum and the rest were just downright interesting. Working with Alfonso and Joan was great and even though the work was kind of strenuous, I was learning a lot about rocks and plants. Now, if I could just find a night to get to the nightclub, one of the big mysteries would be solved.

I arrived at the quarry and waited in the parking area hoping to see Iggy and Eric drive in but they were nowhere to be seen. Since nobody had spent the night at the quarry as far as I knew, everyone who had already arrived was busy lugging their bags over to the bunkhouse. Joan pulled up with Georgie a few minutes after I arrived.

"Hey OD, good to see you! Looks like you made it back from Georgetown in one piece! How was your weekend?" Joan asked me.

"Pretty excellent," I responded. "And yours?"

"Pretty excellent, too! I'll tell you about it later."

My buddies were still nowhere in sight, even after everyone else had dumped their bags off and began milling around outside the office building. Just as Sugarloaf Sam let out with his rodent yell, I saw Gus barreling down the driveway. Eric and Iggy leapt out of the bus and joined the queue just in the nick of time. As I walked through the door next to Iggy, he whispered, "I almost had to kill him."

The scene inside the office building was familiar by now. Big Larry and Rhonda were at the head of the table, the crew chiefs, Dickie, Zelda, Quesnal, Harry and Alfonso were across from them and everyone else found a seat or a wall to lean against. I was sitting in a chair on the farthest edge of the room mentally trying to remember everyone's names before the meeting began. Of course there was Joan, Junior and Georgie from the landscaping crew and some of the other ones were completely unforgettable such as Hector the Animal and Laverne, then there were the two Felixes (although I couldn't yet tell which one was which even though they didn't resemble each other at all), and the rest of the women; Barbara, Yolanda and JK. The other men were Buster, Frederick, and Juan Antonio who was so small that he might have made a good jockey. I made a note to myself to ask him about this at some point.

Big Larry no longer had the bandage wrapped around his head but there was a chunk of hair missing on the side above his ear where it had to be shaved in order for him to get some stitches. He stood up and kept glancing down at a stack of papers he had on a clip board.

"Good mornin', everyone. I hope y'all had a good weekend. How 'bout you Hambone?" Big Larry asked. I wasn't sure why he was singling out Iggy.

"Not the best one ever. My former girlfriend got sent to the psyche ward for observation on Friday night while I was away with some friends so I spent a fair amount of time when I got back to Boulder on Sunday trying to help with that situation," Iggy said sounding pretty somber.

"Sorry to hear that," Big Larry said "but look on the bright side, she's your former girlfriend, right?"

"And are the Three Musketeers going to be joinin' us at the nightclub this evenin'?"

"I will be but Beans here, I mean OD was all set to take the plunge tonight with me, so to speak, but he met some actress this weekend on a bike trip but she called him this morning and now she wants to meet him for drinks tonight in Denver so he's bailin'," Iggy explained. I'm thinking that he's going into way too much detail for this crowd.

"Oh, so that's who I saw you with in Georgetown, right OD?" Joan interjected.

"Yep, that was her," I admitted.

"Well ain't that the cat's pajamas! How about you, Whitey?" Big Larry asked.

"I hope to start spending time here soon," Eric explained, "but it won't be tonight. My girlfriend and I are celebrating our three month anniversary so we've got dinner reservations at the Greenbrier."

"Well, enough of the social hour. Let's get down to business," Big Larry said, changing his tone. "Some of you might have noticed that things are startin' to look a bit more spic and span around here. We've got the Fish and Wildlife Service comin' to do their inspection in about three weeks and I really want to see the quarry lookin' as good as possible. Alfonso and his landscapin' crew are sprucin' the place up nicely but we also need to make sure that our quarry is more appealing to the black rumped pygmy gnat than any other place on the landscape 'cause that's just how those honchos in the government think. Remember, this is partially why we hired the Three Musketeers, 'scuze me, I mean the White guy, ODD and Boney, that's why we hired them in the first place so's we could focus on this project. Now, I know that most of you are probably askin' yourselves, if I were a black rumped pygmy gnat, what would I be lookin' for in a potential restin' spot? Anyone got any ideas?"

Nobody was willing to jump into his trap but I knew if he didn't get some sort of response soon, he might fly into a rage. I decided to be the sacrificial gnat. "Well, funny you should ask, Big Larry. I've been doing some thinking about that very topic. I had some time to ponder that very question," I said, stalling for time to see what sort of ridiculous answer I could conjure up.

DAVID W. GOODWIN

"And what did you come up with there, OD?" Big Larry asked staring me down and opening his beady eyes as wide as they could possibly get.

"I was thinking about their trip from Downer's Grove to Waco and thought about how exhausted I might be if I were a pygmy gnat fighting those fierce headwinds over the plains, kind of like I did this weekend on my bike. My needs probably weren't that different from the bug's needs. If I was tired, weak, hungry and insanely horny and I looked down and saw some sweet granite cliffs, I might take a break in my two thousand mile journey and get a little R and R."

"And . . ." Big Larry said willing me to cut to the chase sooner rather than later.

"And I pictured a wall of fractured granite with hundreds of perching spots enjoying a southern exposure so that the sites would be sunny and warm but protected from the wind as well as from human and avian interference, a veritable gnat heaven. To further entice the swarms of gnats that are certain to be coming this way in the fall, I might even sprinkle a selection of freeze dried insects on each ledge for sustenance and as an added bonus, put out bottle caps filled with a little water on each ledge. That way, each ledge would be a black rumped pygmy gnat paradise, giving them the exact thing that each gnat is craving, except of course, their waiting par amours they will be reunited with in Waco. They spend a restful and blissful night at the Sugarloaf Quarry, similar to most of your employees I imagine, and then get flying on their way in the morning. They leave happy, the Fish and Wildlife Service leaves happy and you're happy because they're happy. What do you think?"

"Pretty good 'cept for one major hole in your argument. You said 'protected from avian interference' and what you describe would actually create a bird smorgasbord because if we set a perfect table for the gnats to rest, it would also be the ideal place for birds to come git some free eats," Big Larry said gleefully, exposing the weakness in my spur-of-the-moment concept.

"So how about if we construct a big fine mesh that covers the entire bug resting area and suspend it a few feet away from the rock? The gnats could get in and out easily but birds couldn't," Rhonda suggested.

"Excellent idea Rhonda!" Big Larry exclaimed. "This is what we're gonna to be workin' on ladies. I don't think their food source has to be freeze dried, just dead, and we need to confine their habitat to one end of the quarry so we can continue doin' business at the other end. Dickie, where do you think that most of your blastin' will take place in the next month?"

"Mostly up the Bobsled but I was thinking about heading to the far end of the quarry up the Fanny Packer since most of the orders coming in lately have been for curbstone. There are a few new housing developments that are starting up out beyond the greenbelt towards Longmont and they'll need a lot of curbing," Dickie explained.

"Sounds like this would work then. Here's what we do—we quarantine the Juiceway from any stone removal for the next month and prepare it accordin' to the new plan. I'm gonna call this the 'Black Ass Project' and I'll assemble a crackerjack crew that will work under the direction of Rhonda to create the perfect restin' habitat for those little black ass bugs. First, we'll scout out the best ledges to define the area where the bugs will perch, then we'll make sure each ledge has some sort of waterin' device, bottle caps or whatever, then we'll install the nettin' and finally, right before migration season starts, we'll use a series of ropes to get down to each ledge and fill up each cap with water and sprinkle dead bugs around so that each gnat will feel like they've just checked into the Ritz-Carlton."

"There's one small refinement we should make. Do you know anything about the dietary needs of gnats?" Eric asked.

"I just assumed they eat other insects," Big Larry stated. "Why, what do you know about it, Whitey?"

"I took an entomology course last year and I'm certain that they don't eat other insects and I'm also pretty certain they don't lap water out of a puddle. My understanding is they feed on molds and fungi," Eric said as I watched Big Larry's face get redder and redder by the moment.

"Listen, college kid, first of all, I don't know what the hell *empty-knowledgey* even means and second, if you're so smart, how the hell do we gather up molds and fungi for them to feed on?" Big Larry barked.

"Simple, all we need is some rotting wood. Each piece will contain all the molds and fungi that a gnat needs."

"Now that sounds easy enough. I hope you're right and not just shittin' me there Whitey. So here's the revised Black Ass Project plan—instead of catchin' other insects and puttin' out bottle caps for water, we simply gather up some rottin' logs from the woods and distribute them on each granite ledge. Whaddya think, Rhonda?"

"Sounds good to me," she answered. "Who do you think should be on this team?"

"Depends on who has some rock climbing experience," Big Larry said. "Any volunteers?"

Without hesitation, Iggy, Eric and I immediately raised our hands. Looking around the room, I saw that Juan Antonio, Joan, Barbara and JK raised their hands as well.

"There's our applicant pool," Big Larry said looking at Rhonda. "We only need three people so I'm gonna eliminate Joan right off the bat because we need her on the landscapin' crew."

"Darn," Joan said. "That sounds like a cool assignment."

"We'll definitely take Juan Antonio because he just looks like he could go up and down rock cliffs easily and since OD and Whitey seem to be full of good ideas, we'll take them too," Big Larry stated. "How do you feel about losin' them from your crew Alfonso?"

"Aye dios, mio!" Alfonso lamented. "You just took half my crew and Junior last week! I'll either need one of them back or you need to give me someone else to replace them, preferably two people. As you know, we have a lot of work ahead of us."

"You're right. I'll give you Whitey back and put Barbara on the crew. That would be Juan Antonio, OD and Barbara. Does that work for everyone?" Big Larry asked.

The rest of the crew chiefs nodded their heads, looking like bobble heads sitting at the table nodding in unison. Big Larry looked down at his clipboard another time, shuffled through some of his papers, looked out into the room and took a quick inventory of the personnel he had to work with. He made the assignments for the day and Eric and Iggy were back on the landscaping crew with Alfonso and Joan.

"Don't forget to get your lunches today. Bunny made some special sandwiches from what I hear. I'd like the Black Ass Project team to stay behind briefly so the rest of you should move on out. Get a lot of work done and see you back here around 4:50," Big Larry said, "and don't forget to bring your sense of humor to Comedy Night, especially you Hambone!"

Everyone else left the office building while the BAP crew remained with Big Larry and Rhonda. Juan Antonio was wearing the smallest Sugarloaf Quarry issued clothing ever made and they still were a bit too big for him. Barbara was wearing a sweatshirt over her outfit since the day was still on the cool side. She was probably somewhere in her mid to late thirties, maybe early forties, had thick black hair that was styled in a rather dated messy beehive hairdo and wore black cat eye glasses that she probably thought were extremely trendy. They had rhinestones embedded in the part that swooped upward. I think these may have been popular in the 50s but were more of an oddity in the 70s. She also wore an overabundance of bright red lipstick and my guess was that she probably spent a lot of time in a poodle skirt in her free time. She seemed like one of the least likely people to be on the BAP crew.

"Rhonda is going to be your new crew chief," Big Larry repeated once everyone was settled around the table. "I've got a lot of other things that need my 'tention today but I'll be checkin' in with her from time to time to see how things are goin'. Rhonda, how do you want to proceed with this?"

"I think the first thing we need to do is head up the Juiceway and do some reconnaissance work. Once we figure out which wall we want to designate for the gnat ledges, we'll need to take some measurements so I can calculate how big the netting and support structure needs to be. What kind of budget do we have to work with here?" Rhonda asked.

"Wha 'cha anticipate needin'?"

"We'll need four or five good climbing ropes, a bunch of carabineers, four climbing harnesses, a whole bunch of webbing for each intersection, two figure eight descender belay devices, and a lot of expansion bolts. The stuff we don't already have we can buy locally at Holubar. In addition to the netting, we'll need some sort of support structure to make sure that it sits a foot or two away from the rock ledges so that the gnats can get in and the birds are kept away."

"Let's try to keep it under a grand. After your crew scopes out the site and takes some measurements, maybe you should call around to some of the other local climbin' shops and price out the equipment," Big Larry suggested. "I think we've got a good plan here."

"Yeah, we may need to make a few minor adjustments. I assume all of you have some climbing experience," Rhonda said looking at the three of us, "I'm picturing this as a top rope situation. I think we can set up a bunch of great anchors at the top of the quarry since we've got good drilling equipment. We will simply rappel down from the top to the ledges and then climb back up. We should be able to reach each of the gnat ledges this way to place the rotten wood on each one. We'll also need to rappel down to drill holes for the bolts that will support the netting. None of these pitches are longer than the ropes so I think it will work out really well. Are all of you up for this?"

Everyone nodded and Big Larry gave his final approval. We grabbed our bag lunches and left the building. Biggie looked like a man with a mission as he walked over towards the supply building while the three of us on the BAP crew followed Rhonda over to her truck.

"Let's head up the Juiceway and start our reconnaissance work. We don't need any special tools or equipment just yet. I think I have everything we need in the truck," Rhonda said as we got into her pickup truck. Juan Antonio and I took the open truck bed and let Barbara take the passenger seat. Given my past experience driving with Rhonda and Big Larry up the Juiceway, I braced myself for ten minutes of torture.

"What sort of climbing experience do you have?" I asked Juan Antonio as Rhonda drove away at a reasonable speed.

"None," he answered with a laugh.

"So why did you say that you did?"

"Because Big Larry keeps putting me on the maintenance crew and I was looking for a change of pace. Since I'm so small, I always got stuck doing the jobs in tight places and I tend to get a little claustrophobic. I like the crew boss Harry and I don't mind working on the equipment but this job sounded pretty good so I lied about my experience. Don't tell anyone, okay?"

"That's cool, don't worry about me," I assured him.

"How hard could it be, really? What's your experience?"

"I've done some technical climbing. One of my friends during freshman year was a really good climber and he took me with him on various trips that year. He dropped out of college after that so I haven't done much climbing since then. It's a lot of fun but the climbing part can be pretty tough, depending on the route. However, if we're just rappelling down from above, you can learn all you need to know in a few minutes. It seems like Rhonda is quite experienced so I don't think you'll have anything to worry about. How do you feel about heights?"

"Scares the living shit out of me!"

"Oh, well, I'm not sure this is right for you then. The first step backwards on a rappel can be pretty scary, especially if we're starting from an overhang. From what I've seen of the quarry so far, however, the rock walls are really steep but not more than vertical so you should be alright if you don't look down."

Rhonda started heading up the Juiceway so conversation became impossible. At the first switchback, Rhonda pulled to a stop and we all got out of the truck.

"We're going to stop at each switchback and assess the rock conditions up slope. Since the road zigzags all the way up to the top of the quarry, we've got some breaks in the walls made by the road. Here's a clipboard with paper and a pen," Rhonda said handing it to Barbara. "I'd like you to take notes on our observations. Let's call this Wall One."

I looked over Barbara's shoulder as she wrote down "Wall One" at the top of the blank sheet of paper, underlined it and drew a flower with a smiley face on the "O" in "One". Rhonda took out a pair of binoculars from the space behind the driver's seat and scanned the rock face.

"Juan Antonio, I'd like you to go over to the left, OD to the right and start free climbing up the rock a little ways. Stay within ear shot because I'm going to call out some questions. You need to hear me and I need to hear you. Don't get up any higher than you want to fall since neither of you have any protection!"

The granite rock face made for good climbing as it was uniformly fractured from the extraction process both vertically and horizontally. Every ten feet or so another layer of granite had been removed so there were nice ledges that were about a foot deep. The challenge was to get up to each ledge in order to reach the next pitch. I was able to use a combination of natural fractures and the edges created by the drilling equipment to work my way up to the first ledge fairly easily. I could look down and easily see Rhonda and Barbara who were only thirty or forty feet away. Over on the other side, I saw Juan Antonio struggling to work his way to the first ledge as his reach was a lot shorter than mine. I was worried that he wasn't going to be able to do it but then he figured out how to use his strength to weight ratio to his advantage and pull himself up a crack to the ledge. Once he was standing up, Rhonda yelled up to us.

"How deep is the ledge that you are standing on?"

"About a foot," I replied.

"Same here," Juan Antonio answered.

"How's the condition?"

"Good and solid, some loose gravel," I reported.

"Same here."

"Okay, head up to the next ledge and then keep going. Barbara and I will drive the truck up to Switchback 2 and meet you there. Keep mental notes on the ledge condition so that you can give us a full report when you get up to the road," Rhonda called out.

The first pitch was fine since it was close to the road but from what I could tell, there were probably about four or five ledges between us and the next switchback. This made me a little nervous, especially since we weren't using any ropes. I could probably do it if I had to but I was thinking that maybe this wasn't a great idea and perhaps even less of a great idea for Juan Antonio. I waited for a moment to see if Juan Antonio was going to respond. I glanced over and I could tell that he was starting to panic a little.

"Rhonda, if we were top roping this, I would feel more than comfortable but I'm worried that one little slip could be nasty. Perhaps free climbing this wall isn't a good idea," I yelled down and could see that my partner agreed with me. "I'd like to climb down and discuss this."

"Okay OD, that's fine. Why don't the two of you come on down," Rhonda yelled back to us.

I slowly retraced my route downward which was a lot harder than going up. Juan Antonio was struggling as well since he couldn't rely upon his light weight and relative strength to descend.

"Trust your handholds and feel for a foothold with your toes," Rhonda yelled out when she saw him hesitate for a long time.

Juan Antonio made a few unsuccessful tentative attempts before he was finally able to support himself enough to get to the next secure spot down below. Eventually, he worked his way down and joined us at the truck.

"That was a little scary," he admitted when he walked up to us.

"Sorry," Rhonda apologized. "I wasn't quite sure how difficult it would be so I'm glad that both of you were honest with me about it. I think we'll just observe the wall conditions from each switchback with the binoculars until we get the ropes. We can assume that the conditions are pretty similar throughout since the rock is so uniform here and the way that it gets quarried is very predictable. We can tell from below how may pitches there are between each switchback so we should be able to use simple math to estimate the dimensions."

"I propose that we use Avogadro's number divided by the square of the hypotenuse of the rock face created by intersection of the road and magnetic north," I suggested.

"Good idea there, OD," Rhonda said in a seriously perturbed voice. "Did you by chance attend any of your high school math classes?"

"Everyone one of them, as well as two years of accelerated algebra, trig and calculus," I replied with theatrical indignity. "I just thought that we should view this as a three dimensional calculation rather than a simple two dimensional one that would introduce a certain amount of error."

"Hey, welcome to the real world, college kid. This ain't no brain surgery here. All we need to figure out is how much netting we need," Rhonda said, sounding suddenly exasperated with me.

She walked over to the apex of Switchback 1 and paced the distance to Switchback 2 as we stood around and watched. She came back and I could see that she was doing some calculations in her head.

"Barbara, here's what you should write down for Wall One: two hundred and fifty feet wide and six pitches high. That translates to about sixty feet. Also write down that the ledges are a foot or so deep and they appear to be in good condition." Once she felt that Barbara had recorded all the information she took big strides towards the truck and motioned for us all to follow.

This process continued at each of the four switchbacks and Barbara dutifully recorded the numbers that Rhonda dictated while Juan Antonio and I provided whatever additional information we could glean from walking along the base of each wall. The quarry wasn't one huge sheer wall of granite, more like a series of walls created from the extraction process separated by natural breaks in the topography, like huge granite steps if you were a really big giant with really tiny feet. The Juiceway, and the other two roads that snaked up to the top of the quarry took advantage of these breaks by following the original landscape.

By the time we arrived at the top of the Juiceway, it was time for our morning break. We sat on the edge of the highest granite wall and ate our snacks while enjoying an impressive view out over the valley with Boulder and the plains out to the east and the Continental Divide with the snow capped peaks behind us to the west. From this vantage point, we could see some really dark looking clouds heading our way quickly.

"Looks like we're in for a pretty nasty storm," Rhonda said. "I better get on the horn to warn everyone to take cover as we're probably the only ones who can see it coming."

She pulled her walkie-talkie off her belt holster and turned up the volume so we could hear the steady sound of static. "Attention all crews. This is Rhonda. I'm at the top of the quarry and can see a full tilt thunderstorm bearing down on us from the west. I advise everyone to take cover as soon as possible as I expect the storm will be on us within ten minutes. Repeat, take cover as soon as possible. 10-4."

DAVID W. GOODWIN

I sat in amazement and watched the sky starting to boil and churn its way towards us. Rhonda said we should all squeeze into the cab of her truck. In the meantime, I marveled at the approaching storm and watched the lightning strike way off in the distance. As it got closer and lightning flashed nearby, the thunder rumbled up and down the various canyons that surrounded Sugarloaf. The effect was incredible. I had experienced this phenomenon a few times in the past couple of years but it is one of those sensations that was always impressive. You could follow the thunder's trail from somewhere in one of the canyons and hear it moving down and up until it hit a place where the canyon split and then follow each roll of thunder as it split into two and then branch out into different canyons, losing its strength with each split until it disappeared completely. Multiply this effect, however, by twenty, each corresponding to a bolt of lightning hitting in a different area and it was like a timpani symphony of thunder rolls, all moving in different directions at different velocities and at different noise levels. The effect was quite melodious. The rain started and I joined the crew in the truck, squeezing into the passenger side next to Barbara.

The noise from the rain pelting the metal roof of the truck added to the brilliant flashes of lightning nearby and the subsequent thunder explosions made any conversation impossible, not to mention unnecessary. The windows immediately became steamed up as a bolt of lightning hit one of the surrounding peaks followed almost simultaneously by a loud crack of thunder. Barbara grabbed my thigh and buried her face in my lap as she let out a scream. It gave me quite a tingle.

The storm quickly passed over us and worked its way off to Boulder and out into the plains. The sky began to lighten up again as the rumbles of thunder got further away and more muffled, with a pleasing vibration that made my whole body happy to be alive and experience such things. The rain had stopped and we got out of the truck sauna.

"I think we've got all the information we need here," Rhonda said. "I'll take Juan Antonio and go do the shopping for the climbing gear. OD and Barbara, when we get back to the office, I want the two of you to take the green truck and head out into the National Forest to scrounge enough rotten wood to fill the back. Are either of you familiar enough with the area to know good places to look?"

Barbara looked at me to see who would speak first. Right as I opened my mouth she said, "I don't really know the area that well since I live out near Loveland, at least on the weekends." I realized that I hadn't actually heard Barbara speak words before and was a bit taken aback by her voice. It was really deep and husky, like she had been a jazz singer in a smoky nightclub her entire life. It was kind of sexy.

"I've hiked around these hills a lot and can think of many places where we might find some rotting wood and drive to easily," I offered. "I'd be happy to take the lead on this one."

We took the same seats in the truck on the way down so Juan Antonio and I had to be careful where we sat since the bed of the truck had a few inches of water in it. This quickly drained out as soon as Rhonda started driving after sloshing around a bit at our feet. She pulled up to the office, went inside to grab the keys and threw them to me when she re-emerged.

"Make sure it's topped up with gas before you leave and I would suggest that you not go too far away. Also, keep in mind the load limits because if you destroy the suspension, Big Larry will not be a happy man," Rhonda warned me. "Good luck and make sure that you're back here by five."

Barbara jumped into the passenger seat and looked like she was about to head off on a weekend trip with her husband and car full of kids. I was feeling a bit anxious about working with her for the rest of the day since I had never talked with her before and sensed we had absolutely nothing in common. My fear was that conversation would be extremely difficult.

"So, Dean," Barbara began as soon as I got into the driver's seat, "I'm glad that we have this chance to work together. I hope you don't mind that I buried my face in your lap but it was instinctual."

"No, that was fine. The thunder startled me a bit too."

"I've been hoping to get to know you and your two handsome friends a little better. I never had a chance to go to college as my husband and I got married right out of high school, it was within a month of graduation. I got pregnant with our oldest daughter on our wedding night and our youngest child was born less than a year later. I was a virgin up until that point in my life but I've always wondered what my life would be like if I had gone to college instead of becoming an instant wife and mom. How do you like college? Do you ever think that it was a bad decision to go?"

When Barbara finally paused long enough to take a breath and I tried to process the implications of everything she had just told me, I responded directly to her questions, "I love college and I never thought it was a bad decision to go. It wasn't an option in my family not to go to college so I never really gave other ideas any serious consideration." As I thought for a moment how that might sound to her, given what she had

DAVID W. GOODWIN

just said to me, I added, "It was the right decision for me but maybe not for everyone."

"I may have the opportunity to go to college some day when my daughters are older."

"How old are they?" I asked, knowing that it would give me a pretty good idea of Barbara's age which I suddenly thought I might have overestimated.

"Well, Janna, the oldest, is fifteen and Hanna is fourteen," she replied and then did the math for me, "which puts me at thirty four. How old did you think I was?"

"That's a little older than I would have guessed," I lied a little.

"You're so sweet for saying that. How old are you?"

"Twenty. By the way, how does it work for your family with you living up here at the quarry during the week? Does your husband take care of your daughters while you're away?"

"Well I certainly hope so! He understands the situation and I always go home on Wednesday and Friday nights after work so I'm only away three nights a week. He has a business that he runs out of our home so things work out pretty well. I miss my kids and Richie, my husband, most of the time but I have to admit, it's great to be out of the house some too. The girls are old enough at this point to take care of themselves," she explained as I pulled out of the quarry driveway and started driving towards Four Mile Canyon.

"I have to say that's an interesting arrangement. I'm glad it works for you."

"The hardest part is not having sex every night. Richie and I did it every night from our wedding night until I came up to the quarry to work about a year ago," Barbara explained proudly.

This kind of took me by surprise. "You've had sex every night for the last fifteen years? Holy crap! But wait, you have two daughters. How can that be possible?"

"No, you're right. We took about a week off after each one was born, well, that is, I took a week off. Richie still needed some special attention those nights too, if you catch my drift," Barbara said with an exaggerated wink. "And come to think of it, I guess I needed some special attention too. Maybe we didn't actually take those two weeks off, we just didn't have intercourse. Those were the two toughest weeks of my life."

"So given those circumstances, how can you handle being away from Richie even three nights a week?"

"I take matters into my own hands and he does too, at least that's what he tells me. Is it alright to be saying these things to you? Do you find my blunt talk too shocking?"

"No, I love talking about sex! I just didn't expect you to be so into it. I find it quite interesting, actually. I've never been in a long term relationship and I've often wondered what its like to be with the same person for a long time. Do you lose interest in them? Do they lose interest in you? Do you get tired of having sex with the same person all the time? You know, things like that."

"Well, tell me Dean. When was the last time you fucked someone?" Barbara asked, this time using the non-clinical description. I was a bit taken aback by her rough language but she said it in a surprisingly sweet and tender way that didn't sound harsh like it might coming from one of my friends.

"Let's see, it was Saturday."

"With your girlfriend?"

"Well, she's a friend and she's a girl but no, she's not my girlfriend."

"You have sex with your female friends?" Barbara asked sounding a bit surprised.

"Friend, singular, and it isn't a regular occurrence. We took a shower together and one thing led to another."

"See, this is one of the things that I missed out on by not going to college. I bet you have sex with two or three different girls every week. Tell me about your shower with this friend of yours and don't leave out a single piece of information."

I decided to be as graphic as I could in my description, including the way that Kate's soapy body and my soapy body were rubbing and squirming against each other in the tight shower stall and how aroused we both eventually became as we groped and fondled each other and how once the runaway freight train left its track, there really wasn't any alternative but to have sex right there.

"I wish I had sex with two or three different women each week but the truth is I don't," I said after I managed to shift gears from the Kate story to answering Barbara's questions. "I'm the sort of person that can usually only focus on one woman at a time."

"So tell me who you're dating now."

I told her briefly about Sarah and Windy but stressed the non-dating aspect of my budding relationship with Sarah.

DAVID W. GOODWIN

"By my calculations, that's more than one woman at a time and then there's the shower woman and that adds up to three."

"Yes, I guess you're right about that. I get your point."

"See, that's what I mean. I hope you don't mind my saying this but thinking about other people's sex lives makes me kind of horny," Barbara said while she squirmed around in her seat a bit. "And I like to hear all of the juicy details."

"Well, I wish I was having sex with Sarah or Windy but I haven't quite gone that far with Windy due to circumstances beyond my control and I just met Sarah this weekend. It seems to me, Barbara, that you still have a lot of sexual energy."

"Still? Like for an old lady? Well, yeah, I do get horny a lot. Look, I'm a normal, healthy, happily married woman. Like you just said, you love to talk about sex. Well I do too, especially with young men, so I hope that you don't get the wrong idea here."

"No, I would have to agree that talking about sex is almost as good as having sex. It's on my mind a lot, too, as you can imagine. You certainly seem to be comfortable talking about it around me so that makes me comfortable. Does your husband know this about you?"

"No, some things are better off left a secret. Say, where are we going?" Barbara asked, abruptly changing the subject.

I told her about a place I had in mind near Gold Hill where we could drive up into the woods. It was an old jeep trail that had once been a mining road but was currently the long driveway for three houses. Barbara was worried that this might be a bit awkward but I assured her the place we were going wasn't near any of them.

"How do you know this area so well?" Barbara asked. "Wait, let me guess, one of your girlfriends lives up there, right?"

"Again, she's a woman and she's sort of a friend but not a girlfriend. She's actually more of a friend of Eric's and I think she would like to be his girlfriend."

"I think Eric the White is a very attractive man but then again, so is Iggy the Ham. I've fantasized already at least once about having sex with all three of you."

"You have? Individually or all at once?" I asked after I got over my shock.

"Both, to tell you the truth," she responded shyly.

"Wow, you don't waste any time. We've only been here a few days. I'm flattered. What other quarry workers have you fantasized about?" I asked.

"Probably most of them. Maybe it would be easier to list the ones that I haven't thought about. Let's see, there's Georgie, Frederick and of course, Big Larry. He just doesn't do it for me. I'll admit too that I get a little hot thinking about Rhonda. Do you find her sexy?"

"Of course I do. She's super hot but so is Joan," I responded looking over at her in the passenger's seat.

"Do you find me sexy? You can be honest," Barbara asked as the expression on her face tightened up a bit.

"If I tell you the truth, promise me that you'll keep it between us, okay?"

"Absolutely, that's the quarry way," she answered.

"Your look says the 1950's to me and that's the decade when I was born. But now that I'm getting to know you a little, I see that you're a very attractive and extremely sexy woman," I answered and I really didn't have to stretch the truth all that much. Her personality and over-the-top sexual obsession was rather titillating and her quarry girl outfit made it obvious that she had a killer body. I could tell that she was very busty and considering that she was the mother of two, her hips and butt were rather fleshy but in a good way.

"That's sweet of you, thanks," she replied, looking down at her feet.

"Have you had sex with anyone at the quarry?" I ventured.

"That I'm not willing to talk about but I did tell you that I'm a happily married woman and I honor the bond between Richie and myself. I think you and Rhonda would make a good couple. She's kind of bossy and a little rough around the edges but I can tell that you've got a good sense of humor and can dish it out and take it as well. There probably aren't many people that she would be compatible with. I love meeting people and figuring out who would work well together as a couple."

"What do you think about Whitey and Georgie together? I think that's a match made in heaven," I observed, tongue-in-cheek.

"I'm not sure Georgie would be compatible with anyone that presently works at the quarry or the entire state of Colorado for that matter. Kind of sad, actually, because I think she's pretty lonely."

I warned Barbara that we would soon be banging a sharp right turn up a pretty rough and steep road to get to the place where I wanted to scavenge for some rotting wood.

"Just don't drive too fast or reckless because in my aroused condition, all that bouncing around rubs my nipples against my bra and gets me a little wet you-know-where. I'm just warning you, it might trigger something," Barbara explained without any noticeable embarrassment. "I just didn't want to startle you when it happens."

"Your husband is one hell of a lucky man!"

The road we were now traveling on was a real workout for the truck and I needed to get out to turn the lugs on the wheels to put it into four-wheel drive. Once back inside, conversation between Barbara and I ended as we both had to concentrate on the task at hand—me to maneuver around the rocks and holes in the road and try to give the truck just enough gas to move forward up the steep incline but not enough for the tires to spin out and Barbara to do whatever she was doing to keep her mind and body under control. Apparently, she lost the battle because right when we finally crested the steepest part of the hill, she let loose with a loud, deep moan and then yelled out "Sweet Mother of God!"

"I say amen to that, sister!"

Barbara was panting loudly as we drove past the house of a mountain homesteading family whom I had gotten to know a little in the past year. As I passed by Fritz's place, I saw him, his wife and young daughter all out in the driveway working on loading a bunch of firewood from a huge pile into his old pickup truck. From what I knew, this was how he supported his family. The interesting thing too was that they lived without electricity and he had several donkeys that he used to haul trees out of the woods to his truck. I slowed down to say hello while Barbara was leaning back in the passenger seat still breathing quite heavily, looking very flushed and somewhat bewildered.

"Hey Fritz, man, how are you doing?" I yelled out through the passenger side window. Since I was driving a pickup truck with the Sugarloaf Quarry logo on the side, I'm sure he wondered who the heck I was and what I was doing driving up the road to his house. Every other time he had seen me, I was on foot.

Fritz walked over to try to figure things out and eventually recognized me.

"Hey Eric, what are you doin' working for that cretin?" he asked me as he leaned into the truck.

"By the way, I'm Dean not Eric. You always seem to get the two of us mixed up. You know Big Larry?"

"Only that the noise from his damn quarry blows over here every so often reminding us that we no longer live in the wilderness, plus there's all that confounded dynamite blasting, plus he's a complete asshole," Fritz said in his slow western drawl.

"Well, I've only worked there a few days now but I could see where it might be a little disruptive. Fritz, this is my coworker Barbara," I said hoping that Barbara had recovered enough to be semi-communicative. "Barbara, this is Fritz."

"Pleased to meet you, ma'am," Fritz said politely.

"Yeah," was all Barbara managed to say with considerable effort through her dreamy haze.

"Is she alright?" Fritz asked me, realizing that he needed to bypass Barbara if this conversation was going to continue.

"Yes, she's fine. I think the ride took a lot out of her. Hey, it's a really long story but Big Larry and Rhonda, his assistant, gave us the task today to gather up a bunch of rotting wood fragments. I thought that a good place to look might be some old logging areas that you worked in two or three years ago. I was hoping that you might be okay with this and could direct us to some lands on the National Forest that you logged in, like maybe up on the road to Gold Hill."

"Why the hell are you wanting to find some rotting wood?" he asked.

I quickly explained about the rock ledges, the mold and fungi, the black rumped pygmy gnat, the U.S. Fish and Wildlife Service and the netting. Since Fritz was the epitome of anti-establishment, I wasn't sure which side of this issue he might come down on plus, since he seemed to have a predisposition against Big Larry, I wouldn't have been surprised if I didn't get a single ounce of cooperation from him. Instead, he seemed to embrace the idea and gave me very specific directions on a few places where he thought we would have easy pickings of rotten wood.

"But let me give you a bit of advice, son. Since your friend Barbara here seems to be on a trip to never never land, I would suggest that you not combine business and pleasure if you want to keep your job. I have to tell you, the inside of your truck smells more like sex than anything I've ever smelled before, even when I'm actually having sex with the wife."

Since I didn't want to dispel any thoughts Fritz was harboring, I smiled, thanked him and headed up the road to go find the wood that we were after. Barbara was slowly starting to rejoin the physical world. After a few hundred yards, we passed the last house on the road and began yet another series of steep sections of the road with switchbacks as we entered the National Forest.

"That was one humdinger of an orgasm," Barbara announced suddenly. "That's easily the best one I've had all day!"

"All day? How many do you usually have in an average day?" I asked incredulously.

"At least one but usually not more than three. How many have you had today?"

"Not a single one."

"Well, we should do something about that. That's just unnatural. Men, especially young oversexed men like you, shouldn't have to suffer like that. Your plumbing just isn't designed for it. You should make sure that you release your pent up juices at least once a day. That's what Richie tells me anyway. It's not healthy to store it up. Maybe I could help you out a little. How can you concentrate on your job when all you're thinking about is sex?"

"That's only been since we've been in the car together. What do you mean, 'maybe you can help me out a little?' What are you suggesting?"

"That depends. Would you like to release the pressure that has certainly built up inside you?"

"Given all that has transpired in the last twenty minutes, I'm sitting here in this truck trying to concentrate on our job but now I've got a large boner and it is threatening to take over all of my normal brain functions," I admitted. "It got me quite aroused when you were masturbating and now that Fritz has mentioned the aroma, it's making me even hornier."

"That does it. Pull the truck over right now. I'm going to have to do something for our own safety. I'm afraid that you might drive us off a cliff so it is absolutely essential that I remedy the situation," Barbara said emphasizing and drawing out the 'it is absolutely essential' part of the sentence.

I pulled the truck to the side of the road, we were in the middle of the forest and there weren't any houses around or other signs of civilization. Barbara got out of the truck, walked around to my side and opened up the door. She extended her hand to me and pulled me out of the truck so that I was standing beside her.

"What are your favorite female body parts?" she asked point blank with her big black crazy glasses enhanced eyes looking deeply into mine.

"There aren't too many parts that I don't like—eyes, lips, ears, necks, the curve of a thigh, an ankle, a butt with some meat on it, hands, you know, pretty much everything. But if I had to choose one thing, I'm especially partial to boobs," I admitted which I'm sure didn't come as any surprise to her.

"That I can do," she said as she pulled off her sweatshirt and Sugarloaf tank top, exposing a fancy black bra. Reaching around behind, she quickly unclasped it and was topless, much to my delight. Her breasts were big and round and a little droopy but in a very sexy way, especially when they wobbled to and fro after being released into the fresh mountain air. Her nipples certainly responded appropriately. She cupped each one in a hand and alternated hoisting them up to her mouth to give her large, erect nipples a few slow licks while maintaining eye contact with me. I found her magnified brown eyes to be almost as sexy as what she was doing to her boobs but I was able to break eye contact long enough to watch her performance. Her areolas were huge and dark brown and contrasted beautifully with the pale white skin of her breasts. I was aroused beyond belief and stood there paralyzed, not sure what, if anything, I should do or what was acceptable behavior with her.

"I have to warn you, once I get started, it's hard for me to stop. Let's take off our boots," Barbara instructed. When our boots were off, we continued the process. "Now, take off your overalls." When I complied with that directive, I took the initiative to step out of my boxers while she slid off her jeans and then tugged at her saturated black panties so they slid down around her ankles. With a little kick move, she sent them skyward and I grabbed them in midair. I put them in the back of the truck with the growing pile of other clothes. When I took off my tee shirt, we were both standing next to the truck completely naked.

"Now remember, I'm only doing this for our own well being, not because I want to be unfaithful to my husband. Come sit down on the tailgate of the truck."

I walked over to the back of the truck while Barbara followed me, opened the tailgate and sat down. Barbara stood directly facing me and placed her hand between her legs and began rubbing herself slowly. She was so moist from her previous experience that the sound alone was enough to arouse me to the point of no return. The little squishy sounds from her well lubricated intricate girl parts and the snap, crackle and pops of various bodily secretions as she touched herself and moved her fingers faster was incredible.

"I want you to do the same thing to yourself," she instructed in an even deeper and huskier voice than usual and I knew that I had better comply. She even shared some of her natural lubricants with me by taking my erect friend in her hands and spreading her juices all over it. She repeated this four or five times until I was crazy with pressure and desire.

DAVID W. GOODWIN

In a very short time, I had my own religious experience. Right before I was about to give my offering, Barbara knelt down in front of me and made an alter of her breasts by pushing them up and tightly together, with her nipples poking out from between her fingers. The effect was more than I could handle and I quickly anointed her with a release that seemed to go on for a long time. She took a large amount of pleasure in my pleasure as she had her second orgasm in the last ten minutes.

She rubbed my juices all over her boobs until the entire area was glistening. After a moment to admire our collective work, Barbara stood up and slowly got dressed while I watched. It took me a longer period of time to transition from this experience to the mundane task of getting dressed as I sat there thinking back on the most recent events. Eric and Iggy were going to have a hard time believing this story; I was there and I wasn't entirely certain that I believed what just happened.

"Do you feel like you are able to drive now that you can concentrate on it a bit more?" Barbara asked rhetorically.

"Barbara, that was one of the best experiences I have ever had. Thank you."

"I thought you might like it but I figured you were too shy to ask."

"Well, I can't say the thought ever occurred to me to ask a married woman to do anything like that before. I've been with more than a few women in the past but I've never had an experience quite like this," I admitted.

"I just ask that you not tell anyone else what we did up here today, okay? It will be our little secret. If we ever get any other chances like this again, I want you to think about what your wildest fantasy might be. Tell me about it and maybe it's something we can do. Understand? I'm open to almost any suggestion."

"It's a deal. I'll let you know what I come up with," I answered as we got back into the truck and continued driving up the road. That was twice I had gotten that same offer in the last few days. Maybe there was something in the water in Colorado.

CHAPTER 12

BARBARA AND I drove in silence for a short while until we got to the turnoff that Fritz had told us about. We followed his skid road into the heart of the old timber harvest area. Just as I had hoped, in the last three or four years since he had cut the trees, some of the smaller branches that were in contact with the ground, especially the ones in seasonal drainage ditches, were starting to rot perfectly.

"This is just what we're looking for Barbara. Let's load up the truck with as much of this wood as we can comfortably haul."

"How can you be all business after what we just went through?"

"Would you rather we climb in the back of the truck and do it again? I probably could."

"No but let's have some transition time. Maybe we should relax and have lunch before we start working. Remember, Rhonda said that we just needed to be back by five so we have all afternoon to do this. I'm guessing that it will take us about an hour to load up and an hour to get back to the quarry since we have to drive down that crazy road with a full load. It's about one o'clock now so we could take a nice long lunch and still do what we have to do. Don't you agree?"

"I guess you're right. I'd lost track of how hungry I've become given the recent events," I agreed.

We got comfortable leaning up against the cab of the pickup truck with our legs stretched out into the bed. She made a little cushion out of her sweatshirt and settled in. We grabbed our bag lunches and the large jug of cold water and ate a leisurely meal while enjoying the warm sunshine, the good food and the memory of our recently shared experience. I must have dozed off for a while because I woke up to the vibration of Barbara's whimpering since I suddenly noticed that her head was on my chest.

"Hey Barbara," I whispered loudly, "time to wake up and start collecting some wood."

"Baby, come lick me some more," she purred.

"Barbara, wake up. You're having a dream."

"Richie, darling . . ." she started to say and then I could see her coming out of her dream, open her eyes, stare right at me and say, "oh, sorry, I thought I was home in bed with my husband."

"That's quite alright. It sounds like you were having a pretty nice time there. I think maybe we should get back to work soon, when you're ready."

"Yes, just give me a moment to get my head screwed on straight."

She put her face right up to mine and gave me a sweet little kiss on the lips. Then, as if nothing happened, we put our lunch remains away, got our clothes readjusted, grabbed our gloves and climbed down out of the pickup truck bed. Barbara's cheeks were all flushed, perhaps from her two orgasms, perhaps from her dream; perhaps it was just what she looked like in her perpetually aroused condition. All I know was that it was a blast to work with her.

"Just be careful when you lift each branch as you may get a little surprise underneath," I warned.

"Like what?" she asked suspiciously.

"Well, maybe a snake, an amphibian or some sort of spider. Make sure you're wearing your gloves, okay? I wouldn't want you to get hurt."

I put on my gloves and picked up the nearest rotting branch that looked like it contained the requisite amount of fungi and molds for gnats to feast upon. There weren't any critters that crawled out from underneath it and I placed it in the truck. "No surprises under this branch," I said. "Let's load up what we can find here and then we'll drive up the skid road a little farther. We'll just keep going until we have a full load."

Working in a several hundred foot radius, we were able to gather enough wood to fill about a third of the pickup truck. Barbara jumped in the truck and drove it a ways down the road while I walked alongside scouting out good source material until she reached a good stopping spot.

This routine continued a few more times until we had enough wood to call it quits. I checked out the clock on the truck and it was around 3:30, right on Barbara's schedule. "That looks pretty good to me Dean," she announced. "Maybe we should head back to the quarry."

"Yes, I think Big Larry and Rhonda will be impressed with our accomplishments today, don't you think?"

"Especially if they knew about all of our accomplishments," Barbara said with a girlish giggle.

We retraced our route back to the Sugarloaf Quarry. Fritz was nowhere to be seen so we didn't need to stop and chat with him again. The truck was full but not overloaded so we were able to get down the long road without too much trouble as long as I rode the brakes. We pulled into the quarry right around 4:15 and saw Rhonda and Big Larry talking in front of the office building. They walked over to see our booty as we approached them.

"This stuff looks excellent!" Rhonda exclaimed as she examined our load. "Great job you two! Where did you get all of this?"

"Dean knew of a place up near an old girlfriend's cabin," Barbara explained, sounding like a jealous lover.

"Not an old girlfriend," I said, trying again to set the story straight, "but it was up near her cabin where another friend of mine had done some logging a few years back. Is this what you had in mind?"

"Zactly," Big Larry said enthusiastically. "You two make a pretty good team from the looks of things. Maybe you should work together more often."

"I'd like that," Barbara said in an overtly flirtatious way. "I like the way Dean handles his wood."

"Take this stuff back to the nursery and unload it. Be sure to cover it with a tarp to keep it from drying out and put some rocks around the edges to anchor it. We'll need to keep it for a month before we haul it up to the ledges," Rhonda said. "Barbara, you might want to wash up a little before the meeting."

As we drove away, Barbara grabbed the rear view mirror, looked closely at her face and wiped something off her chin. We drove the short distance to the nursery in silence and quickly unloaded our gnat bait. I found an old tarp in one of the greenhouses while Barbara scrounged some rocks to hold the tarp down.

"Do you think it was a good idea to be so blatantly suggestive in front of Big Larry and Rhonda?" I asked. "Aren't you worried at all about how they'll react?"

"Nah, he's so self-absorbed and dense that I doubt he even noticed and I was trying to make Rhonda a little jealous. I think it worked. She has always kind of looked down on me and gives the impression that she can have any man she wants at any time so I just wanted her to know that maybe this old mom has a trick or two up her bra. I was just feeling a little vixeny and wanted to express it."

"Fair enough."

DAVID W. GOODWIN

We drove back and joined the rest of the crew as they arrived at the office building. Folks sauntered into the room and everyone took their positions around the table. Big Larry barked out his military-like orders for reports, including Rhonda who described the progress made with the wall reconnaissance, the climbing gear shopping expedition and the work that Barbara and I completed gathering up the rotten wood.

"And everyone should remember," Big Larry added, "that we've got a rookie night on our hands."

"Yeah, I've been meaning to ask, what happens on rookie night?" Iggy asked a bit nervously.

"We don't want to give too much away there Hambone," Rhonda said, winking to the crew, "but one question I need to ask, are you a virgin?"

"Of course not," Iggy said somewhat indignantly. "Why do you ask?"

"Well, do you remember the first time you had sex?"

"Of course, it was 1971, a little redhead that I knew from biology class. Big knockers and a tight little butt. We did it in the bushes of a park near our high school. Right at the most critical moment, a dog came by and peed on my foot. Quite memorable."

"Spare us the details. The reason I ask is because that was a pretty important event in your life, right?"

"Absolutely," Iggy answered.

"Well, your first night at the Sugarloaf Quarry Nightclub is going to be one of those important events. You'll remember it your entire life," Rhonda predicted.

With that, Sugarloaf Sam's scream blasted the airwaves. All the workers were released out into the afternoon sunshine to spend some time taking care of their personal business. I went over to hang out with Eric and Iggy since I hadn't seen either of them all day.

"Beans, what a great assignment you got there today," Iggy said in his usual boisterous voice. "You and Barbara must have had one hell of an afternoon together. Did she teach you how to do the Twist?"

"Did she agree to take you home to meet the husband and kids and maybe even to a Sock Hop?" Eric teased.

"You guys can't even begin to imagine what it was like to work with her today. I can't stand around and chat because I need to quickly get down to Denver to meet Sarah for drinks. Eric, are you driving back to Boulder with me?"

"For sure, man. I've got to get ready to meet Tina for our dinner date tonight too. You still staying here Hambone?" Eric asked.

"You bet. Maybe you guys will stay here tomorrow," Iggy said. "It would be even more fun if you joined me."

"Good luck, man, hope you have a fun rookie night!" I said.

We began our gravity assisted trip down to Boulder in the Cruisemobile. Eric told me about his day on the landscaping crew and how difficult it was to work with poison ivy all over his upper body. I told him about the quarry wall climbing and the assignment with Barbara to gather up the wood, leaving out most of the important details.

"We went up by Fritz's house, past the turnoff to Kylee's cabin and then on past that tall house built on an old gold mine up towards Gold Hill," I explained.

"Did you see Dan Fogelberg hanging out up there?" Eric asked. Kylee had told Eric a few months ago that a woman had just moved into the gold mine house who was dating Dan and that she had seen him hanging out there with her from time to time. He lived up the canyon in the town of Nederland and since all of us were big fans of his and had seen him in concert a few times, this was a big thing.

"No, it didn't seem like anyone was home when we drove by," I said. "But there was a brand new Land Rover there. Maybe that was Dan's car."

"What else would he drive? That had to be his!" Eric exclaimed.

"Yeah, maybe, but I had other more important things to deal with," I said cryptically.

"What could be more important than hanging out with Dan and his hot girlfriend? Kylee tells me that she's always naked on the front porch when she goes by."

"Well, I can't really get into it much but I had a ticking time bomb on my hands."

"What does that mean?"

"First Barbara was the ticking time bomb and then it was me and then it was Barbara again."

"You'll have to explain that in a bit more detail."

"I've been sworn to secrecy."

"By whom?"

"Barbara."

"Come on, you can tell me. I tell you all the details of my relationships," Eric said even though we both knew this wasn't true.

DAVID W. GOODWIN

"All I'm going to say is that there were three orgasms," I said knowing that it was going to drive Eric bonkers.

"Wait a minute. What do you mean 'there were three orgasms'?"

"Just that. Do you know what an orgasm is?"

"You've got to tell me more, like the circumstances, who did what, wait, did you have sex with her?"

"There wasn't penetration, if that's what you're asking," I admitted.

"Then what?"

"Let's just say that she pleasured herself and then she helped me to do the same and then she had another one."

"Geez, man. Here I was stuck hauling and stacking rocks around all day and itching like a mother and you're off having sex with some middle aged married bobby soxer!"

"I think you're being pretty harsh calling her a middle aged married bobby soxer. Even though she's a little strange looking by Boulder standards, I have to say, for a mom with teenagers, she's pretty hot. Oh, and she thinks that you're pretty hot too."

"She said that?" Eric asked changing his tone a bit.

"Yep, she said that she fantasized about having sex with you, Iggy and me."

"All at once or as individuals?"

"I asked her the same thing and she said both!"

"Holy smokes! What's up with that?"

"She is one sex crazed woman. I think that she thinks about sex even more than us."

"That would be hard to imagine," Eric said. "Oh, by the way, before I forget to tell you, Joan told me that we all get Monday, July 5th off as a holiday so you might want to work that into your plans for next weekend."

"That's great! I keep meaning to ask someone at the quarry about it."

I was already feeling that I had told Eric more than I should have and decided to shut up in order to honor Barbara's request, at least marginally. The truth of the matter was that I was dying to tell Eric the details but didn't think that it was the right thing to do. I needed to start getting my brain focused on my date with Sarah and less on the experience with Barbara. The thought of seeing her made me feel a little anxious and I began thinking about what I might wear and what our conversations would be like. I was picturing Sarah and then got a case of the butterflies thinking about the time we had spent together just yesterday. Eric was lost in his own reverie too.

The Cruisemobile found its way to Pleasant Street and I eased it into a parking space right in front of the Zoo. The frat boys across the street were having a fairly subdued cookout in their spacious side yard but since it was summer, there were only a few handfuls of them and even fewer sorority girls. The few women who stuck around Boulder for the summer must have been in high demand and the boys at Sigma Kappa probably felt lucky to get the ones they did. I almost felt a little sorry for them. I wondered briefly what they did to occupy their time in the summer. I often saw them hanging out on their porch or washing and waxing their shiny muscle cars but since our lives intersected so rarely, it was hard for me to imagine what they did. Maybe they spent their summers taking the classes that they had failed the previous two semesters. I was curious if they were even aware of things what went on at the Zoo.

"You've got to tell me some more details one of these days about what happened between you and Barbara today, Beans," Eric said breaking the silence.

"I will, just not now. I've got a little more time than you. Do you want to take the first shower?" I asked as we walked into the Zoo, past an empty front porch. "Your evening might be a bit more time sensitive than mine but it has to be a quick one."

"Sure, thanks," he responded as we each veered off towards our own bedrooms. "I'll be fast."

"That's what your girlfriends always tell me," I joked.

As I entered the kitchen, I saw Crystal and Hazel making out again in a corner.

"Hi ladies, what is it about the kitchen that makes you both feel so horny?" I asked with wonder.

"Oh, hi Dean. Well, you know, it must be something about the smell of food. Oh, and maybe Hazel's oral fixation," Crystal said giving Hazel a very big wet smack on her lips.

"I think it's her that has the oral fixation. She just always wants to have something in her mouth," Hazel said "and I'm usually the closest thing around."

"Could be a lot worse than that," I responded. "You two are cooking dinner tonight, right?"

"Yep, we're doing a spaghetti meal," Hazel answered.

"Did you see the note that I left on the board this morning about not being here?" I asked.

"Yeah, but it looks like you *are* here. Where are you going?" Crystal asked.

I explained to them about my date with Sarah and then excused myself to get ready. I probably had about half an hour before I needed to leave and wanted to make sure that I wasn't rushing around like a crazy man to get there on time. I was an absolute stickler about being on time to just about anything.

Although I wasn't that experienced when it came to first dates, having only really had three or four of them in my life, I remember one experience I vowed never to ever repeat. It was the first real date of my life. I was a really puny tenth grader and I had somehow managed to summon enough courage to call up a particular girl from my health class. I probably hadn't spoken to her other than a word or two in class and even this might have been a stretch. Regardless, I couldn't get her out of my mind. One afternoon while I was on a break at the shoe store where I worked after school, I corralled all of the spare testosterone that my body was just beginning to produce and very nervously dialed her phone number that at this point I had committed to memory. This was, however, the first time I actually dialed it.

To my utter surprise and horror, Louise answered. Other than the fact that she was probably a good three or four inches taller, was clearly working her way through puberty at a faster rate than me and lived on the wealthy side of town, I managed to resist the urge to immediately hang up and go back to being an invisible pre-pubescent coward.

"HiLouise, thisisDeanfromyourhealthclass. I'mcallingtoseeifyoumight liketogotothemoviewithme atthehighschoolthisFridaynight?" I asked in a voice that didn't sound like my own, more like one that was being filtered through vocal cords that were being squished by several sets of invisible hands with a firm grip on my throat. I had rehearsed my lines so often that I forgot to breathe.

After an excruciatingly long silence, she responded, "Are you the small guy with the really big feet?"

"Probably, I sit next to Brian," I answered, relieved that the first part of the conversation was over but now I had to think on my big feet, which my dignity was slowly draining out of. I quickly remembered that she and Brian were friends so maybe this would give her an idea who this idiot was calling to ask her out.

"Yeah, I remember. You're the one that did the report recently on the heartbreak of psoriasis, right?"

"That's me!" I said feeling relieved that at least we had gotten this far into the conversation.

"I liked your report, it was very funny. Sure, I'll go out with you on Friday. Why don't we meet at the high school at 7:15?" Louise suggested.

This wasn't the painful part of the date. That would be the embarrassing clothing that I selected thinking that it would make a good impression. It actually seemed fine at the time but looking back in retrospect; I cringe at my complete lack of fashion sense. Maybe in 1970 it was considered cool to wear a pair of super tight and way too short baby blue corduroy pants and a bright yellow button down dress shirt. This outfit became especially uncomfortable as I was walking Louise home from the movie and she took my hand. After a few utterly euphoric moments reveling in the joy of holding hands with a girl that wasn't my mother and feeling like I was Mr. Smooth, she stopped walking, pulled me around by my hand to face her and planted a full kiss right on my lips. I became so totally aroused that my budding boy part became completely engorged and started throbbing madly. Since my pants were so tight, it had nowhere to go but up or bust through the fabric. I was afraid that if I looked down, there was a good chance that I might see that it had escaped through the top of my pants and was out in plain sight for all the world and Louise to see. It was nearly impossible to thoroughly enjoy the moment thinking that I might be having one of the defining embarrassing moments of my life. Walking was pretty difficult too once our kiss broke up and Louise continued our stroll. I pretended to have an urgent need to retie my shoelaces in an effort both to make sure I was semi-presentable and to try to readjust myself. The problem was that there was nowhere to hide so I simply tried to walk as upright as possible without hurting myself.

It was with this experience in mind that I went into my bedroom to select a more appropriate outfit for my rendezvous with Sarah. Luckily, my date with Louise was the last time those blue pants were ever seen again since when I made it home that evening; I threw them in my mother's rag box. Looking through my very small closet with a very limited selection of shirts, I chose my cleanest, least wrinkled button down white shirt and then a pair of modestly patched and roomy jeans. My ensemble was completed by a pair of Rainbow sandals. Not too bad I thought as I checked my look in the mirror.

DAVID W. GOODWIN

By the time I came back through the house, Wayne, Kate and Peter had arrived and were sitting out on the porch while Crystal and Hazel were busy putting dinner together in the kitchen. I said goodbye to the ladies and hung out briefly with my porch-bound housemates.

"Hey, is there any update on Jackie?" I asked.

"She's still being held for observation," Wayne said. "I went over there to see her during visiting hours this afternoon before I had to be at work."

"That was nice of you Wayne," Kate said. "How'd she seem?"

"I don't know. You contacted her brother and he's planning to come to Boulder to be with her in a few days. She told the nurse that she didn't want to see any of her housemates when they told her that I was there to visit."

"That doesn't sound too good," Peter said slowly.

"No it doesn't. I talked to one of the nurses about her and she said that it might be a while before she gets released," Wayne reported. "She wouldn't tell me a lot about her since I'm not part of her immediate family but she whispered to me that Jackie was quite delusional. She asked me if Jackie was studying to be an animal trainer because she kept talking about punishing the animals at the zoo. I explained what that reference meant and she went over to Jackie's chart and wrote something down."

"Well, I'm off to Denver to meet up with Sarah. You guys have a great evening. Maybe I'll see you late tonight," I said as I walked down the stairs towards the Cruisemobile.

"Yeah Dean, that's fine! Just leave us all here to eat all of the yummy dinner!" Kate yelled out in a teasing way. "Don't expect there to be any left when you come home tired and hungry. Maybe you should cancel your plans and stay with us tonight. We're going to have another group massage!"

"That's tempting," I called back. "See you all later."

The drive to Denver was an easy one and quite enjoyable, especially in the early evening as the sun was just beginning to settle behind the Rockies. The rangeland between Boulder and Denver was bathed in low sunlight and became golden. The cattle that were out grazing looked surreal in the light, almost like they were full scale glossy photographs cut out into their real shapes and propped up from behind in the fields, looking almost too bright and shiny. After cresting the hill outside of Boulder, the skyline of Denver immediately came into view making an abrupt departure from the comfortable safety and familiarity of Boulder and a quick entry into the sphere of the urban jungle. The gravitational pull of Denver caused all of my senses to perk up to high alert mode, knowing I was now out of my element. I knew pretty well where I was heading but looked down on the piece of paper that had my handwritten notes on the various exits and turns that would deliver me to the Oxford Hotel.

At the final turn onto Wazee Street, I had ten minutes to find the hotel, park and then find Sarah. I drove down three blocks and saw the hotel. Parking was virtually non-existent on the street by the hotel so I circled around a few of the nearby blocks and eventually found a spot. With a few minutes to spare, I walked through the main lobby of the hotel and towards the bar.

The place was very quiet and almost empty except for a group of five or six off in the far corner. I quickly scanned their faces to see if any of them were Sarah. They were all dressed quite flamboyantly so I assumed this was her group. However, when I didn't see her there, I had a brief moment of panic wondering what I should do. Instead of going over to introduce myself and ask if they knew her, I decided to have a seat at the bar and wait things out for a while. Maybe she hadn't arrived yet.

The bartender slowly walked over to me and asked if I would like to order a drink.

"Sure, but I was hoping to meet someone from the Aspen Shakespeare Festival cast here at 7:30 but I have the feeling that she's not here yet," I said.

"That's your group over there," he said. "They're the only ones in the joint at the moment. That's not who you're lookin' for?"

I felt a hand on my shoulder and turned around to see Sarah standing there with a drink in her hand. "Perfect timing, 7:30 on the dot! I like that in a man. I was just in the ladies room when you arrived," Sarah said putting her drink on the bar and giving me a hug followed by a delicious cold and vodka flavored kiss.

"This must be your date, fella," the bartender announced. "Either that or you just experienced the easiest pickup of your life!"

Sarah looked quite similar to how I had left her yesterday only with a different dress and fancier high heels. She was wearing a bit more makeup than she had in Georgetown and it made her face look very ripe and juicy and very kissable. I wanted to whisk her off her feet and take her to my penthouse, that is, if I had a penthouse instead of a small bedroom in a dive student house.

"Come on over and meet my friends, Dean, but maybe you should order a drink first," she said.

I told the bartender that I'd have a rum and coke because it's the first drink that I could think of on the spur of the moment. I usually drank beer but thought I would appear a bit more sophisticated if I ordered a mixed drink. A sloe gin fizz was probably the last mixed drink I had and that wasn't the impression that I was going for, especially if it arrived with a tiny paper umbrella and a copy of *Better Homes and Gardens* magazine. He told me that he'd bring it over.

Sarah took my hand and led me over to the table. All of her friends were watching us and I felt a sudden stab of nervousness. This was a crowd that I had never associated with before. However, Sarah's presence was having a calming influence on my jitters and since I was with her, I reasoned, I must have something positive going for me.

"Everyone, this is my new friend Dean. He's a student at the University of Colorado, works at a quarry that has its own nightclub, rides his bike all over the Rockies and is a great kisser!" Sarah said by way of introduction.

"Hi everyone. Let me set the record straight, though, right from the start. Everything Sarah says is true except that I'm not really a great kisser, I'm just average!" I said.

After introductions were made and promptly forgotten, I grabbed a chair from a nearby table and sat down next to Sarah. The bartender brought over my drink and we all had a toast to spending the summer in Colorado.

"You look familiar to me," said a guy dressed in what looked like a pair of clown pants and a patchwork vest. "Have you ever been involved in the theatre?"

"No, except for getting the lead in my sixth grade play. It was an original script written by my teacher that was supposed to teach us kids all about making good decisions in life. I was the one that would always intercede when one of the characters was about to make a bad choice and present them with a range of options, all of which were nicely printed on a signpost that pointed in a different direction. Let's see, there was 'Satisfaction' that was a really popular one with all the boys, 'Greed', 'Respect', 'Humiliation', you know, heavy things like that."

"No, I'm not talking about your sixth grade play. Have you ever performed on stage as an adult in any capacity, like being a part of a band or stand up comedy or a magician?"

"Sorry, I often get mistaken for someone else. There must be a lot of guys out there that look somewhat similar to me. I think the long hair and beard must make us all resemble each other."

"No, that's not it. I know that I've seen you before," he continued.

"Maybe your paths crossed somewhere else," Sarah interjected. "Why do you think it was on stage, Ralph?"

"Because I never forget a face that I've seen and I know that I've seen you in some sort of performance before," Ralph insisted.

"Well maybe something will give you a better clue as the evening progresses," Sarah said trying to move the conversation along. "How was your day at the quarry?"

"You wouldn't believe it if I told you," I responded to her. Looking around the table, I explained, "As Sarah said, I got this crazy summer job working at a quarry outside of Boulder and it's a rather unique place. It's run kind of like a summer camp because most of the workers spend the nights there during the week. They get fed breakfast and dinner in a mess hall and the chef, a woman named Bunny, even makes us all bag lunches and snacks everyday. They sleep in a bunkhouse and the whole situation is a big mystery to me. The strangest part is that each night, they go to this dirty, cramped building and have what they refer to as a nightclub. Everyone just goes absolutely crazy for this and they almost seem like indentured slaves during the day just so they can get to the nightclub each evening. I've worked there for less than a week and haven't yet been to the nightclub."

"Well that's just nuts! Why don't you go some night and check it out?" asked a woman sitting next to Ralph.

"Funny you should say that," I said. "I was planning on going tonight but I got a phone call from Sarah this morning inviting me to meet you all here for drinks. How could I refuse that?"

"You know, this sounds like an interesting premise for a play," said one of the other guys at the table. "I've got a couple of scripts in the works but none of them are really going anywhere. Do you mind if we run with this for a moment to brainstorm on some ideas?"

"Just so you know, Dean, Ellis is the director for *The Tempest*, which we are now rehearsing. As you probably gathered, he has written a number of plays, several of which have been performed and from what I hear, very good," Sarah explained.

"So, the location is a quarry and every day the workers are like drones, slaving away at their grueling jobs, not ever saying anything to anybody, just doing their jobs, trying their best to avoid any additional forms of punishment. Their bosses work them hard, hurling insults at them, yelling, maybe even whipping them to get them to do their jobs like in *Spartacus*. Only, instead of being sent away to gladiator camp for a chance to escape the mind numbing slave existence, the cream of the crop is instead treated to the slave camp nightclub for a night of fabulous entertainment and drinking. Does that describe your quarry pretty well?" Ellis asked me.

"Yeah, that pretty much describes my job," I said, "except for the insults and whippings and the fact that our jobs aren't quite as slavish as you are describing."

"But you described your coworkers as indentured slaves, did you not?" Ellis asked pointedly.

"Yes, but I meant it more figuratively. However, I am a little concerned about actually getting paid. A friend of a friend that used to work there said that they often got shortchanged."

"So that sounds somewhat like slavery if you work without pay," a woman whose name I forgot suggested.

"Or an internship," Ralph said.

"Or volunteer work," Sarah added.

"Alright then, I might want to tone down the slave scenario a little and instead portray the workers as disgruntled and angry. How does that sound?" Ellis asked.

"I wouldn't characterize us as disgruntled or angry. Most of the folks I work with are pretty cool and interesting and fairly positive, optimistic types. There's a wild assortment of characters from Georgie, who no one knows what gender he or she is, to Laverne, a middle aged truck driver who has taken one of the bewildered young men on as her lover, to Juan Antonio, a tiny Spaniard who is working with me on a rock climbing project even though he's afraid of heights, to Barbara, a sex crazed housewife who can't get through more than four hours without having an orgasm, to Rhonda, Big Larry's assistant, who parades around all day in the skimpiest cut offs and tank top that you've ever laid eyes on. She pulled me and two of my housemates off the street where we were throwing the Frisbee around last week and hired us to work on the landscaping crew. She drove past our house in a car with huge rocks on the roof and the logo of a martini swilling rodent on each door and told us to hop in."

"No shit! Man, are you kidding me? There's enough material here for several story lines and we haven't even gotten to the nightclub yet! I would love to talk to you about this more but perhaps this isn't the right time. After you go to the nightclub, call me, collect if you want! I'll give you my number before you leave. This sounds like it has some serious potential!" Ellis said with an extraordinary amount of enthusiasm.

"That quarry of yours does sound like an interesting place to work," Sarah interjected.

"Well, it seems to be so far. However, I'd love to hear about what it's like to be part of an acting troupe and what some of the wild experiences are that you folks have," I said. I assumed that most actors and theatre types were extroverts and would jump all over each other to get the opportunity to talk about themselves and their experiences. I was also hoping to take some of the attention off of me so that I could relax a bit, enjoy my drink and Sarah's company and maybe even get a bite to eat.

The conversation quickly shifted gears while each person took a turn to talk about their road to the theatre and what their experience had been like so far working in Aspen. Most of them were from either coast with the exception of Sarah. Maude and Valerie were both from the San Francisco area while Danielle, Ralph and Ellis were East Coasters. All of them seemed pretty excited about having the opportunity to work in Aspen with the exception of Danielle who was hoping to get accepted at Stratford but settled for Aspen when that fell through.

"My boyfriend got in, I didn't, so we're spending the summer apart. We're both grad students at Brandeis so it will be interesting to see how we reconnect when we get back this fall. I'm sure he's not pining away in my absence or spending too many nights alone since he has always been kind of a lady's man. He's surrounded by so many tarts with British accents that I'm sure they're falling all over themselves trying to teach him the Queen's English," Danielle lamented.

"It looks like you're not doing too badly for yourself either!" Ralph interjected. "How many guys from the cast and crew have you slept with so far this summer?"

"Only a couple but that's different. It's just a casual thing, more out of boredom than passion," she responded.

"That's probably how he would describe his exploits as well, don't you think?" Valerie asked.

"Maybe but he gets emotionally attached quite easily. I think that's the difference."

"I think the funniest experience so far for me this summer was during the scene in *Dream* when all the fairies are in the nest with Bottom and he started tickling mine," Maude said. "I started laughing so hard I broke. I totally went up on my lines. The stage manager was not at all happy with me after that."

"She's talking about *A Midsummer Nights Dream*," Sarah whispered into my ear.

They shared their various experiences for a while as I quickly scanned the bar's menu. I announced that I was going to order some food and asked if anyone else was interested in ordering anything. We got an order together and I went over to talk to the bartender.

"The kitchen closes in about half an hour so make sure that everyone orders everything now," he said. "And the bar closes early on Monday nights, nine o'clock."

I went back to the table and we added a few more items. Everyone wanted another round so I relayed this information to the bartender as well. Sarah walked up behind me while I was at the bar and waited until I was done placing the order.

"Are you glad that you came down here tonight?" she asked when I turned around.

"Definitely! We seem destined to only see each other around crowds of people though."

"I know what you mean. It's kind of frustrating but it's great to see you in a different outfit! The worst part is that we all need to head back to Aspen in a little while so we won't get any time to spend together alone tonight."

"I understand. Seeing you with your theater buddies in this setting gives me a better idea what your life and lifestyle is like. It's radically different than mine."

"I wouldn't be too sure about that. I'll bet there are more similarities than differences."

"You might be right. Say, have you given any more thought to coming to Boulder this weekend?"

"Yes I have and I would love to come visit if at all possible. There are a few details that need to be worked out but we can talk about it later in the week."

"I may not be anywhere near a phone until Friday night since I was planning on staying at the quarry this week. When do you think you could get there?"

"I'd probably leave Aspen Saturday morning so I wouldn't get there until the afternoon. Would that work out for you?" Sarah asked.

"Sure, that would be great! That would give us time together on Saturday, our party is on Sunday and we both have Monday off, right?"

"Yep, so I could stay over and leave sometime on Monday, if that's okay with you."

"That would be great. I can look into availabilities at some local motels if you'd like or see if any of my housemates are going to be away so you could stay in one of their bedrooms," I suggested.

"What? Are you serious?"

"Just checking, I didn't want to be too presumptuous!"

"If you made me stay in a motel, I wouldn't come. The whole idea for coming down this weekend is for us to spend some time together. Do you have your own bedroom?"

"Yes, but I have to warn you, it's tiny."

"Just like something else that you told me was tiny and it turned out to be quite large!" Sarah said with a lascivious laugh.

"True, however, I'm not joking about my bedroom. It's two tiny rooms, my bedroom is literally my bed room and it's just large enough for the mattress and the other room is just big enough for my desk and dresser."

"Sounds cozy! I can't wait!"

The bartender was walking over to our table with the next round of drinks so we followed him and joined the others. Conversation flowed as did the drinks and eventually the food. I hadn't eaten for quite a while so the food tasted especially good. Eventually, the bartender told us it was closing time so we all started wrapping the evening up.

"Hey, don't forget to call me when you get a chance to tell me about the nightclub. I'm already formulating some ideas about this story and I'll want to flesh it out with your real experience. I also have a title in mind—*The Nightclub of the Slaves*—what do you think of that?" Ellis asked.

"Pretty catchy but how about *The Nightclub of the Interesting Characters* instead of the slaves? We should probably discuss my percentage though before you get too far into it. My standard rate is 40%," I said deadpan.

"We can discuss the details once it gets written," Ellis said, missing my humor.

DAVID W. GOODWIN

"It was great to meet all of you. I should probably get my butt back to Boulder as tomorrow's a working day," I said standing up at the table.

"I still haven't figured out why you look so familiar," Ralph said "but I know it will come to me eventually."

"Let me know when you figure it out," I said.

"Let me walk you to your car," Sarah said, standing up as well. Turning towards her friends she said, "I'll meet you all by the van in a few minutes, okay?"

I quickly checked the bill that had been left at our table and took out enough money to cover Sarah's and my part.

"You didn't need to do that," she said when she saw how much money I left.

"Remember our breakfast at the Three G's? I promised to get the next one. Plus, I owe you a massage."

Sarah and I walked out of the hotel together and took the short walk to the Cruisemobile. I took her hand as we walked in the warm, surprisingly quiet evening in the middle of a fairly large city.

"I think they all like you," Sarah said softly.

"They seem like a nice bunch of people. How serious do you think Ellis is about wanting to write a play about the quarry?"

"Who knows? He's a good writer and fairly prolific. There was certainly something in your description that piqued his interest. I have to say, it almost sounds too crazy to be real though. Did you make any of it up?"

"Not a word and I even left out some of the real interesting stuff," I admitted.

"It sounds fascinating!"

"Indeed. There's my car over there," I said pointing to my green monster.

"That's your car? It isn't at all what I imagined you'd be driving."

"No, me neither. It was given to me by my parents so it's better than nothing."

We stood by the car and gave each other a very long hug, neither person wanting to let go. Sarah looked up into my eyes and put her lips in the perfect kissing position so I was happy to seize the opportunity. We eventually let go and said our goodbyes.

"By the way, you're a fantastic kisser," I said. "I look forward to some more of that, hopefully I'll get another chance on Saturday."

"I hope so too. Bye Dean!"

The drive back to Boulder went quickly as I was lost in a world of sensory overload. By the time I pulled up in front of the Zoo, it was almost ten o'clock and things on our street were very quiet, like everyone was already safely snuggled into their warm, comfortable homes. I heard music coming from inside Eric's room and light visible at the bottom of the door so I figured he was probably inside with Tina. I went into the kitchen to make myself a quick bedtime snack and heard the door to his room open.

"Beans, I thought that might be you. How did your evening go with that woman you met this weekend, I'm sorry, I forget her name," Eric said.

"Sarah and it was very nice. She does something to me that makes me feel all wiggly inside, if you know what I mean."

"Kind of and I'd guess that's a pretty good thing."

"Indeed it is. How was your dinner with Tina?"

"Not so good. I hadn't yet told her that Phoebe is flying out from Missouri this weekend. I was hoping I could somehow avoid telling her but she wanted to go camping so I made up something about having other plans. She got all bent out of shape when I told her that I wasn't available to spend time with her. She pressed me for details because apparently she had heard about the Zoo party on Sunday and didn't believe my story about going to visit a friend out in Grand Junction. Well, one thing led to another and eventually I had to tell her the truth."

"How did she take it?"

"Not well. We had just finished our dinner and she left the restaurant before our dessert came. I followed her outside after I paid the bill and she was already walking down the road hitchhiking towards Boulder. I was just about to catch up with her when she got a ride with someone in an old pickup truck. I got in my car and drove to her house but she wasn't there. I have no idea where she went so I just came home."

"Sorry, man, that sounds pretty rough. I can't say as I blame her though, can you?"

"No, I feel like a real jerk. We were having such a great time so it was an unfortunate way to end the evening and maybe even our relationship."

"That sucks. It's pretty tough juggling relationships, especially if your goal is to keep them from knowing about each other. I already told Sarah about Windy, not exactly by choice but since there's a good chance that she'll be coming here next weekend for our party, I didn't want her name to come up and have it be really awkward. She's not too pleased but at least it won't come out as a nasty surprise at an inopportune moment."

"You're not helping me much here, Mungo," Eric said looking a bit hurt. "Did you also tell Sarah about Barbara?"

"No, that would have been incredibly embarrassing but I get your point. I'm not saying I'm perfect or haven't made my share of relationship mistakes, it's just that it's pretty easy to get bitten in the butt if you're not careful. I'm about to head to bed but I was thinking about staying over at the quarry this week. Want to join me?"

"Absolutely! I was thinking about doing the same thing."

CHAPTER 13

WAKING UP ON this Tuesday morning, I quickly tried to anticipate what I would need for the rest of the week, pulled together a bag of stuff, left a note for my housemates and made sure that Eric was ready to go in time. He and I drove up the canyon in his strange muscle car that looked like it should have been parked in one of the fraternity lots. We arrived at the quarry and saw Iggy standing around in front of the office building with the rest of the crew, looking at ease with himself and his new lot in life.

"Good to see you guys," Iggy bellowed from across the parking lot. "Is today the day you guys are finally coming to the nightclub?"

"Tina and I had a big scene over Phoebe's visit this weekend and we aren't currently speaking to each other. The quarry will be a great place to hang out until things blow over a bit," Eric said dejectedly. "How was the nightclub last night?"

"Pretty cool. I think you guys are going to love it! Sorry to hear about you and Tina."

"And I'll be staying over too. All I'll be missing at the Zoo are some cool orgies," I added.

"Great, it will be nice to have you guys up here with me. We've got a few minutes. Why don't you grab your stuff and I'll show you the bunkhouse where you can stash your bags."

Eric and I took our small duffle bags out of his tiny trunk and followed Iggy. Since I had never actually set foot in the bunkhouse before, I wasn't quite sure what to expect. My only associations were of summer camp with the Boy Scouts where we slept on wooden platforms covered with thick canvas tents that smelled like a mix of mold, mildew, mothballs, insect repellent and pre-teenage boy body odor. I associated bunkhouses with the television show *Gomer Pyle* so I was expecting military type quarters with everything neat and tidy, no wrinkles on the sheets and blankets with metal frame beds all neatly aligned and everyone's belongings in perfectly ordered matching geometric piles.

This bunkhouse was a bit more chaotic than my sanitized vision. The beds were the metal frames I had expected but they were set up in a semi-haphazard arrangement. Each of the four corners of the room had been arranged as a private suite with sheets suspended from the ceiling to create personal spaces for the occupants. There were a bunch of additional beds along the remaining wall space and they looked like they had already been claimed. Looking around the interior of the large room, I saw a handful of beds scattered randomly and about half of them were in use. On the far wall was an open door that led to the women's half of the building.

"The corner suites are for the four crew bosses," Iggy explained. "The beds along the walls are for the guys with the most seniority and the beds in the middle are first come first served. Why don't you claim two near me? Just throw your bags on one for now. You'll have time later to arrange things. There are sheets, blankets and pillow cases over in that closet."

We put our stuff on empty beds and left the bunkhouse. All the men from the five crews were already milling around outside and we saw the parade of women coming towards us from the women's bunkhouse. Sugarloaf Sam began his near ear piercing shriek as we entered the office.

"Looks like you guys are finally going to take the plunge," Joan said to Eric and me as she joined the queue into the building. "It's about time!"

"Yeah, Whitey's girlfriend isn't speaking to him at the moment so he thought this might be a good time to check it out," I said as Eric looked at me with sad eyes and a sad mouth.

"That's too bad, Eric. I'm sorry. And what's your story, OD?" she asked.

"Curiosity," I responded, "and to see how closely it resembles the dream I had last week."

We entered the office and took our places. Both Big Larry and Rhonda were moving around the front of the room looking like they were both supercharged with more energy than their bodies could deal with. Apparently, the only way to dissipate it without exploding was to move around quickly so the visual effect was quite comical. Big Larry's head was darting all around the room and he looked down at his clipboard about once every half second while his feet looked like he was dancing the tango in triple time. Maybe he just had to pee really badly. Rhonda was a bit more subdued, moving to a slower tune but her arms were flapping like a duck trying to get airborne. I was worried that something major had happened since yesterday that had them so riled up.

When everyone was settled into their places, Big Larry cleared his throat and started the meeting. "Listen up folks. Today is gonna be a humdinger. Early this mornin', I got a call from a Mister Biff Bojangles from the Colorado Department of Public Health and Safety. He's comin' to the Sugarloaf Quarry this mornin' at 9:30 in response to a complaint his office received about a noise issue. Apparently, one of you, and I'm not namin' names but I have a good idea, called his office last week and told him, and I quote," Big Larry said looking down at his clipboard, "the ambient noise level at the Sugarloaf Quarry may exceed the maximum limit set by OSHA for the occupational noise exposure, regulation 1910.95 of 90 dB for an 8 hour period or 96 dB for a 4 hour period or 115 dB for any time period under one quarter of an hour."

"Excuse me, Big Larry," Eric interrupted, "what's OSHA?"

"Good question, I think it stands for the Obnoxious Shit Head Assholes," Big Larry answered.

"No, it's the Occupational Safety and Health Administration. They're a federal agency that issues regulations on acceptable working conditions across the country that states are required to enforce," Rhonda patiently explained. "Even though Big Larry may not like their regulations, they are designed to protect all of us from unnecessary harm and injury."

"Thank you Rhonda. I've got another question. What's a dB?" Zelda asked.

"It stands for douche bag," Big Larry said. "OSHA standards say there can't be more than 90 douche bags on a job site for more than 8 hours and we're mighty close to the limit."

"Larry, now you're being a douche bag. Zelda, and everyone else, it's the abbreviation for decibels and it's a measure of sound intensity. Apparently, someone complained that the noise might be reaching unsafe levels and if this was the case, we either need to find a way to extract the rock in a quieter way or we need to issue proper hearing protection to our workers, or both. My guess is that most of you wouldn't want to wear big honkin' hot ear muffs most of the time. We have another concern and that's if you can't hear things well, it might become a bigger danger since you might not be able to hear someone yelling at you to get out of the way of somethin' that might knock you on your butt."

"Anyway, Mr. Bojangles is gonna be here this mornin' to investigate. In the future, people, if you have concerns like this, please talk to me or Rhonda first and maybe we can deal with the problem ourselves. Stuff like this just makes more work for all of us. Bojangles said his office took the call on Wednesday so, you three college boys, listen up and listen up good. Don't go pullin' shit like this again. I've got a right mind to fire the lot of you right now."

"You said someone called them on Wednesday?" Eric asked.

"That's right Whitey."

"Just for the record, we didn't even start working up here until Thursday."

"It might not even have been someone who works here. I know of at least one neighbor that's a bit disgruntled about the noise this place generates," I added.

"In that case," Big Larry blustered on while looking around the room, "I'm puttin' the rest of you on notice. Don't go pullin' any more funny stuff, understood?"

"Yeah, except for one thing," Frederick said in a rather timid voice, "if we do have a safety concern, will you listen to it or just ignore us?"

"I'll listen if you have a valid worry," Big Larry responded.

"Then why haven't you done anything about the safety catch on the shaker? We told you about this weeks ago and it still hasn't been fixed. I'd hate to see another accident like the one that happened to Vince," Dickie, the quarry crew chief said. "Is he out of the hospital yet?"

"He's getting out next week," Rhonda responded. "We're still waiting for parts that are being shipped from Ponca City so it's not like we're ignoring your concerns. Trust me on this; we have a big interest in keeping all of you healthy. Not only does it cut into our productivity if you get hurt on the job but it's also bad for morale."

"Rhonda's right. We feel awful about Vince but it was partially his own fault for playin' around on the conveyor belt. True, if the safety gate had been operatin' correctly he wouldn't have been thrown into the shaker but it's also true that if he hadn't been trying to show off for Barbara by conveyor surfin', he wouldn't have gotten hurt in the first place," Big Larry reminded everyone.

"As it was, however, I was quite impressed," Barbara said in her low leopard growl of a voice, "but not so impressed when he went into the shaker. He's fortunate that the emergency shutdown switch was close to where I was standing."

"Alright, I assure you that any complaint or concern any of you have, even from you college boys, will be dealt with like it is comin' directly from the Pope. Now, we've wasted enough time and we've got a lot of work ahead of us today. If there is any way to keep the noise down while Bojangles is here, do it. Dickie, are you doin' any blasting today?"

"We can wait off until later in the afternoon if you'd like," he responded.

"That would be helpful. Zelda, do you have enough sorted material for the day?"

"I think so. We did a lot of work yesterday so I was planning on spending most of the day loading up trucks for deliveries, if that's what you would like," she responded.

"That's right. I think everyone else knows their assignments. Landscaping should continue on the front entrance way, Rhonda and the BAP crew should continue on with their netting project, maintenance is working on the monthly sorter machine regreasing and Quesnal, you have all your delivery work orders so I think we're good to fly. Oh, one more thing, you all remember Tuesday nights are talent night and I think we've got two rookies joining us this evenin', am I right boys?" Big Larry asked looking at Eric and me.

"Talent night?" I asked nervously.

"That's right rookie. Be thinkin' about your talents, known, unknown, undiscovered, unbeknownst and otherwise. But don't think about it too hard 'cause, after all, it's the Quarry Nightclub!" Big Larry said sounding much happier than a few minutes ago. "Let's get out there before the day slips away from us and get some work done. I'll be meetin' shortly with Bojangles and take him on a tour of the quarry. Just do your jobs to the best of your abilities and try to do it as quietly as possible. Grab your lunches on the way out!"

Everyone started leaving the building except for Juan Antonio and Barbara who walked over and intercepted Eric and I before we got out the door. Juan Antonio had a serious look on his face that wasn't very different from his usual look so I wasn't too concerned. Barbara, on the other hand, had a huge ear-to-ear grin on hers and this definitely did concern me.

"You guys should have picked a different night than tonight to come to the nightclub. Any night would have been better than Tuesday," Juan Antonio said with genuine concern.

"Oh, don't be such a Nervous Nellie, Juan Antonio," Barbara said as she approached. "These boys can probably handle themselves pretty well. At least I know Dean can." Barbara gave me a wink and leaned in close to me to whisper into my ear, "I'm still pretty horny today. Maybe we can get another job to do, just the two of us."

"Beans, you're blushing, man!" Iggy cried out as he witnessed this interaction. "Come on; share your little secret with the rest of us!"

"Sorry, no can do. I've been sworn to secrecy under the articles of the Woodstock Accords of '69," I said. "To violate those articles would result in having all of my tie dye shirts confiscated."

"Hey, Barbara," Big Larry yelled over from the other side of the room, "stop botherin' those boys and herd them out to pasture!"

"Aye aye captain," Barbara said coming to full attention, giving Big Larry a salute and clicking her heels together. She started walking towards the door, exaggerating each step by swiveling her hips from side to side and thrusting her deliciously wiggly boobs in the same direction. "Come on boys and follow me to the Promised Land!"

"That's more like it!" Big Larry said.

The BAP crew met in the parking lot to discuss our strategy. Since the ropes and climbing gear had already been purchased and the rotting wood was safely stockpiled, there were a few remaining details that needed to be completed.

"Let's discuss the support structure design and the bird-proof netting," Rhonda began as we gathered around her. "Big Larry and I agreed that the structure needed to be really light so it would be easy to handle during installation. We came up with the idea of using small diameter PVC pipes and elbows that can be glued together easily in place. You should be able to handle it while you're on the ropes and won't need any special tools for assembly other than a jar of glue and a brush. We can assemble the individual sections up at the top of the quarry and lower them down the cliff. How does that sound?"

"How will the structure be anchored to the rock?" I asked.

"Since each intersection of pipes will form a 'T' at the base and then have a section that leads to a 90 degree bend to keep the structure about a foot off the rock wall, these base intersections create a perfect point for attachment. If we drill anchors into the rock at each of these points, we can use nylon webbing to attach each pipe intersection," Rhonda explained.

"Can you draw us a sketch? I'm not sure I'm visualizing this," I said.

"Good idea because I'm not following this either," Barbara admitted as Juan Antonio nodded his head.

Rhonda used her foot to smooth out a section of the dirt and then squatted down as far as her short jean shorts would allow without having them disappear entirely. Using her finger, she drew her concept in the dirt. Since she was limited to two dimensions, three if she drew in perspective, which she didn't, it wasn't helping me to get clarity. When Rhonda saw the blank look on our faces, she decided to use her body to demonstrate. She stood up, held her arms straight out to either side and then bent her elbows so that her forearms were facing towards us, parallel to the ground.

"Imagine that I am the structure, my upper arms are the horizontal pipes and are parallel to the rock wall, my elbows are the 90 degree bends in the pipes and my forearms are the pipes that head towards the rock. Dean, use your arms to be the base of the structure. Here, come up behind me good and tight."

I stood behind her, keeping a respectful distance so that we weren't quite touching and held out my arms so they were straight out on either side of her and then bent my elbows so that my hands were pointing straight up. It was a comical position to be in, like two mimes stuck in a glass box.

"Press in tight so that your arms are in the right position," Rhonda commanded authoritatively.

As I got as close to her backside as possible, I realized that not only was it not going to work but I became embarrassed by the position that we were in.

"How about if I do this from the front?" I suggested. "It's certainly nice back here but I think we would have to be dating for me to get any closer."

"Is that all you ever think about?" Rhonda asked sounding exasperated.

"Yes."

"Me too," Barbara chimed in.

"Yeah, me too," Juan Antonio added.

"Christ! Okay, come around to the front and stand facing me," Rhonda suggested as we assumed a new position.

"Now I get it," Barbara said with a new found enthusiasm "but I want Dean and Juan Antonio to come demonstrate on me. Juan Antonio, you get behind me good and tight and Dean, I want you in the front, also good and tight. When I say go, squeeze me from both sides until I say to stop. Don't stop until I say so, got it?"

"I don't think that will be necessary, Barbara," Rhonda said, throwing a wet blanket on our party before it had a chance to get started. "Let's talk about the netting next. According to the information we gathered yesterday, I think the best rock wall is Number 4. It's the highest and I think because of that it will be the most appealing to the gnats. Our calculations showed that it's a bit narrower and not quite as high as the other three. We don't need to cover the entire wall. I found the supplies we need down at an agricultural supply business east of Denver. They have orchard netting that is designed to keep birds away from the fruit so this will be perfect. We can get rolls of the stuff in a variety of lengths and widths to meet our needs. There's also a place down near there that's a wholesale supplier of PVC pipe so after I do some calculations of how much we need, we'll each drive a pickup truck down to pick this stuff up. One more trip to the climbing supply store to get anchors and webbing and we'll be all set. Are all of you comfortable driving a fully loaded truck on the highway?"

We all nodded so Rhonda gave us keys to the trucks she wanted each of us to drive. Each set had the license plate number on a plastic tag attached to the key ring. "Go find your truck, make sure the beds are empty, if they're not, put the tools in the tool shed, get four tie-down straps each, fill each one up with gas over by the scales and then bring them over here. I've got to go into the office to calculate out the piping and I'll meet you all back here."

We followed her orders and got all of the trucks ready to go. Each of them had the Sugarloaf Quarry logo on the sides but none had the fake rocks on the roof. These were only on the two quarry cars. We had the trucks lined up ready to go when Rhonda came out of the office and asked if someone would go do the same thing to her truck. Juan Antonio volunteered and she threw him her set of keys.

"I just need a few more minutes to double check these numbers. I'll be ready to go as soon as you get back with my truck," she said.

After the dust from the truck settled, Barbara came over to where I was leaning against one of the trucks. "How was your night last night?"

"Quite interesting. I drove down to Denver to have drinks with Sarah, the actress that I met this weekend up in Georgetown."

"Is that the same woman that sexy Iggy mentioned during the morning meeting yesterday?"

"Yep, that's her. She was in Denver with a bunch of people from her theatre troupe to do a radio interview so we met at a hotel afterwards."

"Did you get frisky with her?"

"Do you mean, did we have sex?"

"Yes, did you get frisky with her and have sex?"

"No, not even close. I've only seen her twice now and both times were in groups of other people so we haven't really had any private time."

"Well, you were well primed after our afternoon experience, if you know what I mean."

"Yes, I do. That's a pretty good strategy."

"When Ritchie and I were first married, he would frequently pleasure himself before we'd go to bed so that he wasn't quite so eager and trigger happy when we made love that night. It worked; I'm still with him partially because he is such a good lover."

"I'm happy for you. Like I said yesterday, he's a lucky man!"

Rhonda came out of the building and said she needed to grab something out of the supply building. Meanwhile, Barbara asked me if I had any ideas about what I could perform for talent night tonight.

"Are you all being serious? Talent night? This makes me really nervous. I'm not much of a performer. My father used to make all of us kids do some sort of family performance periodically. While my sisters used to ad lib some sort of song or dance, my claim to fame or infamy was to try to tell jokes. I was the only one that saw any humor in them and my problem was that I would dissolve into a heap of uncontrollable laughter before I would get to a punch line that probably wasn't even funny in the first place. What kinds of things do other people do?"

"Things you just mentioned, songs, dances, play instruments, little skits, things like that. Maybe you could team up with Iggy and Eric to do a skit about what it's like to be a college student and be having sex with so many different women. I'll take a load off your mind; you really don't need to worry about it because at the nightclub, things just happen spontaneously. You'll have so many creative ideas that the challenge will be to decide which one to go with," Barbara said somewhat reassuringly. "Everyone's a performer, the nightclub will bring it out in you and you'll have a very appreciative audience."

Juan Antonio came driving back with Rhonda's truck and Rhonda reemerged from the supply building around the same time. "Let's head out. Follow me and make sure you don't let me out of your sight. I'll wait if any of you get stuck at red lights but here's the route we'll be taking. From Boulder, we'll drive south on 36 to I-25 south, then east on I-70 to exit 280. Try to remember this if you get lost but it's a pretty straightforward route. Got it?"

"I think so, I don't get out of the area too much so just make sure that you don't lose me," Barbara said. "My husband's got some relatives that live out in Punkin Center so we've driven the route that you describe a few times."

"I'll try to stay close to everyone else," Juan Antonio added. "36 to 25 to 70, exit 280."

Our four-truck caravan finally left the quarry. To anyone who saw us coming or going, it must have looked a bit strange, four matching pickup trucks traveling in parade formation, all with pictures on the doors of a smiling rodent in a tuxedo and the words "Sugarloaf Quarry" written underneath his stool. We drove down the canyon through Boulder, down the highway to Denver and arrived at our destination in a few hours without losing anyone. At the agricultural supply store parking lot, Rhonda told us to sit tight while she went inside. When she came out a little while later with a sheet of paper in her hand, she motioned for us to follow her in our trucks. We drove around to the side of the building and approached an area with pallets containing rolls of orchard netting. Each pile was marked and she stopped near one that said "40 x 150".

"We're going to get two of these large rolls. That will give us the netting we need to cover all of Wall 4. I think both rolls will fit in the bed of one truck so let's load them into mine."

Juan Antonio and I were easily able to lift a roll off the stack and place it in Rhonda's truck as long as we had the rear gate in the down position. The second one fit on top nicely and we used the straps we brought and the tie down hooks inside the bed of the truck to secure the load.

"This is excellent," Rhonda remarked. "Our next stop is a few miles down the road at a plumbing supply warehouse to pick up the PVC pipe. Follow me."

A short distance down the highway was a large rectangular and featureless metal industrial building with a sign out front that said "Colorado Plumbing Supplies". Rhonda went in and out quickly and then motioned for us to follow her again. We drove around to one of the loading docks and waited as six forklift loads of bundled PVC pipes were dropped off at the edge. Two bundles were put into each of the remaining three trucks and then secured tightly.

"Good math skills, there Rhonda. How did you know that these six loads would fit so well?" I asked.

"Simple volume calculations. It was easy to calculate the volume of each truck; the big unknown was how much space the netting and the pipe bundles would take up. Luckily, when I called each supplier, they knew the dimensions of each bundle so it was easy to figure out how many trucks we would need."

"Is there any chance we could stop for an early lunch before we head back to the quarry? I'm feeling a bit hungry and I noticed a cool looking diner a little ways back," Barbara said.

"Did you forget to get your lunch bag from Bunny this morning?" Rhonda asked.

"No, I've got it inside my truck. I just thought it would be a fun thing to do for a change since we're already down here and it's on our way. What do you think?" Barbara asked.

"You'd be on your own to pay for it," Rhonda warned, "since I know Big Larry wouldn't cover the cost. Do you guys want to go?"

"Well, I already ate all of my snacks and started on my lunch on the drive down here," I said, "so that's a yes vote for me."

"Yeah, me too," added Juan Antonio, "I already ate both of my snacks."

"For lightweights, you two sure eat a lot! I wouldn't mind if we stopped for a short while," Rhonda said, "but only for a short while, understand?"

Our motley crew, driving matching trucks and wearing gender specific matching outfits followed Barbara's truck as she pulled into the diner we passed on our way to the plumbing supply place. The sign out front said "The Little Baby Jesus Diner" but their slogan underneath had me feeling a bit uneasy. Maybe it was because I knew we weren't in Boulder anymore, maybe it was the way we were all dressed, maybe it was the way Rhonda and Barbara looked, maybe it was the way that I looked but for some reason, when I saw "Food for the God Fearing—Best Eats in All of His Earthly Kingdom", I wasn't certain this was the right place for us.

We found four parking places scattered around out in the back lot. I waited behind Rhonda's truck while Juan Antonio and Barbara maneuvered their trucks into the two far parking spots. I was hesitant to go in alone so waited until we could all go in together.

"Rhonda, I'm not sure about this place," I ventured as she pulled herself out of the driver's seat exposing about three feet of naked legs that seemed to end somewhere around her exposed belly.

"Why, are you a sinner?" she joked.

"Absolutely but as an atheist, I don't need to worry too much about that."

"What is it that worries you, OD?"

"I think we've somehow landed smack dab in the middle of the Bible Belt and I'm not too sure these kind folks are gonna take much of a shine to us," I said in a southern accent.

"This place looks great!" Barbara said loudly as she and Juan Antonio joined our twosome. "Let's go see what's on the menu!"

When I was a youngster, I was force fed religion and hated every second of it. I was given no choice but to attend church with my family every Sunday, even made to become an acolyte where I had to be at church every Sunday for the seven o'clock service and then wait around until the eleven o'clock service that my family attended "religiously". My mom was in the choir, as were my sisters when they were old enough to graduate from the kid's choir that performed at nine. My dad was an usher. I hated having to put on the layered, voluminous robes to be an acolyte. I hated having to walk around slowly with a pious look on my face. I didn't do pious too well. I hated having to change into a jacket and tie for the later service. I hated waiting around in between services and then there was all the kneeling and sitting still and the organ and the long silences and trying not to fart too loudly or giggle. I had a lot of excess energy stored up in my body and church was just the wrong sort of place for me. This was Sunday, after all. My day was tied up from six in the morning to about one in the afternoon. I wanted to be outside riding my bike or playing with my friends. I wanted to be doing almost anything other than being at church. I actually hoped that I would get deathly sick on Sunday mornings followed by a miraculous recovery right after the rest of my family left for church. I think I might have gotten away with this once so the thought was always in my head.

About half way through the eleven o'clock service, all the kids were excused to head off to church school while the adults stayed behind for the sermon. I'm not sure which one was worse. Church school was run by well meaning but poorly equipped adults whose unenviable task was to educate us adolescents in the way of God. Only one or two of the girls in our class paid any attention, the rest of us spent the entire time trying to make the others laugh so uncontrollably that either we wet our pants or got punished for being disruptive and had to stand in front of the class and read some sort of poignant passage from the Bible. I was usually the one that wet his pants since I found almost everything to be extremely humorous, especially crudely drawn pictures that my friend Dean of the Double Dean Wheelie Club would create on notebook paper and slip to me showing something like Baby Jesus wearing a diaper with devil horns, tail and pitchfork riding his bike over a cliff while yelling, "Get me the hell out of here!"

However, my one way ticket out of the religious life was simple and clearly laid out by my father—once you went through Confirmation, you were considered an adult in the eyes of the Lord and could decide for yourself which religious path to take. My older sister went through months of rigorous training, on Sunday's during church school but also one night during the week and it seemed like she did this for years. She eventually got confirmed and chose to continue going to church, which surprised the hell out of me. Why anyone would chose this option was beyond my comprehension. When it was my turn, I saw this process as a bitter pill to swallow but the rewards far outweighed the costs in the long run.

When I became a seventh grader in the fall of 1967, I saw the light at the end of the tunnel and it wasn't an oncoming train or the white light of the heavenly glow. By the spring of 1968, I knew I had a good chance to become a free man, free to make my own choices and start living the carefree life of the devout atheist. Our church happened to be in a transitional time in the fall of 1967 as the only priest our church had known during my lifetime announced that he was leaving to accept a bishop's position elsewhere. His congregation bid him a fond but sad adieu and immediately set about the task of finding a suitable replacement. As September rolled around, the time that Confirmation classes were set to begin for twenty five of us seventh graders, there wasn't anyone around to indoctrinate us. Weeks rolled by, then months and our traditional Confirmation ceremony was rapidly approaching without any of us having attended a single class. Panic must have set in with the church deacons so they quickly assembled a volunteer team to give us kids a crash course on how to transition from children of God to young, Confirmed adults of God. I think maybe we met as a group two or three times in total and the volunteer team was in such disarray that in the end, they simply asked us one question. No tests had to be taken, no memorization of Bible verses, no loyalty oaths, no blood lettings, no animal sacrifices, they simply brought each of us before them one by one, in front of the entire class and asked us if we believed in God. If you said yes, you passed, if you said no, your future looked bleak. In my case, my future would be to continue going to church until I was old enough to run away from home with a red bandana loaded with Pop Tarts attached to a stick searching for the nearest train tracks.

The Confirmation Team was working their way through the alphabet and was getting all of the expected answers from everyone from A through the early M's. My name was called and I went up in front of the table full of parents I had known my entire life. They asked me if I believed in God. I said yes without a second of hesitation and other than the actual Confirmation service to formalize our passage, I never set foot inside another church again. Free at last! It was almost enough to make me believe in God.

For some reason, as the four of us quarry-people were walking towards the Little Baby Jesus Diner, I felt like I was heading back into church, against my will, figuratively kicking and screaming. My stomach was in knots but since Barbara was so gung ho about this place, maybe she would run interference for the rest of us. I kind of felt like maybe I owed her one.

"There's a diner like this in Loveland. Maybe it's part of a chain. My family and I go there almost every Sunday after church," Barbara announced as we approached the main entrance.

"Is it called the Little Baby Jesus Diner?" Juan Antonio asked.

"No, it's called the Search for the Holy Grill but it looks pretty similar."

We entered the diner and waited at the hostess stand for someone to seat us. The lunchtime noise that was rebounding around the diner immediately stopped when we entered. All eyes turned towards us. I imagined the four of us standing there looked like maybe the circus was in town. One kid dropped his fork while another knocked over her glass of milk. The scene wasn't like anything I had ever seen in Colorado before, more like what I pictured a diner in deep, rural Alabama might look like. There were farmers and ranchers dressed how you would imagine but the rest of the customers were all dressed up for a Tuesday lunch. Eventually, after standing in the front of the diner for a little while, a hostess came over and asked us how many in our party. Thankfully, the gift of gab seemed to return to everyone already seated and they went back to their meals.

"Just the four of us," Rhonda said.

"Are you folks part of a traveling singing group?" she asked.

"Uh, no, why do you ask?" Rhonda replied while I started warming my voice up with a 'me me me me' only to get my foot stepped on by Rhonda by the fourth 'me'.

"I guess I would have to say that it's the way you're all dressed alike, like maybe you were on your way to a performance or something."

"No, we all work up at the Sugarloaf Quarry near Boulder and are just passing through here to pick up some supplies," Rhonda explained with a touch of irritation. "Can we get a table?"

"By all means, darlin'," the waitress answered sweetly. "Do you prefer the 'Fire and Brimstone' or the 'Earthly Delights' section?"

DAVID W. GOODWIN

CHAPTER 14

"LET'S TAKE THE 'Fire and Brimstone' section," Barbara responded in her deep voice, taking a step out from behind Rhonda before she had a chance to answer. "This is just like the Search for the Holy Grill! My family always sits in the 'Fire and Brimstone' section."

"You've been there, hon?" the waitress asked Barbara.

"All the time!"

"They're owned by the same person. The Holy Grill was so successful that the owner decided to open up this place a while ago and has plans for another one down in Pueblo."

"What's the difference between the two sections?" Rhonda asked suspiciously.

"The 'Earthly Delights' section is just if you want desserts and coffee, you know, things like that. The 'Fire and Brimstone' section is if you want full meals and alcohol. You can break any one of the commandments except for killing or stealing in that part of the diner. However, if you break two or more, you have to go to confession. See that booth over there? That's where Father Lola sits and will see you on your way out, if you've been naughty," the waitress explained.

She pointed in the direction of the confessional booth and a person, dressed like a priest but clearly an older woman, bent out of the booth and waved at us with a big angelic smile on her face like maybe she had already broken a few commandments herself today. I would have been hard pressed to even name more than two or three of them (given the non-rigorous nature of my Confirmation training) but luckily for me, on almost every available wall surface of the diner were large posters with all ten listed in order. To complement this, the motif of the place was all Baby Jesus. There were crèche scenes of all shapes, sizes and depictions; some small enough to fit on little end tables, some large ones occupying corner spaces that were almost life-size and even a few paintings of the Baby Himself, one on black velvet and another that appeared to be autographed by some blasphemer. Each booth had the name of one of the apostles written on a plaque on the wall next to it which undoubtedly helped the waitresses to identify the tables and also gave the customers a chance to pick favorites.

"Do you have a preference? Looks like we have John, Paul, and Bartholomew open at the moment, and of course, Judas Iscariot. It seems that the only folks that ever want that booth are teenage boys hell-bent on sinnin'."

"What about the Ringo booth?" I asked.

"There is no Ringo booth," the waitress told me. "Do you know how many times people ask me that?"

When Rhonda said that we didn't have a preference, she took us over to the Bartholomew booth. This would have been my choice if I'd had some time to weigh the options more carefully. It had the Three Wise Guys arranged in a processional across the far end of the table and it looked like they were bendable, like Gumby, and I thought that we could have some fun playing with them.

Our waitress was a woman named Marge, clearly written in script embroidery thread above her breast pocket. She came over to our table and handed us our menus with a heavenly smile like maybe she was about to audition for a job as a tele-evangelist. "Praise the Lord! Have any of you gotten any black marks in heaven yet today?" she asked.

When I was a young boy, there were these two red headed girls that were my neighbors. Our backyards abutted each other and since I played in mine a lot as did Donna and Mary Ann, our paths crossed fairly frequently. These girls were raised in a very strict Catholic family and always wore matching dresses with full petticoats so the bottom parts of their dresses flared wildly out below their tiny waists and showed a lot of their little pink, freckly stick legs. They were often outside playing with their dolls or playing house or some other domestic girl play. I would sometimes go over to their yard to check on what they were up to as it seemed very foreign to me even though I had three sisters of my own. They wore these dresses regardless of the weather; during the hot and sticky New Jersey summer or the cold and snowy winter.

Mary Ann was my age and Donna was a year older. My guess is that Mary Ann and I were in second or third grade at the time. Now, to my way of thinking, the only reason a girl would wear a dress like this was so that boys would pull them up in order to see what was underneath. They never really seemed to mind me doing this so I did it a lot. They always wore very interesting underwear with lots of frills on their little heinies. One day, they must have recently picked up a new expression at church because after I had lifted their dresses a few times, Donna said to me, "Dean, that's another black mark in heaven for you!"

I just assumed this must be a good thing. If my name was in heaven and I got a mark next to it, black, white, red or whatever, it must mean that I was doing something noteworthy. I continued with the dress lifting for many weeks before news of my behavior finally reached my parents. It was my dad that explained that black marks were a bad thing, much to my dismay, and that I should immediately cease and desist. I was reluctant to let go of this behavior so figured I'd risk the black marks.

I quickly scanned the menu and wasn't too surprised to see some of the names of the meals. I mean, how could you call yourself the Little Baby Jesus Diner and not carry the concept all the way through?

"What do you recommend, Barbara?" Juan Antonio asked after we had a few moments with the choices. "I'm trying to decide between the Manger Tuna Melt, the Beans and Franks-in-sense and Saint Andrew's Anchovy Pizza."

"Those are all good. My youngest daughter always gets the Beans and Franks-in-sense but I usually have either the Last Supper Special or the Great Gospel Goulash, depending upon the weather."

"I think I'm going to get the Saint John's Jumpin' Jambalaya,' Rhonda said. "That's usually a pretty good dish, if they make it right. What are you going to order, OD?"

"I've narrowed it down to the Bible Baloney Sandwich, Heavenly Hash with Ham, Christ's Blood Sausage Sub Sandwich or the Angel Hair Pasta Special of the Day, depending on the weather," I responded, teasing Barbara a little.

Marge returned with four glasses of water and asked if we were ready to order. Juan Antonio decided to ignore Barbara's advice and got a small Saint Andrew's Anchovy Pizza with peppers and onions while the rest of us were forced to make up our minds quickly. Since the Angel Hair Pasta Special of the Day was artichokes with black olives, I decided to give it a try.

We were settling into our booth and taking in our bizarre surroundings. Barbara pointed out a few of the more subtle accoutrements of the diner that we missed like the halos around the overhead light fixtures and the numbers of various favorite Bible verses on the floor tiles.

Juan Antonio said that he needed to use the men's room and asked if anyone noticed where it was located.

"Go back around the right end of the lunch counter," Barbara said while pointing in the general direction. "Just make sure you know the difference between the silhouette of a monk and a nun!"

Marge brought the ice teas we ordered and took a second to sit down in the space vacated by Juan Antonio. "I'm not supposed to sit down on the job but I need a second to rest. It's not easy being on my feet all day. Do you mind if I join you folks for a moment?" she asked.

"Not at all. Take all the time you need," Rhonda said.

"We don't get many customers from Boulder down here. I have to say that most folks think that everyone who lives up there is a deviant drug crazed hippie. You people look rather normal, well, except for the matching outfits and maybe you," Marge said pointing at me.

"Thanks, I'm touched. My friends would tease me mercilessly if they thought that I didn't look like a deviant drug crazed hippie," I said. "Even though I am."

"He's just kidding Marge," Rhonda said giving me a kick under the table and a stern look when Marge wasn't looking at her. "Always a jokester!"

"Do people really run around on the streets without any clothes on?" Marge asked and I honestly couldn't tell if she was being serious.

"If they did, I might try to get my husband to move there with me," Barbara responded. "Seriously, where do you hear things like this?"

"From customers."

"What else do you hear?" Rhonda asked.

"Oh, things like the mayor is the biggest drug dealer in Colorado and that there are orgies on almost every street corner, you know, stuff like that."

"It's true about the orgies but I think the mayor's drug dealer ranking has slipped a few notches this past term," I said. "The city council didn't get their pay raises so money's a little tight now."

"Dean, stop! No, Marge, Boulder is a city with a lot of college kids running around but it really isn't that different from most college towns. Have you ever been there?" Rhonda asked.

"No, my husband won't let us go near the place. I think he's afraid of getting sucked into a life of sex and drugs, like the moment you cross the town line you become instantly addicted. So that's not true?" she asked sweetly.

DAVID W. GOODWIN

"You should visit sometime. I think you'd be surprised how normal it is," Rhonda said.

"I'll think about it. I guess I better get back to work," Marge said as Juan Antonio returned.

"I guessed wrong on the first door," Juan Antonio said with a touch of embarrassment. "Both of them appeared to be wearing dresses so it was hard to tell which one was the monk. I finally figured out that the monk had the beard because both of them looked like they were bald. Why do they make it so confusing? Why not just say 'Men' and 'Women'?"

"Did you see anything?" I asked.

"Just an old lady brushing her hair in front of the mirror," he replied.

"Praise Jesus!" I said. "So, since we're in the 'Fire and Brimstone' section, we get to break one of the remaining eight commandments. Which one should we focus on?"

All ten were on the wall next to our booth so we glanced over to remind ourselves what they were although my sense was that Barbara probably knew them all, in order.

"Usually, when we're at the Holy Grill, my daughters break number five, in jest of course, and say something mean about their father and me like 'My father and mother are total morons'. We all have a good laugh and then they tell us how much they love us. It really is kind of a fun game to play because it brings us all closer together," Barbara said.

"How about if one of us commits adultery?" I asked.

"That would be a little tricky since Barbara's the only one here that's married," Rhonda said. "Juan Antonio, you're not married, are you?"

"No, definitely not."

"What do you say Barbara?" I asked with exaggerated lasciviousness as I put my arm around her and licked her ear.

"Not today, sorry kid," Barbara said with a giggle, quickly putting me in my place.

"I think we should pretend to covet someone else's meal," Rhonda suggested.

"Or make a graven image in Juan Antonio's pizza. It could become a big tourist attraction. Pilgrims would flock from around the world to the Little Baby Jesus Diner just to see the Anchovy Pizza with an image of the Virgin Mary in it. That would be really cool!" I said. "They would see a huge increase in their business, depending on the weather."

"Okay, Dean, I think you've killed that joke," Rhonda admonished.

"We could bear false witness against one of our booth neighbors and accuse them of stealing our ketchup bottle," Juan Antonio suggested.

Our conversation was interrupted by Marge as she brought our meals so our foray into the world of commandment breaking was interrupted, at least for the time being. I noticed that Father Lola had left her confessional booth and was heading in our direction. I hoped and prayed she was heading somewhere else but it was clear she was coming over to see us. I told Juan Antonio to quickly rearrange the toppings on his pizza to look like Jesus' mom and gave him a couple of olives from my dish to help out.

"Have you decided which Commandment you would like to break today?" Father Lola asked very sincerely as she positioned herself at the end of our table. "It's not mandatory that you break one but since I hear that you people are from Boulder, it seems likely that you'll want to."

"Well, Father Lola," I began, "we've toyed around with numbers two, seven and ten but I got shot down on the adultery one. Are you running any Commandment-breaking specials today?"

"No my son but we get a lot of number nines broken with people falsely accusing their neighbor of some heinous crime, all in the name of fun, mind you," Father Lola responded.

"And which one do you rarely see broken?" Juan Antonio asked stalling for time to work on his pizza creation when Father Lola wasn't looking.

"I would have to say we've seen some pretty creative things on almost all of the rest."

"Did you notice the image that miraculously appeared on Juan Antonio's pizza?" I asked her.

Father Lola looked down at the pizza and saw a very crudely arranged image of what looked to me like a sea creature, maybe even a sea monkey. It had olives for eyes, an anchovy nose, several pepper slices for a mouth and onions arranged around the face that were supposed to look like hair. Given the short timeframe that Juan Antonio had to work with, he did a pretty good job.

"Sweet Mother of God!" Father Lola yelled out so that everyone in the diner could hear. "Everyone, the Virgin Mary has appeared on this man's pizza!"

People emptied out of their booths and came over to look at the face on the pizza, even the people sitting on stools at the lunch counter. There

DAVID W. GOODWIN

was a crowd of twenty or so gathered around Juan Antonio's pizza and this generated much excitement.

"I think it looks more like Joseph than Mary," one diner offered.

"Or Ed Sullivan," said another.

"Or Topo Gigio, the Little Italian Mouse," observed someone else.

"Did your pizza actually come this way or did you do some arranging?" Marge asked Juan Antonio after she had a good look. "It didn't look that way when I brought it over. I would have noticed."

Juan Antonio sheepishly admitted that he had arranged the face in order to break Commandment number two.

"Well, that technically doesn't break it since you weren't really making any graven images but we'll count it as your one free pass. Anything else you do will now count against you," Marge said, laying down the rules. "Understand, you sodomites?"

"Sodomites! How dare you call us sodomites!" Rhonda said angrily as the crowd dispersed.

"It's only a figure of speech here, hon. Just a little Little Baby Jesus Diner humor. We call each other sodomites just to be funny. Please, don't be offended," Marge said kindly.

"Yeah, I should have warned you all about this before we came in," Barbara explained. "Humorous insults are definitely a part of the scene here."

"Well, okay, but given the talk about Boulder and all, I took it as a personal insult. However, if you didn't mean it in that way, I'll let it slide," Rhonda said.

Things eventually calmed down and we finished our meals without any further incidents or Commandment breaking. Marge came back and asked if we would like to see the dessert menu but we passed. She produced our bill and we each threw in enough money to cover it. On our way out of the diner, Father Lola stuck her head out of the confessional. "Nice try there Boulderites. That was a good one! Hope to see you again sometime!"

We sauntered back to our loaded trucks and retraced our morning route in reverse, arriving back at the Sugarloaf Quarry during the middle part of the afternoon. Things were unusually quiet and then I remembered about the visit from Biff Bojangles. The usual racket and dust that was a normal part of quarry life was almost completely absent, you could actually carry on a normal conversation in the parking lot. Before leaving the Little Baby Jesus Diner, Rhonda instructed us to meet near the greenhouses when we arrived at the quarry where we would be doing the preliminary assembly work since it was one of the few places that was level and open.

As I drove through the parking area near the office building, Rhonda stopped and motioned for the rest of us to continue driving back to the greenhouses to unload our supplies. Standing beside the far end of the office building, I saw Big Larry having a discussion with a tall, slender man wearing industrial-type clothing that I assumed was Mr. Biff. Biggie's head came up about to his armpits but only because I think he was wearing his cowboy boots with three inch heels.

We unloaded the pipe bundles from the trucks but my thoughts were on the diner and how a place like that would have gone over in Boulder. Probably not too well unless it was even more outrageous than the place we had just been and that would have been a tall order.

Rhonda pulled up in her truck and we unloaded the netting. She whipped out a small notepad that was in the back pocket of her jean shorts, consulted a few pages filled with her calculations and looked at her watch.

"We've got about an hour and a half left in the workday. Why don't we take a short break and then we'll regroup and I'll explain our first assembly task?"

"Sounds good to me," Juan Antonio said. "Even though I ate the entire face of the Blessed Mother, she didn't really fill me up! I could use another snack."

"How does it feel to have her in your belly?" I asked.

"A little funny but the idea of having Topo Gigio in there is even less appealing."

Afterwards, we spent some time cutting PVC pipe and gluing elbows to form the beginnings of the framework. The work day came to an end so we jumped back into the trucks and drove down to the office building. It was a funny feeling I had about going to the nightclub, I almost wanted to keep it stored inside my brain as the experience I had in my dream. Like any kid growing up in the 60's, I had some fairly lofty expectations that never quite lived up to the hype.

As a young teenage boy, I really liked the Monkees, both the TV show and their music. I had all of their albums and hardly ever missed an episode of their show on Wednesday nights at eight. I ended up quitting the Boy Scouts, much to my father's dismay, because our troop changed their meeting night to Wednesdays and I really hated to miss the

　　　DAVID W. GOODWIN

show. I had worked my way up the ladder from the Cub Scouts to the Boy Scouts, starting as a Tenderfoot, then Second Class and was about to make First Class. The troop leaders then decided to change the night that we met and I was very upset, you might even say distraught. I much preferred to watch the antics of Micky, Davy, Peter and Mike to the dull tasks of making rope quoits or carving neckerchief slides out of balsa wood or playing Steal-the-Bacon in the gym when the weather was bad. The bottom line was that I really hated wearing a uniform and having to follow a strict set of behavioral guidelines. Missing the Monkees was the last straw.

In order to get out of the Boy Scouts as quickly as possible, I had to come up with a really good excuse. I couldn't tell my father that I wanted to quit because the meetings conflicted with a TV show because, first, it sounded really lame and second, he never would have allowed it. My being a Boy Scout was as much about fulfilling his need for his only son to lead a normal boy's life and do normal boy things, activities he probably never had the chance to do as a youngster but would have liked to do if they had been options in his depression-era childhood. Instead, I had to concoct a complex story that would be water tight. Eventually, I settled on a scenario that involved being bullied by the bigger, older boys since I was unusually small for my age (only somewhat true), my intolerance of winter camping due to a complete absence of any body fat and proper equipment (totally and completely true) and a growing fondness for dressing up in girls clothes (an almost total fabrication). It must have broken his heart but he let me quit and had to radically re-evaluate his hopes and expectations for me from that moment onward.

I got to watch the Monkees, I got to listen to the Monkees on the albums I bought using money that I saved from my allowance and supplemented with income from my burgeoning lawn mowing, leaf raking and snow shoveling businesses. The only one real thing left to complete the total Monkees experience was the MonkeeMobile. This was the 1966 Pontiac GTO convertible that was customized with a bunch of body enhancements, a third row of seats where the trunk had been and the cool Monkees logo on the sides in the shape of an electric guitar, even cooler than the Sugarloaf Sam logo. My heart started pumping pretty hard when I heard about the Kellogg's TV Screen-Stakes contest you could enter every time you bought specially marked boxes of Rice Krispies or Raisin Bran, two types of cereal that I loved anyway. I begged my mom to buy as many of these boxes as possible when she shopped at the local

A&P every Saturday so I could use the form on the side to enter the contest multiple times. The first place prize was a brand new 1968 GTO convertible and a guest appearance on the show that one person would win. The second place prizes were fifteen 1968 GTO hardtops while third place was the latest, yet-to-be released Monkees LP and there were going to be fifteen hundred of them. Fourth place was three thousand scale replicas of the MonkeeMobile.

I must have entered the contest twenty times over the course of the time that it ran. My odds of winning one of the prizes seemed pretty good and I started becoming a serious daydream believer that I would win one of the prizes; even fourth place would be really cool. I waited and waited, knowing that once the contest closed on August 31st of 1967, it would only be a matter of days before I was notified what I won. I imagined there was even a good possibility that I might win more than one of the prizes. Weeks went by and then months and I hadn't heard anything at all about the contest. My disappointment grew with each passing day. Then, one day as I walked into my house after school in the winter sometime, my mother came running up to me with a shoebox-sized box addressed to me festooned with Monkees logos.

"Look what came in the mail for you today, Dean!" she said with genuine excitement, knowing my obsession all to well.

I tore it open quickly but carefully, not wanting to destroy the box that I undoubtedly would want to preserve since it had the logo on all six sides. Inside I found my very own MonkeeMobile. In my mind, for months before this, I pictured a model that was perhaps twelve inches long and five or six inches tall, something that I could put in a prime position on the shelf beside my bed and look at lovingly many times throughout the day, maybe even picture a shrunken version of myself sitting inside with the shrunken Monkees while we drove along the street in our double breasted Monkee shirts leaning out the side and waving to the camera, our longish Monkee hair blowing in the breeze and looking super cool while the Monkee theme song played loudly on the state-of-the-art 1960's era sound system. Girls that I had crushes on almost my entire life would see me and suddenly realize how cool it would be to be my girlfriend. I looked inside the box, tore away all the packing material and found a MonkeeMobile that was about the size of a Matchbox car. It was so small that I couldn't even picture myself inside, let alone me and the four Monkees, even shrunken to near microscopic size.

DAVID W. GOODWIN

So, I knew disappointment. I fully understood the challenge of staring into the eyes of reality when reality was so far below expectation that it wasn't even in the same time zone. I felt that I needed to lower my expectations for the nightclub and accept whatever came my way.

We all entered the office building for our daily debriefing session. Our crew was the last to arrive and we entered as the rest of the quarry staff watched. Rhonda went up to the front of the room, had a brief, whispered chat with Big Larry and then the meeting began.

"Our meetin' with Mr. Biff Bojangles went hunky dory today. He ended up not citin' us for any violations but gave us a written warnin' for a few things that we need to do a little different. Nothin' too serious but as long as we implement these requirements, we'll be sittin' pretty as a ten dollar whore at a penny arcade, pardon my French," Big Larry began.

When it became apparent that he was dying to be asked what these requirements were before he continued, Alfonso did.

"Glad you asked there big guy," Big Larry responded. "All blastin' and sortin' needs to be done between the hours of eight and five and all truck deliveries need to be completed by six."

"How is that any different from what we currently do?" Quesnal asked.

"Ah, that's the beauty of these requirements. It's not!" Big Larry said triumphantly. "After all the sand kickin' and knockin' of chips off of shoulders and drawin' of lines in the dust and changin' each other's diapers once or twice, ol' Bojangles gave us just what we wanted in the first place."

"And to top it all off," Rhonda added, "nobody has to wear any additional hearing protection!"

"So that's the good news," Big Larry continued on, clearly impressed with his own performance, "and there's no bad news! How do you like them apples?"

Big Larry had each crew chief give their reports and was wrapping the meeting up when Rhonda spoke up. "We've got another rookie night on our hands. I guess ol' Whitey and OD here finally decided to put their college lives on hold for a while and join us for an evening at the nightclub. Hambone, will you show them around after the meeting and prepare them for the evening?"

"You bet, Rhonda," Iggy said enthusiastically. "I've already shown them the bunkhouse. I'll give them a tour of the showers, laundry and mess hall too. Should I also tell them about the song they need to sing?"

"That's up to you," Rhonda said chuckling. "Are you sure you want to scare them off that way?"

"Are there any more questions or comments before we adjourn for the day?" Big Larry asked, clearly wanting to wrap things up.

Barbara asked, "Can I sleep in the men's bunkhouse tonight?"

"Barbara, how many times have we gone over this?" Big Larry said sounding exasperated.

"I was only kidding," Barbara said shaking her head like this was a recurring conversation between the two of them and Big Larry never quite understood her form of humor.

"Anything else?" Big Larry asked again.

"Yeah, I've got a question," Laverne said, "Can Junior sleep in the women's bunkhouse tonight with me? Would any of you women mind?"

"Would you all work this stuff out on your own? This ain't no kindy garden," Big Larry whined. "Let me rephrase myself here—are there any questions or comments pertainin' to our day of work here at the quarry?"

When nobody had anything else to add, Big Larry dismissed the crew. Sugarloaf Sam hadn't even let loose with his wail yet and everyone was already heading towards the door. It wasn't until Eric and I were walking over to the bunkhouse with Iggy that his screech was heard.

"Men, it's finally official," Iggy announced. "Welcome to your first night at the quarry. We've got some time before dinner. Usually folks use the time to do their laundry and shower but I find that if I let everyone else go first, I can usually fit everything in quite easily. I went for a walk yesterday up into the woods to play my guitar but we need to make sure that we're back here by six. What do you guys feel like doing?"

"Let's get our beds squared away first. I wouldn't mind going for a short hike around and get to know the place a bit," Eric suggested. "I'd also love to take some photos."

"Sounds good to me. Maybe hike up to the top of the quarry and look around some. It's really cool up there," I added. "Great views and a nice place to hang out."

We quickly made our beds up with the supplies from the big closet. Iggy showed us two old trailers that were out behind the mess hall where Big Larry and Rhonda lived. He then gave us a tour of the bathhouse where the showers, bathroom and laundry were located. Many of the quarry folks were already queuing up for a turn in one of the four shower stalls so I could see why Iggy wanted to wait until later. Barbara was there in her robe and flip-flops with a bag containing her toiletries, I imagined, and a big fluffy towel hanging out the side. Most of the other women were there as well. I assumed they had first dibs on the showers.

"Hey Whitey and Hambone," she said winking at me, "do you boys want to come in and take turns scrubbing my back?"

"Careful guys, that's a trick question," I said while Eric and Iggy looked embarrassed.

"Just kidding, fellas. Don't get any crazy ideas. I just wanted to know if you wanted to. I wasn't actually inviting you to join me!" Barbara said with a laugh.

"Barbara, leave those poor college boys alone," Zelda said as she was preparing to enter one of the empty shower stalls. "You'll confuse them. And besides, I'm not sure any of them would know what to do with an experienced older woman like yourself."

"Hey, I'm not that old but I'm certainly experienced, if you know what I mean," she said, again giving me her now trademark conspiratorial wink.

Iggy continued the tour and showed us the laundry facilities. There was a big red plastic laundry basket where folks had already started throwing their dirty quarry clothes. On the wall next to the washing machines was a list of all the quarry workers in alphabetical order and a yellow arrow taped to the wall and pointing to a name. Our names had been added to the list in pencil at the bottom.

"Each day, one person is responsible for doing the laundry for everyone on a rotating basis. Today you see the arrow is next to Georgie's name so if you want to get your washing done, just make sure you get your stuff here by 5:30. We'll go back to the bunkhouse and change into different clothes before we go on our walk so we can start tomorrow with clean stuff. You should also use this big marker to put your initials inside each item so you'll know which items are yours since almost everything looks the same; just cross out any other initials that are already there," Iggy instructed. "Your clean clothes will be stacked up on those long tables over there."

We did as Iggy suggested and then started hiking up the Bobsled towards the top of the quarry. Iggy had his guitar, Eric had his camera and I had my Frisbee. The day was still beautiful and warm. Colorado continued to amaze me with the near perfection of the weather, almost every day. On days when it would rain, it was almost as good as a sunny day because it happened fairly infrequently. Long stretches of bad weather were unheard of, quite the contrast to my experience growing up in New

Jersey where you could get four or five rainy days in a row on a regular basis. As we got higher and higher up into the quarry, the view became more and more spectacular.

"This is awesome, man!" Eric exclaimed. "I haven't had the chance to get all the way up here other than our first day of work last week. Working on the landscaping crew is pretty good but since we've been working mostly on the entrance way and around the buildings, I haven't been able to check this place out."

"Yeah, I've only been up here once so far but now that we're working on constructing the frame for the bug netting, most of our time will be spent up here and rappelling down the granite walls," I explained.

"Beans, you really lucked into a great assignment there," Iggy said. "Mungo and I are jealous!"

"It's a pretty interesting assignment alright. It would certainly be more fun if we could all be working together. I mean, I like working with Rhonda, Barbara and Juan Antonio, they're an interesting bunch but it would definitely be more fun if you guys were there. We stopped at a diner for lunch today east of Denver after picking up pipes and netting that was the weirdest place I think that I'd ever been to."

"What was so weird about it?" Eric asked.

"Well, first, it was called the Little Baby Jesus Diner."

"Yeah right! You're making that up!" Iggy said accusingly.

"No, I'm not. Barbara wanted to stop there since apparently its part of a small chain of religious themed diners. There was a confessional, apostle themed lunch booths, but the craziest thing was that they encouraged you to break one of the Ten Commandments. If you broke more than one, you had to go talk to Father Lola."

"Father Lola? Did you break any?" Iggy asked.

"I encouraged Juan Antonio to make an image of the Virgin Mary in his pizza using some vegetables, which he did, but our waitress said that it didn't really count."

"You should have committed adultery, were there any hot married babes there?" Eric asked.

"Depends if you count Rhonda or Barbara."

"I'd count Rhonda as a hot babe and maybe Barbara as a former hot babe," Eric responded.

"Well, since Rhonda's not married, that wouldn't work but I did ask Barbara if she was interested."

"And was she?" Iggy asked.

DAVID W. GOODWIN

"Not really but you'd never know that by her behavior yesterday."

"Yeah, what was that all about?" Eric asked. "You told me some of the details but I'm having a hard time picturing it. Iggy, I don't think you've heard any of this yet."

"You're right, what are you talking about? What happened yesterday?"

"Barbara and I were given an assignment to gather up some dead wood for the black rumped pygmy gnat project so she and I drove up past Fritz's cabin and then past the turnoff to Kylee's place, you know, the back way to Gold Hill?" I then told them the complete uncensored version.

"Good God! You're kidding, right?" Eric exclaimed.

"Not at all. See what I mean? It was unbelievable! Plus, she told me that she fantasizes about having sex with all three of us."

"Alone or all at once?" Iggy asked.

"That's what I asked," Eric said.

"Me too," I added.

"So anyway, she asked me to keep this as our little secret. I haven't been too good about that so please don't ever say anything to anyone about this. I feel like a jerk betraying her confidence but I had to tell you guys. Whatever you do, keep it to yourselves, okay?"

"Absolutely! No one would believe it anyway!" Eric said.

We arrived at the very top of the quarry and were all breathing heavily from the exertion. All three roads joined together at the top in a big grassy field that was punctuated with large ponderosa pine trees and some smaller juniper bushes. This was pretty much the top of Sugarloaf Mountain and it was all owned by the quarry. There was a massive chain link fence a hundred feet beyond the field to mark the property boundary and was probably there to keep people from wandering into the quarry and accidentally launching themselves over the steep cliffs.

We sat down at the edge of one of the rock walls between the Juiceway and the Bobsled and dangled our feet over the cliff. There was a drop off of about ten feet down to the narrow ledge below that didn't seem too dramatic until you considered all of the other terraces made by the cut granite the entire way down to the bottom. The scale became apparent when you saw the tiny buildings of the quarry below. It kind of made your stomach feel funny and the bottoms of your feet tingle. It would also be a great place to hang glide from since the thermals produced from the sun warming up the south facing rocks were probably ideal.

Iggy took out his guitar and started tuning it. Eric took his camera out of its bag and began fiddling with the various settings and lining up a few shots through his viewfinder. I felt the steady rush of air moving up the rock walls and decided that it would be a good time to play with myself. I took the Frisbee and began testing the interaction between disc and updrafts. Slowly, I was able to wing the wham out into the thermals, very conservatively at first, only to have the updrafts push the disc right back towards me, as long as I threw it out into the void perfectly level. With a little bit of practice, I was able to wing and catch, wing and catch, each time going out into space a little further.

I was deadly accurate with a Frisbee. There was a Frisbee tournament at one of the local high schools the first summer that I lived in Boulder. There were a variety of different competitions from freestyling, to the longest distance that you could throw a Frisbee, to the longest distance that you could throw, run and then catch your own Frisbee, to throwing a disc through a hula hoop that was on a stand from increasingly farther distances. I entered the throw, run and catch competition first and would have won it except that right when I was about to catch my longest toss, one of my Rainbow sandals got tangled up in someone's macramé bag that had been left right in my path and I landed flat on my face only to have my Frisbee smack me right in my head. That was a real crowd pleaser!

Trying to get some sort of redemption, I then entered the throwing accuracy competition and easily won it. I think everyone else that entered was so stoned that they might not have been able to understand the complicated rules which were to stand behind a line and try to throw your Frisbee through the hula hoop. Some of the stoners would run up to and then past the line, coming mighty close to the hoop before releasing their disc and were immediately disqualified. Some would throw their Frisbee in the general direction of the hula hoop, follow it and then make a second toss towards the hoop, perhaps thinking they were playing Frisbee golf. One other person tried to create the illusion of a toss by balancing the spinning disc on his finger, running at the hoop and then whipping it through when he was right in front. Needless to say, the competition wasn't too fierce. I even made the evening news in Denver as I threw my Frisbee through the hoop with a TV camerawoman filming it from behind.

Iggy had launched into a bluegrass version of a Grateful Dead song that he had been working on recently. Eric began taking some photographs of Iggy and then me with my Frisbee and then eventually some close-ups of some weeds. Iggy stopped playing for a while and began rolling a joint, big and sloppy looking, but a joint none-the-less.

"I think it's time to get mellow. What do you guys think?" Iggy asked.

"I don't know. Do you think that's a wise idea considering that it's our night to debut at the nightclub?" Eric asked cautiously.

"Yes, especially because it's your night to debut at the nightclub. You'll thank me for doing this later, I guarantee it."

We took turns sucking on the mini-spliff, dodging small explosions that happened whenever the glowing end would ignite a seed. "Hey man, don't you ever clean your pot? This stuff is loaded with seeds," I complained in a stoned hippie voice.

"Yeah, I guess I missed a few. What can I say?" Iggy responded in kind.

We finished off the joint and I continued tossing the disc out into the thermals. I was able to angle it slightly so that it would return to either Iggy or Eric who were sitting on either side of me. They were pretty skilled at the art of winging too so we all got the knack of it rather quickly.

"So our job for the next few weeks will be to construct this massive structure on the face of this wall and then lay bird netting over the top. Pretty cool, wouldn't you say?" I stated.

"And you'll be doing all of this work while repelling from up here?" Eric asked.

"Yeah, I actually think it will be pretty easy. You see how fractured the rock is? There are tons of handholds all over the place so you can actually free climb on this stuff quite easily."

As I was talking, one of my tosses went a bit astray and didn't quite make it back all the way to Eric. He tried to kick it upward with his foot but wasn't able to redirect the path up high enough to grab it. The disc smacked into the wall and luckily, only fell down to the first ledge below us.

"Oops, I was wondering when this would happen. I guess I'll have to climb down and get it," I said.

"Or you could just wait until tomorrow when you have the right equipment, don't you think Beans? We've got to head down in a few minutes so we have enough time to shower before dinner," Eric cautioned.

"I might as well get it now while I'm thinking about it. You guys want to join me?"

"Normally, I'd say yes but I'm not sure I would want to do this now under these conditions," Iggy said which surprised me. It was unusual when he wasn't up for a little challenge.

"Suit yourself. I'll be right back," I said as I began climbing down the wall backwards.

Eric was playing around with various camera angles and took a few pictures. "This is really cool! From this perspective, it almost looks like you're descending into the Grand Canyon if I keep the lower ledge out of the frame."

"Hey Beans, man, watch out for that peregrine falcon that's about to swoop in and grab you with it's giant talons," Iggy said, channeling the biggest stoner person any of us had ever met, a guy who used to live in Iggy's basement room at the Zoo before Iggy moved in. Iggy had a pretty robust repertoire of stoner imitations but saved this particular one for special occasions. He used an extremely high pitched and nasally sounding voice.

I started laughing because whenever Iggy did his Stu Mellons imitation, it was always funny. I was holding onto the rock with only one hand and one foot since I was searching for the next hand and foot hold but Iggy continued his imitation since it was eliciting such a great reaction from Eric and me.

"I mean, man, like if you want to end up high in some falcon nest and be fed piece by piece to all the little falcon chicks, well, that's cool with me but, man, I wouldn't do it if I were you 'cause it might be a major bummer, that's all I'm sayin', man," Iggy continued.

My laughter was getting the better of me out there on the rock, half way between the top and the first ledge down. My sides began to ache, cramp and then spasm while Iggy continued with his shtick. I was powerless to ask him to stop since I couldn't find my voice through my laughter and now muscle spasms. It was all I could do to hang on where I was. Iggy and Eric were apparently unaware of my predicament.

"Beans, man, which parts do you think the falcon chicks will dig the most?" Iggy continued. "I think your eyeballs will be the first to go, you know how baby chicks like eyeballs, right man? I'm tellin' ya, they love it almost as much as horny goat weed, man!"

I tried to yell out for him to stop so that I could get a better position on the rock wall but before I was able to get a sound out, my hand hold slipped and I slid down the rock face about six feet and landed on the ledge feet first. The impact of the hit caused my body to fall backwards and I flipped over and somersaulted down the next pitch and luckily came to a stop face down on the second ledge. My lights went out momentarily as I tried to get a handle on what just happened.

"Shit, Beans, are you alright?" I heard Eric yell from above.

"Poindexter, answer us!" Iggy yelled when I didn't immediately respond.

I was busy trying to get my bearings and do a quick assessment of my injuries. Part of my body was hanging over the ledge so I scooched in a bit to make sure that I didn't fall down another section. An inventory of my body parts was reassuring as I seemed able to move all of them. My head had smacked against the ledge pretty hard and I could start to feel the pain intensifying in my forehead. I reached up to feel the damage and was alarmed to see that my hand was covered with blood. I slowly moved my body into a sitting position on the narrow ledge and tried to convince myself that I probably wasn't hurt too badly.

"I smacked my head pretty bad," I yelled up, suddenly aware of the throbbing and how much it hurt to yell as the sound of my own voice seemed to be amplified about ten times inside my skull.

"Don't move, one of us is going to come down and help you up," Eric instructed. "Just sit tight for a few minutes."

"Okay," I said as loudly as possible without hurting my brain too much.

I sat on the second ledge and tried to figure out how it was going to be possible to get back up to the top. My whole body was kind of shaky from the shock of falling and blood was running down my face into my eyes and mouth. If only I had some water to wash my face and a clean rag to stop the bleeding. I got the idea to use my tee shirt so I carefully striped it off while sitting a bit precariously on the ledge. By tying it around my head, the bleeding seemed to stop and it made my head feel a little better.

I heard movement coming from up above and saw that Iggy was making his way down to the first ledge. Eric was standing at the top and watching and I'm pretty certain that he was taking some pictures. I decided to stand up and see what I could do to start climbing but as the blood rushed out of my head, I started to feel faint and quickly sat back down again on the ledge. By this time, Iggy was on the first ledge and peered down to where I was.

"Dean, holy shit, you look awful!"

"Yeah and I feel even worse"

"Are you able to stand up?"

"I just tried and felt like I was going to pass out."

"Try it again only go real slowly."

I gathered my thoughts and concentrated on doing everything in slow motion. I was able to get onto my feet this time without feeling faint. Iggy was surveying the cracks in the rock and suggested that I try a route off to my right since he thought it was the most promising.

"I'm willing to come down and help but why don't you see if you can do it on your own first?"

Following his advice proved to be a bit more difficult as I had lost almost all of my confidence, I couldn't see all that well, my head was pounding and my arms and legs felt like they were made out of rubber. This was not a good combination for rock climbing. Once I started to move, I realized how much pain there was in my legs and hips. However, I began a very slow ascent and Iggy gave me encouragement from above. After I had successfully climbed about half way up, I started to feel better and tried to fill myself with positive thoughts. As I approached Iggy, he pulled me up the last few feet to the first ledge.

"Great job, Beans! I wasn't sure that you were going to be able to do that."

"Me either but I was channeling the energy from the group massage the other night and felt like I had six people pushing me on."

"Good idea. Do you want to rest here for a while before doing the next section?"

Before I could answer, I saw Eric's head appear over the edge.

"Beans, man, you look nasty!"

"So I've been told."

"There's someone up here who has a little surprise for you once you get to the top. She says her name's Sarah and she's totally naked. I'd get up here in a hurry if I were you 'cause she says that she has to leave soon plus she's really hot. Wait, she's saying something else to me, hold on a sec." Eric's head disappeared for a few seconds and then he reappeared. "Plus, she said that if you aren't in too bad of a shape, she might do a Barbara for you."

"You're funny!" I said.

"What do you say, man, are you ready to head up?" Iggy asked.

"As ready as any other time, let's go."

"You go first. Hey Eric, we're coming up the route that we went down so get ready to help us up as we get close," Iggy said loudly and then to me, "I'll follow up behind you."

DAVID W. GOODWIN

The climb up this pitch was challenging but not too terrible. At one point, I lost my grip and slid backwards a few feet to where Iggy was. He stopped my descent rather easily by giving me a cross body block that pinned me against the rock so that I could get my hand and foot holds re-established. We were eventually able to reach the top and over the lip with Eric's assistance. Once we were all safely off the rock, I realized that I had completely forgotten about retrieving the errant Frisbee.

"I've got to go back down and get that damned thing," I said in a serious voice.

"Oh no you don't. We're heading back down the road to get you some medical attention," Eric said emphatically.

"I was only kidding."

"Man, you're lucky that you didn't kill yourself," Eric said with genuine concern. "If you kept bouncing off ledges all the way down, you'd be a big piece of hamburger right now. You're gonna have to get your head wound checked out. From the amount of blood that's soaked into your shirt, you might need some stitches. Do you want my shirt? Are you cold?"

"Not at the moment, Mungo, but thanks. Let's get down so we can get cleaned up and have dinner."

We began walking down the Bobsled and I was aware of how sore my entire body was starting to feel. The impact of hitting the ledge feet first must have compressed my ankles, knees and hips pretty well so all those joints were throbbing. Landing face down on the second ledge might have been a blessing in disguise since my entire body must have absorbed most of the impact. Other than a pounding headache, I figured that maybe I had been somewhat lucky.

As we got closer to the quarry buildings, I began to worry about how everyone would react to my blunder. I wondered if Big Larry might just fire us for screwing around up at the quarry. I was also worried that the other folks might think that I was a total idiot for doing what I had done.

"Hey, guys, let's not tell anyone about this if we can avoid it. I'll just go over to the bathhouse and clean as much of this blood off as possible if one of you guys bring me some clean clothes, towel and toiletry kit out of my bag. Maybe even a first aid kit if you know where they keep it."

"It's going to be impossible to hide this from anyone," Iggy said. "You look pretty awful. There's a first aid kit in the bathhouse. I have the feeling that people get hurt around here fairly often given the nature of the place."

"Maybe after I get cleaned up it won't be so bad. Head wounds have a tendency to bleed a lot so it might not be as bad as you think. One time, my father dropped a fireplace grate on his head as he was trying to put it up into our attic. Man, you would have thought that his head was severed considering all the blood that he lost. After a few stitches, you could barely tell that anything had happened."

"We can try but I think you might have some injuries that someone will need to check out," Eric said seriously.

"Let's evaluate things in a little while. In the meantime, I'll shower; we'll go to dinner and then see how things stand, okay?"

"Fair enough," Iggy said.

We were approaching the bunkhouse and didn't see any activity. I tried to remove the bloody shirt from around my head but it had dried in place.

"I'm going to quickly duck into the shower and try to get this shirt off. See you guys in a few minutes. Hey, thanks for your help today."

The bathhouse was empty so I jumped into one of the shower stalls without anyone seeing me. I soaked the tee shirt in warm water under the shower nozzle and watched the red tinged water drain out past my feet. Once the dried blood bond was broken, I was able to carefully remove the shirt and gingerly wash out my sliced forehead with soap and warm water. My biggest worry was that the blood would start flowing again but I had to take that risk. From what I could tell with my fingers and the sensitivity of my face, it seemed like most of the damage was at the top of my forehead near my hair line.

Eric entered the building and yelled out that he had all the stuff that I had requested. "I'll leave it on this bench out here. How are things looking?"

I poked my head out from behind the shower curtain. "Not too bad, I think, at least from what I can feel. What do you think?"

"Wow, it's a lot better than I imagined," he said as he took a closer look. "It's kinda raw and is somewhat swollen but it looks like you're going to live."

Iggy came in with a first aid kit and took a look at my gash as well. "It's sort of nasty but it might not need any stitches, maybe just some creative bandaging. I think there are some butterfly bandages in here. I'll help you once you're out of the shower. Be sure to clean it out well."

They both disappeared for a few minutes and then returned for their own showers. I dried off and went to look at my head in the mirror to assess the damage. Just as I sensed, the slice wasn't too bad, only an inch or so in length and fairly straight since I think I cut it on a sharp rock. I rubbed a bunch of first aid cream on the wound and began looking around for bandages that would work well. Iggy had finished up with his shower and threw on some clothes as he came over.

"I've got a lot of experience patching people up," he explained. "Why don't you just sit over on that bench and I'll take care of you?"

"Okay, Nurse Hambone, I'm all yours."

Iggy examined my cut closely and then rummaged through the first aid kit. "These bandages work best when you can apply pressure from both sides since they pull your cut together. Unfortunately, in order to get it to adhere properly, I'll need to cut a small patch of your hair. How do you feel about that?"

"I guess that's fine if you really think it needs to be done. I really don't want to head down to the hospital so do what you have to do," I said feeling rather light headed and just wanting this ordeal to be done.

"Just a small patch. There are some surgical scissors in the kit. Let me grab those and see if they work well enough to cut some of your hair."

Iggy got the scissors, cut my hair and then applied the butterfly bandage. I could feel the pull on either side of my skin so I figured that he knew what he was doing. Eric had finished his shower and came over to admire Iggy's patch job.

"I would also suggest putting some ice on it to keep the swelling down and also take some aspirin for the inflammation. I'll go get you some of both," he offered.

We heard a bunch of activity outside the bathhouse and guessed that everyone was heading over to the mess hall for dinner.

"Maybe we should deal with that stuff later, Eric. I can't go to dinner looking like this though," I said. "What do you think I should do?"

"How about wearing a bandana to cover the bandage?" Eric suggested. "It wouldn't look too suspicious since you wear one sometimes anyway."

"Great idea! I've got one in my bag. Give me a second to get it and then we can all go over to dinner," I said.

We waited until it sounded like everyone from the bunkhouse had left for dinner and then snuck out of the building and walked quickly to the bunkhouse. When we arrived, we saw Junior sitting on his bed. He looked up when the three of us entered the room.

"What happened to you?" he asked.

CHAPTER 15

M Y FAVORITE BLUE bandana was going to get me out of another jam. It was used mostly to keep the hair out of my eyes but I found that it came in handy for lots of different situations, like if you found a stray dog and needed to make an emergency collar so you could tie a rope to it that you found in the woods and be pulled around on the ice if you happened to be up in the mountains in the middle of winter and ran across a beautiful frozen lake and the drugs that you had taken about an hour earlier were just starting to kick in full time. I laid the scarf out on my bed to form a triangle, smoothed it out and then put it on my head, taking care to completely cover the rather large bandage.

"Oh, nothing too serious," I responded to Junior's question. "I just hit my head on a low hanging branch when we were out hiking a little while ago. Aren't you going to dinner?"

"I'm not all that hungry."

"Does this have anything to do with Laverne?" Iggy asked.

"Well, maybe a little bit. I just don't understand why she keeps bothering me."

"You're quite a catch, man. You're probably one of the studliest guys here and she just wanted to snatch you up before Joan or Rhonda got the idea," Eric managed to say without laughing. "Why don't you come to dinner and sit with us?"

"I guess that would be fine," he responded.

"How does my bandana look?" I asked.

"Perfect," Iggy said. "I'm starving, let's go get dinner."

The four of us walked over towards the mess hall. We heard loud voices, the tinkling of silverware on plates, glasses making contact with tables and the general ruckus caused by twenty or so people assembled in a fairly small space for a meal. Iggy led us into the building.

"It's about time you all showed up," Big Larry said. "You know how I feel about bein' on time. It's now 6:40. Bunny was starting to worry and some of the boys were takin' bets on whether you college boys had gotten lost somewhere out in the wilderness."

"No, we didn't get lost," Iggy said calmly. "I took Dean and Eric on a hike around the quarry and it took a little longer than expected. My apologies to everyone. Is there any food left?"

"Come and get it!" a woman sang out from behind a serving table. This must be the chef, Bunny, and I realized that I had never seen her before, only heard her name mentioned on a regular basis. She was wearing a white chef's apron and chef's hat that looked like a giant marshmallow. Windy's name was perfect for her but I was having a hard time with Bunny's. She was a huge black woman. Her dark skin contrasted magnificently with her big, juicy red lips and sparkling white teeth. Her radiance, beauty and luscious smile made me immediately want to become her best friend.

We walked over to the food table and lined up to wait our turn to serve ourselves dinner. There weren't any choices but Bunny described what she had made and it was clear that she took a lot of pride in the food she prepared. This was evident from the few lunches that I had already had the pleasure to eat.

"Tonight's meal has an Asian theme going," Bunny explained. "We've got pork egg rolls, sweet and sour soup, chicken fried rice, and a broccoli and Chinese cabbage stir-fry. You boys grab a bowl so I can start you off with some soup. Mustard and homemade duck sauce are on the tables as are chopsticks and soup spoons. When everyone is done with the first course, you'll come back up here for the main course. Here are some egg rolls."

"I can't wait. We haven't been able to eat any meat for a long time," Eric said.

"You're not vegetarians, are you?"

"None of us are but we live in a vegetarian house," he explained.

"Well, dig in. I hope you'll like it."

There was one empty table in the corner so we took our seats. Almost everyone else had finished their first course so we had a little catching up to do. When we were settled in, Bunny cleared away the appetizers and folks lined up to get the next course she was bringing out.

"How are you feeling, Beans?" Eric asked me quietly. "You're looking rather pale."

"I think I'm going to be really sore tomorrow based on how I feel right now. I was hoping that my first night at the club would be under different circumstances."

"Just take it easy," Iggy advised. "Maybe the food and some relaxation time and ice will help."

We finished our fabulous appetizers and then went up to get the main course. Dinner was so good that I almost forgot about my discomfort. The level of Bunny's culinary talents made me wonder why she wasn't working at an upscale restaurant in Boulder or Denver. After everyone had been served their meals, Bunny came over to our table to check in with us.

"This is one of the best meals I've ever had," Eric said as she sat down at our table.

"Yeah, I'd have to agree," Iggy added. "Every bite is like a flavor bomb!"

"Glad you boys approve. I like to experiment with a variety of cuisines; Asian, Mexican, Mediterranean, African, French, Greek, pretty much anything that's not boring."

"Bunny made a ratatouille over couscous last night that was better than anything my mom ever made and she grew up in the south of France," Iggy said.

"What's your background? Where have you learned how to cook like this?" Eric asked.

"Oh, darlin', it's a long story. Let's just say that I've worked in a lot of restaurants in my life and been exposed to many different styles. Right now, however, I've got to start cleaning up before the nightclub."

"Do you have anyone to help?" Eric asked.

Before she could answer, Iggy told us that just like the rotating laundry duty list, there were two people assigned to meal clean up each day.

"Thanks so much for the great meal," Eric said.

Even in my altered and semi-comatose state, it registered with me that I loved her enthusiasm and energy and her smile was making me feel all happy and warm inside. As she was walking away, Laverne walked over and sat down in the recently vacated chair. "Why didn't you sit with me, lover?" she asked Junior. "I saved you a seat."

"These guys invited me to join them," he answered rather lamely.

"Are you mad at me? Did I say something that hurt your feelings? Didn't you like our lovemaking last night?"

"No, I mean yes, well yes to some and no to the others," Junior said tripping all over himself.

"I just can't get enough of you and want to be around you all the time. Is that wrong?"

"No, I just need some space sometimes. Is that alright with you?"

"I guess so, as long as we'll be together tonight," Laverne said as she got up and gave Junior a big smack on the lips. "Ta ta for now, my love. See you in a little while!"

We finished our meals and cleared the dishes, separating out the various items into big plastic tubs that were clearly marked on a table near the half wall separating the eating area from the kitchen.

As we were leaving the room, Big Larry turned his attention to us. "I'm not sure what you boys have been up to but in the future, make sure you get your butts here on time. Understood?"

"Sorry Boss, it's my fault. We'll be more cognizant of the time in the future," Iggy responded taking full responsibility for my mistake.

"You better be more cogyzant, whatever that means, as long as it means bein' on time."

We left the building and I immediately felt so tired that all I could think about was lying down in my bed. Inside the bunkhouse, everyone was busy doing some sort of task like arranging their belongings, making up their beds, writing, reading, or playing cards. I collapsed on my bed with my clothes on and told my friends to wake me up when it was time to head over to the nightclub.

My next conscious memory was feeling someone touching my shoulder in the fading light of the early evening and telling me it was time to get up. I was so deeply asleep that I didn't have the slightest idea where I was or even the year.

"Beans, time to go to the nightclub," a voice said.

"Whaaaa?"

"Everyone is heading over to the nightclub now. Why don't you get up and come with us?"

"Can't get up," I mumbled semi-coherently. "Too tired, my head hurts, go without me."

Someone grabbed my legs and swung them around off the bed onto the floor. Someone else pulled up on my shoulders and then pushed my upper body into a sitting position. When my feet were on the floor, the person behind me pushed my back to get me to stand up. I made some initial progress in that direction but ended up slumping over sideways and eventually came to rest lying on my bed again except in the opposite direction.

"This is useless," I heard one of them say.

"You're right. We're going to have to leave him here tonight," the other one said.

"Sweet dreams, man. Don't accuse us of not trying."

The twilight became total night in one or two heartbeats. I woke up enough at some point to walk over to the bathroom and was marginally aware of loud voices and music coming from one of the buildings. Each step I took seemed to jostle my brain like it was an overripe melon loosely packed inside a globe of Jell-O so I had to move as slowly and deliberately as possible. Getting back into my bed felt like a major victory and I eased myself down into a lying position, falling back to sleep immediately.

My dreams came in torrents, at first I relived my fall down the rock wall as it really happened and then they became surreal interpretations of the same event over and over. I started to hear a voice from above and someone was gently touching my hair.

"Dean, I heard you hit your head really hard today. Are you alright?" the voice said in a soft whisper that sounded very sexy to me.

I liked the direction this was going so I responded, "I think so."

"I'm worried about you. Is there anything I can get you?" she asked sweetly.

"I'm fine for the moment. My head hurts a bit but not too bad."

"Do you feel well enough to come do something with me?" she asked as she sat down on my bed and began gently massaging the back of my neck. It was so dark that I couldn't see anything but the outline of her body.

"That really feels good. When I stand up, my head starts pounding, although if this is a dream, I can do whatever I want, right?"

My dreams have been so realistic my entire life that I can't recognize them as dreams while they're in progress. I could feel the heat from her body and smell her scent but I often experienced all five senses vividly in my dreams anyway. I began to wonder who I had conjured up for this role and tried to figure it out based on her voice.

"Yes, you can do whatever you want but this isn't a dream," she said.

"You know, that's what all the characters in my dreams tell me in order to fake me out. Even though you say that, I still think this really is a dream," I said confusing even myself.

"Is it alright that I'm here with you?" she asked ignoring my suspicions.

DAVID W. GOODWIN

"Sure, why not, as long as you're not here to throw me over a cliff again. How did you know that I was injured?"

"I heard your friend Eric mention to Barbara that you had hit your head pretty hard and I wanted to make sure you were okay."

"That was kind of you. I was hoping that nobody found out that I whacked myself."

"Your secret is safe with me."

"Who are you?"

"Maybe you should guess."

"Well, let's see, your voice sort of sounds like Joan. Is that who you are?"

"No," she said laughing. "Nobody has ever mistaken me for Joan."

"Hmm, okay then, do you work at the quarry?"

"Of course I do, we've worked together a few times."

"You don't sound like any of the other women who work here. Give me another hint."

"Maybe you should touch me a little, that might help."

I carefully sat up in bed until I was facing her. I began to touch her starting with her head and her shoulder length straight hair. I then ran my hands up and down her upper body over loose fitting clothes and observed that she had a slender but athletic build.

"Don't be shy," she prompted. "Touch me anywhere you want."

I ran my hand up and down her back and noticed that she was wearing a bra. I then did the same thing in front and found that she had somewhat smallish breasts which surprised me since the women in my dreams usually had large boobs and their bodies were a lot fleshier.

"So, you're not Bunny, Zelda, Rhonda, or Laverne and you're certainly not Barbara. Are you Yolanda?"

"No, I'm not. Maybe you should touch me down below," she whispered.

This dream was getting pretty cool so I followed her advice. I moved my hand down to the top of her pants and then slowly rubbed in wide circles centered on the zipper of her jeans. As my circles got smaller and the pressure on my hand increased, I was startled to discover lumps and bumps where I expected to find tight smoothness, like tiny triangular pillows on either side of her zipper.

"Gad zooks!" I exclaimed pulling my hand away quickly and suddenly felt wide-awake. "You're a man too!"

"Don't be alarmed, Dean," she and/or he said. "Do you know who I am now?"

"You're Georgie, right?"

"Yes and even though I've got man parts down there, I've got female parts up here as you just discovered. I'm stuck somewhere in between and it's really frustrating."

"Wow! In the dark I was certain that you were a woman since you talked like a woman and I sensed your female energy."

"It's tough, I never really fit in anywhere. Men don't treat me like a woman and women are generally more accepting but rather cautious. People generally avoid me so I lead a pretty lonely life. Are you afraid of me?"

"Not at all, I'm rather fascinated. Do you feel more like a woman or a man inside?"

"That's a good question, I'm not sure I know the answer. I was kind of hoping that maybe you could help me answer that."

"How can I do that?"

"Are you willing to perform a little experiment? Joan has agreed to help out and she's waiting for us right now over in the women's bunkhouse."

"What do you have in mind?"

"Come with me and I'll show you."

"Let me see if I can stand up first."

With Georgie there for support, I got out of bed and stood up for a moment until my head stopped spinning around. When I felt fairly normal, I took a few steps and seemed to be alright. We slowly walked through the dark room and entered the women's side where I saw Joan lying under some covers in her bed with a bunch of candles lit around her on tables, chairs and the floor.

"Joan, Dean has agreed to be a part of our experiment."

"Wait, I haven't agreed to anything yet but if this is a dream, I'll probably try just about anything," I said a little hesitantly.

"Dean, don't be worried, we're just here to help out Georgie," Joan said.

"Okay but what's the experiment?"

"I want to find out if I'm more attracted to men or women and I'm hoping you can help me," Georgie said. "Joan and I talked about this yesterday and we came up with an idea."

DAVID W. GOODWIN

At that moment, Joan slowly pulled her covers off and revealed her nakedness to us. She had a stunningly beautiful body from head to toe.

"I can tell you both without any hesitation that I'm definitely attracted to women, especially right now," I said trying to keep my salivary glands from actually squirting out into the room through my open mouth.

Joan stood up and walked over to me. She made a show of removing my clothing very slowly so that Georgie could get the maximum effect. She went over to do the same thing to Georgie. Within a few short moments, the three of us were standing naked in the cool evening air and were bathed in the warm glow of the candle light.

The contrast between Joan and Georgie was monumental as I'm sure the same could be said about me and Georgie. I'm certain that I had never seen a person with the sort of mix of parts that Georgie had and it was very confusing but somehow erotic. After touching him earlier, he seemed more male than female but now seeing his full naked body, there was something decidedly female about her. Her entire body, if viewed without regard for her small penis seemed more female but when the penis got thrown into the mix, it seemed to trump everything else.

"What would you like to do next, Georgie?" I asked tentatively.

"I want both of you to let me caress you and kiss you and I want you to do the same to me. I want to see how I respond and then maybe I'll figure this thing out once and for all. Are you willing?"

"Yes, I am," Joan said, taking this task very seriously.

"Can I just watch?" I asked.

"No, that's the deal. You have to be a participant otherwise this experiment won't work," Joan said. "Maybe you should pretend that Georgie is your new girlfriend Sarah."

"She's not my girlfriend but I'll give it a try," I said with some hesitation.

Georgie came towards Joan and started touching her shoulders and arms. I moved away from them a little so I could watch from a comfortable angle and distance. Joan seemed to relax into Georgie's caresses and it looked like she was enjoying herself. Her breathing became slower and her body seemed to come to life. She began touching Georgie in return and eventually they started kissing. Joan looked like she was on a different wavelength all of a sudden. Watching them do this to one another had a very powerful effect on me as they seemed like two women together. Joan was slowly getting aroused and it was even more obvious that Georgie was too, much like me. They began touching each other all over, cupping each other's breasts and then took turns licking each other's nipples. They rubbed and squeezed each other's various parts and then Joan reached down and began massaging Georgie's swelling mini member. Georgie returned the favor and slid her hand between Joan's legs and started moving her hand in slow circles around her delicious girly parts. I had to sit down on the bed since I was starting to lose my bearings a bit.

"Don't go too far away," Joan whispered. "Maybe you should come join us instead of sitting on the sidelines."

Joan welcomed me to the group by giving me a soft kiss on my mouth. Georgie did the same and much to my surprise, the effect wasn't entirely unpleasant. Joan's kiss was soft and sweet and very juicy while Georgie's was a little rougher and muskier. Even with a penis, in some way, Georgie seemed more like a woman to me than a man. Maybe it was the presence of Joan and maybe it was the dreamlike quality of the encounter but all of a sudden none of that really seemed to matter anymore and things took on a life of their own. It all became an intoxicating blur of activity and then the next thing I remembered was lying on my bed back in the men's bunkhouse with Georgie sitting on the floor beside me.

"What happened?" I asked.

"You seemed to pass out when the three of us were lying on Joan's bed so we put you back into your own bed."

"And did the experiment work?"

"Let's talk about it later. You should get some sleep."

I either fell back asleep almost immediately or the dream ended because the next thing I heard was the 6:30 wake up call that I remember Big Larry telling us about on the day we were hired. At least that's what I assumed we were hearing. Would there be any other reason to be hearing the Chambers Brothers *Time Has Come Today* over the loudspeaker? From the opening tick tick tick, to the drums, the opening guitar piece and finally the lyrics, I guessed that it was time to wake up for another work day. I looked around the bunkhouse and saw everyone starting to stir.

When I looked over in the direction of Iggy and Eric's beds, I saw that Iggy was awake and slowly getting out of his bed. Eric, on the other hand, was still sound asleep.

"How are you feeling, Beans?" Iggy mouthed in a whisper.

"I'll let you know in a few minutes," I responded as I slowly got out of bed. I had a pretty intense headache but the dizziness that I had

DAVID W. GOODWIN

experienced the day before seemed to be mostly gone, much to my relief. I was able to stand up and walk around without any light headedness.

Iggy went over to Eric's bed and gave his shoulder a shake. Eric shrugged him off and rolled over to his other side.

"Not so fast there buddy," Iggy said to Eric giving him a more substantial shake and sang along with the music into Eric's ear.

Eric started laughing at Iggy's singing and gradually woke up enough to realize that this was the wake up call and he had better begin mobilizing. Since this routine was new to both of us, Iggy filled us in.

"Breakfast is served in fifteen minutes so if you want to grab a quick shower, you need to do it now or wait until after breakfast. Some of the ladies shower before they eat but most of the guys wait until after work."

My bandana had fallen off sometime during the night and I asked the boys how things looked.

"Not too bad, you've got some dried blood around the bandage but it seems to be doing its job. The swelling has gone down some but you should clean it out and I'll put on a fresh bandage," Iggy said after giving me a quick examination.

I gathered up the items that I needed and went over to the bathhouse. Two of the four shower stalls were empty so I grabbed one and washed up. Once I got back at the bunkhouse, everyone else had finally gotten out of their beds and was getting their clean work clothes on, even Eric. I had my towel draped over my head like a pharaoh, hoping to conceal the cut on my forehead. Iggy had a fresh bandage waiting and carefully applied it after putting some ointment on the small gash as I sat on his bed. I put on a clean bandana over the bandage and we took off for breakfast.

"How was the nightclub last night?" I asked Eric as the three of us sauntered over to the mess hall.

"Pretty cool, for sure. If you can try to stay out of trouble today, you'll get to come to Dance Night tonight since it's Wednesday, isn't that right Iggy?" Eric asked.

"Yep, although missing out on Talent Night was unfortunate for you. What a blast!"

"Say, did either of you see Georgie or Joan leave the nightclub sometime during the evening?"

"Not to my knowledge but nobody really keeps track of those things," Eric said.

"Did either of you tell Georgie or Barbara about the blow to my head?" I asked.

"No, definitely not," Iggy said and Eric shook his head.

We entered the mess hall and joined the line with everyone else. Big Larry was standing behind the serving table with Bunny and walked over when he saw us enter the building.

"Did you enjoy the nightclub last night there Whitey?" he asked.

"It was awesome! I didn't know there was so much talent at this place."

"How about you Hambone?"

"Ditto, man!"

"And where were you, DO?" he asked staring directly at me with his intense beady eyes.

"I came down with a really bad headache. Every once in a while, I get a migraine that can last for a while. I can't even remember the last time I had one, it was so long ago. Anyway, I'm feeling much better this morning so I expect to make it tonight."

"Well I hope for your sake you do. A square dancin' friend of mine is comin' by this evenin' to lead us all in a hoedown so you're not gonna wanna miss that action! And don't be knockin' anythin' before you try it. Did you ever think that Talent Night would be so much fun before you came last night? I bet not! We're gonna have ourselves a hootenanny, with ladies chains, promenades, do-si-does, allemandes left and rights, and you'll get a chance to honor your partner. You're gonna have more fun than you ever thought possible with your britches on!"

I have to admit that when we were taught square dancing in second grade, I kind of liked it. It was one of those activities that all the boys pretended to hate but I think maybe some of us actually liked it more than we were willing to admit. True, I would have preferred kickball to square dancing but it was a heck of a lot more fun than singing. We all wore brightly colored yarn on our right wrists so that we could remember our lefts from our rights and we got to hold hands with girls. That was the best part, especially when Eve London was in my group of eight. I especially loved it when we were partners and I could promenade with her.

"Can't wait," I responded to Big Larry.

Breakfast was a great spread of eggs and sausages with a few juice selections and a big pot of coffee. Eric and I didn't drink coffee and he asked Bunny if there were any teas to choose from.

DAVID W. GOODWIN

"You boys don't drink coffee? Well, I'll be! I don't think we've ever had anyone work at the quarry that didn't drink coffee or eat meat. I make a special blend, you should try it," she said. "But I do have a stash of teas in the kitchen. Hold on a second and I'll see what we have."

I have only had one cup of coffee in my life and I remember the time quite well, at least as well as I could considering that I was absolutely plastered. It was on the day I had gotten my driver's license. I celebrated by bringing two young ladies I knew from a neighboring town I had met at a church camp a handful of summers ago over to my friend's house for a pool party. It was just the four of us as the rest of his family were away someplace. I must have met them during the summer before my church confirmation because I'm absolutely positive I wouldn't have agreed to go to a church camp after I was deemed old enough to become a freewheeling atheist. Anyway, I drove over to pick them up, took them back to our cozy little pool party, swam, consumed massive quantities of alcohol supplied by my friend's older brother and then had a little make out session once we figured out who was going to get paired up with whom. The plan then was to drive them back home.

Things were going great until the massive quantities of alcohol found their way into my not-so-massive body. Before long; I realized I was in no shape for anything productive and was barely semi-functional. When it was time to take them home, my friend forced a cup of coffee into me so I was at least a fairly alert drunk. Fortunately for all of us, I got them home safely, although I have little memory of anything having to do with that part of the evening.

Bunny brought out an assortment of teas and we made our selections. After helping ourselves to the food, we joined Iggy at one of the tables where he was sitting with Joan and Alfonso.

"That's a nice look on you, OD," Joan said pointing with her coffee cup towards my scarf.

"Thanks, Muffy," I responded, hoping she both remembered the reference and the conditions under which the joke had been made previously.

"Not that again! I thought we had put that joke to rest!" she said laughing.

"Consider it officially put to sleep," I said. I was looking for any sort of sign from her about our activities last night but she wasn't showing any of her cards. I figured that I could play this game too so I ignored the elephant in the room and asked how things were going with the landscaping out front.

"Really well," Alfonso responded. "We're hoping to wrap things up today with the rock wall. How's your special project going? I know Joan is chompin' at the bit to do some rock climbing, eh chiquita?"

"Sí, Señor," Joan responded.

Once we finished our breakfasts and conversations, we headed back to the bunkhouse. While I was making my bed and organizing my few possessions, I saw Georgie enter the building and watched as he walked over to his bed.

"How's your poison ivy doing, Eric?" I asked, diverting my attention back to him.

"Much better, most of the itching is gone and all I'm left with is a little rash. If I don't think about it, I almost forget that it's there."

"Just in time for your double girlfriend weekend!" Iggy said.

"Yeah, don't remind me. I don't think I have to worry about that problem too much anymore. I doubt that Tina and I will cross paths much in the near future but maybe by the time I get back to Boulder, she'll have calmed down some."

"Or have worked herself into a bigger frenzy," I suggested.

"I suppose that's possible too. Phoebe's flight gets in Saturday morning so that's got to be my focus. After all, it's only Wednesday so the weekend's pretty far away."

"Do you think you guys will be around for the Zoo's Fourth of July party?" I asked.

"I hope so. How about you Iggy?" Eric asked.

"For sure man, wouldn't miss it for the world!"

Time had come for us to start our work day so we joined the mass exodus and entered the office building with everyone else. There was something about the various routines at the quarry that I found very soothing. In contrast to the irregular structure of being a college student with each day being different from most of the other days, time at the quarry flowed in a very linear fashion. As much as I liked college, I found myself enjoying the rhythms and predictability of the working life.

Big Larry began the meeting and talked about the day's schedule. When the various assignments were made, he looked around the room, looked over at Rhonda, looked down at his boots and looked back at Rhonda again. He opened his mouth but nothing recognizable as words came out. Rhonda stepped forward.

DAVID W. GOODWIN

"Since Biggie doesn't seem comfortable leading this discussion, I guess it's up to me to talk about a sensitive subject. Some of you folks might have noticed at the nightclub last night that Georgie and Joan disappeared for a while during the middle of the Talent Show. First, as you all know, Georgie is one of our best and quietest employees; she's been here longer than me and Big Larry. Her father used to run this place. I'm not sure how many of you knew this but she has a job here for life. Georgie, are you still okay with this discussion?"

"As ready as I'll ever be," Georgie spoke up softly.

"Last night, Georgie made a decision that's going to change her life forever," Rhonda continued. "You see, she and Joan hatched a plan and it involved a visit with OD here. OD, would you be so kind as to tell everyone what happened last night?"

"Uh, um, I'm not sure what happened last night was real or if it was a dream. I had a really bad headache," I said feeling a bit startled that I was being put on the spot like this. "Georgie, were you in the bunkhouse with me last night?"

"Yes, I was. You see, I've never been with a man or a woman before and I wanted to see what it was like so I could make a pretty important decision. Why don't you describe what happened."

"If you're sure you want me to, okay, here goes. Since I wasn't feeling well, I needed to go to bed really early and wasn't able to go to the nightclub. Georgie came to me in the night and I wasn't sure who it was. As I said, I thought I was having a dream, especially when she encouraged me to touch her. I was a bit surprised by a few things that I discovered."

"Please continue," Georgie said looking me right in the eye. "You have my permission to say exactly what happened."

"Well, for one thing, she is both a he and a she, a she on top and a he down below. We went over to Joan's bed where she was waiting for us and tried a little experiment. I don't remember much after that so maybe Joan should continue the story."

"Sure, if you'd like. The idea was that we would help Georgie figure out if she was more attracted to men or women. She felt this would help her make a decision about which type of surgery she wanted to get," Joan explained. "And what did you conclude, Georgie?"

"I was more attracted to you Joan. I think with some testosterone treatments, I could transition to being a full man. I've already got the equipment, it just needs a little power boost. When I saw how Dean reacted to you, I realized that that's the path I want to pursue because I was feeling the same way in my head and heart."

"Well I'll be!" Big Larry exclaimed, unable to control himself. "I think everyone in this freakin' place would probably react to Joan that way. Maybe you should try the same experiment on Bernice the Flamboyant or my ex-wife. Now that would be a serious test of your resolve. Let me give you a little piece of advice, Georgie, maybe you should become a woman and just be one of those lesbos that seem to be crawlin' all over each other down in Boulder."

"Big Larry," Rhonda interjected, "that's not being very helpful. We need to be giving Georgie constructive feedback, not confuse the issue. Just shut your mouth if you can't be more supportive. What do others think?"

"I can picture Georgie going in either direction," Yolanda offered.

"And I don't think it's anyone's business but Georgies. If she feels that she wants to become a man, that's what should happen," Laverne said.

"Maybe she could find someone who has the opposite problem, like maybe from the circus. That way, they'd be like two peas in a pod," Quesnal offered.

"That's enough of this pussycock, I mean poppycock," Big Larry said. "I can see that we're just not gonna make any progress. See Rhonda, this was a bad idea, just like I told you earlier."

"Georgie, the bottom line is that we support whatever decision you make, even if it's no decision," Rhonda said ignoring Big Larry.

"And if you want me to get my ex-wife up here for another experiment, just let me know. I'll even ask her to shave her beard off if you think it might be helpful. Now, let's all get out to work before the day disappears."

CHAPTER 16

THE DAY WENT by in a blur. Maybe it was the residual headache and dull throbbing I felt, maybe it was the experience with Georgie and Joan the night before, maybe it was the cloudy cool day but it was probably because everyone seemed in a strange, remote, untalkative mood. Somehow, the business with Georgie seemed to have a major impact on everyone's behavior and everything just seemed out of whack. Rhonda was all business as usual trying to get the gnat netting framework pieces transported up to the top of the quarry and then assembled, Barbara was acting weird towards me like I had somehow betrayed her by going along with Georgie's plan and Juan Antonio was nursing a serious attitude like he was pissed off at the world and refused to go anywhere near the rock walls or move at anything but a snail's pace. Maybe he had been having special feelings for Georgie that he felt were now getting trampled.

"I . . . just . . . need . . . to . . . keep . . . my . . . head . . . balanced . . . on . . . my . . . shoulders," he slowly and methodically responded when Rhonda asked him to get another can of glue from the truck. It took him about five minutes and I got a case of the giggles watching him move in slow motion, trying to keep his entire upper body perfectly still. It looked like he was walking on sheer ice and was afraid that if he didn't maintain perfect contact with the surface, he might go skidding out of control at any moment.

"Hey, Juan Antonio, watch out for that water molecule near your foot. It's a biggie!" I yelled out as loudly as I could without blowing a hole through the top of my skull.

"You're . . . funny . . . Mr . . . ACDC," he answered in a soft voice. "You . . . sure . . . you . . . didn't . . . like . . . Georgie's . . . bottom . . . half . . . more . . . than . . . the . . . top?"

"No, I'm not sure. I think I could become a homosexual any moment now. Geez, I just noticed, you've got a pretty cute ass!"

"Alright you two, that's enough," Rhonda interjected. "Would you both just concentrate on the tasks at hand?"

This is how our morning went. We were like alien zombies going through the awkward motions of our working day having as few interactions with our coworkers as possible. The energy just wasn't flowing like it normally did. We were busy putting together each section of pipes to make twenty five foot squares. At one point I asked Rhonda how many sections were going to be required.

"What do you think, doofus?" she barked.

"I think that I don't know which is why I asked, fart breath!" I responded half insulted that she called me doofus and half amused at my own response.

"Who you calling fart breath, droopy drawers?"

"You, dork nose!"

"Oh yeah, well you're a dirty hippie head," Rhonda responded with a forced laugh as she lunged at me and pulled the scarf off my head, revealing my bandage and the missing chunk of hair. She stood there for a moment with my blue bandana in her hand and stared at my head. "What happened to you?"

"Georgie took a bite out of me last night, mistaking my forehead for Joan's left nipple," I answered shooting a quick glance at Barbara. She averted my gaze by looking out over the quarry.

"Right!" Rhonda said sarcastically.

"No, really, it was something like that. I can't say for sure what happened but when I woke up this morning, I had a whopper of a cut."

"So why are you missing part of your hair?" Rhonda asked.

"Iggy helped me to dress the wound and thought the bandage would work better if it could adhere well."

Rhonda examined the dressing up close and got perhaps a little too personal but I didn't mind much. Even though she was a difficult person to be around sometimes, she was still pretty hot. She hovered around me, examining the cut from several angles and I could feel the heat radiating from her body and it made me feel like I was starting to come down with a mild fever. Eventually she pulled back and agreed that Iggy had done a pretty good job.

Her voice and demeanor then abruptly changed back to that of our crew chief and she told us to all get back to work. She had to go over and rouse Juan Antonio who had used the time to take a quick siesta in the back of Rhonda's pickup truck. The day became dull again and worked its way through lunchtime and eventually arrived at late afternoon. Even with the lack of any serious collective energy, we were able to get a fair amount of work done on the structure and Rhonda seemed pleased with the progress. She herded us into the truck and we made our way slowly down to the office building.

We arrived a few minutes before anyone else. Rhonda silently motioned for me to follow her into the building when Barbara and Juan Antonio were over by another building drinking some water out of a hose. "Quick, come here with me for a moment," she whispered from the doorway. "I want to talk to you in private before the others arrive."

I did as I was told and followed her into the building. "What is it, Boss Lady?" I asked as I was staring at her tanned lower butt cheeks disappear into the darkness of the room.

"Did you, Joan and Georgie really have the experience you described at the meeting this morning or did you all just make that up?" she asked after turning on some of the lights.

"Like I said, my memory from last night is a little cloudy but I'm probably 95% certain that it happened. Why do you ask?"

"It just seems so . . . what should I say? . . . uncharacteristic of both of them. Neither really seem like the adventurous types, if you know what I mean."

"I have to say that it surprised the hell out of me too especially since I was sound asleep when Georgie came and woke me up."

"Did you really touch his private parts?"

"Yep, for sure."

"That's amazing! All this time, I was convinced that he was a she."

"You should check him out yourself if you have any doubts or don't believe me," I suggested.

The crew started entering the room, Iggy and Eric came in together with Joan and Alfonso and we were soon joined by everyone else except Big Larry. Rhonda asked if anyone had seen him recently. Harry said he had been in the garage checking out some equipment around lunchtime but hadn't seen him since. Rhonda decided to run the meeting and took everyone's report, wrote down some notes on a pad of paper she extracted from the back pocket of her jean shorts and opened the floor to any comments.

"Yeah, I'd like to ask about square dancing at the nightclub tonight. Is Big Larry serious?" Hector asked. "I have to say, that doesn't really sound like a whole hell of a lot of fun."

"I'm just sorry I'm going to miss it," Barbara chimed in. "You know this is the night that I spend with my family. I'm jealous. Does everyone remember the time a while back when we had Hokey-Pokey night? Well, I'm sure this is going to be even better than that!"

"What was Hokey-Pokey night like?" Eric asked innocently.

Almost everyone in the room started chuckling and looked at Eric. Finally, Rhonda said, "Whitey, do you know how to do the Hokey-Pokey?"

"Of course I do."

"So, imagine the nightclub, imagine the Hokey-Pokey, and then imagine all of the various things that you can put in, take out and then shake all about, then maybe you'll get the idea!"

"Ohhh, I see!"

The door to the building came flying open and in blasted Big Larry like he had been shot out of a cannon. He had so much velocity that he ran right into the first object in his way, which happened to be Rhonda.

"Whoa, where's the fire, Biggie?" she asked as his head landed smack between her breasts. She caught him in her arms, stopping him dead in his tracks, preventing him from serious injury in a way that most of us probably envied.

"Dang, that was a close call. Everyone, I want you to swear on a stack of Bibles that I've been here in this room with y'all for the last five minutes," he said in a very loud whisper.

Big Larry started the meeting over again. Rhonda whispered into his ear so that everyone in the room could hear, "We've already done this."

The door flew open again, this time it was Bernice the Flamboyant that came charging into the room. I hadn't seen her since she was being carted off to the hospital last week with a broken collarbone. Her arm was in a sling and stabilized against her body with a few Ace bandages.

"You little weasel, how dare you run off with my car keys!" she yelled.

"What are you talkin' 'bout, my little love button?" Big Larry responded, trying to look as sweet and innocent as his genetics allowed. "I've been here at this meetin' all along."

"Well, I'm missing my keys. I was in the little girl's room, freshening up. When I came back to the trailer, they were gone. I know that I left them on the counter. Why would you take them?"

"You got the wrong man, Sweet Lips. Maybe you left them somewhere else. We're in the middle of our meetin' here, darlin', why don't you go look around and I'll come help you in a few minutes when we're done?"

Bernice turned around, muttered something under her breath and left the building. Big Larry wiped his brow in an exaggerated gesture and then dismissed us all for the afternoon.

"What was that all about?" Rhonda asked him as the crew made a half-hearted attempt to leave. I know that I wanted to hear his response.

"I'm hopin' to convince her to stick around for the nightclub tonight and if she doesn't have her keys, she can't leave," he explained as he pulled a set of keys out of his pants pocket and held them up for Rhonda and the rest of us to see. "We had a little spat but I think she'll calm down in a little while."

The room then emptied out and we went back to the bunkhouse. I was determined to keep my body in one piece so I could attend my first nightclub and wasn't going to do anything between now and then to jeopardize my chances, even if Iggy or Eric had some sort of mini-adventure planned before dinner.

"Let's go wing the wham around for a while but not by the quarry this time. How about we go over by the greenhouses?" Iggy suggested.

"Yeah, that sounds like a good idea," Eric responded. "Let's make sure to get our dirty clothes over to the laundry first. You up for it Beans?"

"Well, I was thinking about just hangin' out here until dinner. My head feels almost normal again but I could use a little change of scene, especially now that the sun has finally come out. Sure, let's go. Do either of you have a watch?"

We quickly changed into our shorts and tee shirts. Eric grabbed a watch from somewhere deep in his duffle bag and I grabbed my backup Frisbee since my main disc was still at the quarry. We went over to the laundry drop off and then out into the sunshine.

"Where are you guys heading?" Georgie asked as our paths intersected. I told her what we were up to and invited her along. "Sure, that sounds like fun. But I have to warn you, I'm not very good."

"No problem, we can help with that," Eric said.

The four of us walked down the road to the greenhouse turnoff and found an open grassy area near one of the huge compost piles. We threw the disc around for a while without talking much, just enjoying the increasingly warm afternoon. Eventually, the three of us stripped off our tee shirts and were down to just our shorts before I realized the implications for Georgie.

"I hope you don't mind if I don't follow suit," she said.

"Whatever you're comfortable with," I said. "It doesn't matter to any of us either way."

"Yeah, really, it's not like we've never seen topless men or shirtless women before," Iggy said kindly, trying to increase Georgie's comfort level and trying his best to be all-inclusive and cover all options. He then added, "Or bottomless men or women for that matter."

"But probably not all in the same person," Georgie said.

"You're right about that!" Eric exclaimed laughing.

Georgie actually was a pretty good Frisbee tosser compared to most women that I had played with. She did that thing that most women do when they are throwing a ball or skipping a stone where they try to get all of their power from just their wrists.

"Try stepping into the throw and rotating your body to get more power and spin," Eric suggested. "You've got a good throw but you could easily throw it twice as far and fast if you put more into it. Watch."

He demonstrated by throwing the Frisbee to Iggy who then threw it to me and then back to Georgie. "See the difference?"

She did, immediately, and within a few throws had improved significantly.

"Wow, I've never had much success trying to teach this to anyone before. You got it immediately."

"Maybe I have more testosterone than the others. Were they all women?"

"Yes," Eric admitted.

"Well, I have that part too, as you all now know." With that, Georgie joined the bare-chested men club but as I discovered last night, she didn't really qualify for membership. This clearly was another step in her new mission of full self disclosure and her choice to come out to the quarry community.

"Yeah, that's what I'm talking about!" Iggy yelled using one of his redneck cowboy voices. "To be honest, Georgie, with a beautiful rack like that, I think you should stay a woman!"

"You're making me blush, Iggy, but thanks. I've always thought that these were more like swollen mosquito bites than actual boobs."

"You're wrong there! You've got nicer boobs than half of my old girlfriends. I happen to like that size and especially your large nipples. How about you Eric?"

"Me too, haven't you noticed Tina's A cup? I think Beans here is the only one that has never met a boob that's been too big. Am I right?"

DAVID W. GOODWIN

"Personal taste, I guess. If only I had been breastfed for more than two days I might not be so attracted to women with large tits."

We continued throwing my spare Frisbee around for a while but the three of us guys were having a hard time concentrating on much of anything other than our own mass of confusion over Georgie's naked chest and the concealed man parts under her jeans. She, on the other hand, seemed to be reveling in both the freedom of her newfound comfort with her body, the relief that probably came with not trying to hide her sexual identity and her new found skill throwing a Frisbee. It was, undoubtedly, a powerful combination.

Eric said that it was time to head back for dinner so we put our tee shirts back on and started walking back towards the compound.

"That was a lot of fun," Georgie said, "Thanks for letting me hang out with you guys. I haven't done something like this for a long time."

"Hey, any time Georgie," Eric said.

We quickly washed up for dinner and made ourselves as presentable as possible. Bunny had a Mexican theme going and it was almost as good as Señor Miguels plus we didn't have to pay for it. The two other amigos and I sat with Georgie, Felix 1 and Laverne who seemed upset that she kept getting thwarted in her efforts to spend time with Junior. He seemed to have perfected the art of finding a table to sit at without any available spaces before Laverne arrived.

Not only was Laverne a good conversationalist but she also had a bawdy sense of humor that us college boys were especially partial to. There are a few people I know that are encyclopedias of jokes, like they remember every joke they have ever heard in their entire lives. Laverne was one of them. I think you could throw out any topic, like foot fungus, and Laverne would have ten or twenty jokes on the subject, half of which would be raunchy.

The six of us were devouring our meals when Felix 1 asked Iggy if he had always been a hippie. Hearing the word 'hippie' set Laverne off immediately, even before Iggy had a chance to respond.

"Two hippies are walking down the street and see a dog licking his balls. One says, I wish I could do that. The other says, man, you better get to know him first."

"That's nasty!" Eric said laughing.

"Okay, here's a better one," Laverne offered, "What did the hippie say after the drugs wore off?"

"I don't know," I said.

"Man this music sucks!" Laverne said loud enough for everyone in the room to hear.

"That's pretty good," Iggy said. He decided to join the joke fest and told a long one involving a hippie, a nun and a bus driver. Laverne then reeled off three or four more jokes that were even dirtier.

Dinner came to an end, we walked back to the bunkhouse and then all went our separate ways. My downtime was spent reading a book I had started a few weeks ago and rarely seemed to find time to read. The other guys in the bunkhouse all were busy doing any number of things like the previous evening. I made it through a few more chapters before the sun started going down.

CHAPTER 17

IT HAD BEEN a solid week of hearing about the nightclub. Everyone who worked at the quarry had been to it except for me and none of them were talking, even my best friends. Other than a whacked out dream about the place and seeing the physical location in real life, I still had no idea what to expect. The sun had set a while ago, the sky had faded from blue to pink to red and finally it became the color of night. Up here in the mountains, this was a deep rich dark blue that seemed transparent, more three dimensional than possible, maybe even four dimensional, like the entire universe suddenly revealed itself to us earthlings in a way that the daytime sky couldn't or wouldn't do. When the stars started coming out, first off on the darker eastern horizon, then overhead and finally in the western sky, it was clearly time for the magic of the nightclub to begin, or disappoint.

Folks in the bunkhouse started getting themselves ready. I was keeping a watchful eye on their activities to figure out how much effort to put into it. Of course, in my dream, we all showed up in our work clothes so this part appeared to be wrong. Guys were putting on nice clothing, nothing too fancy, mostly clean blue jeans and button down shirts. Iggy and Eric had been off playing cards with Juan Antonio and Frederick and ended their game to begin changing into their nightclub clothes.

"How dressed up do people get for this thing?" I asked Eric as he searched through his duffle bag.

"Not too much. There isn't a dress code or anything. It doesn't really matter, just wear something that's comfortable," he suggested.

I pulled out a pair of khakis I had when I needed to dress up a little and a light cotton v-neck sweater. It was the kind of outfit I would wear when I was at my parent's house and they would inevitably say something like, "that's a nice outfit, much better than the ratty jeans and tattered work shirts you usually wear". I knew it made them happy to see me out of the college student uniform of the mid '70s so it seemed like a good choice for this evening.

I waited around for someone to make the move out to the supply building nightclub and wondered what might trigger it. The quarry loudspeaker suddenly crackled to life. After a brief moment of silence, the big band sound began to fill the quarry and Frank Sinatra started singing *Fly Me to the Moon*.

Apparently, that was what everyone was waiting for because as soon as Ol' Blue Eyes started his smarmy warble, everyone got up and walked over. The women arrived on cue and had taken a little extra effort as well to clean up. The effect was quite pleasing. Iggy and Eric each gave me a big smile as we approached the nightclub door.

Frankie was still wailing away on speakers inside the supply building as we made our entrance. I was expecting to see the inside of the supply building as I remembered it from my last visit—college student quality tables with folding metal chairs, crappy floor to ceiling shelving units filled with clothing and appliances, dusty light bulbs hanging from the ceiling and the massive switch on the wall by the door. The only thing recognizable was the massive switch on the wall.

Instead, the inside of the supply building had been transformed almost to the nightclub of my dreams. There was a large raised circular stage in the middle of the room with fancy leather and chrome stools arranged around tall glass topped tables on the edges of the stage. The stage was ringed with floor lights and illuminated from above with theatre lighting. The scary looking lightbulbs hanging from the rafters had been replaced by classy and elegant track lighting and the rafters were no longer rafters and had somehow become a mirrored ceiling.

I took a seat at a table with my buddies and Georgie. Everyone else settled into the remaining chairs. Frankie's song ended and we were left with the quiet sound of anticipation. I looked around the room and saw almost everyone that worked at the quarry.

Leaning over towards Eric, I whispered, "How the hell did this place get transformed to this? What happens next?"

He put his finger to his lips and in a few seconds, the lights went up a notch and some great jazz came on over the sound system. In from a doorway I hadn't noticed before walked Big Larry, Rhonda and Bunny, all carrying trays loaded with elegant shot glasses filled with a bright green liquid that seemed to be sparkling more than possible, like they were their own light source. Additionally, the lights from the nightclub reflected at every conceivable angle off these drinks. The crew all applauded and the

DAVID W. GOODWIN

glasses were distributed throughout the room onto the tables. Nobody touched their drinks and sat patiently.

Big Larry and Rhonda went onto the stage and Bunny took one of the remaining seats as the music faded out. They both took a shot glass and then Big Larry spoke with much fanfare, sounding almost like a circus announcer.

"Ladies and gentlemen, welcome to the Sugarloaf Quarry Nightclub! I'm your Master of Ceremonies, Thad Flapper and I'd like to introduce my lovely assistant, Wanda Ladowski!"

Everyone broke into another round of applause. If Big Larry was going to assume the alter ego of Thad Flapper, I kind of expected him to look different but he just looked like the same old Big Larry that slunk around the quarry looking for trouble. Wanda Ladowski was identical to Rhonda except that she had traded in her short jean shorts for medium short dress shorts and her quarry tank top for an elegant cashmere sweater that was unbuttoned down at least half way to her glorious belly button barely reigning in her equally glorious breasts.

"Tonight's another rookie night. We've got Mr. OD for his first nightclub experience so I'll ask him to high tail his rump up here." I stood up and began walking towards the front of the room. "With your drink!" he commanded so I reversed my tracks and grabbed my electric looking drink off the table.

When I was standing up front with them, Thad raised his glass to the room. Wanda followed his lead and then he said, "We welcome OD to the brethren and sisteren of the Sugarloaf Quarry. We welcome you into our secret society and ask that in return for your induction into our world, you honor this privilege and speak of this experience to no one outside of the quarry. Lift your glass and indicate your acceptance of these rules by repeating after me,"

"I, insert your name here . . ."

"I, insert your, oops, I mean, I, Dean Morrison"

"Do solemnly swear to follow the Sugarloaf Quarry rules . . ."

"Do solemnly swear to follow the Sugarloaf Quarry rules . . ."

"And honor the privileges bestowed upon me to the best of my abilities . . ."

"And honor the privileges bestowed upon me to the best of my abilities . . ."

"Or suffer massive negativity, bad karma and possible multiple blows to the head . . ."

"Or suffer massive negativity, bad karma and possible multiple blows to the head . . ."

"So help me Thad and Wanda."

"So help me Thad and Wanda."

"You are hereby welcomed into the Sugarloaf Quarry Nightclub Club. You may now kiss the bride."

"You are hereby . . . oops, never mind."

I wasn't sure who the bride was so I stood there with a confused expression on my face until Thad said, "It can be anyone you want—go kiss her or him—your choice, and then we'll drink to your health and happiness."

I knew this might be a once in a lifetime opportunity so I walked over to Bunny, took her large, fleshy, mocha colored hand as she stood up, embraced her enormous body in my arms and planted a kiss on her luscious lips as we dipped slightly away from the table towards Thad and Wanda. She had lips that were equal to two or three of any combination of my past girlfriend's lips and I immediately felt lightheaded and giddy and didn't want to stop. However, since this apparently was the signal for everyone else to drink, I wrapped up our kiss, handed her the glass from the table and then drank mine. It tasted a little sweet, a little sour, a little bitter and had a distinctive taste of licorice, all at the same time and was unlike anything I had ever tasted before.

I whispered a quick thank you to Bunny and went back to my table. Eric, Iggy and Georgie gave me high fives and Eric said, "Good choice, Beans! I chose Rhonda." Iggy told me he had chosen Joan.

All eyes returned to Thad and Wanda once I sat down. Big Thad made an exaggerated survey of the room to make sure all of the drinks had been consumed. When he was satisfied with what he saw, he declared the nightclub open for business and walked over to the monster switch on the wall by the door. I was beginning to feel like I had just been to the dentist and instead of injecting some Novocain into my gum; they instead injected it into every appendage of my body, from my feet all the way up to my head. I looked over at Iggy to try to figure out what was happening but noticed that he seemed to be shrinking rapidly with a sublime look on his face. I looked the other way and saw Eric starting to hover above his chair and his body had a strange aura around it, like maybe a bunch of sparklers were going off behind him. Georgie, sitting directly opposite me, was spinning rapidly in his chair like a cartoon barber's seat gone haywire and was just a blur. The feeling I had wasn't in any way unpleasant but in no way could I say that I felt like myself anymore.

Big Thad put both of his hands on the switch and, just like in my dream, used his entire body weight to slowly pull it down. When the switch lost its connection with the upper contacts, the lights went dim for a few seconds until it contacted the lower part. When this happened, all of the lights came on in a bright flash, the door opened that Big Larry, Rhonda and Bunny had entered through and a miniature Conestoga wagon came roaring into the nightclub. The wagon had the Sugarloaf Sam logo on either side and was being pulled by a team of four of the largest rats I had ever seen in my life. Each one was wearing a set of custom made-for-rats Sugarloaf Quarry tee shirts and overalls. They were hell-bent on speed and had been trained to run laps around the inside of the nightclub. Strapped securely into the driver's seat of the wagon and sitting up as much as an extremely large rodent could was Sugarloaf Sam. He had the reigns and a miniature martini glass in one of his front paws and a lit mini-cigar in the other. Over the sound system was an extended version of his starting and quitting time scream. The crowd went nuts as the rats did a few laps and then disappeared back through the door from which they came.

When the rats were gone, the door opened again and out came the band. They joined Thad and Wanda on stage and started playing a fabulous tune. This was probably the best music I had ever heard in my life and I made a mental note to myself to go buy some square dancing records the next time I was in Boulder, maybe even trade in all my rock and roll albums. It affected me deep into my corpuscles, perhaps even deeper.

Off to the side was an elegant bar and people were going over and ordering drinks being served by a woman dressed and made up to look like Dolly Parton, complete with massive balloon enhanced boobs. She looked familiar but I couldn't quite place her in her current outfit. Before the first song was over, everyone had a fresh drink in their hands and was back at their tables enjoying the music. Before the second song, we were called up to the floor and the fiddle player gave us a quick lesson of the basic steps and patterns and walked us through a number of square dances and then things went even crazier.

The music started again, the fiddle player called the first dance and thanks to the quick lesson, we all seemed to know what to do and how to do it. We formed easily into three groups of eight and then paired up within our groups. Men were with men, women were with men, women were with women, it really didn't matter. The fiddle player began calling a dance and it was like one of those dopey musicals where a bunch of random people are walking into a subway, the music starts and complete strangers launch into a perfectly choreographed number where everyone's movement is totally dependent and intertwined with each other. This is the movie I was suddenly cast in except that instead of the subway entrance, it was the square dance nightclub at the Sugarloaf Quarry.

The evening flowed in a series of dances, music, drinks, and laughter. It was the best party I had ever been to, which, coming from Boulder, is really saying something. I had been to Halloween parties, Fellini parties, naked dance parties, end of finals parties, beginning of finals parties, formal sorority parties, stoned hippie parties, and impromptu Tuesday night mushroom parties but they all paled in comparison to this party. We were an integral part of a cohesive mass; movin' and groovin' with each other. At one point, I was called up to perform. Since I didn't know any square dancing songs and had never even sung a song by myself in public before, I had a brief moment of panic. However, when I was up on stage and in the spotlight, it all came to me, like suddenly being fluent in a foreign language I had never known before. I could sing, I knew the lyrics, the rhythm and the syncopation.

After my song was over, the band played a slower number they called *Saint Bruce's Reel* which segued into the *Boulder Bi-Breakdown*. At this point, the square dancing constructs broke down and we formed a large circle filling up the entire stage. Rhonda and Joan went into the middle and improvised a dance that probably raised everyone's libido to near dangerous levels. They were circling with their arms interlocked and reversed direction at the start of each new stanza. When the chorus came around, they unlocked elbows and each managed to quickly take their shirts off and then resumed their circling. At the next chorus, their brassieres came flying off and were launched into the appreciative crowd. They took each other in their arms and danced close together, their breasts pressed tightly while my head spun from the sensory overload. The quarry folk loved this and began stomping along with the music as we continued dancing in the outside circle.

Iggy and Eric, seizing the opportunity of a lifetime, joined them in the center and managed to become a part of their dance. Eric was dancing with Rhonda, Iggy with Joan and they tore off their shirts too. Before long, everyone else followed suit. The whole nightclub, except for the band members themselves and Dolly Parton, was topless and dancing to the rhythms. The band took the tempo up a notch with the *Mountain Meltdown Jig* and I found myself partnered with Georgie. Any inhibitions I had ever felt in my life when it came to dancing and living in the moment were gone and it was a moment of pure bliss, like any worries or self doubts I ever had just disappeared into the nighttime quarry air. Georgie and I danced like there was no tomorrow and the fact that she was packing a penis in her pants barely entered my mind. I saw Eric and Rhonda off in a corner making out while Iggy was dancing with Joan, pressed tightly behind her while she wiggled her hips into him in an exaggerated, slow motion to the rhythm of the song.

The pace of the music then increased in tempo and volume and we slowly worked ourselves into a full frenzy. A bunch of songs were played that I had never heard before. Some couples were clearly paired up for the remainder of the evening as they were having too much fun together, like my pals and Junior and Laverne. Georgie left me for Big Larry, of all people, and it gave me the opportunity to dance with Bunny. I can't say that I had ever seen a woman as large as her naked from the waist up before. When we began doing a rock and roll inspired do-si-do together, her abundant flesh was flying in every direction and I wanted to be smothered by her enormity. I hoped for another slow song but had to settle for a fast one with her. Finally, the band finished the evening with an over-the-top up tempo song, *The Camel Toe Traveler*. At this point, we were all bumping, jumping, pumping, and thumping so when the music finally ended, we collapsed in place on the stage. It was a moment of utter and complete exhaustion and satisfaction.

The band received a huge round of applause as we all struggled back to our feet. The Dolly Parton bartendress came around with large glasses of ice water for everyone which apparently signaled the end of the evening. When she was close enough to hand me my drink, I realized that it was Bernice underneath all the makeup, wig and balloons and should have noticed she was only using one arm. We all drank deeply, returned the glasses to the bar, and found our shirts. I thanked Bunny for the fabulous dance and she gave me a friendly kiss goodnight. I made my way back to the bunkhouse in a haze of delirium. Nobody spoke because I don't think there was anything that could be said after such an experience.

The effect from the green drinks seemed to be wearing off some at this point and my brain was filling up fast with questions. There was so much I wanted to talk to the guys about but I wasn't sure where reality ended and where my own distorted perceptions began. They both stumbled into the bunkhouse a few minutes later.

"Were those really giant rats pulling a covered wagon around?" I asked Eric.

"Pretty cool, eh?"

"Well, yeah, but were they real rats?"

"For sure, man," Iggy chimed in. "Rhonda raises them. Remember our first day here when she dropped us off because she forgot something in town. She came back with a box full of animals. That was her new batch of Giant Gambian Pouch rats for breeding purposes."

"Remember in our animal ecology course, man?" Eric asked. "*Cricetomys gambianus?*"

"No, not really."

"And they're the quarry mascots, in case you hadn't figured that out yet," Iggy said.

"Yeah, I did but they're massive. They're big enough to be confused for hairless poodles," I remarked. "And what was in those green drinks?"

"Mystery juice. I'm not sure anyone knows but they're pretty good, wouldn't you say? You won't have a hangover tomorrow and they completely wear off in a few hours. What could be better?" Iggy asked.

"I'm not complaining, I just never experienced anything like it before."

"Did you have a good time tonight, Beans?" Eric asked.

"Absolutely."

"Then don't think about it too hard and get a good night's sleep."

"But how did the supply shack get transformed to the nightclub?" I asked.

"Like I said, don't think about it too much, just enjoy it," Eric repeated.

I was so sweaty from all the dancing and thought a shower would feel good before I hit the sack. Laverne and Junior were waiting around for one of the already occupied shower stalls. She couldn't keep her hands off him and was wildly pawing him, removing whatever articles of clothing she could over his mild protests, all the while trying to remove her own clothes with one hand. Junior was acting like a store mannequin and had about as much romantic energy. He looked at me while I was brushing my teeth and rolled his eyes.

Before they were both completely naked, a shower opened up and Laverne pulled Junior in with her. She was down to just her industrial

DAVID W. GOODWIN

strength semi-white underwear which came off before she actually made it into the shower, giving me a glimpse of what kinds of treats Junior was feasting on. She looked at me and said, "You could be next if you're interested."

I wasn't, so my strategy was going to be to make myself as scarce as possible. Another shower opened up so I quickly jumped in, rinsed off the evening's square dancing sweat and toweled myself dry, but not before I was serenaded by the grunts, groans, squeaks and yelps of the March/September couple going at it in the next shower stall. I wasn't sure what Laverne meant when she told Junior to rope a big one, pull it tight and give it a brand but fortunately, I didn't stick around long enough to find out.

The scene back at the bunkhouse was quite a bit mellower as most everyone was settling in for the night. I heard a woman's voice coming from Alfonso's sheeted off area and I guessed that it might be coming from Joan or Yolanda, I couldn't tell. Eric and Iggy had both disappeared. I had enough excitement for the night so went over to my bed and fell asleep within ten seconds, maybe less.

Sometime in the middle of the night, when I was off in a dream that involved being at the Georgetown hot springs with Sarah, I heard someone calling my name. I ignored it at first since it didn't seem to be coming from Sarah or anyone else in my dream. I looked over at the group of folks that I had been swimming and hanging out with that day last weekend and saw the heads of Rob, Candy, Jimbo and Orville but their bodies were Giant Gambian Pouch rats only human sized. The fact that they had rat bodies didn't really seem to cause them or me much concern. The Rob rat came over, dragging his long hairless tail over the rocks and through the icy water and asked if I had brought any cheese.

"There might be some in the stash that Jimbo packed," I answered. "By the way, when did you get turned into a giant rat?"

"Sometime last night. Do you remember seeing all of us at the nightclub pulling the Conestoga wagon while Sarah got to sit and steer?"

"I saw four rodents pulling Sugarloaf Sam who had a martini and a cigar. You're saying that was you and your friends?"

"Yep."

"How did you get shrunk down to that size?"

"And how did we get turned into rats? I'm not sure what the answer is to either of those questions but I'm wondering why Sarah is no longer a rat. It's kind of fun to be a different species for a while and I'm glad I have my normal head but I'm having these strong cravings for cheese and an insane desire to dig holes in the dirt."

"Yeah, I woke up looking like the rest of you this morning but when I looked at myself in the mirror, I immediately became myself again," Sarah explained. "I wasn't too happy to have a rat's body so I'm glad that it was only temporary."

"Do you have a mirror with you?" Rob asked.

"Sure, there's one in my purse over by the towels. You can go grab it if you want."

I heard someone saying my name again but ignored it as I was too interested in seeing what was going to happen to Rob when he looked at himself. Sure enough, when he gazed at his reflection, he became fully Rob again. I thought he would be more excited but he seemed to accept the change without showing much emotion. He walked back to the rat pack and explained the antidote to them. One by one they all returned to their old selves.

"Here's what I remember about last night," Sarah began explaining. "We all thought it would be fun to come surprise you at the nightclub so we jumped into Candy's car and found our way to the quarry, arriving right around sunset. We parked a little ways away from the buildings so we wouldn't ruin the surprise. Rob volunteered to do some reconnaissance and ran into a woman coming out of one of the buildings. He said she was wearing really short jean shorts and a tight tank top. She asked him what he was up to and he told her we were there to surprise you. She said that wasn't allowed but instead invited all of us back to her trailer. When we got there, she gave us these really great bright green drinks and the next thing I knew, the bitch locked us into a cage somewhere out behind her trailer. She then said some words that sounded like Swahili and we were turned into rats and shrunken down to the size that you saw—bigger than any rat that I've ever seen but smaller than our normal size. She made us put on these funny little outfits and explained that we had to drive this wagon around for a while inside the nightclub. Once we did that, she said we would revert back to ourselves and then we'd be free."

"Is that what happened?"

"Yes, except for the reverting back to ourselves part. We got back to our normal sizes and got our normal heads back but the rest of our bodies were still rats. It was tough driving back to Georgetown without anyone seeing us as rats and, as you heard, I didn't get my body back until this morning."

"Well, I'm glad you did. You're much sexier as a woman than a she-rat. Did you see me at the nightclub? I don't remember seeing you driving the wagon. You looked like Sugarloaf Sam."

With that, my dream abruptly ended as someone was shaking my shoulders while I heard them say my name again. I slowly opened my eyes to see Iggy and Eric standing there in the moonlight filtering in through the bunkhouse windows.

"Beans, man, wake up, you can get some cheese later," Iggy said again in a loud whisper. "We need to show you something."

"Leave me alone, I'm in the middle of a great dream," I mumbled.

"No, you've got to get up. You'll thank us for this later," Eric said. "We don't want to wake anyone else up so come quickly and quietly with us."

Realizing it was fruitless to try to fight these two Poindexters, I begrudgingly got out of bed, threw on some shoes and followed them outside into the bright moonlight. In Colorado, away from city lights up in the mountains on moonlit nights, you could clearly make out buildings, trees and other features almost as well as during the day except for the absence of color. Everything looked like it was part of a black and white infrared photograph and objects took on a kind of eerie glow that made familiar things look vaguely unfamiliar but wholly recognizable. We were heading straight for Rhonda and Big Larry's spooky looking trailers and it made me feel really uncomfortable.

"Where are we going?" I asked grabbing both of them by the arms in an effort to slow down before we got too close. "Whatever you guys have going on, my guess is that it's a real bad idea."

"Don't worry, just follow us," Iggy said as he and Eric broke my grasp and walked around the two trailers. "Just be really quiet from this point onward. Don't say a thing, got it?"

Fortunately, neither one of the trailers showed any sign of life. We went around the end of Rhonda's mobile home and continued down a path that went through the woods for a few hundred yards. Eventually, we came upon a huge fenced in animal pen set in a lightly wooded area. I had never ventured over to this part of the quarry before so it was all new to me. Inside the pen was an entire Giant Gambian Pouch rat community, with youngsters, oldsters and inbetween-sters. There were smallish wooden houses, feeding bowls and a water trough and piles of excavated dirt and holes in the ground scattered throughout the entire pen area. The pen was a rat hive of activity which made sense since most rodents are nocturnal. The youngsters were busy chasing each other around and the babies were squealing to try to get reattached to their mommies who were half-heartedly trying to get away from them. Some of the other adults were busy digging while others were gnawing at various food items that were strewn around the massive caged area. Fruits and vegetables, recognizable from the previous day's menus, were heaped in several piles at either end of the pen.

"This must have been the cage that Sarah and her buddies were talking about," I whispered.

"What are *you* talking about?" Iggy asked. "You've heard about this rat farm?"

"Only what Sarah and Rob told me. They said that they came up to the quarry this evening to surprise me at the nightclub but Rhonda caught them first, made them drink some of the wonder juice, threw them into this cage, turned them into rats and then hooked them up to the wagon for their laps around the inside of the nightclub," I explained before remembering that maybe that was part of my dream. "Or something like that."

"Are you making this stuff up?" Eric asked.

"Um, well, actually, now that you mention it, maybe that's what I was dreaming about when you guys woke me up," I replied, starting to get confused about which part was true myself. "Regardless, this is all starting to make some sense to me now. How does Rhonda train them to do their nightclub act? Iggy, you've been there three or four times now, do they do the same thing each night?"

"Not exactly, there is usually some sort of tie in to the nightly theme of the club. Since it was square dancing night tonight, having them come in pulling a wagon seems logical."

"And the night before was talent night so a bunch of them came in through the door and did a few laps of clown rolls and rat acrobatics. That was pretty cool!" Eric exclaimed.

"With Sugarloaf Sam riding a little trike behind them holding his martini and cigar. He's always part of the show, that's a constant," Iggy added, "and something that everyone looks forward to each evening."

"We'd better get back to bed before anyone sees us here. I have the feeling that Big Larry and Rhonda wouldn't want us to be poking around much," I said.

We quietly walked back down the path the way we had come in, tiptoed around Rhonda's trailer and, quiet as rats during the daytime, snuck back into the bunkhouse. As soon as my head hit the pillow, I was out for the count again.

Morning seemed to arrive almost immediately and I was aware of the Chambers Brothers song beginning to fill the airwaves. I sat up in my bed, swung my feet onto the wooden floor of the bunkhouse and felt the coarse wood on the soles of my feet. Looking around to do a brief survey of the scene, I did a double take when I saw Georgie get out of Iggy's bed.

CHAPTER 18

IGGY DESERVED HIS reputation for being the most open minded person who lived at the Zoo. Most of the rest of us were kids fresh from some Republican suburb and were trying on a new, alternative life style for the first time. Iggy, even though his upbringing wasn't radically different from the rest of ours, had first generation Europeans for parents and probably had been exposed to a different set of world viewpoints growing up. This was also reflected in his views about his own sexuality. Other than being part of Georgie's experiment with Joan the previous evening, it was unlikely that I would have jumped into bed with him or her. Iggy, on the other hand, must have seen this as a once-in-a-lifetime opportunity and seized the moment. I had to give him credit for that.

Georgie gathered up her clothes while Iggy stayed in bed. As she was about to leave, she leaned over and gave him a quick kiss. I looked over to see if Eric had seen any of this but he was still in some transition period between sleeping and waking. He wouldn't have seen the *Guinness Book of World Records* record setting largest streak that we at the University of Colorado had set two years ago in March where we broke the record set by the University of Maryland, even if all 1,200 of us had streaked right through the middle of the bunkhouse. He would have probably also missed the University of Georgia's streak of 1,543 later in the month as well so the subtle departure of Georgie from Iggy's bed this morning was entirely lost on Eric.

We all made our way over to breakfast. Eric and I were on cleanup duty for the day so we helped Bunny do the dishes and straighten up the room. Once this was done, I stayed and talked to Bunny for a little while and told her how much fun I had with her last night, especially the kissing part. She thought that was hysterical, for some reason. As I walked out into the parking lot, I saw Barbara getting out of her burnt orange Chevy Vega.

"Mornin' Barbara," I said, happy to see her.

"Oh hi, Dean. How was your rookie nightclub experience?"

"Unbelievable! I was surprised how much fun square dancing could be!"

"Honey, you'd be surprised how much fun anything could be at the nightclub. Heck, even if the activity was playing 'Go Fish', it would be fun. That reminds me, since its games night tonight, maybe that's what Big Larry has in mind, you never know. Say, did you miss me?"

"I most certainly did. It would have been fun to dance with you last night. Did you have a good time with your family?"

"Let me just say that it was great to see my daughters and even greater to see my husband. He gets so worked up when I'm away for two days that he's like a sex crazed stallion when I walk through the door. Wow, I can barely walk this morning! What a delightful soreness! Anyway, I had to give my daughters ten bucks to run down to the pizza parlor so Richie could have his way with me. Luckily, he'd been storing up for a few days so he filled me up quickly before they got back."

"Yikes! That sounds like fun. Is this typical of married couples?"

"I don't know, probably. I'd better go drop my bag over at the bunkhouse before morning meeting. Want to come over with me and help me unpack my undies? I brought some extra sexy pairs thinking that I might get a chance to show them off."

"To me?"

"You or anyone else. I just like to think that if everyone knew what sort of panties I was wearing during the day, they might have a hard time walking around the quarry trying to keep their stiffie under control, if you know what I mean."

"Oh yeah, I know what you mean. Sure, I'll come over with you but I have to warn you, I'm planning on spending the weekend with Sarah so I want to save up as much as I can, just in case I get lucky."

"Oh that's so cute! But, hey, you're twenty years old, right?"

"Yes but what are you getting at?"

"Come on, you could have five or six explosions a day and not show any signs of slowing down. I remember what Richie was like when he was your age. I don't think I ever had a chance to dry out. I usually needed to change my underwear at least twice a day, sometimes more. Hey, maybe we'll get sent on another secret mission today."

We walked over to the women's side of the bunkhouse and climbed up the wooden stairs. I felt a little uncomfortable barging in unannounced so I let Barbara lead the way. We entered the room just as Yolanda was pulling her shirt over her head and I felt a bit embarrassed to invade her privacy.

"Nice bra, Yolanda," Barbara said in her deep husky voice. "Where'd you get it? It's very flattering."

Yolanda adjusted herself once the shirt was over her head, pulled her long, curly hair out from under the collar and then noticed me standing there behind Barbara.

"Oh, you should have told me that we had a visitor. I got it at the Boulder Boulder Houlder Store out on 30th. By the way, how'd you like the nightclub, OD?"

"I had a blast. It was so much fun. I can see why you all look forward to it so much."

"It seemed like you were having a good time."

Barbara had gone over to her bed and was busy unpacking her things and putting them carefully into a nearby dresser. She was holding a pink lacy pair of panties up for me and everyone to see. "This is my favorite pair. Maybe I'll put them on today."

"I don't think you'll have time there girl. Work starts in a minute," Yolanda said laughing. "We'd better get ourselves over there pronto."

I was feeling a little apprehensive about the fuss Big Larry was going to make about my inaugural nightclub experience so was trying to brace myself for the worst. My suspicions were raised when he came stomping into the room wearing an oversized cowboy hat. He could barely see out from underneath it and it made him look even smaller than he actually was. It looked like it might just swallow him whole and then there'd just be a hat with feet moving around and bumping into things.

"Yeeee hawwwww!" he screamed like he was riding a kid sized bucking bronco for a quarter outside of a supermarket. "I seem to recall a certain group of college boys thinkin' that maybe a square dancin' hoedown might not be within their narrow minded idea of fun. Well, I s'pose you're all whistlin' a different tune this mornin', am I right there college boys?"

"You're right about that, Big Larry," Eric said, taking the bait. "That was more fun than I imagined possible. My face hurts from all the smiling last night."

"See, you boys just got to learn to trust me. How about you OD, does your face hurt too 'cause it's killin' me!"

"Not my face so much as my butt. I think maybe I did a hundred too many 'swing your partners' and not enough 'sit this one outs', but in a good way," I responded. "Thanks to you, Wanda, Bunny, Dolly Parton and everyone else for a great evening. That was a lot of fun."

Big Larry then took off his hat and got down to the business of the day, giving everyone their assignments. After pushing all of us out the door, the BAP crew jumped into Rhonda's truck and made a brief stop over at one of the supply buildings where she had been storing the equipment purchased for the project. A few more gallons of PVC pipe glue and a box of disposable brushes as well as the new climbing gear, ropes and hardware were thrown into the truck. Juan Antonio was asked to drive a truck over to the garage where we picked up two air compressors and two portable pneumatic rock drills. With the two trucks fully loaded, we slowly made our way up the Juiceway.

The rest of the morning was spent assembling the remaining pipe sections at the top of the quarry. The plan was to piece them together eight sections wide and three sections high to make the final frame. When the last one was finally finished, we took our lunch break and Rhonda eventually began discussing the next step.

"We've done about all we can do up here on the top and now it's time to begin installing the frame sections on the wall. The first eight sections will be fairly easy since we can do most of the work from above. However, we'll need you two guys to be on ropes in order to drill the holes in the wall at the proper locations so we can secure each section. You'll then glue the next section that Babs and I will lower down to you. We'll use the drills to establish a series of anchor bolts up top. These will secure the frame and also hold the ropes you'll work from. We want to make sure these anchors are super strong. I'll do the first one so you can see the proper technique."

After lunch, we got the air compressors positioned and then brought over the drills and the rest of the equipment, arranging them for easy access. Rhonda pulled out a hunk of chalk and put a series of marks at the top of the rock wall that she established by using a tape measure from her belt. She then primed the compressor engine, pulled the cord to fire it up and then connected the hose to one of the drills. At the first mark, she knelt down and began drilling a hole with the industrial quality drill and an extra large drill bit. After a few minutes of effort, she had drilled a hole about three or four inches deep.

"See, it's pretty easy," she said as we surrounded her to look at her hole. "Just go in straight, take it down almost the full length of the drill bit and then we'll set the expansion bolt and hanger. Let's drill all the holes first."

The other compressor was turned on and a hose was connected to the second drill. We all had a chance to drill a few holes and finally completed the task by mid afternoon. Rhonda walked over to grab a bag of anchor bolts and hangers from the truck.

"This is the most critical part of the process," she explained. "These stainless steel expansion bolts have to be installed perfectly since they'll be supporting you and the netting structure. We'll slide a bolt inside a hole, slide a hanger over each one, screw on the nut and then tighten it down to expand the bolt firmly inside the hole. If done properly, it can hold hundreds of pounds, like two Juniors, three ODs and maybe four or five Juan Antonios."

We installed the bolts and hangers under Rhonda's supervision. She checked each one by attaching a carabiner and a long harness and then pulled on it with all of her weight from different angles to make sure it was acceptable.

"These bolts will be used to support the structure along the top of the wall. That's why we've installed so many of them in order to distribute the weight evenly. Tomorrow, we'll attach the top sections, drop one of you guys over the edge so you can glue them in the middle and then repeat the process with all twenty-four sections. The drills will be lowered down on ropes so that you don't have to be holding them the entire time since they'll get pretty heavy in a hurry. You'll have a jar of pipe glue hanging from your belt as well as a bag of bolts and a bunch of hangers. I think this will work well."

"How are we going to get enough leverage to drill horizontally into the rock? It was fairly easy up here but we were drilling straight down using all of our weight," I observed.

"First, those holes only have to be in an inch or two deep since they won't be carrying much weight and second, the expansion bolts on the rock face are a lot skinnier so the drill bits are much smaller. The entire process will be a lot easier."

"What are the chances that we'll die doing this?" Juan Antonio asked softly, clearly scared out of his gourd.

"Pretty slim, I'd say, but we're going to take every precaution to make sure that you guys are well protected. Are you having second thoughts?"

"Well, sort of. I'm just thinking about me and the structure hanging from one of these bolts and it doesn't really seem like it would be strong enough."

Rhonda asked, "How much do you weight?"

DAVID W. GOODWIN

"About a hundred and five."

"Well, let's just say that I weigh quite a bit more than that. Would you feel more comfortable if you saw me hanging from one of these bolts first?"

"That would help," Juan Antonio admitted but I knew that wasn't his real issue.

"First thing tomorrow, we'll set up a rope and I'll show you how strong they are. I think you'll be surprised by how much weight these can take. But that's tomorrow, now it's time to pack it up and call it quits."

We loaded all of the equipment into the trucks and left the PVC pipe support sections on site. Rhonda had us stack up all of the extra pieces we didn't use since they might be needed later on in the process; depending upon how the installation went. She threw me the keys from the other truck and Barbara jumped into the passenger seat with me leaving Juan Antonio to ride with Rhonda. I slowly followed her vehicle as we made our way down the Juiceway.

"Have you been thinking about my skimpy, lacy panties all day, Dean?" Barbara asked once we were on our way.

"Are you a mind reader? Of course I have, how did you know?" I exclaimed with mock surprise that apparently went over her head like an errant Frisbee toss.

"If there's one thing I know, it's how men think. Why do you think I planted the thought in your mind this morning? I want you to be brimming with lust by the time you get to the nightclub."

"And what do you think's going to happen at the nightclub, Mrs. Horner?"

"My guess is a lot of sweet man juice will be flowing like honey and I hope to be there to rub it all over myself. That's one of the sexiest thoughts imaginable."

"Does that sort of thing really happen at the nightclub?"

"Absolutely!"

"Even on Games Night?"

"What do you think?"

"I think the chances are slim."

"You'd be wrong."

I felt it best to change the subject but it was difficult since I was beginning to feel that familiar tightness in my jeans that was starting to strain the limits of the denim. However, I tried to erase the images out of my mind and replace them with things like laundry, food, a shower, relaxing in my bed reading my book, dinner and Eric's poison ivy but all I could think about were Barbara's fabulously fleshy and bouncy boobs, her hand skillfully playing with her delicate folds of womanly things and parting the way to showcase her juicy pink delights. I guess it was no use to fight the lust.

"I think you've achieved your goal. I'm brimming," I admitted.

"Never fails. I'm brimming too because I didn't get a single chance for any quality time today. I was hoping that Rhonda might have sent us on another task and we could have taken a small detour. I'm supercharged!"

We arrived at the office and I followed Barbara into the building. She was making every step count since she knew that I was behind her and seemed to take a great amount of pleasure in knowing that I was watching. As we were about to walk up the stairs leading into the building, she stopped abruptly and pretended to bend over to tie her shoelace or something. I rear ended her and she wiggled her hips into me, giggling like a teenager at her ploy.

"That's cheating," I said.

"Hardly, that's just priming the pump."

The afternoon meeting went quickly, reports were given and Big Larry went on a short, confusing toot about a former employee that ended up quitting his job during Games Night a few years back. Most of the crew were around during this time and remembered both the person and the incident. He started wrapping the meeting up and asked if there were any questions.

"Yeah, Big Larry, I've got a question. Can you tell me what's in the green mystery drink?" I asked.

The room became deadly quiet and I realized too late the error of my ways. You could hear a rat breathe and Barbara's libido drop and one of Laverne's jokes fall flat simultaneously. I immediately regretted asking as Big Larry reacted like I had asked him about his comb over.

"Let me answer that lame brain question with another question, there OD. Tell me, is there somethin' in your college boy life that you just accept as fact without needin' to know the details?"

"Well, probably, but that's not really why I'm asking. Don't get me wrong, it's an incredible drink and I really like how it makes me feel but I'm asking more out of curiosity than needing to get the recipe or anything," I said, digging myself in deeper since I didn't see any easy way out now that I had begun.

"Well, stop bein' curious then."

DAVID W. GOODWIN

"Just tell me then is there anything in there that might cause a permanent change in my chromosomes or psyche or physiology?"

"Only if you're a complete retard to begin with."

"What does that mean? Have there been any bad incidents from people drinking it? Is it alcohol based? Does it contain any psychotropics? I might want to have children some day and I want to make sure my kids aren't born with two sets of nards." I immediately realized the implications of this for Georgie and hoped she didn't take any offense.

"Slow down there slim. I'm not even sure what some of those high falootin' words mean that you're throwin' around like confetti at a funeral. Here's what I'll say about it and it's the same thing that I've told folks for years—it's safe, no one has ever had a bad reaction and if you're such a namby pamby about drinkin' the stuff, don't drink it. Meeting adjourned."

Not only did I now feel like a complete moron for asking, but the issue was even more perplexing. I wanted to have some idea what I was subjecting myself to. It all came down to faith and trust. Did I have faith and trust that Big Larry knew what he was doing and wouldn't intentionally or unintentionally harm us?

On the way out of the building, people were avoiding me like I was Trickie Dickie, even my best friends. I guessed this was the biggest forbidden topic of the quarry, even worse than talking to outsiders about the nightclub or asking Rhonda why she cut her shorts so short. The scene inside the bunkhouse was subdued as everyone went about their usual routine and seemed to be concentrating more than necessary on their tasks in order to insure that I wouldn't continue my line of inquiry with them. However, since I seemed to be riding this wave to the end, I was determined to get some answers from what certainly was the one question on everyone's mind.

Approaching Iggy and Eric as they busied themselves with their dirty laundry, I said quietly, hoping that I was out of earshot of everyone else, "So, guys, in the three years we've known each other, we've drunk just about every form of alcohol available, we've dropped acid a few times, ingested mushrooms and peyote, snorted some coke, taken a Quaalude or two, and done a few hits of speed and mescaline. Each of these drugs has a unique feeling, each has its downside. Wouldn't you agree?"

"Yep," Iggy agreed while Eric nodded.

"And from my experience last night, that green concoction wasn't like any of those things; wouldn't you agree with that as well?"

"Yep," Iggy agreed while Eric nodded.

"Aren't you curious to know what's in it?"

"Yep," Iggy agreed while Eric nodded.

"So why is it such a federal case that I asked? Don't you feel that we all have a right to know?"

"Yep," Iggy agreed while Eric nodded.

"You guys are a lot of help. Listen, I'm going to look into this a little more on my own. Maybe snoop around behind the scenes to figure it out. There are so many things about this place that just don't make any sense."

"Not a good idea Beans. You'll end up getting all of us fired. Is that what you want?" Eric asked.

"No, but why is everyone so complacent? Why is Big Larry allowed to run this place like this? There are a few big secrets that he's keeping and something's just not right."

"Come on, let's go for a walk," Iggy whispered, looking around the room, grabbing me by the arm and leading me outside. "We can't be talking about this in here." We walked until the buildings were out of sight and took a path into the woods away from the quarry. Finally he said, "I strongly suggest that you not go sleuthing around. It can only lead to trouble. There's something we need to tell you, something Eric and I discovered Tuesday night when you were knocked silly and decided to have a ménage a trois with Joan and Georgie. Yeah, there's something fishy going on here alright but it's probably not what you're thinking. You've got to promise to keep this to the three of us and not say a word about it to anyone, not to anyone who works here, not to any of your other friends; it has to be a secret. Do you promise?"

"I can't promise if it's something so nefarious that it needs to be reported."

"Don't worry, Beans, it's not. Just promise that you keep this to yourself. We weren't even going to tell you about it until you decided to open your big fat mouth and force the issue," Eric said. "Deal?"

"Sure, deal. What's the big secret?"

"Do you think there's so much money selling granite that Big Larry can afford to pay his employees a good wage, outfit them with all the clothes and equipment they need, feed them around the clock, house them, take care of all their needs all week and then create a kick ass nightclub complete with fabulous drinks and entertainment?" Eric asked.

"That's one of the mysteries, for sure but I'd guess that the granite market is rather lucrative."

DAVID W. GOODWIN

"That may be but probably not this lucrative. We think we stumbled upon the answer Tuesday night. Right before we went into the nightclub, we happened to be sneaking back through the woods from the rat farm and were back behind the trailers. We stopped and watched because we saw Rhonda hand something to a guy who had just pulled up in a big shiny black Lincoln Continental in exchange for a big wad of cash."

"What was it?"

"A baggie with a handful of gold in it."

CHAPTER 19

" SO HERE'S OUR theory about the Sugarloaf Quarry," Iggy began, talking slowly as if he was still formulating his thoughts, "Eric and I think that we've figured out the connection between Big Larry and Rhonda's strange behavior, Big Larry's sometimes generosity, the nightclub, the rodents, and the electric green drinks. It's all based on gold."

"I'm not feeling that analytical right now so you're going to have to connect the dots for me."

"Let's break it all down. Let's start with the assumption that they've discovered a vein of gold in the quarry. That would certainly be rare but as we learned in our geology courses, there's an association between this type of granite and gold. Are you with me on this one?" Eric asked.

"It's possible," I admitted.

"So, although they both run the quarry, they're not the owners so they probably work on salary. If the owners knew there was a gold vein here, theoretically, all of the value would go to them, right?"

"Most likely, go on."

"So we think that together, Big Larry and Rhonda are mining the gold out secretly and then selling it at a handsome profit on the black market, all for their personal gain. Obviously, that's what the black Lincoln was doing here the other night. Big Larry and Rhonda must be raking in tons of money on the side."

"So how does this explain the nightclub, the drinks and the rodents?" I asked.

"I think they have so much cash hanging around they need to do two things. First, they've used some of it to finance the construction of a nightclub that is electronically wired so it can be transformed from what looks like a tiny, dingy supply building to the super cool nightclub easily. Haven't you noticed how big the building is from the outside and how small it seems on the inside? Since the owners are unlikely to ever show up at night, they have to maintain the illusion of a normal quarry operation and supply building by day when the owners would most likely be here. My guess is they don't even live around here and just look at the balance sheets each month," Eric said.

"And what's the second thing?" I asked.

"They need to keep their employees so happy that nobody questions what goes on here all day. Except for the daily meetings, you hardly ever see them together. You're working with Rhonda on the wall. Is Big Larry ever around?"

"Never up on the wall," I admitted.

"One of them is always on gold duty. Think about it—all your needs are met and you get to have a party every night during the week—all expenses paid! So for you to question that today really rocked Big Larry's boat."

"How do the rodents fit in?"

"Right, the rats. They're very intelligent animals and have a remarkable sense of smell. We've already seen how trainable they are but I think that's just a little smoke to throw people off the track. I think they somehow use them to sniff out the gold in the granite."

"Interesting. So there's one last connection. How do the emerald drinks fit into this theory?"

"Glad you asked because this is what ties it all together. Did you notice how light reflects off these drinks?"

"Yeah, that was incredible," I remarked.

"And did you notice that they tasted like licorice?"

"Unmistakably."

"I think the drinks contain little bits of gold dust and I'm certain they are made with a lot of absinthe," Iggy said, visibly proud of his powers of deduction.

"What's absinthe? I've never heard of it."

"It's a type of liquor that has a certain chemical that's a mild hallucinogen. It's not legal to sell in the US but in my travels through France and a few other countries in Europe with my family when I was in high school, my older brother turned me on to this stuff. It's made from a bunch of herbs like anise and fennel and is derived from a plant called wormwood. There's a chemical in the wormwood plant, I don't remember what its real name is but Europeans call it the green fairy. It's chemically similar to THC that's in marijuana, only a lot stronger. I think that when the absinthe is combined with the tiny flakes of gold, it produces the kind of reaction we all have at the nightclub."

"Holy shit! That makes total sense," I exclaimed. "So they've got the gold, they've got the money but how do they get the absinthe if it's illegal?"

"I haven't figured that part out yet but they must have some connection somewhere that's able to smuggle it in. I don't think that part is really too important because they're getting it here somehow and they have the cash to grease the skids. So, not a word of this to anyone. Let's just keep cool and keep our eyes and ears open to see if this theory holds water. From everything we know now, it all makes sense. There may be a few details that we've gotten wrong but I think the overall concept is plausible," Iggy said. "The bottom line is that we can't let on that we know anything about this or our jobs are toast. Come on, let's go back and eat some dinner."

We sat off to the edge of the mess hall with Georgie, trying to keep a low profile. I could feel the tension in the room and my mind was racing with the implication of the new theory that Eric and Iggy came up with. Conversations were muted but the food was fabulous. Bunny had put together an almost traditional Thanksgiving-like meal with roasted curried chicken, sweet potatoes, chipotle stuffing, garlic mashed potatoes, cranberry sauce with fresh limes and green beans with pine nuts. Since I had missed the last three Thanksgivings being far away from home, it was a very comforting and satisfying meal.

Eric and I waited around until everyone had completed their meals and then helped Bunny with the cleanup again. This took quite a bit longer than the breakfast process and I was thankful for the distraction. Afterwards, I spent some time relaxing in my bed with my book until it was time to get ready for games night.

When I finally heard the speakers come to life with *Fly Me To The Moon*, it was a welcome relief. I was determined to be as friendly as Bunny, as passive as Junior and as agreeable as Mr. Biff Bojangles. I'd drink my crazy drink and have a great time at the nightclub, no questions asked.

The nightclub routine was the same as last night with the exception that Barbara was there. She chose to sit at our table which made me happy since she had such a devious sort of energy about her. The transformation of the supply building was identical and when the lights went up a notch, in walked Big Larry, Rhonda and Bunny with the trays of the sparkly green drinks. Rhonda came over to our table and as she set the drink in front of me, whispered, "Don't think about it too much OD, just enjoy."

I nodded and smiled and watched as Bunny took her seat and our two bosses took the stage. I had a close look at my drink in the modest light of the nightclub and could see that maybe they did have gold particles in them since they were so sparkly.

"Ladies and gentlemen, welcome to the Sugarloaf Quarry Nightclub! I'm your Master of Ceremonies, Thad Flapper and I'd like to introduce my lovely assistant, Wanda Ladowski!"

As I experienced last night, wild applause greeted Thad's opening line and he did an exaggerated deep bow while Wanda curtsied. Everyone drank their drinks, pounded them on the table and Thad declared the nightclub open for business. He again made a show of pulling the oversized switch down. The lights dimmed and then came back on again even brighter. At that moment, the door opened and out came five Giant Gambian Pouch rats only this time each one was dressed in an outfit to match a deck of cards, from the ace of spades down to the ten. They ran in single file around the room three times as the crew roared their approval. When the final lap was done, they paused momentarily by the door while the ace stood on his hind legs prompting the other four to line up and do the same thing displaying a royal flush on their five little rat bellies. They held the pose until the cheers and hoots started to die down and then disappeared back through the door. The bar was officially open so people went over to get a new round of drinks. This seemed unnecessary to me as the kick from the absinthe was almost as much as I could handle. The effect of this concoction was the same as before and I was already in an altered state.

Thad got on the microphone again and asked everyone to settle back into their seats for a moment. When he was satisfied, he went back over to the big switch and moved it to the middle so the lights went dim again. When he moved it back to the down position and the lights came on, there was a giant custom-made round Twister mat that almost filled up the entire stage.

"Yes, it's Twister night ladies and gentlemen!" Thad yelled at the top of his voice into the microphone so it came out all distorted sounding. Wanda wheeled out a large easel with a huge spinner and all four colors and all four appendages listed. Twister night apparently was a big crowd favorite.

"You all know the rules. I'll be the first caller, you all line up around the outside edges and the last person standing wins and is the next caller," Wanda explained. "Thad, what's the first prize?"

"Well Wanda," Thad said as he took the microphone back, "the first prize tonight is a one hour paid vacation tomorrow. You choose the hour and you can take it off to do anythin' you want. You can sleep in an extra hour, you can go into the supply buildin' and try on women's clothin' for an hour, you can go home an hour early but then you won't get your paycheck so I wouldn't recommend that option, you can take an extra hour for lunch. I think you brainiacs get the idea."

Wanda called everyone up onto the stage as Herb Alpert's *A Taste of Honey* started playing on the sound system. It was perfect, I wanted to go back to Boulder and trade all my rock and roll albums in for Herb's entire record catalog instead of square dancing music now. When Rhonda spun the wheel and called out "right foot yellow" followed by "right hand blue", I knew this was going to be a fantastic evening.

We were all getting pretty wrapped up in each other and it didn't take long before some of the less agile folks fell over and had to take their seats. By the time the second song, *Green Peppers*, came on it was down to just Juan Antonio, Thad and Yolanda. Eventually, Juan Antonio won when the call was "left foot red" and Thad fell on his back as Yolanda collapsed on top of him, much to the crowd's delight. To me, it looked like Juan Antonio defied gravity as his body position seemed impossible and his arms and legs stretched at least two times their normal length. Thad seemed to melt into the floor like the Wicked Witch of the West after the bucket of water was dumped on her.

The drinks were flowing, the bodies were pressing and gyrating, the music was floating along and everyone was having a great time. In one of the games, it came down to just Eric and Barbara. They managed to stay out of trouble for a while but when Laverne called left foot green, Barbara made sure to position her butt right in his face. Eric was barely holding his position but lost it on the next call when he had to reach his left arm between her legs to get to a yellow patch. She used this opportunity to put him in an Egyptian thigh squeeze which flustered him so much that he lost his balance and rolled over on his side, pulling her along for the ride because she wouldn't let his arm free. She ended up straddling him and dry humped him for a while although maybe she was pretending to be riding a horse. Either way, the crowd loved it! Her prize for the match was the honor of setting off the dynamite the next time some blasting was needed. When the next round began, I noticed the two of them had disappeared into a dark corner of the nightclub to try some special moves.

As the effects from the drink intensified, my grasp of the evening seemed to slip away bit by bit. Each match seemed to have a new concept and new rules. One time we paired up in tag teams and could tap out to our teammate if we felt like we were going to fall. Hector and I paired up and he used his massive head to take up as much space as possible, knocking most of the competition out before I even needed to tag in. He would let out a lion roar every time someone was eliminated and it sounded even better than a real lion. In another match, all our moves had to match the music, like a Twister dance, and the mostly dance-impaired men were eliminated early, leaving just the women to wiggle it out. Another time it was each crew against the other. It took a while to decide who was on which team until Big Larry finally decided it should be based on today's crew assignment. The BAP crew made a great showing. Since all teammates had to maintain contact with at least one other teammate and we were all pretty flexible to begin with, we pummeled the competition in no time. The match culminated when Rhonda stuck her boobs into Iggy's face and he needed to come up for air, losing both his position and the match. We must have gone through the entire *Whipped Cream and Other Delights* tape three or four times so I was getting very familiar with each song. Eventually, the final match was announced.

"For our Grande Finale, we will take the winners from each of the matches held so far in a winner take all, no holds barred competition," Thad announced. "Will Juan Antonio, Barbara, Laverne, Junior, Hambone, Joan, Georgie, Alfonso and Felix 2 please come to the stage?" They each took a position on the outside edge of the Twister mat.

"In the last event of the evenin', as long as your foot or hand is on the color patch, you can do anythin' you want to throw your opponent off. You can talk trash, you can bump them, you can rip a fart in their face, you can insult their grandparents, you can do anythin' to get them disqualified. And the prize for this championship event—well, you tell 'em Wanda!"

"Well Thad, the winner of this final event will get a one time 'get out of cleanup duty' pass," Wanda explained to the appreciation of the crew.

The competition began and it was cutthroat. There was dirty play, foul play, devious play and every other kind of play. At one point, Laverne gave Felix 1 a hip check that sent him completely off the stage. Juan Antonio was crushed like an insect under Junior in an unfortunate choice of color patches. Joan made the mistake of getting too close to Georgie and was tickled out of the game. Finally, it came down to Iggy and Barbara. Right when it looked like Iggy had the upper hand, Barbara stuck her tongue inside his ear which caused his arm to buckle and he lost the match.

Wanda crowned Barbara the "Quarry Queen of Twister" and put a plastic gold crown on her already elevated hairdo. She took a victory lap around the nightclub, giving everyone a big hug and a kiss, taking some extra time with Eric and I'm sure that she slipped him a little tongue since when she broke it off; there was a shiny thread of saliva that kept them connected for a moment. Thad poured out a bunch of glasses of ice water at the bar and eventually the nightclub came to a close.

We all slowly walked out of the building and made our way back to the bunkhouse where my evening quickly came to an end. Apparently, other folks had different plans as all that body contact got some couples riled up. I barely stayed awake long enough to floss, brush, change my bandage and wash up. I was probably the first person asleep in the quarry that night but had a vague awareness of a lot of people walking around, in and out of the building or through the door to the women's side, sliding of bed frames on the wooden floor, giggles, and muffled noises. The night seemed like a long one and by time morning arrived, I woke feeling fresh and ready to face Friday.

CHAPTER 20

MORNING CAME AND it sounded like the Chambers Brothers again. Not only was I excited about putting the pipe frame together and doing some rock climbing but I was hopefully going to get my first paycheck and spend time with Sarah this weekend. I looked over at Iggy's and Eric's beds and both were empty. I glanced around the rest of the room and saw that more beds had double occupancy than single and many were empty.

I was used to seeing and occasionally participating in brief casual relationships as a college student but I figured this was the one time of my life where this sort of thing could happen. It wasn't like this in my high school where the kids mostly had long term relationships since we knew each other from a young age and felt a certain responsibility to stay on good terms. However, I didn't expect it would be like this out in the real world of adults, if in fact, this could be considered the real world. Most of these people were adults, some married and some with children and quite honestly, it surprised me that it was happening. I witnessed first hand Barbara's definition of fidelity but thought she was the exception, rather than the rule. Obviously everyone had their own story, made their own moral decisions and I certainly wasn't one to judge but it was still somewhat unexpected. I calculated that there were fifteen and a half men, eight and a half women and I suppose the mathematical combinations were quite numerous. However, some of those combinations could probably be ruled out as highly unlikely.

Breakfast was about to be served so I walked over on my own. The mess hall was really quiet, just Bunny, Frederick and me. We served our meals and Bunny had a nice assortment of teas for me to choose from. I sat down with Frederick as a few others started to enter the building.

"I have the feeling that it was a pretty wild night for everyone," Frederick said.

"It certainly was at the nightclub but I was out like a light the second I got back to the bunkhouse."

"Yeah, me too. I'm not as young as some of you bucks so after a day of hauling rock around and then partying at the club, I'm beat."

Soon the place was pretty full. Eric, Iggy, Barbara, and Georgie all came into the room together. By this time, Alfonso and Joan joined us at our table and the energy of the place started to pick up. I think Fridays always did this to people who worked hard for a living.

Dishes were cleared, beds were made, teeth were brushed, and toilet seats were warmed. The day was brilliant and cool and I found a protected spot outside against a building and sat alone in the soothing warmth of the early morning sunshine. When the time came, I joined my colleagues and went into the quarry office building. Everyone had settled around the table but Big Larry and Rhonda hadn't appeared yet. I didn't remember seeing them at breakfast either.

"Did y'all have a crew chief meeting this morning?" Yolanda asked looking at Zelda.

"No, they didn't show up for that one either," she responded.

We sat around for another few minutes when Dickie, the biggest person at the quarry, decided to take control of the meeting and do some imitations. "Alright now you pinheads, listen up," he said in a little whiny high pitched voice, "we've got a lot of work to do today. Here are the assignments—I want all you women to go into town and bring your hottest girlfriend up here. Then, I want all you men to leave so that I can have them all to myself."

"You wouldn't know what to do with them," Hector heckled.

"Oh yes I would. I'd dress them up in quarry outfits and have them pull me around in my chariot all day!"

"Are you havin' fun there, Dickie?" Big Larry softly asked from the doorway.

"I, uh, it's um, well, no, not really. We were just waiting for you to show up," Dickie said mostly in his normal voice as it took a few words to get Big Larry's squeak out of his mouth.

Big Larry strode into the middle of the room with Rhonda right behind him. I couldn't tell if he was perturbed or amused by Dickie's imitation but my guess was that he was probably perturbed. They quickly consulted each other before Big Larry addressed the crew.

"Sorry that Rhonda and I are late today. We got distracted by a phone call early this mornin' from the quarry owner, Mr. Modus Tollens. Most of you have never met Mr. Tollens so you should be grateful for that but for those of you that were around a few years ago and had the irritation to

DAVID W. GOODWIN

meet him, well, you know what I'm talkin' about. So, here's the bottom line—Mr. Tollens is passin' through Colorado next week on his way from Salt Lake City to Dallas and wants to spend a day or two here. He got the noise report from OSHA and already knew about the Fish and Wildlife's worries about the migratin' gnats so he just wants to check up on things. What does this mean for all of you? Not a lot but we might have to suspend the nightclub for a few nights since he doesn't know anythin' about this and might not approve. Since you all have Monday off and Tollens is expectin' to be here on Wednesday and maybe Thursday, let's just plan on no nightclub next week until he's completely out of our hair. Any questions?"

Big Larry looked around the room that was buzzing with sounds of disappointment but everyone slowly nodded their acceptance of the change in plans. He then made the assignments and said that he'd hand out our pay this afternoon. "Oh, one last thing, if Rhonda or me don't show up on time for meetin' again, I suggest you amuse yourselves by makin' fun of each other or one of the college boys, not me. Got it?"

All of us shuffled out of the room, making sure not to make eye contact with Big Larry and concentrated full time on watching our shoes move across the worn wooden floor after the reprimand. I felt guilty and I didn't even have anything to do with Dickie's humorous impersonation.

Our BAP crew assembled outside next to the landscape crew as each team waited for their leader to show up. I had a few moments to talk to the other two college boys.

"Where were you guys last night?" I inquired.

"Well I got an offer too good to refuse," Eric said quietly looking over at Barbara who started to laugh.

"And so did I," Iggy said. "You wouldn't even begin to imagine the possibilities."

"Oh, I think maybe I would," I answered as Rhonda came bounding out of the office building and directed us into her truck. "I guess we'll have to continue this conversation later."

"Bye Eric," Barbara said in her sexy tiger growl. He blushed.

Juan Antonio and I had a bumpy ride up the Juiceway in the back of the truck after stopping to get the equipment we needed for the day. When we arrived at the top of the quarry, we laid out all of the tools and pipe sections. Rhonda explained how she wanted to position the first top section on the ground near the top of the wall and then attach four ropes along the edge farthest from the abyss. The other ends were attached to hangers with some extra rope that would be cinched up once the structure was over the edge and in its proper place.

"So the idea here is for all of us to be on this side," Rhonda said. "We'll push this section out over the cliff until it goes past the middle. When it starts to fall down the wall, we need to hold onto these ropes and try to control the fall so it doesn't break apart from the impact of hitting the wall or when it comes to an abrupt stop when it reaches the end of the ropes. The whole section doesn't weigh more than fifty pounds so I doubt that we'll have any problems. The glue should be stronger than the pipes so I'm not expecting it to fall apart."

We worked together to push the pipe section slowly out into the void. As we got closer to the half way point, the structure started to bend more and more and we could hear the creaking of all the joints. Once the tipping point was reached, our end shot up way out of reach, becoming vertical immediately and Rhonda yelled for us to grab our ropes. Everything happened so fast that none of us managed to secure our ropes before the structure fell down the wall and came to rest dangling from the ropes. Since I didn't hear the sound of the pipe pieces smashing against the rock ledges, it sounded like maybe everything worked. We got down on our knees and peered over the edge to see what happened. There below us, hanging from the ropes was the PVC pipe section all in one piece.

"Woo hoo!" Rhonda yelled. "It worked! All we need to do is pull it back up into place and secure it with the hangers. I can see that we should use shorter ropes on our next section so that it doesn't fall down the wall so far."

We pulled the section up to the desired position, attached the hangers to the bolts and then slipped them over the top pipe. Once this was secure, we removed the ropes and the web hangers that held our first section in place. This process was repeated three more times until four of the eight top sections were over the wall. We took a break and Rhonda told us we were going to have a rope safety lesson next.

"Remember you were going to demonstrate how strong these bolts are before I trust them?" Juan Antonio asked.

"Right, that will be a part of the lesson, you'll see."

After our break, Rhonda showed us the proper way to put on a harness.

"That reminds me of an outfit that I wear for Richie except the nylon webbing is lace and it's a pretty pink and black pattern," Barbara observed daintily stepping into her harness as Juan Antonio and I followed suit, although not as daintily.

DAVID W. GOODWIN

Each of us attached a figure eight descender to the fronts of our harnesses and then added a carabineer. Rhonda attached a carabineer to each of two adjacent anchor bolt hangers and then threaded the rope through both. She pulled the rope through until the ends were even and then threaded both ends through her descender.

"One thing to remember is to tie a big knot in the end of your rope to prevent yourself from rappelling beyond the end. You definitely wouldn't want to do that. I'm going to prove to you that these anchors are strong. But first, I want to set up a belay rope so that we have an extra layer of protection."

She set up another rope on the same two anchors and attached one end to the carabineer on her harness with a special knot. She then showed me how to wrap the other end of the rope through my carabineer and keep proper tension on the rope.

"OD, your job is to be my backup support if something messes up when I'm descending but also to give me rope tension if I slip when I'm climbing back up. You've always got to be ready, always keep tension on this rope, not too much so that I can't climb or descend but enough so that you can back me up. Got it? Tension, remember that if nothing else, but not too much."

"Yep, I've done this before and I haven't let anyone die yet."

She then yelled out "are you on belay?" and waited, staring a hole through my head. I had a vague memory that I was supposed to say something but couldn't remember exactly what it was. The best I could come up with was "yep". Rhonda didn't move.

"I need to know that the belay is set and that you are ready to start belaying me. You say 'belay on' and that's my signal to begin. This is really important."

"Right, sorry, belay on. Now I remember."

Rhonda backed over the lip of the cliff and yelled out "on rappel" followed by "ready to lower", again waiting for a response from me. I then remembered to say "lower away" and Rhonda reminded me the proper response was first "on me" and then "lowering" to let her know that I was awake and taking responsibility for providing backup for her. She then went down the wall slowly to the first ledge, using the friction of the rope and her descender to control her speed while I made sure to feed her belay rope out at an appropriate rate. When she reached the first ledge, she called out "off rappel" to which I responded, "belay off".

"No, damn it, I thought you knew what you were doing?" Rhonda yelled from twelve feet below us. "You need to keep the belay on. 'Off rappel' just means that I've reached the bottom. You can say 'received' or 'yippie' or 'let's boogie' but never say 'belay off' while I'm still on the rope. That means you're no longer giving me protection. I'm going to start climbing now so I'll say 'climbing' which means that I'm coming your way. You say 'climb on' so I know that you're alive. Climbing."

"Climb on." I thought of a few funnier things to say but realized this wasn't a good time for humor.

Rhonda got back to the top and tossed my lost Frisbee to me without saying a word. We went through this sequence a few times with Juan Antonio and Barbara each getting a turn as the belayer and made sure everyone understood the proper sequence of climbing commands. Once she was satisfied that we were all trustworthy, she had me take a turn rappelling and climbing. It was a great system and I felt perfectly safe without any worrying thoughts of my previous tumble here.

"Now, OD and I are going to do a tandem rappel off the same anchors while you two belay us. Juan Antonio, this should ease your fears about the safety issue."

We set up the ropes and Rhonda and I rappelled down side by side. We climbed back up and I could see that the bolts were up for the task. "Your turn my man," Rhonda said to Juan Antonio. "I'll belay you."

The two of them got everything set while Barbara and I watched. I could tell that he was extremely nervous and was trying hard not to let it show but his trembling knees and the lack of color in his normally brown face gave him away. Rhonda guided him to the edge of the cliff against his will, almost having to push him as she was starting to get impatient and he wasn't being very cooperative.

"What's the deal here? You saw how OD and I did this. You saw how safe it is. We have double backups, two bolts and two ropes. Come on!"

"I just remembered that I have to go pee first," Juan Antonio said in a voice that sounded like he was six years old.

"Come on, let's do this first. You can pee in a few minutes. We're all set up to do this now."

Seeing that his options had been reduced to zero, I could tell that he was trying hard to summon the courage. He backed up to the edge of the cliff like he was getting into place for a back dive off a diving board, moving backward in fractions of inches instead of feet like Rhonda and I did. He was like a cat that had to swim across a large puddle to get safely to the other side, dipping a paw into the water, quickly pulling it out, shaking it a hundred times, licking the water off and then repeating the process, and all the time you doubted that it was ever going to do it. He just couldn't take that first step.

"It's now or never. If you can't do this, say the word and I'll get someone else from the maintenance crew up here," Rhonda said with only about five grams of patience remaining.

Juan Antonio immediately launched himself backwards over the cliff and was on the ledge in no time. Luckily, Rhonda was ready with the belay rope as his descent was more like a freefall.

"You forgot to ask 'are you on belay'," Rhonda yelled over the edge.

"Are you on belay?" we heard from below.

"Too late for that. Belay on. Let us know when you're climbing, remember? I've already told you several times how important these details are."

Juan Antonio yelled out "climbing", Rhonda responded with "climb on" and she started taking in the slack of the belay rope. In a few minutes, we saw Juan Antonio's curly black hair appear at the top of the wall. He was back with us and seemed quite relieved to have this ordeal behind him. We practiced this sequence a few times until we were experienced climbers and belayers, at least in Rhonda's eyes. Barbara was a natural climber as she was very flexible and surprisingly strong for someone her age. She didn't show anywhere near the fear that Juan Antonio had and seemed to love the new challenge. Juan Antonio got a little more comfortable with the process and slowly began to trust the hardware and himself.

The rest of the day was spent putting the remaining four sections into place and gluing them together. This turned out to be a bit tricky as we had to rappel and then climb back up under the structure but we got the hang of it pretty quickly. Rhonda decided that all of us should take turns being on the rope and doing belay duty. The afternoon flew by and for the first time since I had started working at the quarry, I almost wished the day had been longer.

We gathered up the supplies and drove down to the office building for the final meeting of the week. I was mentally calculating what my paycheck would look like. I had worked 2.5 hours on Wednesday and 9.5 hours on Thursday and Friday so that totaled 21.5 hours last week. Since I was getting $4.55 an hour, my paycheck would be close to $100. Not bad for part of a week. We were the last crew to arrive at the meeting and quickly took our places around the room. Rhonda reported on our progress and was quite pleased that we finally had something tangible to show for our efforts. This also made Big Larry happy.

"I reckon Juan Antonio can scamper up and down those rocks like a lizard on sandpaper," he conjectured. "Am I right?"

"More like a duck playing tiddlywinks," Rhonda said. "He's getting the hang of it but it's actually Barbara that looks to be our best climber and of course OD's not too bad either."

"Well folks, this week has been a big pile of horse donuts, if you know what I mean. You've all done slightly above average work, nobody got injured that I know of and as far as I can tell, no new cases of syphilis have been reported so let's hand out your pay envelopes. This is from last week, college boys so don't be expectin' a full week's pay."

Envelopes were handed out and the three us opened them simultaneously. Mine contained $73.87 in cash and I looked over at Iggy and Eric. We all had the same looks on our faces. I mouthed my total to the boys and they all nodded their heads.

"Um, Big Larry," Eric said, "we worked over 21 hours last week. This paycheck should be a lot closer to $100 than $73.87. Can you explain that to us?"

"I had the feelin' you boys would be taxin' your brains doin' some funny mathematics. First, we have to pay Uncle Samuel, then we have to pay the guvner, and then finally, I don't pay you for your lunch hour so durin' a typical 7:30 to 5 o'clock work day, which is nine and a half hours in case you got your numbers wrong, you're only really workin' for eight and a half hours. If you multiply that out and subtract the taxes, you'll get to your bottom line. Is that plain enough for you nimrods to understand?"

"Yeah, I guess so but I thought you'd pay for the entire work day."

"Jesus H. Christ! I already pay for your clothin', lodgin', food, drinks and entertainment. I think you boys got a pretty good deal here."

"You're right Big Larry," Iggy said stepping into the fray. "We're cool with that. Thanks!"

"Can we work through lunch and get paid for it?" Eric asked right before some guys nearby hit him from both sides on his shoulder.

"This meeting is adjourned. See you on Tuesday. Have a wing dingy of a Fourth of July and somebody knock some sense into that boy," Big Larry said as he left the building.

DAVID W. GOODWIN

CHAPTER 21

EVERYONE GATHERED UP their belongings from the bunkhouse and the grand exit happened within about five minutes. Farewells were exchanged and most of the cars roared out of the parking lot as people seemed eager to begin their long weekend. I decided to ride back to the Zoo with Iggy since it was more fun to ride downhill than uphill in Gus and it went more with my image than to be seen in Eric's Firebird, even though it could go two or three times faster.

"I can't believe Poindexter made such a stink about his paycheck. Hasn't he ever had a job before where they took out taxes?" I asked rhetorically.

"You know how he is about money. But Big Larry has a good point. There are so many other perks of the job that it seems silly to get all bent out of shape about not getting paid for lunch."

We stopped to pick up some beer and arrived back at the Zoo well after the Firebird. Eric was already hanging out on the porch with most of our other housemates and a guy that I'd never seen before. It felt good to be home after being gone most of the week. Iggy and I grabbed our bags out of Gus and joined them.

"Hey everyone, what's been going on around the Zoo all week?" Iggy asked.

"You'd better have a seat and we'll fill you in on all the juicy details," Crystal said. "But you might want to get yourself a cold beer first, my treat. I bought a case to celebrate and they're in the cooler over there."

"Excellent, what are we celebrating?" I asked.

"Well, the Bicentennial for one thing. A massive tip I got from a parent of one of my voice students, for another. We're talking the biggest tip I've ever gotten in my life, seventy five dollars!"

"Wow, what was the occasion?" Iggy asked. "That's more than the three of us got for working two and a half days at the quarry."

"She's an interesting kid, very shy, doesn't want to join in anything at school, no sports, no music, no yearbook staff, no reindeer games, nothing. Somehow she agreed to take voice lessons but had a really bad attitude. She wouldn't try anything. Finally, I asked her what sort of music she listened to and since then, we've been working on a few songs. She's really opened up, her parents are thrilled and they gave me a big tip today. Pretty cool, huh?"

"Yeah, what sort of music does she like?" I asked.

"Promise not to laugh? It's the Bee Gees and the songs we're working on are *Jive Talking* and *Be Tender With My Love*! Hey, it wasn't my choice."

"Wow, that's so ironic! Those are my favorite songs too," Peter said and started singing the few words that he knew from *Jive Talking* and I was worried that he was going to get a hernia. Luckily, none of us joined in so the song died a quick and relatively painless death.

Iggy grabbed a beer for both of us. Hazel said everyone was dying to hear about our jobs and the nightclub experience since they asked Eric when he arrived but he wanted to wait until we got there.

"We'll get to that soon. It looks like everyone's here except Wayne and Jackie. I expect Wayne will show up around dinner but I'm afraid to ask, what's going on with Jackie? Has she been released from the hospital yet?" Iggy asked.

"No, not yet," Kate said. "Things haven't changed much since you left on Monday. Her brother Chuck here is staying with us to try to help with her process. Chuck, this is Iggy and Dean."

"I was wondering who you were. You're Jackie's brother? Wow, I see the resemblance," Iggy said giving him the soul brother handshake. "How long have you been here and where did you come from?"

"Kate called me this past weekend. I live down in Taos and came up a few days ago to see what I could do. Jackie's pretty agitated right now but I'm not really sure what's going on with her. Our parents came into a lot of money when Jackie and I were young so they decided to spend all of their time traveling around the world as missionaries. We were basically raised by a constantly changing cast of family friends and relatives and had pretty weird childhoods."

"Yeah, Jackie told me a little about that. Is there any guess when she might be released?"

"No, I think it's going to be a while but there's not much we can do at the moment that hasn't already been done. Iggy, I'd like to talk to you in private sometime this weekend."

"For sure, man. By the way, has anyone thought about dinner tonight? I'm sure that the three of us being away all week has really screwed up the cooking schedule."

"You're all scheduled to cook over the next few days since the rest of us have been doing double duty but tonight, Peter and I have it under control," Kate said.

"You know that Phoebe's flying in tomorrow morning, right?" Eric asked.

"And Sarah will be arriving tomorrow afternoon," I added.

"And Sunday is our big Bicentennial Blowout!" Crystal said.

"We're gonna have a full house. This is gonna be a great weekend!" Hazel exclaimed. "You should also know that we've scheduled a house meeting tomorrow at eleven to plan the party. Can you all be there?"

"Phoebe's flight gets in at nine so I'll be there if everything happens on schedule."

"Alright 'cause we've got a fair amount of work to do. By the way, what happened to your head, Dean?" Kate asked.

"He decided to hang glide off a cliff at the quarry but forgot the hang glider," Eric responded.

"It was Iggy's fault. My Frisbee fell down the cliff and I climbed down to get it and Mr. Moron here started in with his Stu Mellons imitation. I started laughing so hard that I nearly wet my pants and couldn't hold on anymore."

"He's lucky to be alive," Eric said somberly.

On that note, I decided to put my stuff away and get cleaned up. Kate and Peter went inside to put dinner together. After a while, I rejoined most of my housemates on the porch and started feeling a nice mellow buzz from working all week and from drinking a cold beer. Dinner was served and the three of us tried to tell everyone else what it was like to work at the quarry. How can you adequately describe that crazy cast of characters and capture the essence of the nightclub without actually experiencing it and still honor the quarry oath? We did our collective best to convey to our housemates what it was like, much to their amazement, leaving out the gold theory and the mystery drinks.

Most of us hung out on the porch after dinner and slowly let the evening drift away. It wasn't too much longer before the dead of night was upon us and the three quarrymen started to fade out. I was the first one to actually give in and got up to leave the porch. Soon, I was fast asleep in my little bedroom.

Early the next morning, I heard someone in the kitchen trying to be quiet but instead was making more noise than three people combined and figured it must be Eric getting ready to go get Phoebe at the airport. After he left, I dozed off again because the next thing I heard a whole gaggle of Zoomates scrounging breakfast. I checked my clock and saw that it was close to ten.

We had a leisurely meal out on the porch, the ladies wearing their tantalizing sleepwear that always piqued my interest even though I tried to pretend not to notice. I'm sure they noticed my not noticing. Crystal and Hazel wore matching outfits only they had their tops and bottoms switched. Kate had on the unforgettable tank top and boxer combo and the guys were all wearing cut off jean shorts and worn out tee shirts. I tried to be as objective as I could and come to some sort of understanding about what any woman ever saw in any man. Women could be so darn cute and yummy. Guys were just guys, with very few redeeming qualities. Luckily, not all women saw it that way although two out of three women on our porch this morning apparently did.

As the morning rolled on, Peter and Iggy eventually joined us as did Chuck. Wayne worked really late on Fridays so we'd be lucky to see him by noon. He wasn't big in the helping around the house department so we had lowered expectations for him anyway. As eleven o'clock approached, the blue Firebird pulled up and out stepped Eric and his high school girlfriend Phoebe, fresh off the plane from St. Louis.

"You're just in time for our party planning meeting," Kate called out before they had even gotten to the sidewalk.

"Sorry guys but that's about the last thing we're in the mood for right now," Eric said somewhat apologetically.

"And what's the first thing?" I asked knowing full well what it was.

"Eric, you agreed to this party. You can't just disappear with Phoebe for the next two hours and expect us to do all the work," Crystal said with agitation in her voice. "This will only take ten or fifteen minutes."

"They're right Eric; I knew that you guys were having a party this weekend. That's partially why I came out here," Phoebe said. "Let's see what we can do to help."

Begrudgingly, Eric accepted his fate. We discussed the various tasks to be done and everyone had their assignments to be completed by noon tomorrow since the party started at one. I was on food shopping duty with Kate and we decided to go do it immediately. I wasn't planning on using my precious time with Sarah to go shopping so I wanted to get it out of the way as soon as possible.

"So Kate, are you going to go dressed like that?" I asked.

"Sure, if it would make you happy."

"It would but it might cause riots at King Soopers."

We both put on real clothes and took Kate's car to stock up on party food. It was fun shopping with her because she was so sassy and made even mundane things fun. Our shopping cart was loaded up with veggie burgers, tofu pups, buns, rolls, chips, salsa, condiments, ice cream sandwiches and all the fixings for a potato salad and a green salad. At the checkout, our total bill was $73.87.

"That is so ironic, that's the exact amount of my paycheck yesterday!"

"That's all you made working at the quarry?"

"It wasn't a full week, just two days and a few hours."

We got back to the Zoo and began putting the food away. Peter came into the kitchen and told me that Sarah had called to say that she was leaving Aspen and expected to get to Boulder around three or four.

"Are you looking forward to her visit?" Kate asked all wide eyed and innocent looking.

"No, not really. She's an ignorant slob without much on the ball."

"I'm looking forward to meeting this woman. I hope things go well for the two of you this weekend. I've had a couple of similar situations that didn't quite turn out how I expected."

"Better or worse?" I asked.

"All for the worse, unfortunately, but I hope this one turns out better for you."

"Thanks, Kate. She and I hardly know each other but I get a real strong feeling that there's something special there. Not that I can see into the future but you know what I mean, right?"

"Yes I do. By the way, I decided not to invite Elmo to the party. He's been acting like a real jerk lately so why bother?"

"Poor sucker."

We made the potato salad, that is, Kate made the potato salad and I followed her instructions. We then chopped up all of the salad ingredients and put them into separate containers so that it could be assembled in a hurry tomorrow. This was a college party, after all, and nobody expected that the food would knock your socks off. By mid afternoon, I was starting to anticipate Sarah's arrival and began to straighten up my room and made my bed with clean sheets, just in case. She had given me every possible indication that this was part of her weekend plans so unless she had a sudden change of heart, I fully expected we would soon be enjoying the fresh sheets together. I checked myself in the mirror and thought that I looked as good as I could given the raw materials.

The scene out on the front porch was peaceful. Most of my housemates were out in the world or inside the house doing various activities but I saw Iggy and Peter winging the wham on the fraternity lawn so I joined in. We started trying to show off for each other, flubbing as many moves as we made. A few cars went down our street, none of them were Sarah and then I realized that I didn't know what she might be driving. Eventually, an old Volkswagen bug came slowly down the street and stopped in front of our house. There was Sarah behind the wheel with her window rolled down.

"Hey, you, with the long hair, come over here and give me a proper welcome!" she said in a Brooklyn accent.

Always one to follow orders, I ran over and got to her car right as she stepped out. After a brief hug and delicious kiss, I had to step back and take her all in. She was wearing a beautiful dress, semi-sensible high heels and looked like she had just stepped off the Champs Elysee. I was about to say something, I wasn't even sure what it was going to be yet because my brain was feeling all goofy, when a Frisbee hit me in the back of the head at the same moment that Peter yelled 'Hey Beans, look out!' This seemed to happen to me whenever something monumental was going to happen so I took it as a good sign.

After rubbing my head a few times to regain my composure, I said, "You look stunning Sarah! Thanks for coming down here this weekend."

"Thanks, Dean. Why don't you introduce me to your friends?"

Iggy and Peter walked over and introductions were made. I could tell they were stunned by Sarah's appearance and didn't make much of an effort to hide it. They eventually went back to playing Frisbee and I took Sarah into the Zoo. Wayne was finally awake and eating breakfast. I was relieved when Wayne refrained from saying 'I'm Wayne and I'm hot to trot' when he met her. Crystal and Hazel were busy making out in the kitchen, as usual, their home away from home when we walked in.

"Your house is very, uh, what shall I say, studenty, but in a good way," Sarah observed when she was introduced to them. "We all have to live in dorms and even though the rooms are nice, it's not as nice as having a house. You all are very lucky."

"Where do you go to school?" Crystal asked

"Yale."

"Whoa, that's hard core!"

"Not as hard core as everyone thinks. I'm a theatre major, not one of those stuffy academics. Anyway, it's nice to meet you all. Why don't we continue with the tour, Dean?"

We walked around upstairs, I showed her the rooms and then she asked where my room was. I wasn't sure how she would react to my two tiny rooms off the kitchen so I was intentionally saving it for last. "Be prepared to be underwhelmed," I warned her.

"Oh, it's so cute! It makes me just want to jump into your bed and get cozy! I'm a bit weary from the trip since I'm not used to driving that much. I was lucky to be able to borrow the car from one of my friends but it kind of wore me out. Plus, I'm really thirsty."

"I'm sorry not to be a better host. What would you like? We've got beer, juice, water and a lot of food."

"A beer would be great. I stopped on the way to get a late lunch so I'm not very hungry."

I disappeared for a moment to get her a beer and when I returned, she made good on her word and was stretched out on my bed. I handed her the bottle and she sat up and took a good sized gulp. "Come on, why don't you join me? I've been looking forward to this all week."

The rest of the day, evening and following morning were a blur of extraordinary experiences. Neither of us were shy or modest, we finished each other's sentences when we spoke at all, we breathed the same oxygen molecules, we jumped onto the same runaway train, we laughed at each other's jokes, we ate olives and cheese scrounged from the refrigerator, we napped, we drank, she met other housemates here and there on her various trips between my room, the kitchen and the bathroom, we napped again, it might have been day or night but I had lost track of time and space, my mind orbited around her celestial body, it felt like my entire life had led me to this moment in time. It was poetry and it was magnetic.

There was a knock at the door. It was light outside. My clock said twelve so it had to be Sunday at noon, I think. Could it be Monday? Could it be this light out at midnight? Could time have gone backwards and it was still Saturday? I suppose anything was possible at this point.

"Hey Beans, man, you've got to come out and help get things ready for the party," Iggy yelled loudly through the closed door. "Our guests will be arriving in a little while."

Sarah was coming out of a deep sleep and the sight of her in my bed made my spirits head into the stratosphere. Her hair was all tousled around her face and my sheet covered her quite unstrategically. It was unbelievable!

"Yeah, okay, we'll be out soon."

Sarah and I snuggled again but must have dozed off for a while. I heard my door open and before I could even pick my head up to see what was happening, all of my housemates plus Phoebe and Chuck were standing and jumping on my bed chanting 'Dean', 'Dean', 'Dean'.

Sarah let out a little scream of protest but it was barely a peep compared to some of the screams that she had been serenading the Zoo with earlier. They formed a circle, holding hands while Sarah and I got small in the middle.

"Get up, its America's birthday! Time to parteeeee!" Eric yelled out.

"Uncle Sam wants you two!" Kate cried.

"No more sleeping away the Fourth of July!" Iggy exclaimed.

"We've got some cold ones on ice!" Peter said.

"That sounds fabulous," Sarah said. "Give us five minutes and we'll be there."

The party had begun or actually it continued, just in a different venue. The final touches were put on the food and house setup. Guests began arriving and before long, everything was at full throttle. Iggy got the grill going out in the backyard, the beer and ice were thrown into four large ice chests on the porch, snack trays were set up in the multipurpose dining room and music was playing on the stereo.

All of our non-Zoo friends that were still in Boulder for the summer were invited and by mid afternoon, we had perhaps thirty people there. Kate had a change of heart and invited Elmo after all. The ultimate stoner burnout Stu Mellons made an appearance and he was so wasted that he wasn't even aware that Iggy was doing a better imitation of him than he did, Georgie showed up much to our delight, John and former radio DJ Effie came over, as well as some of Peter's geology friends, a few former housemates, and some neighbors. To everyone's surprise, Tina pulled up in her car and walked up to the porch. Luckily Eric and Phoebe were out back grilling.

"Hi everyone," she said, "I heard there was a party happening today."

"Tina! Great to see you," Wayne yelled out loud enough for anyone in a hundred yard radius to hear. "Come on up and join the fun!"

Tina grabbed a beer and Wayne, seizing an opportunity, took her inside to show her the food options. I was worried that this wasn't going to go well but figured it wasn't any of my business. We all liked Tina and it just didn't seem right that she shouldn't be a part of our party, regardless of the consequences. I filled Sarah in on Eric's history.

"Hey, does anyone know anything about Boulder's parade?" Hazel asked.

"I'm not sure there is one," Iggy responded.

"What, no parade? On the Bicentennial? That's just wrong! There's got to be a parade!" I exclaimed.

"I'm going to check out the paper, it lists all of the activities today," Kate said as she disappeared into the house.

"I thought every town had a Fourth of July parade," Sarah said. "In the town that I grew up in, the entire town was in it. I'm surprised there were enough people left over to watch."

"Well, if there isn't one, we should have our own," I suggested.

Kate returned with the paper and looked through it until she found the schedule. "Let's see, there was the Bicentennial Breakfast that already happened and then the Community Sing Along at eight followed by fireworks at nine at the stadium. There's nothing about a parade. That's rather odd, wouldn't you say?"

"Then it's up to us! Let's assemble all the instruments and figure out a song that we all can play. We'll also need a drum majorette and anyone that doesn't have an instrument can bang on pots and pans. I've got my sister's flute, what else do we have?" I asked.

Peter, much to everyone's surprise, said he had a trombone as well as a guitar. Of course Hazel had her tuba but also had a piccolo and an alto flute. Iggy had a bunch of stringed instruments and a few harmonicas.

"Everyone should go get them and then we'll see what we can put together here," Crystal said. "This is going to be great!"

Tina and Wayne came back with their full plates of food and we filled them in on our plan. Wayne said that he had a kazoo and disappeared to get it. Tina said that she didn't play any instruments but always wanted to be a drum majorette. She found a big stick in the yard and said she could use it for her staff. After getting some aluminum foil for the top from the kitchen, it kind of looked like something a drum majorette might have. Sarah had taken some flute lessons as a teenager and said she could probably learn a song or two. Kate said that she was going to get our percussion section and returned with various pots, pans, plastic buckets and a bunch of wooden utensils.

Eric and Phoebe came through the front door to see what was going on. He stopped dead in his tracks when he saw Tina, the blood drained out of his face and literally turned into his quarry alter ego Whitey.

"Hey Eric and Phoebe!" Iggy said, trying to head off trouble, "we're going to have our own parade so grab a seat while we figure out who will play what."

"Hi Tina," Eric said weakly.

"Hi Eric and I assume you're Phoebe?" Tina said with a bite in her voice.

"Yes, I am," she responded boldly. "Nice to meet you, Tina."

"Yeah, you too. I hear you're taking a break from high school to visit."

"Well, not exactly taking a break, I graduated a month ago. Do you live here? I thought that I had met all of Eric's housemates."

"No, I was Eric's girlfriend until a few days ago."

That was enough for Phoebe. She shot Eric an angry look and stormed off the porch with Eric following. He looked back at Tina from the front yard and said, "I guess I deserved that."

"You sure did, asshole," Tina yelled back.

"Now we've got some energy here to harness," Wayne declared and moved the parade planning ahead. "What song does everyone want to do?"

"How about something sort of patriotic but not too over the top?" Hazel suggested.

"We've got two flutes, a piccolo, a trombone, a tuba—what a great brass section. How about *Be Kind to Your Web Footed Friends*?" Kate suggested.

"Great idea except that's really just a take off on *Stars and Stripes Forever* that is about as patriotic as possible but I think it'd be perfect!" Hazel said. "Let's see if we can make it sound like something."

Instruments were distributed to people that had some rough idea how to play them and everyone else grabbed a pot, pan or bucket. Each member of the Pleasant Street Zoo Marching Band made some noises on their instruments and the drummers tried their best to drown us out. Crystal, who had become our de facto band leader, organized the percussion section enough to have them all working on the same beat.

"Keep the beat steady. This song is in 2/4 time and generally played in E flat but we could do it in a different key, if it's any easier for folks. I'll

DAVID W. GOODWIN

be the conductor now but once we're out marching, it will be the job of Tina as the drum majorette to keep everyone on the beat. Do you think you can handle the pressure, Tina?"

"Absolutely but I better make sure that I have a few more beers and food first." Tina was clearly into playing this role and wasn't going to let Phoebe's presence slow her down.

We all agreed this was a splendid idea and fortified ourselves since we also agreed it was going to be critically important to be somewhat drunk. I thought maybe we'd see that Eric and Phoebe had kissed and made up but so far, this wasn't the case.

Stars and Stripes Forever was starting to take a rough form and I could tell it was going to work pretty well. Sarah played my flute and I abused Hazel's alto flute. She was a lot better than me, without a doubt. The next step was to change into our best Fourth of July clothing, meaning anything that was red, white or blue. Kate had some blue star tights and a red leotard while Crystal was rocking a pair of white go go boots. The rest of us made do with a crazy array of inappropriate clothing, including Sarah and I dressed in identical shorts and tee shirts. Everyone grabbed a few more beers for the road and we fell into formation out in the street.

"Tina will lead us on our route. I suggest we do a tour of neighborhoods on the Hill and then maybe head downtown. Her staff will mark the beats and we'll start the song on her first downbeat. Any questions?" Crystal asked.

We were all crazy with excitement and a small crowd from our neighborhood came out to watch and a few asked if they could join in. Crystal rejoined the marching band formation, Tina stood facing us in front, raised her staff, brought it down and off we went down the street and the noise was so powerful that most of us had to stop because we were laughing too hard.

Eventually, the novelty and silliness factor passed and we were able to march and play without breaking our formation. Tina took a right turn and we approached a large student apartment building on the right. As we neared, people came out onto their balconies and began cheering and applauding like this was the greatest thing they had ever seen. Tina stopped us in front and we played the song in its entirety. Some residents grabbed their own instruments or each other and joined the parade. We continued this way, stopping wherever there was an appreciative audience and before long, our numbers swelled close to a hundred. I would say that Boulder was one parade starved town in 1976.

At one point, our parade was approaching an intersection at the same time that a bunch of mentally challenged people from a group home out for a walk were approaching from a side street. We met in the middle and some of them came with us in our direction while some of us went with them in their direction. Luckily, the two parades reconverged several blocks later and we eventually sorted everyone out properly.

One of the largest apartment building complexes on the Hill was taken over by the Naropa Institute for the entire summer. This was the hippest, grooviest, and coolest subset of the already higher than average cool Boulder population, at least in their minds. They spent their days in intellectual pursuits by reading and attending classes and seminars on deep philosophical subjects. It also happened that in the courtyard of their apartment complex was a pool where they would almost always be hanging out naked. Tina took the parade right through the middle and as we rounded the corner into their private space, they all ran for cover faster than any of us thought people that mellow could run.

The parade continued on for another hour or so. We had to stop at one point to give our legs and lips a break but picked it back up and continued through downtown and eventually back to the Zoo where the party continued. Anyone that was still with the parade at that point was invited to stay and as dusk settled on Boulder, a core group of us grabbed our instruments and marched over to the stadium for the sing-along and fireworks display.

As the fireworks were winding down, I turned to Sarah, looked her in the eyes, took her hands and planted a kiss on her lips. "This has been the best day of my life."

"So far," she agreed.

CHAPTER 22

T HE HIKE DOWN into the Grand Gulch Primitive Area wasn't all that difficult but it was early October in southeast Utah and the heat of the day was about to max out. I was worried that we might not have enough water for our three days of backpacking in the incredible canyons and Anasazi ruins. Also, the three of us, Eric, Iggy and I weren't exactly young foolish college boys anymore. We had celebrated our joint fiftieth birthdays a handful of years ago by going on an adventure that our wives found a lot more appealing than a long hike in the desert with heavy backpacks. They thought a villa overlooking the Caribbean on Tortola was in order so we indulged ourselves. However, a few years later, this desert trip was a guys only, testosterone fueled adventure designed to prove to ourselves that we still had the strength, vitality and spirit to actually go backpacking in spite of our aging bodies and a full litany of physical aches and pains. These included blown knees, bad backs, and pretty much everything else except unexpected rectal discharge and erectile dysfunction, at least speaking for myself. Three days of food, water and alcohol plus the various accoutrements of camping in my backpack felt like I was carrying Big Larry down into the Gulch. We sure the hell had better consume everything consumable otherwise the hike out was going to be seriously difficult.

"Mungo, what are the chances that we're going to find any water down there to filter?" I asked since the landscape looked to be totally devoid of moisture. He did all the trip planning so I figured he would have the best sense of what we might find. "I think each of us needs to carry at least an extra gallon, maybe even two."

"Beans, man, I think you're being overly cautious," Eric said. "I've got my filter and all of us have enough water for a few days. I'm sure we'll find something to drink down there."

"I hate to be thirsty and you heard what the ranger said. I'm going to carry a gallon in each hand."

Iggy decided to take a couple as well but Eric wasn't buying into my argument. He was committed to traveling light, except for his ten pounds of cameras and camera-related equipment. Iggy was at the other end of the spectrum and even brought his own chair and a two pound cast iron coffee percolator. Of the three of us, he was still the biggest and probably the strongest, like a mule deer. In the years since Boulder, he and his wife and two kids had traveled and backpacked around the world extensively, including some epic trips into dangerous territories. He knew what comforts of home were important enough to carry on his back for three days.

It took us about an hour to drive Iggy's four wheel drive truck in from the road and then another hour of hiking to get from our remote parking spot to the edge of the canyon. My arms felt like they had been stretched at least a few inches and began to ache about a hundred yards from the truck. When the trail finally went over the lip into the canyon, I thought this would be a good place to stash one of my bottles. Iggy agreed and then Eric talked us into stashing all four.

"You don't really want to be hiking down this trail for the next two hours without the use of your hands. It's gonna be tough enough with these backpacks to keep our balance and not go for a tumble like you did at the quarry. Remember that?" Eric asked.

"Like it was yesterday. I still have that little reminder if I part my hair to the side a little."

We got about half way down and took a break at the first shady switchback we ran across. Iggy was more acclimated to this kind of weather since he still lived in Colorado. Eric and I had moved to New England after college and thirty-three years later, still lived within ten miles of each other. We remained best friends, were best men at each other's weddings and watched our kids grow up into adults together.

"You know, thinking back on your tumble over the cliff, I'm still amazed that you didn't die," Iggy said. "Maybe it was your experience with Georgie and Joan that night that nursed you back to health so quickly."

"Nursed, yeah, good choice of words!" I said for Eric's benefit. "Georgie, wow, I haven't thought about her for years. Have you two kept in touch? I know you made a pretty special connection that summer."

"How many guys can say they had a threesome with just one other person? We kind of lost touch over the years but I'd like to think that I was instrumental in helping her to decide to transition to a full woman.

The last I heard, she decided to leave the quarry the year after we did and was living in Portland with a transgender partner."

"Are you still sticking with your story about not remembering getting jiggy with Joan?" Eric asked me pointedly.

"My memories are of how beautiful she was, especially how beautiful she was naked. I remember kissing her but I don't think we did anything else," I recalled, bringing up a recurring topic between Eric and myself. "Remember, it was all for Georgie's sake. I don't know why they chose me instead of you for their experiment."

We continued down the trail and eventually got to the bottom of the Gulch where Eric led the way to our first campsite. It was late afternoon, the sun was no longer shining directly into the canyon and the temperature started to drop to a more comfortable level. We hiked along for another hour or so and arrived at a bend in the canyon with a large flat terrace that was perhaps twenty feet above the canyon floor. This looked like a perfect place to set up our tents knowing that in the unlikely event of a flash flood, we would be high and dry.

Our pre-trip agreement was that each person would be responsible for one dinner. Eric had volunteered to cook the first night so after we set up camp, he got busy making the meal before the sun went down completely. Iggy and I went off to do some exploring as it felt great to walk around without Big Larry on my back. Things were absolutely bone dry and I had some vague peace of mind thinking that if worse came to worst, I could hike out of the Gulch fairly easily and retrieve our backup water bottles.

Eventually, we found our way back to camp where Eric was putting the finishing touches on our meal. He took out a bottle of absinthe and passed it around before we ate. "This is legal now in the U.S. as long as it doesn't contain the good kind of wormwood extract," he said as I took a tentative sip. "It doesn't quite have the same kick as the quarry version but the taste will take you back."

The meal was fabulous like most meals are when you're camping. It could be cold hot dogs over granola doused in OJ and it would still taste surprisingly good. We sat on our terrace watching the twilight fade quickly into night while Iggy made a pot of coffee. The stars visible in our narrow view of the sky from the bottom of the canyon were unlike anything we ever see in New England.

"Did you know that the black rumped pygmy gnat is now so plentiful that it was removed from the endangered species list a few years ago?

I read an article on the internet recently that actually talked about the prototype project we worked on at the quarry. I was meaning to forward it to you guys but keep forgetting to do it," I said. "It even had a picture of the structure after we had finished working on it, back in the day. The photo looked ancient, almost like it had been taken right after the invention of color cameras. Are we that old?"

"Afraid so, Beans. I wonder whatever became of the quarry," Eric said.

"I guess I never told you guys. The place went out of business a long time ago. They had pretty much quarried out all the granite that was any good and then the owner, Toper or something, whatever his name was, sold it to a developer. Last I heard, they were turning it into a rock climbing facility and training site, complete with a water system to make it an ice climbing park in the winter."

"That was a pretty incredible summer," Eric reminisced. "Except for that whole Phoebe and Tina thing. That got kind of ugly."

"Yeah, but of course there was Joan, Rhonda and the crazy Barbara thing if you can remember back that far," I said.

"I have to say that when you told me about your first encounter with Barbara, I thought you were a total perv. She was, what, fifteen, twenty years older than us? But remember back at the nightclub when we played Twister that first time? I couldn't believe how much sexual energy she had. Looking back now, thirty five doesn't seem that old to me."

"You're right and I would imagine now as a seventy year old, she's probably still giving ol' Ritchie a run for his money," Iggy said. "And then I got an opportunity the next week during Talent Night to spend some quality time with her. I have to agree with you guys. She was unbelievable."

"Did either of you ever actually do it with her?" I asked.

"Define 'do it'," Eric said.

"You know, actually have sex?"

"Not me. That was her rule. It was kind of a fuzzy distinction she made but it seemed to work for her even though I was dying to find out what it would be like," Eric said.

"Yeah, I never did either but I kind of had my hands full with Georgie that summer," Iggy said. "However, my time with Barbara had to be one of the most interesting sexual experiences I ever had without actually having sex. I'm not sure I ever told you guys about the time during Talent Night at the nightclub later that summer. She and I were sitting at one of the tables together while Eric and Joan were up on stage acting out the final airport scene from *Casablanca*. Barbara leaned over and casually whispered to me that she had a special talent. Of course she wanted me to ask and when I did, she told me she could blow smoke rings. I told her I could too, like maybe she thought this was a big deal. She said she could blow smoke rings, but not out of her mouth. I thought she was kidding and just laughed. She insisted it wasn't a joke and led me back to the bunkhouse and sure enough, she could. We played ring toss for a while, she generated the rings and I supplied the post. Things got pretty kinky after that, if you can imagine."

"Oh, yeah, I can imagine. Peter and I were once picked up hitchhiking by a wild teenage girl when we went on a spring break trip out to California during our Boulder years that claimed she could do the same thing but she never demonstrated like Barbara did, apparently," I said.

We finished every last morsel of food Eric prepared, drank some cups of coffee and then set about making a serious dent in the bottle of absinthe. We talked a lot about our times at the Zoo and the quarry since this was our shared history. The last time we were together was on Tortola and clearly our spouses didn't want to hear much about our college days except when it involved them and certainly not when it involved old girlfriends. This was our first time in a long while to catch up. Iggy produced a joint from his massive backpack and lit it up.

"What's the story on Jackie? Did she ever get her head back on straight?" I asked.

"Well, you know that she dropped out of school for a while after the group massage session but re-enrolled the following year when she was able to cope with life more effectively. I get updates on her occasionally from Kate who has kept tabs on her over the years. After she graduated, she moved in with her brother and apparently has her own counseling practice, specializing in women who had some sort of traumatic sexual experience. Go figure, right? In my practice, I work with a lot of pretty whacked out individuals. Sometimes their shit is so far beyond my comprehension that I can't even begin to relate to their insanity. Maybe Jackie understands them better than most and can help."

"I haven't been in touch with anyone from the Zoo since Eric and I left Boulder. You mentioned Kate. What's she up to?" I asked.

"She became a pediatric nurse. She's perfect for the job as I'm sure you can imagine. She lives in Denver, near where we both grew up. I run into her from time to time when I'm visiting my mom. She's happily married with three kids," Iggy said.

"What about Windy? Was there ever any sign of her?" I asked.

"No, I don't think she ever came back from California. Her house was still vacant when we all graduated as you probably remember. Eventually, she had someone pack up all her stuff and send it out to her, or so one of her old pals told me years later. I thought maybe I'd see her playing out on the streets of Boulder but she just completely disappeared from the scene after our summer of slave camp."

"I'm sure glad that I didn't put my love life on hold waiting for her to come back," I said.

The night had become about as dark as it ever gets. From our vantage point, looking out across the canyon to the other side, where the darker rocks at the top met the lighter starlit sky, we could see an interesting silhouette, outlines that weren't at all apparent in the three dimensional light of day. Eric thought it looked like two people, a man and a woman, lying down in opposite directions with their heads touching and their feet sticking up at either end. Iggy thought it looked more like a single, pregnant woman except that her bulge was much lower on her body than it should be, as if the baby had descended down way too far, like beyond her crotch.

We contemplated the outline for a while longer and continued taking hits off the joint. Other interpretations were offered and got a little more avant garde in nature. Iggy said if you squint your eyes and look at it sideways he could see the profile of the quarry with a pack of Giant Gambian Pouch rats jumping off some of the ledges. Eric thought it looked more like a series of waves that were breaking onto a bowling ball.

"Sorry guys but you're both wrong," I said taking the final toke, "what we're looking at here is a guy and he's got a sheet over him, you know, like first thing in the morning. We might need to call a doctor for him since I'm sure that erection has lasted way more than four hours, more like a million years. The guy's sporting a serious boner tent!"

"Yeah, a boner tent! It's a sign. You know how we've been trying to come up with a name for our men's group? Let's christen ourselves the charter members of the Boner Tent Men's Group!" Eric exclaimed.

"This is weird, I've now been part of two clubs in my life and both of them have a boner theme going. I'll have to contact the other member of the Double Dean Wheelie Club and let him know about this, even though I haven't seen him since high school."

DAVID W. GOODWIN

The stars started to disappear as a thick bank of clouds quickly blanketed our narrow slice of sky. The boner tent was no longer visible and within a few minutes, it started to rain and it rained hard. We could hear the storm moving down the canyon with thunder all around and bolts of lightning lighting up the canyon with each flash. After a short while, water was trickling down the once dry creek bed and in no time at all it became a major flow. We went down to investigate and in a few minutes time, the water rose up about half way to our campsite. I guess my concern about finding drinking water was now completely unjustified.

"We'd better go make sure everything is secure at our campsite," Iggy suggested.

Once we were satisfied that we were still in a safe place, we found a nice dry overhang to sit under, watch the storm, monitor the rise of the creek and continue our discussion while working on the bottle of absinthe.

"Let's have our first meeting of the BT Men's Group," Eric suggested.

"What do men's groups actually do?" I asked. "Iggy, you probably have been a part of some in the past, right?"

"Well, yeah, mostly we talk about our feelings, problems with our various relationships, but mostly it's to get the support of guys who might have some good insights based on similar experiences. Sometimes it's a useful thing, sometimes a waste of time."

"I think we should talk less about our feelings and more about the women that we've had sex with," Eric suggested since this is usually what he wanted to talk about.

"That would be a pretty short discussion for you Mungo. As far as I can tell, you've only had sex with three or four women your entire life," I said.

"How about we focus on some of the best or worst experiences we've had in our lives. It doesn't necessarily have to involve women or sex. One question might be, for example, who was the biggest jerk you ever knew?" Iggy asked.

"Other than you two?" I asked. "I would have to say Big Larry but I think he had a lot of somewhat hidden positive characteristics. I think he wanted all of us to think he was a jerk so he could run the quarry more efficiently but he definitely had some jerk-like tendencies."

"Yeah but by the end of the summer, when our jobs at the quarry finally ended and we went back to school and were living at the Zoo again full time, he actually thanked us for working there. He told us that the landscaping and gnat netting project probably wouldn't have been nearly as good without our help. I think he turned out to be a pretty good guy and he even gave us triple fives after our first month of working there. Remember?" Eric asked.

"But things didn't go too well for him after that," Iggy said. "After we came up with the theory about the gold and the rats and the financing behind the nightclub, it was hard to just accept it without wanting to know more of the details."

"Yeah, remember that night right before our last day at the quarry when I accidentally walked in on Big Larry and Rhonda weighing out the gold in the office building after hours? That was pretty awkward. I honestly went in there looking for my bandana but they got all flustered when they saw me. It was obvious what was going on but Big Larry tried to concoct some sort of story about testing some minerals for their reactivity," I recalled.

"From what Rhonda told me, the jig was pretty much up for them at that point and they were just trying to make one last sale before the owner fired them both. He had been on to them for a while and that last sale was a total setup. You knew that, right?" Iggy asked.

"Yeah, Joan knew about it too and told me about it later. I think the biggest jerk was our Zoo landlord," Eric said getting back to the original topic. "Remember when he threatened to evict all of us when we got a warning from the city for having a parade without a permit? Like, what the hell difference did it make to him?"

"I would vote for the entire Sigma Kappa Fraternity for banning us from playing Frisbee on their front lawn," Iggy said.

"Yeah, what jerks!" I agreed. "Who was the nicest person you ever knew?"

"I'd have to say it was my Dad," Eric said.

"Yeah, the few times I met him he seemed like a really great guy. I would say for me, the nicest person I ever knew would be Kate. She was always so generous and loving; she would have done anything for you. She was always in a good mood, always had a smile on her face, the perfect friend," I said.

"Yep, I agree. She's still like that," Iggy said. "Who would you have died for?"

"Certainly my wife and kids," Eric said.

DAVID W. GOODWIN

"Do you think she would die to save you?" Iggy asked. "Remember on Tortola when you stepped on a sea urchin and she left you to go get a drink up the beach?"

"Oh yeah, you might be right about that but I'm sure she assumed my injuries weren't life threatening, even though my entire leg swelled up and I was having a hard time breathing. She had already gone to get her drink when the helicopter got me so she didn't really know how bad it got until later," Eric said a bit defensively. "Joan always seems to have slightly different priorities. Remember when she and I started dating later that summer? Even though we worked together all week, she would often insist on spending occasional weekends apart saying she needed to feel like she was living her own life and that was the lifestyle she had gotten used to. I think she and Alfonso might have had something going on but she has never admitted it to me. When we moved to New England with Beans the following year, she easily changed her ways and is a committed wife, a great mother and a top-notch businesswoman. Her wetland plant nursery continues to be enormously successful."

"Yeah, it's pretty amazing how your relationship has been so strong all these years," Iggy said. "Okay, next question, who was the horniest person you've ever known?"

"Joan, for sure." Eric said.

"Not Barbara?" I asked.

"Yeah, you're right, I guess I'd have to change my answer," Eric said.

"I'd have to say Sarah, but Barbara is a very close second."

"You're kidding, right?" Iggy asked. "By the way, do you know there is now a clinical name for Barbara's condition? It's called 'Persistent Genital Arousal Disorder' I've only met one other person with PGAD in my life and it was an eighty year old woman."

"That's an unsavory thought! I guess that explains Barbara's situation. How about you Iggy, who was the horniest person you ever knew?" I asked.

"I would have to say Georgie, especially when she started getting estrogen and anti-androgen treatments. Watch out! Which of your past girlfriends or wives had the loudest orgasms?"

"Anita, remember her from our junior year?" Eric asked.

"You're kidding, how could any of us forget her? My ears are still ringing even after thirty-three years. For me, it would be Sarah, no competition."

"Yes, everyone on the Hill would agree with you there. I would have to say my wife on this one. Who would you say was the kinkiest?" Iggy asked.

"Barbara"

"Indeed. Barbara, for sure."

"It's unanimous, Barbara in a landslide," Iggy stated. "Where was the strangest place you ever had sex?"

"Tina and I once did it on her back porch while her other housemates were out there sunbathing."

"And you got away with it?" Iggy asked. "They weren't disgusted by it?"

"Well, yeah, but that's beside the point. How about you Dean?"

"Sarah and I were driving back to Aspen that summer and we both got insanely aroused as we drove up Cold Creek Canyon. We pulled off, climbed up to a little rock ledge above the highway and did it right there, entirely in plan sight of all the traffic. It must have looked pretty interesting. How about you, Iggy?"

"Rhonda and I were in the Andes with our kids when they were really young. We were at Macchu Picchu and put them down for a nap in the tent and went off to one of the restricted areas and had sex there. We got caught right when we were in the middle of things. It triggered both of our orgasms and the park ranger guy just stood there and waited until we were done. Kind of like the time at the nightclub during one of the dance nights. Georgie and I were doing the twist or the frug or something and Rhonda cut in to dance with me. All that time I thought she could barely stand the sight of me. She took me off into a corner and gave me what today we would call a lap dance. Damn, she was sexy, still is for that matter! Juan Antonio, who I think had a bit of a crush on her, was watching and I think he might have pitched a serious boner tent himself. So here's another question, if you could go back in time and make one different decision, what would you have done differently?"

"I probably wouldn't have invited Phoebe out for the Fourth of July. That was the last time I ever saw Tina and Phoebe turned out to be a total space case. Last I heard, she was living in a commune somewhere in Arizona and changed her name to something unpronounceable with a lot of apostrophes and hyphens and has five or six kids, all with different fathers."

"Yeah but it opened the door for you and Joan to hook up. If I could have done one thing differently, I would have never gotten involved

DAVID W. GOODWIN

with Jackie," Iggy said. "It seemed like a good idea at the time but those memories are still difficult. How about you, Jacque?"

"I would have never let Sarah out of my life for so long. We had that long time apart when I moved out to Massachusetts with you and Joan and then Sarah went on to grad school and eventually settled in New York City to pursue her acting career. We kept in touch as much as our situations allowed but our lives were moving in such different directions at the time. When all six of us got together to attend the premier of Ellis's play, *Quarry Quagmire* at the Bleecher Street Theatre, I think she and I finally realized that our fates were intertwined."

"I'm not sure Rhonda ever got over the way he decided to twist things around even though she loved the spin Sarah put on her character, even down to the short shorts. She was relieved that he decided not to work the entire gold angle into the story line. That's still a sore subject for her and she still doesn't want to talk about those days. When the quarry owner found out that she and Big Larry were trafficking in gold and threatened to press charges, they had to make some restitution to him and both lost their jobs. Things worked out for the best, I suppose. It sort of forced Rhonda to go back to school and become the sexiest teacher in the Denver school system. It also paved the way for Big Larry to open up the first adult book store in Boulder. It still gets picketed regularly."

"Funny that all this might not have happened if we hadn't been out in front of the Zoo that day winging the wham when Rhonda drove by," Eric noted "and turned us into slaves."

"I guess any event has the potential to turn your life onto a completely different course," Iggy said philosophically.

"Yeah, you're certainly right about that. After the play had its run, I think the faculty position that opened up at Amherst College was also guided by fate. Sarah was probably set for life living off her various residuals but the universe seemed determined to get us back together again."

"How are your kids doing?" Eric asked. They all hadn't hung out together for years but we always asked each other about our children.

"They're great. I have to say that I look forward to every day with Sarah and my kids when they're in town or when we can work in a visit. It's like the best of all worlds, nightclub magic, green sparkly drinks, great sex, true love and no boulders to roll uphill all day, unless you think about life's little challenges metaphorically."